Praise for *Seraphim* by

MICHELE HAUF

"A rich medieval tapestry woven of fantastic tales of revenge,
women warriors, faeries, and demon fire.
Michele Hauf captures your attention with vivid,
powerful, sexy characters. What I wouldn't do
for a man like Dominique Saint Juste!"
—Award-winning author Lyda Morehouse

"From her first word to her last,
Hauf weaves a magic spell.
You'll root for Seraphim and sigh over Dominique as they risk
heaven and hell in this heartstopping adventure."
—Emma Holly, author of *Hunting Midnight*

"This book kicks butt—in a lush and lyrical way."
—Susan Sizemore, author of
"The Laws of the Blood" series

Seraphim

MICHELE HAUF

LUNA
www.LUNA-Books.com

LUNA

First edition May 2004

SERAPHIM

ISBN 0-373-80206-4

To Jesse Marvel Hauf aka Bob
Because this story is filled with all the things guys like:
danger, adventure, sword fights, giant bugs, fire demons,
poison-dripping castles—with just a touch of romance.
But you know what? We girls like that stuff, too!
Love, Mom

❧ PROLOGUE ☙

France—1433

The black knight's sword-tip drags a narrow gutter in fresh-fallen snow. The tunic of mail *chinks* against outer protective plate armor. Footsteps are slow. It is a struggle, the short walk from horse to a wool blanket laid upon the snow. There, a squire stands waiting to disassemble the heavy armor and remove it from the knight's weak and weary shoulders.

Thick white flakes have begun to blanket the muddy grounds surrounding the Castle Poissy, making foot battle difficult, slippery. Yet successful.

Mastema de Morte, Lord de Poissy, Demon of the West, has fallen, his head severed by the very sword that now draws a crooked line in the snow.

"You did well," the squire says, not so much encouraging, as merely words spoken to break the hard silence that follows the soul-shredding events of the evening.

The squire, lank and awkward in a twist of teenage limbs, takes to the removal of armor. Gauntlets are tugged off and deposited on the blanket with a cushioned *clink*. He unscrews the pauldrons starring the knight's shoulders, and lifts the heavy bascinet helmet off the mail coif. Working from shoulder to leg the squire carefully, noiselessly, sets aside the pieces of armor. Wouldn't do to draw attention to their dark hideaway a quarter league from the castle. Earlier, the squire had found the perfect spot tucked away inside a grove of white-paper birch limning the river's edge. The Seine flows in quiet grace, accepting with little protest the fallen soldiers who have given up the ghost in battle.

"Hold out your arms and I'll lift the tunic from your shoulders. Steady."

It is difficult not to sway. The knight's legs feel cumbersome, leaden. Arms are weak from swinging the heavy battle sword. Though forged and designed especially for the bearer, the weapon had become a burden after what seemed hours of blindly swinging and connecting with steel plate armor, chain mail, and human flesh and bone. Though it could have been no more than a quarter of an hour from the time of entering battle to the moment of success.

This act of participating in war, in bloodshed and mindless cruelty is new. But necessary. And not mindless. Not in any way.

The tunic, fashioned of finely meshed mail, is lifted from shoulders, lightening the weight on the knight's tired, burning muscles. Carefully the squire works the mail coif from a tangle of dark, sweaty hair that has slipped out from under the protective leather hood.

Suddenly granted reprieve from the heavy weight of steel and mail—and revenge—the knight's muscles wilt and limbs bend. The hard smack of cheek against ground feels good. Cool snowflakes kiss feverous flesh and melt tears of the new season over eyelids and nose and lips.

The squire, sensing the immense toll battle visits upon his master, allows the silent surrender to rest, a dark oblivion rimmed with promises of salvation that only angels can touch. He lifts the mail tunic and places it in the leather satchel spread across his horse's flanks. Necessary tools this heavy armor and meshed steel, as they travel the unseasonably frigid desolation of France from one village to the next in this insane quest for revenge.

Insane, but certainly warranted.

"You have felled both Satanas and Mastema de Morte," the squire offers, holding observance over his silent master. "But three to go."

"This one...was for Henri de Lisieux." It hurt to stretch a hand up to brush the snow from a bruised and aching face. The knight squinted against the sharp bite of cold. It is not natural, this heavy snowfall. But what since the coming of the New Year had been natural? "Have you caught wind of where the next de Morte plans to strike?"

"Nay," the squire responded. "But I wager word will be bouncing off the tavern walls in the next village. If you can find a de Morte foolish enough to venture out after the death of two brothers. I fear Abaddon de Morte will remain sealed behind a fortress of stone once word of another brother's death reaches his ears."

"He is the...Demon of the North," the knight managed through breathless gasps. Lying in a state of weary triumph, surrender to the bittersweet kiss of winter is effortless. "We shall be on to Creil and meet the man on his own domain."

"Insanity."

"Is there any other way?"

The squire sighed, and kicked at the fresh-fallen layer of white flakes with a tattered boot he'd peeled off a dead man's foot less than a week ago. "There is another way, it is called retreat."

"Not an option, squire. Do you live in fear or faith?"

He wanted to simply mutter *fear,* for of the two 'twas that to which he clung most often. To him, faith was a whole new world, one he'd hoped the abbe Belloc could lead him toward, far away from the sins of his past.

"It is fear…for now."

"Then I shall have to keep the faith for both of us. We ride."

The squire had known that would be the command. As he had come to know every rational suggestion he made would be immediately discounted by this false knight of vengeance. But whom had he left in this world to listen to anything *he* should say? "Tomorrow then, we ride to Pontoise, it is six leagues from here. We shall keep our eyes wide and our ears open for any word of the North Demon's plans."

"We shall ride tonight."

"Six leagues?"

Unhinged, the squire thought of the knight sprawled on the ground. Completely lunatic.

"It is what must be done." The tone of his master's spoken words had changed since the first morn of the New Year. Commands and utterances had become deep and alien, laced with an unwelcome evil.

"Very well." Resigned that he would get no sleep this night— as he had not gotten for the last two nights they had ridden by moonlight—the squire rubbed his itchy eyes. With resolute regard, he toed a mass of the black hair that swirled around his master's shoulder. "If you intend to continue this charade I wonder should you cut this off. These luxurious curls are a dead giveaway that you are a woman, my lady."

"I've no intention of disguising myself as a man. It is unnecessary. Rumors run rampant of a black knight come to exterminate the de Morte clan. Who would suspect a woman?"

"True. But the road is a dangerous ride, my lady. You are a beautiful woman. Would not you prefer the safety of disguise over the possibility of further harm to your person?"

"There is not a brand of harm left in the tattered kingdom of France that can further wound this blackened heart."

"Really?" He hated to challenge her so, but the squire knew otherwise. This woman's heart glowed a brilliant silver.

A lightning swift hand lashed up and unfastened the dagger from the belt the squire wore at his ankle. Another dead man's gift.

Seraphim d'Ange handed Baldwin Ortolano the weapon, handle first. "Do it then."

ONE

Lucifer de Morte tightened his jaw and clamped his eyelids shut. The sheep tallow used to oil his saddle oozed between his leather-gloved fingers.

"Just last night," Mastema's emerald-liveried messenger said in a tone too soft and fearful to blossom from a whisper. "I rode all night, my lord. I beg thee forgiveness."

At a dismissing flick of Lucifer's fingers, the messenger bowed and backed from the private chamber positioned deep in the center of the fortified lair. Lucifer remained stiff, his hand fixed in a scrubbing position on the cantle of his saddle.

To his right, a blazing fire spat angry sparks across the tiled Istrian-marble floor. The hearth—forged of iron—resembled a demon's mouth, complete with curved fangs, and above the gaping jaws, carved recesses for eyes where the flames danced high, animating the macabre face in wicked design. Overhead, suspended from the pine-beamed ceiling, a stuffed eagle, preserved and mounted with its eight-foot wingspan regally spread, silently mocked Lucifer with its glistening ruby eyes.

The black knight, the messenger had said. *Again.*

In a rage of motion, Lucifer pushed away from the saddle stand and crossed the room, scattering tallow and steel saddle furnishings in his wake. His sword, propped by the hearth, flashed violently as he swung the jagged-edge *espadon* through the heat-festered air.

He spun once, his anger, the pure force of his loss, drawing the pain up through his arms and to the end of the *espadon*. With a grunt and a thrust, he dashed his blade against the stone wall. Steel clanged dully. Limestone chips spattered the air. He thrust again. *Clang.* And again. He smashed his sword against the wall until his arms burned with exertion and foul sweat poured from his scalp.

Staggering to the wall, to which his back connected with a jaw-cracking thud, Lucifer finally dropped his sword with a clatter. A spark from the hearth leapt into the air and landed an amber jewel upon the deadly steel.

Lucifer raked his fingers through his tangled mass of dark hair. He squeezed his scalp until he saw crimson behind his closed eyelids. The color of blood.

The black knight's blood.

Some fool bastard had taken it upon himself to exterminate the de Morte clan. Why?

No! It mattered not the reason. Lucifer knew well there were hundreds, perhaps thousands of reasons; the bones and scarred flesh of those reasons buried copiously beneath the frozen French soil or floating down the murky waters of the Seine.

But why now? Why, after nearly two decades of de Morte reign, had some demented soul finally decided to exact revenge? And to succeed?

Mastema had been beheaded in the middle of the battlefield. He always surrounded himself with his own men. Always. After learning of their brother Satanas's death on the field but five days earlier, surely Rimmon, Mastema's Master of Arms, must have been at his side, his eyes peeled for oncoming danger?

With a guttural grunt, Lucifer kicked at the flaming ember that simmered on his sword blade. It sailed through the air, a sizzling missile launched by hatred, to land in the fire with a grand explosion of heat and blue-red flame.

Still panting from the toil of his anger, Lucifer stood before the blaze, fists clenched at his thighs. Heat blistered his face in delicious warmth. He could feel the sweat bubble upon his flesh like the surface of a witch's cauldron. So difficult at times, this sheath of mortality that he wore.

But obviously not a challenge for much longer, if this black knight would have his way.

Satanas had lived south of Paris in Corbeil; his nickname, the Demon of the South, as the villagers had taken to calling him. Hell, half of France used the monikers years of destruction and debauchery had attributed to the de Morte brothers. Mastema, the West Demon, had resided in Poissy. Sammael, the Demon of the East, resided in Meaux. The four brothers surrounded Lucifer, who lived in Paris.

But if the black knight was systematically attempting to erase the de Mortes from the planet, north would be his obvious next move.

Abaddon.

Squeezing his fists so tight the tallow and sweat and his own blood mixed to a hideous ooze, Lucifer decided on his course of action. He would not leave his own fortress to aid his youngest brother. Abaddon was an ox in size and vigor; he did not require Lucifer's help to flick away an offensive gnat like the black knight.

But he would send out a scout—no, a mercenary—to track this vengeful knight, and stop him in his tracks before Abaddon even need worry about defending himself against the revenge the de Morte family surely deserved, but would never tolerate.

The road to Pontoise stretched a long white ribbon this chill January eve. Flakes as light yet massive in size as swan's down fell quietly through the night. Seraphim blew a breath through her nose. Ignoring the ice-fog that lingered in a pale cloud before her, she slipped the leather hood from her head. She scratched a hand over her newly shorn locks and eased her heels into Gryphon's flanks to pick up the pace.

Gryphon had been her brother Antoine's prized mount. A fine black Andalusian bred for battle stealth and stamina, it measured near to sixteen hands. The beast's coat glimmered a blue sheen under sun and moon. "Power," Antoine had always whispered, as he'd brush down Gryphon's coat—a formidable partner to sword and shield.

Behind Sera, Baldwin dutifully followed on his borrowed roan, clad in borrowed clothes and borrowed life. He was a reluctant squire to Sera's bold, black knight. The man—teen—had been studying under the tutelage of the abbe Belloc, an ill attempt at penance against his former life, when Lucifer de Morte's raid upon the d'Ange castle the first morning of the New Year had taken down all but a handful of household servants and knights.

Much as Sera would rather shoulder the quest for revenge entirely herself, she took comfort in the young man's company. There was no favor for a lone woman riding the high roads by night. Even if the disguise of armor and distempered countenance did fool some, it certainly would not fool all. And as Baldwin had implied, she might be physically prepared to fight off attackers, but mentally, there were no promises.

Sera had endured much since her mother's illness had rendered the taciturn matron useless about the d'Ange castle a decade ago. But she had endured so much more in the short days since the New Year had begun.

The moment she allowed herself to stop, to think on what had occurred just weeks earlier, the nightmare would engulf her.

Never. I will not allow it.

"Oh my—bloody saints!" Baldwin hitched a clicking sound at his horse and rode up alongside Sera. "I—I'm so—damn—so sorry!"

She regarded him slyly, for to turn her head any more than a fraction of an arc pained fiercely. Exhaustion from this night's battle clung to her muscles. She needed rest. Even the chill air could not rouse her to any more than dull interest. "What be your concern, Bertram?"

"Your..." He gestured at her head with long, pale fingers that she'd always remember as clutching a bible. Or a toad. The makeshift squire stretched his mouth to speak, but after a few more gesticulations and wide-mouthed gasping, couldn't express his obvious dismay with any more than, "I'm just so sorry."

Sera rubbed a hand over her scalp, assuming his chagrin to be directed at her hair. "'Twill grow back."

The sound of her own voice, abraded and sore, was an odd thing. She did not recognize the deep rasping tones. New, shiny scar-flesh had begun to appear beneath the scabbed wound on her neck. Little pain lingered. Save that which seeped from the tear in her soul.

"But...it's so—oh—Mother of Malice! Why did you command me do such a thing in the dark of night, my lady? It is hideous! You look a sheep shorn by a swillpot. It juts here and there and—Heaven forgive me!"

His dismay made her smile. Briefly. Soon as she realized her swing toward mirth, Sera checked herself and drew on a frown. Much easier lately to touch sadness than any sort of joy.

"It is but hair, Bernard."

"Baldwin is my name, my lady, I have it on very good authority from my mother and father."

"If you insist."

The man was not averse to correct her; nor should he be. His forthright manner was one of many reasons Sera had invited him along on her quest. Baldwin Ortolano would do whatever the situation required to survive, be it honor-bound or criminal. A favorable ally to have.

There was also his plea not to be left behind at the castle d'Ange in the blood-curdling wake of battle. Sera could not have ridden away, leaving the teen alone, fearful, and so lost. Especially when she felt virtually the same. Alone, lost—but not fearful. *Never choose fear.*

One final scrub over her lighter, choppier coif brushed off a scatter of half-melted snow. "It will grow back." Her words did not work to cease the man's sorry head shaking. "Come, *Baldwin,* I find it quite refreshing. I have lived four and twenty years, each morning being a struggle to pull a comb through such a long tangle of hair. So many treacherous curls, all coiling and slipping over my…shoulders."

She made sure her sigh was as inaudible as possible. So much had been lost in so little time. Now, the last vestments of woman had been shorn from her head, making her more an anomaly than she had ever before felt.

But regret would not serve her mission.

"Now, you see, I've only to give my head a shake and it is done."

"'Tis a fine circumstance we've not a mirror in our supplies."

Sera yanked her leather hood up over her head. Lined with thinning white rabbit fur, the hood provided a bit of softness to ease the mental pain. "I shall keep it covered if it vexes you to look upon it."

"That is all well and good, but I fear your reaction when finally you do come upon a mirror. You were always so beautiful, Seraphim——"

A twinge of regret spiked in her breast. "The removal of my hair has made me ugly?"

"Oh, er…nay."

Sera straightened her neck, lifting her head regally. Insistent revenge pounded back the regret with relentless gall. The luxury of her past was no more. Tomorrow only promised trial, which must be faced with iron will. "I should hope so. As you have said, I cannot risk anyone discovering I am a woman."

Mustn't allow any more time to ruefulness. Last night had been for Henri de Lisieux, her fiancé. Five days ago, in memory of her brother Antoine, Satanas de Morte had fallen. The future held justice for her mother and father.

And Seraphim d'Ange.

"With your hood up and those smudges of dirt on your face, I wager you shall pass as a man in the next village," Baldwin offered. "But you mustn't bat those long lashes or allow any man to look upon you too closely."

She felt for her dagger, secured at her waist inside a thin leather baldric. "You could cut my lashes, as well."

"Don't be silly, I would blind you in an instant. What a fine pair we'd make, the blind black knight and the postulant-cum-squire-former-toad-eater, traveling the countryside seeking to extinguish the minions of Lucifer de Morte."

The black knight. At both battles Sera had heard the moniker.

Issued in awed wonder as she'd exacted her revenge with a mighty swing of her blade and then, mission accomplished, had ridden off into the darkness.

The armor she'd plucked from the dead body lying in the bailey of her family's castle had been of smoked steel, dark enough to be considered black. With little time to pick and choose, she'd lifted a set of scaled gauntlets and slid them over her blood-stained fingers, following with a breast plate. It was the only armor that would fit her frame; tall and slender, with broad shoulders and remarkably muscled arms. She hadn't the stout torso or powerful, heavy thighs of a spurred knight. But on more than one occasion Antoine had teasingly accused her of hailing from a lost tribe of Amazons.

Indeed, the lot of d'Anges were a hardy breed. Sera had gotten her height and persistent work ethic from her father; her thick black hair, blue eyes, and undaunted pride from her mother. Years of practicing in the lists alongside her father's knights had gifted Sera with the arm strength to swing her sword and deliver the killing blow.

Ah! Two weeks ago she would have never thought such a thing. The killing blow? 'Twas a term used only by knights and thieves and, well... *men.* Much as Sera had always embraced her power, her freedom and lack of feminine wiles, her mind-set had been irreversibly altered by one vicious act.

And she would not rest until that act was served the justice it deserved.

"I don't like it," Baldwin muttered. "Not at all."

"I have already told you I shall keep my hood upon my head. Cease with your whining, squire."

"I am not a squire, I am a postulant. I've subscribed to the Catholic church. Get that straight. And it is not your damn hair I am whining about!"

Sera chuckled, her breath freezing before her in a manner to match the clouds that puffed from Gryphon's nostrils. "For a man who wishes to serve the church you've quite the cache of oaths spilling from that mouth."

"Aye, and I've paid penance for them a thousand times over. I cannot control my tongue. There are just so many words, and at times so very few of them to express my feelings. I try to control it. I know the Lord cringes with every damn—every bloody—every—"

"Squire!"

"Forgive me, my lady."

"It is, *my lord,*" she corrected with a stern rasp. With a painful jerk of her head, she shot him a steely look. "Don't forget it, either."

He ceased what might have been another tirade at her casting of the eye. She'd honed the evil eye to an art form on the lackwit scullery maids that dallied more than dutied in her father's home. That, and the mongoose eye always served her silence when she wished it.

"Now, pray tell what it is you do not like besides this new coif with which you've gifted me?"

Sera slowed Gryphon and Baldwin sidled up beside her. His pale blond lashes were frosted with tiny icicles. "What you have become," he said boldly. "What you are becoming. This is not you, Seraphim. You have killed two men—"

"I know what I have done." She heeled Gryphon in the flank and the gelding clopped two paces ahead of the squire. "It is what is necessary," she called back, the deep grit in her voice gifting her with an authority more suited to a man. "I am adapting. A week ago my soul was torn to shreds and stolen away by Lucifer de Morte. With that evil triumph in hand he stole my family's souls, as well. I will not rest until I can reclaim what was taken from me. An eye for an eye, squire."

Gryphon dug heavy hooves into the snow and pounded ahead, leaving the shivering squire in a wake of fine, diamond-glittering particles of winter.

An eye for an eye, indeed. Seraphim d'Ange had changed drastically upon the entrance of the New Year. A change Baldwin could attribute to the surprise attack laid on her father's home, and all she had suffered from such.

But she was wrong about her stolen soul. The woman still possessed a soul. The evidence of such blazed brightly in her pale blue eyes, and in the fire that lit her path toward the ultimate goal. Mayhaps it had been damaged, for it had been stripped and beaten and bruised by that bastard Lucifer de Morte, the leader of the de Morte demons.

Was Seraphim d'Ange's soul beyond repair?

Baldwin prayed not. For she would need a soul intact to battle the devil himself.

Tor's breaths powdered the air before his gray suede nose. Dominique San Juste spied a village just ahead, settled like a giant's stone tossed amidst a thatch of forest. A fortuitous discovery, for he was weary, peckish, and he'd already once caught himself dozing.

He knew Tor would not stop should his master fall in a dead sleep to the soft pillowing of fresh-fallen snow. Dominique imagined the elegant white Boulonnais might be waiting for that very incident. The stallion would suddenly notice the loss of weight upon its back and, without pause, pick up into a gallop and be off, never to be seen again.

He leaned forward and gave Tor a reassuring smooth across his withers, then scratched the sensitive spot just below his long feathery mane. "Not yet, my fine one. When this mission is complete, I promise you the freedom you desire. You have served me well over the years; you deserve as much. Mayhaps we shall someday find that which has been lost to you?"

In response, Tor lifted his head and tamped the air with his nose. At the stamp of an agreeing hoof, spray of snow sifted up, coating Dominique's face with a fine kiss of January cold.

Unseasonable, this heavy snowfall. And the frigid chill. There was something amiss in this fine and darkened moon-glittered world. Since the morn of the New Year, Dominique had felt the odd fissure between nature and the mortal realm. But he could not explain it any more than he could reason his acceptance of this bizarre quest he now found himself embarked upon.

One final mission and then he, too, would find the freedom he desired. The Oracle had promised as much. If that is what the ghostly figment of an innocent-faced boy who had been appearing to him over the past few years really was. Could be a damned ghost, for all Dominique knew. Didn't resemble any child—living or dead—he had known. Oracle was as good a title as any.

Leaning forward once again Dominique smoothed his palm over the bald spot on Tor's forehead, reassuring in a manner he knew Tor understood. Perfectly round, the wound never did heal, though it did neither fester. It merely remained pink and moist, as if waiting. *Waiting to become whole once again.*

"We both seek wholeness," Dominique whispered, then straightened, and closed his eyes.

Another battle last night. Mastema de Morte had been executed; his troops had retreated behind the safety of twelve-foot-wide battlements. Word told that a mysterious knight clad in black armor had arrived midcombat. Deftly, he'd woven his way through the clashing, battling men, right up to Mastema de

Morte. One swift blow had cut through leather coif and flesh
and bone to sever the man's head from his neck. That done, the
black knight had turned his mighty black steed and galloped
away in the same mysterious manner that he had appeared.

He'd done the same less than a week ago, when Satanas de
Morte had laid siege to Corbeil for no more reason beyond boredom and the need to see fresh blood purl down the groove in
his sword.

The black knight sounded more myth than legend to Dominique. But he was not the man to dispute the tale. Especially
not in these troubled times, when the common man needed a
vision of heroics to cling to in the face of certain death.

'Twas rumored the de Mortes served the English king who
occupied Paris in his never-ending attempts to possess French
soil. The French king, Charles VII, who had been crowned but
two years ago thanks to the ill-fated Jeanne d'Arc, had yet to
banish all the English from Burgundian France. After almost a
century of fighting, these were surely the blackest years yet.

But at this moment in time Dominique did not care for any
man other than himself. He was on a mission. The finding of this
legend.

Tor's lead took them dangerously close to the prickles of a
bushy gorse. Dominique's spur caught up on the spiny branches
that splayed out over the path. At contact, a cloud of iridescent
particles coruscated into the air.

Dominique eased Tor to a stop and dismounted. "Not at all
favorable," he muttered, as he slapped at his left calf with a
leather-gloved palm. The platelets scaling the back of his gauntlet *chinked* with the motion. "It's been too long." Another slap
released a generous cloud of glitter from his lower leg. The ac-
cursed dust permeated all clothing, even his leather boots and
braies.

A few stamps of his feet and finally, the last of the renegade particles dispersed. It besprinkled the ground and lay upon the moonlit snow like diamond dust.

He had to be cautious. Dominique was destined for the first tavern that offered fire and food. It wouldn't do to wander in and seat himself in a dark corner only to begin to coruscate.

Then rationality overtook peevishness. Anger served no man but to draw him farther away from his own soul. Besides, anger was for the dawn.

Drawing in a deep breath of icy air, Dominique lifted his face to the eerie white moon sitting low and fat in the sky. It hung as if a pearl framed between the black iron latticework of a twisted, leafless elm. Midnight. 'Twas the time of the faeries.

The first time he'd ever heard that phrase—the time of the faeries—Dominique had been nursing watered ale in an ash-dusted tavern, sharing a table with a grizzle-bearded old man. With a bristle of his shoulders, and a hearty swallow of his own ale, the man had then nodded toward the door, where the moonlight seeped through cracks in the boards. "'Tis the time of the faeries," he'd said, as if imparting great wisdom.

And so, Dominique had walked outside, lifted his face to the moon, and had decided that indeed midnight and all its mysterious darkness was a time of magick.

"The stroke of midnight finds the Dragon of the Dawn at his weakest," Dominique muttered now. He closed his eyes and drew upon the moon's glow as if it were the sun and cast beams of heat upon his face. "Avoid the dawn. Triumph beneath the moon."

Seeking to break the cold silence that had settled between the two of them since he'd inadvertently mentioned Sera's new coif was rather ugly, Baldwin hiked a heel to his mount's side, and came upon Gryphon. "'Tis magical, no?"

"What? Your amazing ability to irritate?"

"No, my lady, the air, the sky, the—why the moment. Look all around, the moon glimmering upon the snow. 'Tis as if the faeries have danced about and laid their magical dust over all."

"Speak not to me of the foul creatures," she snapped.

"Foul—you mean—faeries?"

"There shall be no more talk of such."

"Very well." Baldwin smoothed a palm across the saddle pommel. That attempt at lightening the mood had gone over about as well as a cow tiptoeing through a pottery shop.

"They are mischievous, evil creatures," Sera muttered.

Evil? He'd always thought faeries rather whimsical, fey things. Course, should the abbe Belloc discover he had such thoughts— well, it mattered not anymore. That dream had been dashed on the eve of the New Year.

Baldwin pressed his mount faster so he could hear Sera's quiet words. She did not pay heed to her own request for silence. "When I was twelve my mother gave birth to my sister, Gossamer."

He'd not known the d'Anges had another daughter. When Sera was twelve? That would have been, hmm…right around the time Elsbeth d'Ange had taken ill.

"Gossamer was but one month in the cradle when the faeries stole into my mother's solar under the blackness of midnight and made the switch. A changeling they laid in the soft nest of silk and down where once my sister had cooed."

Baldwin cringed at Sera's dour recitation of the word, changeling. The mere thought of such a beast curdled a shiver from his spine up to his earlobes. Everyone knew changelings were hideous, sickly things; far from whimsical.

"The creature lived but a day. My mother was not the same after that. She grieved in silence, would but utter few words.

She closed herself from others. I could see her limbs literally begin to curl in on themselves. Until finally she was so crippled she could not take up a needle or even walk without assistance. 'Twas then I took over her duties as chatelaine."

"I'm so sorry," Baldwin said, meaning it, and wishing he'd never tried to brighten the mood. Brighten? He'd just snuffed out any light that had existed. There was much he did not know about Seraphim d'Ange.

"No more mention of faeries?"

"Most certainly not—" A glimmer of steel flashed in the squire's peripheral view. "What is that yonder?"

They came upon a lone rider dismounted at the edge of Pontoise. Moonlight poured over the sharp angles of his face and glittered in the plush snowflakes capping his shoulders.

Sera did quick reconnaissance of the man. Leather jerkin and braies, a grand black wool cloak ornamented with metallic-black stones around the collar. Hematite, she knew, a stone that quickened the blood. A two-handed battle sword and dagger glinted at his hip, both of simple design, with brown suede wrapped about each hilt.

No doubt a knight—no, his spurs were steel, not gold. Perhaps he was a mercenary, looking for his next purse.

"Good eve to you," Baldwin called, as he and Sera passed by the stranger who had not yet opened his eyes, only appeared to be worshipping the moon. He must have heard their approach.

"It is," the man finally responded.

Gryphon eased by the man's white stallion. Seventeen hands for sure, Sera judged the remarkable beast from the added height it grew over Gryphon's withers. Impressive.

"Headed for Pontoise?"

"If that is the name of yonder village, indeed I am."

Sera wished the squire were not so friendly with strangers.

They could trust no one. But the stranger did no more seem eager to share conversation than she.

As they completely passed him by, she turned at the waist, propped a fist on Gryphon's hindquarter, and saw he still stood a silent sentinel, his face lifted to worship the moon-glow, his eyes closed.

The beginning of a black beard shadowed his square jaw. The trace of a mustache squared his lips in an inviting frame. Black shoulder-length hair glimmered blue, like Gryphon's coat, in the eerie midnight illumination. A graceful, yet sharply boned profile, he possessed. Gluttony was not his vice. Perhaps a bit of pride, though. He could be a knight, valorous and brave, for not all wore the gold spurs when not riding in battle.

It might have been the play of moonlight—surely it was—for the man seemed to give off a glow of sorts. It caressed his figure, romancing him in a cocoon of white light.

"Sera?"

Caught in a silly swooning pose, Sera spun around and took up Gryphon's reins, keeping her sight from what she sensed to be a smirk on the squire's face. "Onward then," she said.

But she could not resist twisting at the waist and stealing one final glance at the moon worshipper. And from deep inside her scarred and damaged being, the damsel she had once been emerged—and sighed.

·⟨TWO⟩·

"Bertrand, what say you?" Sera dangled a chunk of stringy brown food above her trencher, imploring the squire to comment.

"It is meat." Her traveling partner shoved another piece of the greasy fare into his mouth. Whenever they came upon food he became focused and voracious in his endeavor to fill his belly.

"Aye, but what sort?" Pressing her lips together in consternation, Sera turned the meat this way and that. "I cannot determine, there is so much salt."

"Most likely venison," the squire muttered through a slobber of watered ale. "But say naught, for the king's men could be within hearing distance."

"Yes, but which king?" She prodded the remainder of her trencher with a fingertip, wincing at thought of consuming such unremarkable fodder. All her life she'd eaten her meals from plates. Oftentimes a fine silver fork had been provided, as well. This salted, stale, indeterminable fare she'd seen over the past week was enough to make one's stomach close up and choose starvation over death by disgust.

"Certainly, it is not what you are accustomed to, *my lord*." The squire was not one to disguise his frequent bouts of sarcasm. *Not* one of the reasons Sera had elected to have him accompany her on this quest. "You always receive the finest cuts, while the lower table is given this salted ferment, or if we are lucky, your table scraps."

"Bernard, I'm sorry—"

"It is Baldwin," he hissed, spattering his own trencher with spit. "And if you do not wish your portion then I shall gladly consume such, for I fear it will be another full day before we again stop to fill our bellies."

If all went well. Sera figured a two-day journey to Creil. Tonight they would rest, then greet the dawn and ride the entire day through by following the winding Seine. It was critical they reach Creil as quickly as possible. No doubt word of Mastema's death already beat a sweating horse's trail to Abaddon's ears. She did not want to give him more time than necessary to prepare.

"So, is it mine?"

A glance to Baldwin's finger-pocked trencher found it bare of meat and gravy. At that moment Sera's stomach moaned in protest. She had not been eating well, could feel it in the light-headedness that accompanied her yowling innards. With three of the five de Mortes left to hunt down she must keep her wits about her, and her strength. This bitter battle must be fought— or die.

She bit into the hard chunk of salted deer. All she could do was offer a negative nod, for she suspected this small morsel would need a good chewing.

"I do believe we are on Charles VII's land," Baldwin added

quietly. "That damned English king holds but Paris now, does he not?"

"Aye, the bastard," Sera muttered, equally as quiet. 'Twas difficult to know who was one's enemy with the English occupying Paris. Many a Frenchman had deserted and gone to serve Henri VI. They craved the organization and rumored frequent pay dates that were quite the rarity in the French musters.

Never, Sera thought to herself. *I shall serve my homeland until I die.* As had her father and her brother.

Fact was, Lucifer de Morte was allied with the English king. Another good reason to take his head.

"Ah, there," Baldwin whispered. "Yonder comes your moonlight knight."

"Do not speak so loud," she muttered. A glance to the tavern door witnessed the cloaked stranger stroll in with but a nod to the barkeep and a cursory scan of the room. "You will raise suspicion."

"What suspicion worries you? That *my lord* was romancing over another knight?"

"Baldwin!"

"Ah, so she does know my name. When it serves her authority."

"Enough." Sera lifted the pewter tankard to her lips and forced a swallow down her throat. While the watered-down spirits were anything but appetizing, just the feel of the cold liquid running down her wounded throat alleviated the haunting pain.

The large vessel also blocked the moonlight knight's view of her face as he strode by the long trestle table where she and Baldwin sat across from a half dozen dirty-faced men.

The man sought out a lone chair at the back of the tavern. There in the darkness, a single candle set into an iron sconce shone upon his face and the scaled-armor gauntlets he tossed on the table before him. A serving wench, thin brown hair tucked up with a few pins, limped over to his side and, with a few exchanged words that Sera could not hear, she then wobbled away to retrieve—most likely—more inedible meat.

In the main room of the tavern, two knights who had been quietly exchanging defense instruction, now clanged weapons in a good-natured display of method. Metal rivets studded the leather jerkin of the barrel-chested fighter and *clinked* with the misplaced touch of a sword. The moonlight knight didn't pay them a glance. Instead, his dark velvet eyes remained fixed on...Sera.

She quickly looked away and drew a finger along her crusted trencher, as if the food now promised great gastronomic delight. "He's looking at us," she hissed to the squire.

Baldwin, already breaking his rye trencher in half and preparing to devour that as well, glanced to the dark recess at the back of the tavern, making great display in turning his body completely, so anyone who might be looking would know his intentions.

"Don't do that," she pleaded hoarsely.

"He's not looking at *us,*" Baldwin replied around a bite of bread. "He's looking at you."

"Me? N-no. Really?" The damask- and silk-clad damsel that Sera had been but a week earlier shivered beneath the chain mail and scars and butchered coif. To capture the eye of such a dashing man—was no longer thinkable. "Let's be off, Bertrand."

"I'm not finished."

"Finish it in the stables. Our horses need tending." She stood, but the squire made it clear he had no intention of moving until every last crumb of the gravy-soaked trencher swam in his gut.

Sera cast a sideways glance toward the knight sitting in the darkness. He inclined his head in acknowledgment at the pair.

"Aren't you going to answer that?" Baldwin wondered.

"I did nod," she lied. "Hurry. Methinks you are making me wait apurpose."

"Dominique San Juste!" A gray-bearded man, dressed in olive hosen and wool cloak, crossed the room and set his tankard on the table before the moonlight knight.

Dominique? Sera toyed with the name in her mind as she placed a hand on Baldwin's shoulder, staying him for the moment. 'Twas a fine enough name, honorable, elegant and…beguiling.

The one who'd called out the name was a burly old man with young blue eyes flashing above his long beard. A scar pinched the corner of his left eye shut and dipped to his nose. 'Twas a match to the scar that puckered the flesh on Sera's throat.

"Good to see your ugly face again, man."

Sera had to close her eyes and concentrate most fiercely to hear Dominique's reply.

"You say Abaddon de Morte has plans to ride on Clermont in two days?"

"That *was* the word that blows on the wind," the scarred man said. "Was, that is. There's serious doubt the Demon of the North will leave his lair now with half his numbers obliterated by the black knight. They had been sent to aid Mastema's siege, and did but a handful return to their master."

"Ah yes, the infamous black knight. You wager he has set the rest of the de Mortes to a cowardly shiver behind their castle walls?"

The bearded man shrugged, scratched his generous belly. "Abaddon's the biggest and strongest of them all. If any of the de Mortes were to stand off a single, armored man, it would be him. Though rumor tells Lucifer has hired a mercenary to stalk the black knight and cut him down before Abaddon need worry of breaking a sweat."

"A mercenary? Lucifer not up to the task himself?"

"Perhaps shivering like a coward in his stinking lair. The black knight is a force! They say he rides into battle on his great dragon of a steed, the beast blowing smoke from its nostrils."

Dominique waved his hand dismissively. Sera did not miss the mocking gesture. "Gossip tends to grow a man's muscles tenfold and his amours by many hundreds," he said.

"Aye, but the black knight swung his sword and severed Mastema de Morte's head from his body with one swift and mighty blow."

Baldwin shot up like a rabbit bit in the tail by a curious mastiff. He pressed his hooded visage close to Sera's face. "You severed the man's head?"

Sera looked away from the greasy-faced squire, zoning in on Dominique San Juste's furrowed brow. The beguiling knight took great humor in listening to the man's tale. He didn't believe a word of it, she could fathom as much from the smile that wriggled his lips. Such white teeth beneath the thin black mustache. Captivating, in a most alarming way.

A hand clamped over her wrist, forcing Sera to redirect her attention. "You cut off the man's head?"

She shrugged out of Baldwin's greasy clutch and whispered, "So?"

Taking the eyeshot of a nearby traveler as warning she might speak too loudly and reveal more than she wished, Sera turned and stalked out of the tavern, followed closely by Baldwin. The slam of the heavy wood door released a mist of snowflakes upon their heads.

Baldwin skittered up on Sera's heels, her pace intent for the stables. "That's so...so...barbaric!"

She raised a brow, smirked, but did not slow her pace.

"That's not you, you're not that—bloody saints!—wicked!"

"I was mounted in the midst of battle," she hissed under her breath. "The man needed to be taken down. I did what was necessary."

He gained her side, a sad shake flapping the ragged wool hood on his head back and forth over his still-chewing cheeks. "You're changing, Seraphim. This is no life for a woman."

"You are not my lord and master, Bernard."

Breathing in a deep breath, Sera put the squire's comments from her thoughts. It would not do to think on what was wrong with her life. Only, she must focus on what must be done to avenge her family. With that vengeance would come peace for many thousands of French villagers who every day suffered at the hands of the de Mortes. The villains raped and pillaged and burned for reasons no more obvious than that of their own twisted pleasure.

For each de Morte slain, dozens of families would benefit.

The chill of nightfall slipped between her cheek and the rabbit fur lining her hood. Sera shook off a shiver and strode through muck of mud and snow to the stable.

Here in the stables it was warm, dank, and sweet with hay and animal-scent. Gryphon nuzzled into her cupped palm. Sera did the same against the magnificent beast's warm neck. She slipped a hand over the knobby row of witch knots that Antoine kept braided into the glossy black mane. Fond memories of helping Antoine feed the horses and oxen early each morning before the sun broke the horizon filled Sera's thoughts.

She recalled her insistent daily question to her brother. "When will you let me ride Gryphon?"

Antoine would always smile his wide, devil-take-me smile and chuck a knuckle under her chin. "You do have a way with Gryphon, I can see that. This beast won't allow any but the two of us to touch him without putting up a raging fuss."

"Today then?" she'd eagerly wonder, her fingers already curling around the saddle horn in preparation to mount.

"Soon," Antoine would always say.

And Sera's hopes would wilt. She knew he hadn't been ready to share with her his one private passion. For she shared his every other passion, such as sword-fight, tending honor through patience and diligence, and respect for their parents.

"You were good for him," she whispered now against Gryphon's smooth black coat. She drew her fingers over the silky and thick hide, shimmery in the rush-light glow. "I know you miss him, but you serve your former master well in allowing me to ride you now. Thank you, Gryphon. Together we will avenge my family's cruel demise."

"Not if you insist upon such theatrics." The squire's voice echoed in from the stable doors. "Riding into the midst of battle on your great and fiery dragon-steed? A swing of your sword decapitating the enemy? Sera!"

"I don't want to hear it." She pat Gryphon's rear flank and picked up a curry comb that hung from an iron hook on the wall. The horse bristled his coat as she smoothed vigorously over it with the brush. "You may leave my service if you wish."

"I—your serv—" He struggled to place his tongue on the words.

Sera knew the man had nowhere else to go. He was hopelessly lost when it came to religious pursuits. And toad-eaters were certainly out of vogue.

With a curt straightening of his shoulders and a proud thrust of his chin, Baldwin replied, "I would never."

"Then silence your objections from this day forth. Do you understand?"

Baldwin Ortolano, tall and slim, his hands and wrists jutting way beyond the hem of his borrowed shirtsleeves, merely nodded, defeated. "I fear my attempts to cease uttering oaths may have to be renewed should I remain by your side."

"It is not me you must answer to in your final days," she said. The curry comb skimmed through Gryphon's sleek hide, warming her fingertips with the brisk motion.

"You would do well to remember the same," he said.

The fine wire brush stopped on a glossy patch of hide. When her final day did come Sera knew exactly who would ask of her mortal sins. And she did not fear Him. She could not. She was doing the right thing. So many lives would be spared with the swing of her sword.

Though, she sensed there was a deeper reason she had taken on the quest. But that reason was not immediately to hand. Normal females did not take to the sword to sever heads. What was she doing? There was no doubt she had not a clue beyond that she was angry. On the other hand, 'twas very much…a *compulsion* to battle. She knew not why, only that the rage that boiled within pushed her. Enticed her forward. *Someone* had to put an end to the de Mortes' reign of terror.

And that someone would be her.

"Creil is another two days' journey," the squire offered in the silence of torch flicker and horse chawing. "Might we bed down here tonight and start afresh in the morn?"

"That is what I intended."

Baldwin's sigh of relief could have been heard in the dark cacophony of yonder tavern. Sera smiled, but turned her face to Gryphon's flank so the squire would not see such emotion.

"Shall we get a room?"

"Is there one available?"

"I believe there is."

"You have my coin stashed safely?"

"I do." He patted his hip where a conglomeration of baldric, gauntlets, leather bone-bag, and wool cape made it impossible to determine just how slender the man really was. He kept her coin in his codpiece, Sera knew, from the rhythmic *tink* that accompanied his strides.

"We've enough to see us through many months." Though she prayed this quest would end much sooner. "Go ahead. One room. I shall sleep on the floor."

Already eagerly on his way to make arrangements, Baldwin stopped in the doorway. He turned with a pained moan and pinched grimace. "Sera, you know I will not sleep a single wink should you be lying on the floor while I have a straw pallet to cradle my weary bones."

"Are you propositioning me, squire?" Sera peeked under her arm to catch his reaction.

"Why no!"

He blushed a deep crimson. The two of them had never shared more than a brief nod in passing through her father's castle, or whispered morning prayers in the chapel. But she had heard of his former profession, the very reason that pressed him to seek atonement by applying to the church. Baldwin Ortolano had done things to survive—cheating, lying, stealing—acts that branded him a criminal. Those same acts also fashioned him imperfectly human. And she certainly needed human right now, imperfections and all.

"If the bed is wide, we can share. We shall lie so our heads are opposite one another's feet. What say you?"

Baldwin lifted a suede-booted foot and rubbed it along his opposite ankle. "I'm not sure..."

Sera gestured through the air with the brush. "I've smelled worse than your feet in my lifetime. Now be gone with you.

Run up and find us a room with a fire and have it blazing for me when I return."

"Yes, my lady—er, my lord."

A while later, Baldwin strode out of the Dragon's Eye, pleased that his mistress's coin had purchased them a fine room with a wide bed, fresh water (melted-down snow for washing), and clean straw.

Sera hadn't come in from the stables, and an odd twinge of foreboding had prompted him to seek her out. She was, after all, a woman. A young female of four and twenty who should not be left to defend herself against any danger that should approach.

Oh, he knew Sera was not your average amiable, submissive female. He'd lived at the d'Ange castle for nine months, and in that time had learned Sera had taken over chatelaine duties when she was but twelve. Elsbeth d'Ange, Sera's mother, had developed twisted joints that would not allow her to do anything with her hands, save brush aside the bed curtains to receive her maids.

He now knew that affliction had come following the abduction of Elsbeth's newborn daughter. Faeries, eh? Fine enough, the little winged creatures. But the idea of a changeling, mewling in a newborn's crib…well, it just gave Baldwin the shivers.

When Sera could not be found taking accounts in the larder, or purchasing food and fabric at market, or mending clothing, or shearing sheep, she stole a free moment here and there to practice in the lists with her father and brother. An unusual female, Seraphim d'Ange, in that she wanted to do it all. If her brother Antoine could do it, she could as well.

And her father had encouraged her masculine pursuits. Marcil d'Ange, a stalwart lord possessed of a compassionate but fierce heart, had treated Sera as if a son, but not without the occasional gentle smile and knowing wink.

Beyond such knowledge of her abilities, the fact that Sera had beheaded two of France's most notorious villains still troubled Baldwin. When ensconced in the black armor and charging through the roar of battle cries with a steel-clashing sword, Sera rode a strange sorcery that tricked her mind into believing she would succeed.

Baldwin prayed that sorcery would keep its hold on her until this quest was finished. For if and when she did fall, it would be a hard fall, indeed.

Just as he had suspected! A strange man leaned over a figure lying on the freshly spiked straw at the end of the stable. Long, narrow legs and wide hands splayed over the nest—he stood over Sera!

In a cacophony of *tinking* coins, jangling bones, and breathy huffs, Baldwin dashed through the stable door. He tripped up his feet on a block of wood, righted himself with the expert skill he'd developed since his teen years had seen to stretching his limbs to ridiculous lengths, then scrambled to the end stall where Gryphon was tied.

Before Baldwin could blurt out an angry shout, the man turned and backed away from Sera, acknowledging the squire with a nod. 'Twas the dark-haired knight that had set Sera to a swoon.

"That is my lord at rest, and I shall thank you to leave her— er, *him* at rest."

Baldwin knew his eyes bugged at that slip, a response to mistruths he had never been able to tame. Indeed, he'd played a blind toad-eater, wearing a scarf over his eyes to keep the innocents from reading his grift.

He clutched the bag of bones tied at his waist. For strength. "Pray, tell what you think you are doing, sir?"

"Forgive me." The man raised his hands briefly to show he had no ill intentions, then stepped back. "I was just seeking my own resting place for the night. All the rooms are taken."

Baldwin took a moment to look over Sera. On her back, the heavy mail tunic pressed her body into a snug nest of straw. Her hood was still up and her eyes were closed, a soft snore purring from her mouth. So tired, she hadn't even made it to the room he'd rented. But, thankfully, curiously androgynous under cover of sleep.

"What is wrong with him?"

"Hmm?" Baldwin turned and looked over the man. Two black eyes beamed at him. Dark hair slicked over his ears, and a shadow of a beard progressed dash-and-scatter from his cheeks to his jaw. There lived an eerie peacefulness in the depths of those eyes. Perhaps he was a little handsome—ah, hell! What was he thinking?

"Your master." The man gestured to Sera. "To look over his face one would wonder..."

Sweet Mother of Wonder, did the man suspect?

"Is he ill?"

"Ill?" Not the suspicion Baldwin had feared. He swallowed a melon-size gulp and tried to act nonchalant. He pressed his hand to the stable wall, crossed his legs at the ankle—and winced at the pinch of coin digging into his delicates. "Wh-why do you say that?" He quickly uncrossed his legs.

"It is only because he looks it. Those dark crescents under his eyes and the gaunt flesh over bone... Mayhap he is frail?"

"He is no thinner than I, my lord."

The obsidian eyes of the stranger took in Baldwin's lank frame. Dressed in squire's tunic and the tight-fitted brown leggings borrowed from yet another dead man, Baldwin felt awkward and exposed. But better to distract attention to himself.

"You're not a soldier, are you?"

"A postulant, actually. I am soon to become a monk." Though for as much as that was worth anymore, he might just as well go back to eating toads.

"Really? I thought you a squire to this man's knight."

"Well…" Baldwin twisted his head upon his neck, fighting the sin of mistruth even as he babbled a thousand lies. Closing his eyes to avoid discovery, he offered, "That, too."

"Have you a condition yourself, man?"

"Condition?"

"Your eyes—"

"No. No, no…just, you see—I'm terrible exhausted, my lord. Traveling all day, you know. It tends to tire my eyes."

"Indeed." Not a spark of belief in the stranger's condescending tilt of head. "Pray tell, what is your lord's name?"

"My lord?"

"Yes, the man lying here on the straw."

Baldwin shrugged, felt the color of blood flush his cheeks hotly. "My lord?"

"You just said that."

"That is what I call, er…him. My—my lord."

"Ah. But he must have a name?"

"He is of the d'Anges." Yes, and leave it at that, Baldwin thought.

For the week they had traveled the roads the moniker of the Black Knight had served Sera's alibi. He could not just announce to this man that "my lord" was really "my lady." He couldn't tell anyone, for that matter. Much as he wished an entire army backing he and Sera on this suicidal quest.

"D'Ange." The knight, in thought, thumbed the scruff of his beard. "Were they not set upon by Lucifer de Morte? I thought the entire family murdered by that bastard less than a fortnight ago?"

"Yes, well, there were..." Baldwin fidgeted with a stray point that dangled from his shirt, and closed his eyes, "*two* brothers... One survived."

"I see." The knight cast another glance over Sera's inert figure, then flashed his eerie eyes upon Baldwin. "And his name?"

"Who, sir?"

"The man sleeping on the floor. Your master?"

"Er, Antoine." Baldwin gripped the bag of bones tightly. Pity he hadn't been able to procure Jude the Obscure's wrist bone last market day. 'Twas the Patron Saint of Hopeless Causes, he. And this lie was certainly hopeless. "Yes, Antoine d'Ange."

"Antoine d'Ange." The stranger walked a few paces across the straw-littered floor, then turned on Baldwin, drawing his angular face up close until his breath hushed in cold clouds across Baldwin's nose. Within the depths of the steely black eyes, Baldwin sensed the Fates toyed with his string at this very moment. "You're lying to me, squire."

"I am not a sq—er—squire. Yes, indeed. I *am* a squire."

"Liar."

"I am but a novice! I—I am not yet accustomed to answering to that title."

"There is something up."

"What is that, sir?" Damn, but he needed that bone!

The knight fit his hands at his hips. His studded leather jerkin skimmed his knees, and shiny black boots shrouded his legs from thigh down to his spurred heels. He was a tall man, slender, but possessed of thick arms and muscled wrists capable of matching blows in battle. "I had better find my own nest of straw before all the drunkards come spilling out of the tavern. Good eve to you, squire."

"Good eve—" All the drunkards?

Baldwin flashed his gaze over Sera's peaceful form. How

soon before someone discovered she was a woman? And what would they then do to her—no, he didn't want to think of it. He'd heard one perfectly horrific tale of abuse from Sera, had seen enough…

He could not leave her alone.

Baldwin glanced to the tavern, up to the second floor where he and Sera's room waited. Already paid for. A warm bed waiting to cradle his tired, aching limbs. 'Twould be a shame to let it go to waste.

A sniffle, a crunch of hay, and the *chink* of chain mail accompanied Sera's turn upon her makeshift bed. She curled on her side, pocketing her hands up near her chin, her knees arrowing toward her stomach. Sleeping like a babe. A woman's position.

"You will be the death of me yet," Baldwin muttered. "You there!" He hailed the stranger back over to his side. "I didn't catch *your* name."

"Dominique San Juste," the knight offered with a short bow. The black stones set around his cloak collar clicked with the graceful movement.

Just what *did* the man suspect? He hadn't pressed for the truth behind the lie. Maybe he had just been guessing. Baldwin prayed so.

"Sir San Juste, I've a room in the inn with clean water and fresh bedding. But as you can see, my lord has seen to a change of plan. Would you take our room?"

"At what price to me?"

"No price. I've simply no desire to see the room sit empty all night."

San Juste considered the notion, followed Baldwin's pointing finger toward the lighted window, and then, "Thank you for your kindness, squire, I shall accept."

Baldwin raised a finger to correct the man, but stopped. It was too late; he was too tired; it wasn't worth the bother. Squire was perfectly acceptable. For now.

"If I may ask, what is your destination, San Juste?"

"Creil."

"Ah, ours as well."

"Indeed? Perhaps we might share the road tomorrow? I do favor friendly conversation."

A smile captured Baldwin's countenance, so surprising, that he smoothed a hand over his jaw to verify its reality. To touch such an unrestrained emotion had become something of a quest for him this past week. "That is very kind of you, Sir San Juste, I accept your offer."

Though he wagered Sera would not be delighted about another traveling companion, the advantage of having this rather imposing, broad-shouldered knight alongside them could not be overlooked. And beneath the wool cloak there glinted a sword and dagger; an extra set of weapons could not be refused.

"Tomorrow morning?"

"I shall meet you at dawn."

Such luck to procure a room with little difficulty beyond a mere "I accept." Dominique settled onto the bed, for to stand up straight was impossible beneath the angled pine beams that reduced the height of the room from a man's shoulders to his waist in less than a stride.

He splashed too-cold water from a dented copper bowl over his face, then shook his head, dispersing droplets across the bed.

Fresh bedding, indeed. The nest of mice sharing the packed straw on the pallet might argue against that. But with the kitchen's chimney bracing the wall before which the pallet had been laid, the room was warm, so he had no argument about sharing quarters.

It hadn't been kindness that had prompted the squire to offer his master's room, Dominique felt sure. For could not the squire have taken the room in his master's absence?

No, the squire's need to remain at his master's side was more necessity. The lank young man had wanted to protect the sleeping knight. He, a mere squire, thinking to protect a spurred knight! But he would not protect for long with the skein of lies he wove.

Dominique wondered now if the squire realized the wide boggled appearance his eyes took on when he spouted an obvious mistruth. Exhaustion? Would not the man's lids then be heavy upon his sight?

And what exactly was the man protecting? Could it be that his master also danced with an illusory shroud to his steps? Were they thieves?

Dominique had observed the duo in the tavern. The squire had no more thought than most men after riding all the day, to fill his belly. But the other, Antoine d'Ange, had plucked and prodded suspiciously at the fare the tavern offered. So...effeminate his actions. Just not...right.

Perhaps the two were engaged in more than just a partnership of the ride? Mayhaps there was reason the squire chose to bed down next to his master this eve. Dominique knew there were those men whose carnal preferences led them in sinister directions.

He smirked at the thought, then lay back. A few squeaks near his hip protested his position, but soon settled to sleep as well.

⚜ THREE ⚜

She pouted for two leagues, hunched on the saddle, every so often casting Baldwin the evil eye. She did have a knack for the evil eye. 'Twas a shade more intimidating than the lesser mongoose eye. Her pale blue orbs barely revealed color as her lashes meshed in the squint of hell. Baldwin felt its damning power bore deep into his gut, where it twisted his intestines into a nervous knot.

But he could not ignore the advantage of traveling with real muscle. And Dominique San Juste was just what a wayward monk-in-training-playing-squire and a mixed-up-lady-playing-knight needed.

Sera hadn't been able to argue with Dominique's request to accompany them; he had already been mounted and ready to ride. Instead she'd purposely stepped on Baldwin's foot on her passage to Gryphon's side, and had twice knocked him to the ground with an elbow to his ribs before they rode out of Pontoise.

Heaven knew no fury like that of an angry angel.

Dawn gifted the chilled riders with a slash of vibrant color. Pink painted the horizon as far as the eye could see, followed by amber, and orange, then the bright flash of sun, before all too quickly fading. To find the sun in the winter months was rare; most days it hid behind clouds that filled the gray sky, as if that were the natural tint instead of cerulean. And so Baldwin cherished the few moments of color.

Hours later he'd learned little of Dominique San Juste, save that the dawn beguiled him as well, yet it was midnight that truly bewitched the moonlight knight.

"It's too damn dark," Baldwin said. "Especially riding through the forest. A man cannot know when a creepy will jump out and rip him to shreds."

"It is a time when I feel the greatest strength," Dominique offered as his mount, Tor, sidled to a walk alongside Baldwin. "If there are enemies to be felled I shall wait for the moonlight. Perhaps I'm one of those creepies you fear?"

Baldwin shot the mercenary a look. All seriousness in the man's expression. Much as he favored having him along for the ride, he did not have to trust him.

"And yet, you find the dawn most beautiful as well?"

"It is a compulsion I must meet every morning as the sun rises. And yet, I am drained and oddly weak at that moment. A bit testy, too." He offered a shrug and a knowing grin. "I cannot explain it. Never have been able to, for as much as I've questioned it over the years. Have you an hour in the day during which your energy seems most frenzied?"

"I do favor the supper hour," Baldwin said with a grin. "Aye, I challenge any man to stand against me when there's a fine roast boar waiting on table with apples stuffed in its mouth and wine flowing from a fat wench's pitcher."

Dominique cocked an agreeing nod at Baldwin. "I shall see

to remember such when we stop to fill our bellies, lest I might lose a finger to your ravenous appetite."

With renewed interest Dominique changed tactics. "Have you a voice, sir?" he prompted from the other side of Baldwin. The squire's master rode a horse-length ahead of the trio. "While I find your squire's conversation most enjoyable, I wonder how you find this fine gray morning."

A thick cloud of frozen breath blossomed before the rider's face, and he rasped out, "Cold."

Dominique raised an inquiring brow to Baldwin. The squire merely shrugged and looked ahead over the stretch of white-frosted ground. Rabbit tracks stitched a line in the quilting of snow and led to the forest edge where black-striped white birch grew tall and slender amidst the thick trunks of decades-old oak and elm. Within hearing distance, the Seine sang crisply, her waters impervious to frost. Beneath the snow cover verdant earth and grass slept in a moist bed until spring.

"I feel I've offended in some way," Dominique said, more to himself than anyone. Not that *anyone* listened.

The gruff-voiced man who led their motley trio certainly did keep to himself. Fine with him. The squire offered enough conversation to keep a man's jaw oiled in the stiffening chill. "What is your business in Creil?"

Baldwin started, "We're to—"

The squire's master blasted over with a quick, "What is yours?"

"Ah, a tidbit of conversation." Dominique heeled his mount to catch the faster pace of the man.

What was his name? Ah yes, Antoine d'Ange, of the ill-fated d'Ange disaster less than a fortnight ago. So he would allow him the morose brooding. Surely he had lost much to Lucifer de Morte's cruel rampage. "As for my business, I am on a mission."

"Aren't we all—"

"Squire!" d'Ange quickly silenced.

Dominique could feel the air crackle between the two. Tension held both stiff upon the saddle. Something had lit a flame beneath d'Ange's mail chausses.

"I stop in Creil," Dominique added carefully, all the while gauging the vibrations between the two. Though d'Ange spoke little, each word, every movement was charged with a remarkable energy.

"So you are a mercenary?" Baldwin called.

Such perception. Or rather, an obvious guess, for he was a lone rider, fit out with sword and a mysterious manner. No gold spurs on his heels. There was no necessity in remaining a mystery. Clues to finding the black knight were welcome from any and all. And he much intended to get to the core of this intriguing tension that shot back and forth between his travel mates.

"Indeed, a mercenary. I'm sure you've heard much of the dark knight who swoops into battle to claim the members of the de Morte clan? I've been instructed to seek this legendary knight."

"Oh?" Baldwin and his master exchanged looks. There was a glimmer of—something—in Antoine d'Ange's pale eyes. Dominique couldn't place what it was, but it overwhelmed the haggard condition of the man's face. An inner fire, perhaps that is what kept the poor soul going after his entire family had been murdered.

"Don't tell me you've not heard of the black knight?"

"We have not," Antoine d'Ange rasped, and in a stir of hoof-sifted snow, turned his horse from the trail. With a nod of his hooded head he beckoned the squire to his side. "A moment to converse with my squire, if you please, San Juste."

Dominique inclined his head and crossed his hands over the hard, leather saddle pommel.

The twosome dismounted and walked off. D'Ange positively steamed as he pumped his fists and worked his way toward the forest. Filled with a raging force, he was. Their boots kicked up little parallel mountains in the soft layer of snow following their wake.

An interesting reaction to Dominique's mention of the black knight. They must know something. Or perhaps they knew no more than any of the villagers claimed to know? That the knight was all-powerful and stealthy in his pursuit of the de Mortes. A legend amongst mere mortals.

Hmm… Dominique just couldn't get a grasp on d'Ange's physicality. The squire he'd already pinned as faithful, eager to spin a mistruth to protect those he served, and not entirely cut out for the journey he'd most likely been persuaded to embark upon. But d'Ange was a tough read. He purposely kept apart to avoid consideration.

What hid beneath that cold facade of utterly serious silence?

Slipping a hand down the side of his leg, Dominique mined for the itch that had tormented his ankle for the past few minutes. When he returned his gloved hand to the pommel he cursed the coruscation that coated his gauntlet.

"A fine day it is when you've invited the enemy to accompany us like hell's guardian to our deaths," Sera hissed, and punched her gloved fist against Baldwin's tunic.

He gripped his shoulder and groaned, "Sera."

"He is the one," she said in harsh whispers, her eyes alight with accusation.

Dominique San Juste sat out of hearing range, but both were aware he kept an eye on them. Overhead, a hawk spread his wings wide as it skimmed the ground, plunged, and snatched up a field mouse in a graceful act of violence.

"What *one?*" Baldwin wondered, as he pulled his gaze from the death peals of the mouse.

"You recall the rumor we heard in the inn, that Lucifer de Morte has sent a mercenary to stop the black knight before he can get to the Demon of the North." She punched a fist into her opposite palm. "Well?"

"Sera, do you not think if San Juste wanted to kill you he would have done it by now?"

"He knows not who I am!"

"And he never will. If only you would let him know you are a woman, his suspicions would never come to fruition."

"He suspects me? What say you, squire?"

"He does not."

"Then why speak such a thing?"

"I don't know!" He gripped his scalp, then spread out a hand in dismay. "Your foul mood sets my brain aquiver. I cannot think aright with you hounding me like a rabid dog. I like San Juste. He's a personable fellow. And I rather enjoy speaking with him." Baldwin followed her frantic footsteps. "Did you hear he lives on his own? An available man, Sera. And quite the handsome face, too."

"You change the subject to serve your lies. Besides—" she crossed her arms over her chest with a *scriff* of mail to armor "—I know nothing of his looks."

"Come, my lady, every look you give the man is that of a swooning goose."

"Geese do not swoon."

"Very well, but women do." Baldwin playfully tweaked his hand near her cheek.

"Don't touch me, toad-eater!" She slapped his hand and he

recoiled, but more from her words than her actions. "Sorry," she rushed in at sight of his morose expression.

"I am no longer," he managed, feeling the remorse for his past misdeeds coagulate in his throat. "Never once did I take a man's life, only his money. You know I have always done what must be done to survive."

"I should not have said it," she said, punching her fist into a palm. "You coax me to false anger atimes, Baldwick."

"It *is* false, for you use it to cover up those emotions you'd rather not touch."

She did not reply, only fixed her gaze to the knight standing yonder by the brilliant white stallion. Fire had burned her path from the horse trail to here. But now the flames flickered in her cold blue eyes…and settled. Baldwin watched Sera's anger simmer to a nodding acceptance.

Whew, he'd barely missed another punch to the shoulder.

With a thoughtful finger to chin, she finally offered, "He isn't like most men, is he."

"Doesn't sound like a question. More an observation."

"I've observed many a man." She looked him right in the eye. Difficult to escape her arrow-true gaze. "Often."

"Really?"

"How else could a woman blend into a man's world? He's different," she said, as she turned to place the mercenary in eyesight. "Dark, yet peaceful."

Indeed—but she spent all her time observing men? For some reason that information set a tickle to the back of Baldwin's neck. What did she do when she observed these men? Did she think, well…*things* about them? When could she have had the time?

"So you watch men…all the time? Have you ever, er—" he drew a wide arc in the snow with his boot toe, trying to act nonchalant "—observed me?"

"Certainly." Her summation of his expression worked a catty wink and a one-sided smirk to her thick lips. "Castle d' Ange's reluctant postulant, who spends the hours he should be studying religion in the battlements watching the knights practice in the lists. He drinks the holy water after the abbe Belloc has left the chapel—"

Baldwin stifled a gasp.

"And," Sera continued, "he attracts the women with a mere curl of his lips and a roguish wink."

Baldwin released his held breath. "You have observed all that?"

"Aye. You are lithe, agile—now that you have mastered your growing legs—"

"Not quite, but I'm working on it. And about that holy water—"

She smiled, freely. "And—unless it has to do with religious pursuits—you are ever willing to please and learn. Very much opposite our mercenary. For some reason I feel San Juste has no need to learn, that he possesses wisdom untold."

"Quite an observation for a morning spent fuming."

"Aye." She punched a fist into the birch trunk. "You have had your say then, squire. Forgive my rude treatment of you this morning. I remove the curse of the evil eye. Though, I shall not forgive you for inviting the mercenary along."

"But what is wrong with seeking help? And moreso, with allowing softer emotions?"

Her mood quickly changing again, she slammed a clenched fist to her breast and croaked out in her battle-roughened voice, "This heart will not feel until all the de Mortes lie six feet under. And if you can even think I will bat my lashes at the very man sent to kill me, you've eaten one too many poison toads in your lifetime, squire. Now come, we are leaving San Juste behind."

"Oh? And you think he will just sit there and allow us to ride away? Where, then, are you two off?" he mocked the mercenary's proposed question. "Oh, we favor a head-start before you fell us with your sword."

Sera paced in the snow before him, chewing her lip and punching her fist in her glove. The scaled platelets of armor riveted along each finger *chinked*. Erratic the rhythm. So…unsure about this new challenge.

"Men don't do that," Baldwin commented. She looked to him and he gestured to her mouth. "Chew their lips."

She released hold of her lip. Baldwin noticed that what had once been plump pink mounds to tempt every man's dreams of passion were now cracked and dry. Winter and the stress of battle had taken a toll on this precious angel.

Dominique had been right at guessing she was ill. But 'twas not a physical malady that darkened her eyes, but a ghost of weeks ago. A ghost that clung to her with horrid memories of the first night of the New Year.

"We must be rid of him."

"Sera, you mean—" Baldwin sliced a hand across his throat in horrific display.

"It is the only way." She gripped her sword hilt and slithed the blade in and out of the steel scabbard. "I must take him out before he assassinates the black knight."

What could they possibly be discussing beneath the skeletal bower of birch branches? Dominique unwrapped the leather reins from around his gauntlet, then draped them between his thumb and forefinger. Perhaps he should skrit over there?—a series of movements so agile and quick, not even an ultra-alert deer could sense his presence.

No. He wrapped the reins tight again. He didn't have time

for tricks. Much as he had enjoyed conversing with the squire for the past few hours, he highly doubted the other would suddenly be gifted with the urge to speak any more than a few mumbles.

Though, the twosome were involved in a very animated conversation at the moment.

Hmm... Were his suspicions true? Could they possibly know something about the black knight? Mention of the mythical knight had been what set d'Ange into a sudden flurry of motion.

Dominique pricked his ears. He could not hear them talking from here. The only audible sound was Tor's bursts of breath through gray velvet nostrils, and the press of the beast's heavy hooves into the snow-packed ground. And Dominique's own tense breathing.

Just ride, his conscience implored. *You do not require conversation. Ride on to Creil and locate the black knight. End your own search for answers that much quicker.*

Easier to think than to actually do.

Creil was a good-sized village, set apart from the imposing walls of Abaddon's fortified battlements. Would the black knight be so foolish to just ride in to Creil, all glorious black armor and sword held high? The de Mortes had to be fully aware of who, or what, had taken down the first two brothers.

No, if the man had any sense to him at all—and Dominique highly questioned that for the brazen acts of riding into battle and felling two of France's most notorious villains—surely he would lie low. A sneak attack this time. There were no rumors of a siege on Abaddon's part. Dominique had not been alerted to such. And he would know as soon as the idea had birthed in the de Morte camp. For the Oracle was a relentless visitor.

It was decided. He would be off. Those two could offer no

information that would help Dominique. He suspected something sinister between the squire who claimed to be a postulant and his mysterious partner. But that was of a personal nature; it did not concern him.

"San Juste! Dismount!"

Dominique jumped at the sound of the rasping command, which set Tor to a nervous stamp.

"Is there a problem?" Dominique wondered, as he slid from Tor's back and his boots crunched upon the hard-packed trail. A glance to his heels reassured he'd not exposed himself with a cloud of telltale coruscation.

"Yes, there is a problem," d'Ange announced. He paced before Dominique, his scaled black gauntlet working around his sword hilt. "But it shall be solved soon enough. Bertram!"

D'Ange's sword was drawn in a sing of steel. Dominique was fleetingly aware that the squire led Tor away from him and d'Ange. The instinct to unsheathe his own sword worked the action before he realized he stood at the ready to defend himself.

Defend himself?

"What say you this problem?" Dominique barked. "Is it me?"

"Indeed." D'Ange stalked the ground before him, carefully measuring his strides as each step closed him in to Dominique. "You seek the black knight?"

With a simple reply clinging to his tongue, Dominique bent to dodge the sweep of d'Ange's broadsword. A quick riposte brought the blade of finely tempered steel back his way. Had Dominique not stepped back his head would be rolling toward Tor's hooves.

"I," Antoine d'Ange rasped, "am the black knight."

"You?"

Seeing his challenger's overhead hammer-drop slash toward him, Dominique swung his blade to the left, caught the tip in his gloved hand, and thrust it above his head to block the blow. The jar of contact rippled through his bones and shuddered to his feet.

Morgana's blood, but the man had a powerful thrust!

But what the man had just announced. It could not be. *Him,* the black knight? Not this man, this—gangly excuse for a man. Especially a man he suspected to be something entirely different, at least regarding his sexual nature. Certainly not the type to become a knight, let alone, the legendary black knight.

Though he did have strength...

Drawing his sword arm down, Dominique's blade slashed over the chain mail tunic that clung loosely to d'Ange's lithe torso. The hindrance of the tightly meshed rings stymied his intentions and his sword merely slipped, steel over steel.

"Careful!" Baldwin yelled from where he stood by the trio of horses.

Dominique figured 'twas not he for whom the squire was concerned. But should the man not have more faith in his master?

There was something very odd about his opponent. Dominique could feel it through to his bones. And it was not that he suspected the knight and squire shared the same bed. Indeed, the man's effeminate mannerisms in the tavern returned to thought now. Sc delicately he'd held his meat...with slender hands...

By all that is sacred—could he be?

"Why do you seek to stop the man who wishes to aid you in your efforts?" Dominique yelled. He ducked. Another slash of steel *whooshed* over his head.

"Aid me? Is that what you call murder then?"

"Murder? I no more wish to murder you than I wish my own heart to cease beating. Which it yet may if you are successful in this twisted attack. Cease, man! I surrender."

"There is no surrender but death!"

The heavy blade of his opponent's steel skimmed Dominique's thigh. Pain-heat pinged and shivered in his serrated flesh. The blade had sliced through his leather braies.

Still the attack did not cease. "Did you hear me? I don't wish you harm. I've been sent by a higher power to ensure the black knight succeeds in exterminating the de Morte clan."

This time the angry d'Ange heard. He tried to stop a forceful swing, but the sword pulled him forward, and he had to jab the tip into the snow to break his attack. "A higher power? You speak insanity."

"You think I am Lucifer de Morte's mercenary?"

"Can you prove otherwise?"

"Nay." What did the man require? A letter de cachet? The sacrifice of his head? "I do not work for the devil. How dare you? I was called to serve the black knight by one who wishes him success. It is your puny hide I've been sent to protect. And I see now why I was needed."

"A higher power—" Antoine d'Ange spat out. He paused, huffing in exertion "—has sent you to see the de Mortes are murdered?"

"I have been instructed not to interfere in your quest, only to navigate and to provide protection on your journey from one de Morte to the next."

"What is this nonsense? A higher power? Do you speak of God?" Forgetting his sword, the man splayed his arms before him and declared to all, "Murder cannot be sanctioned by the church. What sort of god do you serve?"

"A god that tires of watching the de Mortes reign over the innocent men, women, and children of France. A god that confuses me as well, for he has chosen a gangly misfit of a man to bring down his greatest enemies. Are you sure you are the black knight?" He looked to Baldwin. "He is not, is he?"

The squire stepped to his mount and lifted a wool blanket slung over the leather saddlebags. Beneath was revealed a collection of shimmering black armor.

It took an unnatural amount of control to keep his jaw from dropping at such a sight. Dominique swung back on his aggressor, who stood lean and lithe, yet heaving from a simple tryst of matched steel. Much as he could not believe it—did not want to believe it—this man truly was the legend whispered of in villages stretching from southern Corbeil to Paris and beyond. He'd expected a great and hulking man, virile and strong. A warrior. Not…this.

"I need no protection." D'Ange turned, retrieved his sword that had been stuck into the packed snow, and gestured to his squire that he mount. "Take your sacrilegious beliefs and be gone with you. Creil is but a day's ride. Abaddon de Morte awaits the end of his cruel reign."

Had he known the black knight would be so obstinate, Dominique might have refused the delectable offer the Oracle had used to coax him to such a task. But the fact remained, he had accepted. And he never surrendered to opposition. "Tell me, black knight, how much do you know about Abaddon de Morte?"

"I know he is a bloodthirsty bastard, and the devil's brother; there is nothing more necessary."

How had this fool man succeeded in murdering two de Mortes thus far? Dominique felt sure Abaddon would not be the third. Not when this knight planned to blindly ride into de Morte's fortress of clever ambushes and ensorceled traps.

"So you are aware of the man's penchant for booby traps?"

Already mounted, the knight regarded Dominique with a cold-air huff, and a nod to the squire to get on with it and mount as well.

"You think you can just march into the man's castle and slay him in his own bed?"

Dominique felt laughter most appropriate, and answered the call of humor. It felt good to draw in the cold air and fill his lungs. But this moment of mirth was oddly bittersweet.

"What need I know about Abaddon de Morte that you cherish so to your breast?"

Dominique crossed his arms over his chest. "I will tell you, if you will allow me to protect you."

"Never."

"My lord." Baldwin's voice sliced a sharp edge through the chill air. "Perhaps it would do to hear the man out. If he knows things about Abaddon—"

"Damnation! Already you've turned my squire against me, San Juste. And you wish me to put trust in you after such?"

Dominique tilted his head back to meet the traveler's eyes, shadowed by the dullness of cloud cover. "Abaddon de Morte has many strengths—both physical and occult—that will keep your blade far from his neck. He has a weakness as well."

The knight's brow lifted. Considering. He smirked, pressed his thick lips together. Not a shadow of beard on the man's face. Could he be much more than a child? Insanity! That the people's legend was a mere, why a mere— Dare he think it?

"How do you know so much?" rasped out of the black knight's throat. "Explain exactly why I should trust you and your misguided God."

Certainly the Oracle had not provided a means to ingratiate himself into the black knight's trust. But trust was not necessary to provide protection. Though tolerance would be a fine trade-off.

"I cannot say why, or even *if* trust is necessary. Only that you must take benefit of the knowledge I possess. We have a common goal, to see the de Morte clan terminated. You have taken down two-fifths thus far, I shall join you in the final rounds."

"And how do you know what lies ahead? Have you spies? Inside the de Morte lairs?"

"Of a sort. Difficult to believe," Dominique offered, at surprised looks from both his traveling companions, "but necessary."

"Then why has nothing been done to stop the de Mortes until now?" The knight's steed pawed the ground, impatient as his master. Power and cold air pressed out from the horse's nostrils with each puff of breath. Counterbalance to its master's fiery demeanor. With d'Ange's smoothing glove to its neck, the horse settled and turned its master back to face Dominique. "Why? When so many have suffered and died at the hands of such demons?"

Dominique felt the pain in the black knight's voice as he rasped out his tirade. 'Twas akin to the pain that clutched his own heart, a pain that had forced him to accept this one final mercenary mission. He just wanted to know *why*.

"You hold your tongue to keep me from success. I do not believe you, Sir San Juste. Ride on!" D'Ange hiked a spur to his horse's flanks. "I've a mission, and I'll not have you underfoot to hinder it."

"Abaddon de Morte's castle is a veritable cache of booby traps," Dominique called, as d'Ange pressed his horse toward the trail where he and Tor stood. "Boiling water cast down from the battlements, spikes screaming out from hidden murder holes. Live spiders and locusts. There is a spell of enchantment over parts of the castle that can forever spin a man into a confusion of the senses. But if you can pass through the rumored seven hells your reward shall come with cleverness and planning."

Michele Hauf

"Seven hells?" Baldwin's voice cracked.

"Abaddon de Morte, Demon of the North, Master of the Seven Hells," Dominique said. "You have not heard the moniker?"

"I've heard of the Demon of the North," Baldwin said shakily. "Everyone knows of the four villains set to each corner of the compass, and their ruler, Lucifer, planted in the very center, somewhere deep within Paris."

"The Dragon of the Dawn," Dominique confirmed.

"You say Abaddon has a weakness?" D'Ange stopped his mount alongside Tor. The two horses mustered little regard for one another.

"Yes, but unfortunately it will do none of the three of us any good to know such."

"Why is that?"

No harm in revealing the little he knew of Abaddon. Dominique had no intention of allowing the black knight to press on without him anyway. "He favors women something fierce. The man missed the siege at Poissy because he instead chose to stay home and indulge in a ménage. The man goes through women like a worm boring through a rotting corpse. He's quite vain, as well."

"Baldwin."

Dominique followed d'Ange's eyes to the squire's face, a visage that had grown paler than the snow at ground with mention of the seven hells. The twosome had a way of communicating with a single look—

"Oh, no. If you even think to attempt such," Baldwin said, "I shall tell San Juste all."

"All?" Now this was beginning to sound interesting.

Dominique marched over to the squire's mount and jerked the reins from his hands. "I knew you were a liar." He released his dagger from his waist-belt in a swift move that defied any mortal man's eyesight, and pressed it to the squire's neck. "Tell all," he barked at the black knight. "Now."

"You call *this* protection?" d'Ange protested.

At his move to unsheathe his sword, Dominique pressed his blade harder. A narrow spittle of blood dribbled from Baldwin's neck.

"My lord!" Baldwin managed, his eyes closing to squeeze out tears from the corners.

D'Ange turned on his mount. So he was a coward to allow his squire death while he turned his back?

"The black knight is a woman," Baldwin spat carefully from behind Dominique's faltering blade. "Her name is Seraphim d'Ange."

FOUR

"Betrayer!" Sera jammed her sword in the snow and stomped toward Baldwin.

Dominique lunged right in her way. "A woman?" He couldn't believe he spoke the word. But a strange comprehension fell over him as the lithe, gaunt-faced black knight approached him, anger huffing out in cold breaths of air. "I should have known!"

"And how should you have known?" She slammed fists to her hips. A feminine action. Dominique had suspected something of the sort upon observing the duo in the tavern. Suspected a pair of unusual males. But a woman? A woman had slain Mastema and Satanas de Morte? In the midst of battle?

Seeing Seraphim d'Ange was more intent on reaching her bristling squire than him, Dominique dodged into her path to prevent her from taking her anger out on the youth. If she had beheaded two de Mortes, what would she do to her squire for exposing her identity?

Dominique had heard of these odd, masculine women that

chose to live their lives the way of their betters. Why, Jeanne d'Arc's ashes still smoldered in the square of Rouen. Did Seraphim not see what she might bring upon herself if she were discovered? The label "witch" would be slapped upon her forehead. For the misguided d'Arc wench had seen to that.

"Release me!" she argued, as Dominique wrangled her wrists into a tight clutch. She was much stronger than he had anticipated. And now he could see she matched him in arm strength, as well as height.

"Much as I am stunned at what you have achieved thus far, my lady," he said, twisting and bending to keep the fiery angel in grasp. "Tell me how you expect to continue? The black knight has become a legend, quite literally with the swing of your bloody sword. But you'll not gain entrance to Abaddon's castle without also gaining an arrow to your brain."

"I shall think of something." Her sneer stretched pale, full lips to reveal tightly clenched teeth.

"Damn! I cannot believe this!" With a thrust, Dominique released the struggling woman. He stepped back, half expecting her to explode upon him.

Something fired a mighty rage inside that slender form. And if rage is what compelled her to exterminate the entire de Morte clan, he could only guess it had been put there by one of the five demons.

But the fact remained...she was a mere woman.

"How do you expect to survive? Hmm? Tell me!" Dominique would not allow her the distance she sought. With frantic steps back and to the side he matched her every move, finding agility with ease, even in the thick snow. "Riding into battle upon your great steed and swinging a sword is one thing. But what of hand-to-hand combat? There is no sign Abaddon has even considered siege or attack. He will be tucked away in his lair, surrounded by his minions, lying in wait for you. Make me believe you can survive that!"

"I can, and I will." The dark circles under her eyes had receded since last eve. Rest had served her well. Now only the glow of rage lit her pale eyes. Eyes of an indeterminable color, save the anger that flared there. Indeed, this woman had been sorely wounded by the de Mortes.

And it was now Dominique's responsibility to see she survived to achieve her goal.

A woman? *Il diable!* Had the Oracle known as much?

Of all the fine disasters. He should just mount Tor and ride off, abandoning this fool to her idiotic quest.

There is but one reason you agreed to this insane mission. A reason that had haunted Dominique for over two decades.

So be it.

Using a trick to draw her attention, Dominique skrit around behind her, his movement faster than a mortal man's sight. "Show me your strength!"

She spun round, surprised to find him behind her, but not commenting on his change of location as her anger held her in check.

Fired by this woman's verve, Dominique jutted up his chin in defiance. Certainly he would not allow a woman to best him.

"Here." He tapped his chin and matched her steps, a swift side-to-side lunge, a stride back across the hoof-pounded snow. "Deliver me your best. Come on then," he coaxed at her reluctant pout with beckoning fingers. "Are you afraid to prove your mettle—"

Pain shuddered through his jaw. The retreat of Sera's fist flashed in Dominique's blink of astonishment. He pressed a hand to his jaw and stretched his mouth wide. No loose teeth.

Indeed, she did have strength. But where speed was concerned, she was no match to his fey footwork.

"A child's tap!" he mocked. "You've not leveled me, black knight. Come. Right here. Double me over."

Determined feminine courage eyed his gut as he tapped and taunted. Her right fist hovered near her chin, though it wasn't building to a punch. He sensed she had never before encountered such opposition. The devil take her soul, if she would not encounter such a thousand times over if she were determined to see the black knight's goal to the end.

This had to be done. He had to make her understand just how vulnerable she would be in Abaddon's lair. That she needed him at her side. For he would not allow her to cut him out of this bargain. Whether or not he approved that she was a woman, he would see this quest to its end.

This time Dominique saw her fist lunge toward his stomach—but he didn't dodge. He wanted to feel her anger, to gauge the fire that blazed in this wounded angel's heart.

Her fire was more forceful than he had expected. The initial blow doubled him. Breath wheezed out from his lungs.

"Seraphim!"

The squire suspected his master had actually hurt him? And what sort of name was that anyway? Seraphim? An angelic name for a woman whose punches wielded the power of a demon?

Dominique staggered, but he would not fall—not in front of a woman.

Although—on second thought...

He fell to the packed snow. The cold kiss of winter bruised icy crystals into his cheek, and he rolled to his back. A forced groan was necessary to lure his prey. She leaned over him—

"A-hah!" Dominique gripped Seraphim by her upper arms and laid her on the ground with a deft flip and a foot hooked under her mail-sheathed knee. He pinned her hips with his knees and pressed her shoulders into the snow. Her hood had slipped from her head, exposing a wild crop of black hair. Dominique stifled a chuckle. Had the woman thought to change her appearance by cutting her hair? And who was her barber? A fingerless blind man?

"Off!" she rasped, in what Dominique guessed to be a scream.

Her voice was not natural. Most likely she'd been injured. It had served her well for a day or two as disguise, but now…

She struggled like a pinned weasel, her head twisting from side to side, her eyes closed, and her fists blindly beating at his chest. 'Twas a child fighting for freedom from the monsters that haunted her nightmares.

Enough. She now knew the danger that could befall her.

Dominique pressed against her shoulders for leverage, bringing his weight upright to stand. The fallen angel sprang to her feet. Like a rabbit sprung from a trap, she dashed off to the woods.

"Seraphim!"

"Stay away," she called back to her squire. "Keep him away!"

"What the hell did you do that for?" Baldwin shoved Dominique's right shoulder. About all the man dared, Dominique wagered, for the flicker of uneasiness in the boy's heavily lashed brown eyes. "You've sent her off in horror!"

"She fares well enough." He brushed off ice crystals from his braies and cape. "I wanted the woman to see how truly helpless she is against a man. One single man. And do you know how many men await her at Abaddon's castle?"

Wisely, the squire remained silent, his gaze switching from the woman's retreat, and back to the ground before his feet.

"Morgana's blood, a woman!" Dominique said, clenching his fingers into a useless fist. For what sense could his punches press into the woman's head? She had come this far. And he certainly had no reason to stop her. To see her through this senseless quest would give him the answers he sought.

But a woman?

Dominique sheathed his sword and paced a short tread before the squire. "What devil got into her head to make her do such a thing?"

"Lucifer de Morte."

He found on Baldwin's square-jawed face a chill calm. The lank boy scrubbed a hand through his dirty brown hair and stared off toward the wood where Seraphim had retreated.

Lucifer de Morte. Known to many as the Dragon of the Dawn. "I suspected as much."

"Aye, well you don't know the whole of it." Now the squire dared raise his voice and pound the air with an admonishing finger. "And you would do well to show a little more compassion. Sera's been wounded. And she won't rest until the demon that haunts her nightmares is extinguished."

Dominique toed the tip of Seraphim's abandoned sword. So Lucifer de Morte had set the blaze beneath this angel's wings. Most likely the dark lord had no idea it was a woman who now stalked him and his brothers in the guise of the black knight. If Sera had been beneath the Dragon of the Dawn's sword, or worse, his rutting loins, surely the villain must believe her dead.

Why *did* she yet walk this earth? Mayhap she hadn't been in Lucifer's path, only her family? No. It didn't make sense. Lucifer never made a mistake, nor did he leave a trail. If he'd a grievance against the d'Anges, he would not have left their home until all had given blood to his sword.

But did the reason that Seraphim d'Ange walked this earth really matter? She had survived. And now she sought vengeance. And Dominique had agreed to see her through to the end. They both had their own motivations toward extinguishing the de Mortes. Personal reasons.

Lifting her sword up by the hilt, Dominique tested the weight, found it was surprisingly light for its length, then stabbed it back into the snow. Must have been fashioned especially for her. The black knight had so easily abandoned his— *her*—weapon. Further proof that this woman was well over her head in the thick of things.

What a hell of a way to begin a partnership. Though he mustn't consider it such. He would merely serve as guide and protector. Seraphim d'Ange would be the instrument of destruction.

How odd did that sound? He, following a woman warrior? Though, stranger things *had* occurred in Dominique's lifetime. He'd best accept Seraphim and get on with it.

"I should go retrieve her."

"I will," Baldwin said. "You've done enough for one day."

She clung to the smooth, hard surface of a narrow birch tree. The thin layers of papery bark were cold, like sheets of ice laid around the wooden core. Her breaths worked frantic puffs of condensation before her face, her heart racing—and winning— the pace of each exhale.

Visions, the horrid, horrid nightmares filled her head.

Shoulders pressed to the cold stone floor. Impossible to struggle free. Still groggy; startled awake from a dead sleep—fire everywhere.

One dark man, a face unremarkable in the shadows save the glints of flame flickering in his eyes. Red. Red as the devil's rage.

"I'll see you in hell." The heavy voice curdled over her bones like hoar frost freezing to flesh. He cracked a grin, spat on the floor, and shoved a mail-coated fist against her shoulder.

Pain seared between her legs. Screams pummeled up her throat. Escape. Let loose your voice. Someone will hear.... will rescue.

Where is Father? Antoine? What of Henri? And the guards? What is happening? So much fire, and...this devil grunting above her.

They're all dead. Their throats cut...

Oh...the pain of the blade slicing across her flesh...

Seraphim pressed her forehead to the cold birch. She clasped her hand to her throat. No more pain. No... *Make the memories go away!*

But there is pain. She felt the scream, the cry of lost innocence gurgle up her throat. Heavy breaths, unbidden tears, and finally, the whimper of helplessness.

Fear droned from her mouth. It was not the same vivid scream of that night when her family had been slaughtered. Now the scars inside her throat muffled the pain, made it ache.

She had always slept like a dead man. Since taking over her mother's duties Sera had risen at dawn and worked a long, hard day. At day's end, sleep came easily, so heavy, and quick. Hypnos, the God of Sleep, always favored her with dreamless rest.

She had only wakened that early morning of the New Year when her chamber door slammed against the wall and that dark-haired man with the red, glowing eyes ripped her from bed.

Too late. Too late to scream for help. The damsel had been damaged.

Now, her soul tattered and torn by Lucifer de Morte, the damsel had shed her robes of silk and finery and donned the black knight's armor.

It mattered not the violation, the robbing of her maidenhood. It had hurt. Nothing more. She would survive that humiliation. But in sparing her—in leaving her to live amongst the ruins of her family's home, the silent lamentations of their disturbed spirits—that had been the true destruction. That she had lived to bury her parents, her brother, and her fiancé, had been the ultimate twist to Seraphim d'Ange's soul-raped shell of a body.

And now, there came another, a man who would toy with her hollow carapace, the remnants of a life once lived with pride. Dominique San Juste.

Sera peered through the fencing of birch trunks. In the distance, Tor pounded the ground. His master paced before the brilliant white beast, his head bowed as if in thought.

No moon to romance him into your dreams.

San Juste could not have known what his threats, his forceful ways, would stir in her. *She* could not have known she would react so. And much as she hated to admit it, the man had been right. What would become of her when she stood surrounded by Abaddon de Morte and his minions, far from the advantage of riding Gryphon and swinging a deadly blade? It could happen. It *would* happen.

Mayhap, that is what San Juste had planned all along? To weaken her. To make her question her abilities. She had no idea who he really was. Sent by a higher power? What could that mean? At present, the de Mortes reigned over all of Burgundian France. The English King Henri VI ruled Paris thanks to Lucifer's influence. Even Charles VII feared and bowed to Lucifer de Morte's whim. Had not the d'Arc witch's fate been sealed by Lucifer de Morte's influence over the English?

Dominique's claim that he was not the mercenary sent to assassinate her could be a clever ruse. Though, there was no reason why he should not have killed her moments ago. Follow with a blade across Baldwin's neck and San Juste's mission would have been complete. The de Mortes' reign would be saved from total annihilation.

He is not a killer. He must not be.

Sera smirked at her conscience's foolish pining. She did not want him to be the mercenary any more than she enjoyed this quest. But that did not mean he wasn't dangerous. De Morte's minion or not, he was still a mercenary, a man who killed for coin. She could not trust San Juste. Did not want to trust anyone but herself and the man she had chosen to accompany her on this journey through hell.

Blessed Mother. She pressed her forehead to the birch trunk. Her heartbeats had slowed, and her hands had stopped shaking. San Juste had proven her lack of physical strength. And he'd opened her eyes to the forthcoming dangers. She could not ride on to Abaddon's lair without some protection. Years drilling in the lists beside her brother had given her a false reassurance. Of course, Antoine—why, any of her father's knights—would have never given their all against her, but a mere woman in their masculine eyes. Hand-to-hand combat, as Dominique had just proven, would be a challenge considering her sex.

She *did* want to trust him. She wanted to feel the same relief Baldwin had felt at having the mercenary accompany them. Dare she allow him continue at her side? How to judge San Juste's best interest was for her? What reason could a complete stranger have for joining such a suicidal mission? *She* had not offered him coin.

Blind to all but this stir of conflicting emotion that threatened to fell her to her knees, Sera let out another horrifying moan as she was grabbed from behind.

"It is me, Sera." Gentle arms embraced her shoulders. Not harsh. No dagger. No demon horns formed by shadows dancing in the firelight.

"Release me," she said, with a shove to the squire's hand. Drawing in a breath of courage she expelled it in a thick cloud between the two of them. A decisive nod chased away the foolish trepidation. "I am better now."

"What happened back there? Did he hurt you?"

She managed a mirthless snort. "I am not injured. I merely…needed some time apart. A moment to myself."

She found in Baldwin's silent gaze an understanding that neither need speak. For he had found her the night Lucifer had descended like his namesake upon the d'Ange castle. This man knew. He had seen the blood, her torn skirts, the devastation. He would keep her secrets— "Why did you tell him? I trusted you!"

"For your own good. You know well yourself, we need him, Sera. San Juste knows Abaddon's secrets."

"How? Did you ever pause to think about that? How do you know we can trust the man? We know not who he is. He claims a higher power sent him?" She propped her arm against the birch trunk and vacillated her attention between the squire and the distant mercenary. "To me that is Lucifer de Morte. How else would the man have such intimate knowledge of the layout of Abaddon's lair?"

"You think Lucifer would send a man to watch the black knight extinguish his brothers?"

"Of course not, but perhaps this is San Juste's way—deliver me to Abaddon's hands, then watch a grand slaughter."

"He would have killed you by now."

She found conviction in the spark of white centered in Baldwin's brown eyes. A certain integrity that had not been there during morning rituals in the cool shadows of the chapel. No, the church did not hold solace for this man. Not yet.

"You trust him?"

"I do."

She gazed across the expanse of whiteness that separated her from her self-proclaimed protector. Her running footsteps had made deep prints in the snow, with Baldwin's long strides stamping craters alongside. San Juste stood by his horse, brushing a reassuring hand along the rich ivory mane. He had frightened her something fierce by pinning her in the snow. Had she not seen the glint of violet in the man's dark eyes she might have died of pure fright right then and there.

Violet. The color of peace and royalty. A gorgeous, passionate color. A color she could—*wanted to*—trust.

"If he indeed wishes to protect you," Baldwin said softly, "then you can go about your business without fear. At least you will have someone watching your back."

"And what is wrong with you?"

"Sera, I am not a knight. I've no inclinations to the sword. I am but a miserable toad-eater who relies on a bag of worthless bones to see him through strife. But I do wish the extra protection San Juste can offer."

"And if it turns out he really is the enemy, sent to kill me at the finest moment?"

Baldwin opened his mouth to speak, but Sera stopped him with a curt response to her own question, "Then so be it."

At least she would die knowing she had given her all to avenge her family.

Trust him? Never. But use his knowledge to make her quest easier?

"Perhaps Dominique will share all he knows of this castle of the seven hells?" Baldwin offered.

"He will, or he will answer to my blade."

Baldwin opened his mouth to comment but Sera cut him off. "I thank you," she muttered in the quiet of the chilled air. "You allow me to see through my rage with your simple wisdom."

He shrugged, allowed a smile to wriggle his mouth. "I *think* that was a compliment."

Despite her misgivings, the knowledge of this new *protection* released a cord of tension from Sera's neck and shoulders. She had much to face in the coming days. Instinct must be honed, reaction burnished to mere seconds, and above all, she must keep her senses about her.

But now they were three. And Sera had to admit, this man did not so much frighten her, as put forth a challenge to the heart of the silk-clothed damsel hidden deep within.

FIVE

The moon glowed high in the sky when the traveling trio decided to stop at the edge of the thick forest that bordered the winding green waters of the Seine. Sera, who had been silent since granting San Juste his desire to protect, now settled against the rough, icy bark of an elm. She spread her wool cape out around her thighs and tucked it up over her knees to fight the chill.

They'd passed the Abbaye de Royaumont a half hour earlier. Now its single spire rose up majestically in the distance, decorating its little unpopulated spot of land with quiet grace. A sanctuary from evil, open to all who sought sanctity. Save the English.

Yes, please, Sera thought now, as scrapes of flint striking stone produced sparks at her traveling mate's direction. *Grant me sanctity. I want to be free of this quest, free of the rage and anger.*

But Sera knew that such freedom must be earned. 'Twas the price she must pay for being the only survivor. Her brother and father would have done the same.

Soon a roaring blaze lighted their snug encampment. Fire

sprites danced up toward the unreachable moon. Gryphon, tied close by, had settled to rest and Tor, untied, wandered the edge of the forest, seeking sustenance. The squire followed Tor's un-tethered steps, then looked to Dominique—who offered but a silent shrug.

The mercenary excused himself, and took off over a hard pack of snow.

He needed a few moments away from Seraphim's hard blue gaze to collect his thoughts. Every time she looked at him she gazed straight into his eyes. Not an evasive, coy look, as most women were wont to express. The feeling that she touched his soul with an imperceptible appendage was so strong. What did she spy in his own eyes of such interest?

He also sensed she still did not completely trust him. Wise woman.

But all for naught. He had every intention of protecting Seraphim until her mission was complete. Woman or no, he would not be granted release from the burning question of his parentage until he did such.

The chill air quickly attacked his exposed cock as Dominique drew a line in the snow with steaming urine. A man should won-der if the thing might take up the freeze and fall off for the times he must whip it out just to relieve himself. He could think of far warmer places to put it. Though present company would go unconsidered. The last woman he wanted to expose his starv-ing lust to was a sword-wielding vixen like Seraphim d'Ange. That woman could emasculate with a mere glance. Rather, with the evil eye.

Securing the leather codpiece to his soft linen undershirt with a tug of the points, Dominique then slipped his fingers over the narrow slash in the thigh of his leather braies, courtesy of the black knight. 'Twas shallow, the cut. His flesh had taken on the chill, though the wound had already healed. There was not a drop of blood on his skin or clothing—at least not of the red variety. He smoothed away the congealed iridescent liquid, rubbing it between his fingers until it became powder and glistened into the air.

The only pain he felt was that of succumbing to his opponent's blade. A woman's blade, for the love of the Moon! He most certainly was not accustomed to such a bold woman. She deserved to be put in her place.

No. She deserves as much respect as you wish for yourself.

Indeed, he must set aside petty male/female comparisons. Seraphim d'Ange traveled a perilous course; she deserved nothing but his support. As their path drew closer to Creil, that course would only become more dangerous.

Tugging down his jerkin and drawing his gauntlet back on his hand, Dominique then punched a fist inside his other palm to stir his blood to a faster pace. He hated the chill and was most susceptible to drafts. Especially right between the shoulder blades. Once he exposed a bit of flesh the cold crept under his skin and remained until spring. He much preferred to grow a thick bushy beard to keep in the warmth, but the damned thing would do no more than sprout a thin shadow over his chin and upper lip.

Sorry man he'd turned out to be.

"Damned faery blood," he muttered, as he cupped his palms before his mouth and blew. His warm breath briefly touched his nose and cheeks, but disappeared all too quickly.

"Your mission is progressing nicely."

Dominique spun around, a stealthy movement bending him at the waist and crouching him into fight position, his dagger unsheathed and flashing before his face.

"You?" He relaxed his fight stance and jabbed the dagger-tip into the snow. "Morgana's spine, but you follow me even when I am taking a piss!"

The Oracle remained serene, an odd expression on the figure that appeared to Dominique to be a boy of perhaps nine or ten. Short spikes of palest brown hair spurted here and there, as if bed-tousled. A flat nose only made his eyes appear all the more generous. A sweet fragrance, like a fresh spring meadow, overwhelmed him always.

The wide brown gaze of innocence teased Dominique to question his beliefs every time the Oracle glimmered into form—for that is the only term Dominique could summon for the sudden appearance of the apparition—swept in on a glimmer.

But for as young as he appeared, Dominique suspected the Oracle was decades older in wisdom. And if he were really a ghost of some sort, he could have been dead for ages.

"Do you realize the black knight is a woman?" Dominique asked.

"I…did not know that until now."

Difficult to believe, knowing what Dominique did of the Oracle.

He regarded the vision with a careful summation of his visage. Not a flinch to his smooth features, the brown eyes held a frustrating clutch on naiveté. The Oracle knew everything. He'd given Dominique the layout of Abaddon's castle, provided him with the information that he would meet the black knight en route to Creil, had even relayed details from both battles that saw the first two de Mortes fall. Why hadn't he informed him of this important fact?

"A woman!" Dominique jabbed the trunk of a twisted elm with his boot, not hesitant at letting the Oracle see his disappointment.

"Can you keep her safe?"

"Against Abaddon, Sammael, and Lucifer?" Dominique shrugged a fall of snow from his shoulders then lifted his chin in challenge. "Sounds like a battle already won. And not by the black knight."

"You must believe in yourself, Dominique San Juste," the Oracle said in his whispery adolescent timbre. "You are of the earth; Seraphim is of fire. I chose you, knowing you would be a formidable match—as well a complement—to the d'Ange woman's fire."

"D'Ange," Dominique muttered, shaking his head in disbelief. "An angel riding a quest against the darkest demons in France—wait! You said you did not know she was a woman. And yet—you just said you chose me to match her fire." He raised an accusing finger on the glimmering figment. "You lie to me to serve your own selfish needs? What is the truth of my mission? Who are you, and why did you come to me?"

"You ask far too many questions, and already know the answers."

"And you are a double-talking nuisance."

"Have I yet steered you wrongly?"

The Oracle had first appeared to him three years ago. Dominique had been contemplating joining the English on the raid against Rouen, where Jeanne d'Arc would finally fall. No—contemplation had been all of a moment at sight of a purse gleaming with coin. He'd avoided siding with the English for years. But the coin...oh, that bright and sparkling coin.

The Oracle had appeared, insisting he go home. His mother needed him. Dominique had arrived only to hear his father's dying words. "I have loved you so, son."

Son. A word wrought of pure, priceless gold to Dominique's

troubled soul. Far more valuable than any English coin could offer. Yet beneath the gild lay a bronze core.

"Tell me, do you know *why* she quests so?"

The Oracle shrugged. Actually shrugged, which seemed to Dominique a very odd movement from one so otherworldly. "You have not asked her?"

"The woman is not one for conversation."

"She fears adversity."

"I am not the enemy."

"Make her believe it and together the two of you shall triumph. She fears the same thing you fear, releasing the anger and following her heart."

"I have no anger," Dominique said, his jaw tightening.

"Really? Why then this mission? Perhaps it is not necessary to provide the answer you seek?"

"I am not angry about my past—only—all right! So I *am* angry." He kicked at the snow, his frustration erupting in a powder of cold crystals. "It was not fair to be abandoned. To be left to my own devices in a world so unaccepting and....and wrong."

"You made it your own world, did you not?"

Dominique huffed. Another kick buried the toe of his boot.

"Come, Dominique, you tread too deeply in anger over such an insignificant portion of your life."

His parentage insignificant?

Before Dominique could protest the Oracle's suggestion, the waif of flowing robes and wide brown eyes was gone. Gone in a glimmer, a fizzle of twinkling lights and sweet scent.

"I hate it when he does that. Why can't I do that?"

But the Oracle's words lingered in his mind like heavy flakes of falling snow. Falling, but never landing on the ground. ...*such an insignificant portion of your life.*

No, 'twas not insignificant to his heart. To finally put to rest the decades-old question of who his real mother and father were was no little thing. He would have the answer, one way or another.

Pounding his boot heel against the elm trunk behind him, Dominique noticed the iridescent dust still coruscated from his person. He had to cast a glamour soon or risk exposing himself to Sera and Baldwin. A secret unnecessary to reveal; his mission did not rely on either of them knowing his truth.

Of course, he did not know their truths either. So many secrets. The squire—or was he a monk? And Seraphim d'Ange, the women who hid beneath a mask of male dress and bravery.

Well…he understood the need to hide. And for that reason he would not question.

Dominique pulled his cloak snug around his shoulders and flexed the muscles in his back. He'd hidden his true identity for so long he'd become accustomed to the aching need for release that always tingled between his shoulder blades. But not on this quest. He wanted the woman and her squire to accept him as an equal, not an anomaly.

Sera heard Dominique's footsteps crunch over the hard snow behind her. Settled in for the night, she shrugged her hood down to her shoulders, allowing the heat of the blazing fire to simmer over her face and neck.

"We thought you'd been stolen away by the fair folk," Baldwin offered from his tight little cocoon of wool cape as the mercenary landed camp.

"*He* thought as much," Sera corrected. "I do not speak of such nonsense."

"The nonsense that a man of my skill should allow himself to be stolen away?" Dominique moved close to the fire to draw heat into his chilled bones. "Or the fair folk?"

"The damn faeries," she muttered.

"You——" Sera marveled at the muscle that tensed in Dominique's jaw "——consider them nonsense?"

"You know naught of what you question, San Juste."

"Ah, I see. A nonbeliever. So you believe only in what you can see?"

"Aye, but——"

"You cannot see the wind, yet it is so powerful as to fell trees."

She regarded him with a wry smirk. No need to explain that she did believe, or to reveal her hatred for the hideous creatures. He was most likely a believer in the whimsical and magical ways of the fair folk, could have no idea of the true evil they wrought.

Dominique nodded, the movement of his hood clacking the hematite stones against one another in a canorous ring. "I shall grant you that, for the sake of peace."

"I shall take it without your leave. Did you scan the perimeter?"

"We will be safe here in the forest for the night."

"Your horse wanders freely," Baldwin commented.

"He does." Having no intention of elaborating, Dominique moved between Sera and the squire and picked up a leafless elm branch to poke at the fire. A few jabs raised a flurry of red fire sprites over the blaze in a spiral of escape. "Have you ale or wine?"

"No supplies," Baldwin said with a shudder.

"You should have filled your belly in Pontoise," Sera commented. If the man craved drink he could melt down snow for all she cared. "We travel light, nothing to burden our journey."

"Just wondering," he said, a dismissive tone to his voice. Sera gauged that he was not a man to anger easily. Unless one tried to lie to him about their identity.

She leaned forward, propping her elbows on her knees, and unfocused her eyes upon the brilliant orange flames. In her peripheral view, the mercenary's stallion did indeed roam freely. Curious. But she didn't trouble over the reason. Instead she released a sigh and allowed her shoulders to sag. It felt good not to think. To relax before the blaze. The warmth brought a numbness that spread to her skull. This night she would not worry of what the morrow may bring.

But close, sat San Juste. Too close for the damsel to disregard.

Just one moment for my pleasure?

Very well, Sera thought, being much too tired to conjure an excuse.

From the corner of her eye, she studied the side of the mercenary's face, as he, too, voided out on the flames. His jaw was so sharp as to be deadly. Not a single line of age creased the unnaturally smooth flesh. Though black stubble lended masculine roughness to an otherwise tender visage. Indeed, a handsome man. But she was not taken to swooning, as Baldwin liked to tease. Had Sera ever before favored a man, she had required but a look and a bend of her forefinger to bring him to her side.

That was me, the damsel cooed.

Enough then. Sera lowered her head onto her knees and closed her eyes, forcing the damsel back into the darkness. 'Twas risky to allow such thoughts.

"From where do you hail, San Juste?" Baldwin asked.

"East of Creil, but five hours on a slow horse. Deep in the Valois Wood where my father built a cottage for my mother, far away from any village."

"Your parents await their son's return from a successful mission?" Baldwin wondered.

"I have not been to the wood for over a year. What of you, squire? How long have you been at the d'Ange castle?"

"Let's see...since the May Day festival, I believe. Aye, I re-member sweet Margot and her plump—"

"Benwick."

Baldwin quieted at Sera's terse reprimand. He offered a shrug and slumped into his nest of cape and supplies.

"Did you lose parents," Dominique wondered, "loved ones in the New Year's ordeal?"

"I am an orphan since six. Spent all of my life living upon the discards of others, the swiftness of my fingers, and the finely tuned wit of my brain."

At Baldwin's boastful declaration Sera cast him the mongoose eye. And he saw.

With a resolute sigh, the squire said, "Very well, if you must know, before I became a squire, well, er...a postulant, I was...a toad-eater. Though you mustn't hold it against me," he rushed in. "I atone for my crimes every day. I was seeking orders, for heaven's sake!"

"Toad-eater?" Dominique wondered. The flames danced in his dark eyes. Sera could not look away from the beguiling sight. No red demons there, only violet allure. "Are not toads poisonous?"

"Oh, aye," Baldwin offered. Then with a wriggle of his thick brows, he added, "*If* you really eat them."

"I don't understand. You say you ate them, and then you say you did not."

"Exactly." Baldwin sat up a little straighter. A proud smile beamed beneath his wearied brown eyes.

Sera would allow him such pride, for she was the first to admit the man was not the sort of hardened criminal that belonged swinging at the end of a noose. He was the closest thing to family she had left. She needed family. A place to belong. A place to be loved.

The squire spread his hand open, the long fingers splaying to catch the heat. "You see, I used to work for a magician, Melmoth the Marvelous. You've heard of him? Known through all parts of France and England, also a small portion of the Irish Isle. Anyway, I helped him sell his elixirs at market every summer to unsuspecting dupes—er, patrons."

"I think I begin to understand," Dominique said. "The patrons would witness you eating a poisonous toad. You would go into convulsions or some form of grand death charade. The magician would rush an amazing cure-all elixir down your throat, therefore drawing the poison from your body and curing you before all eyes."

"And only three sous per six drachms!" Baldwin declared in his best hawker's voice. "I never did eat the toad. Well, there were occasions—hell, a man tends to build an immunity by slowly exposing himself to poison. I can munch a whole toad now without worry of dropping dead. Rather tasty roasted."

Dominique leaned across the distance between he and the squire. "And just how were you such a success when I myself have witnessed your remarkable inability to cover a lie?"

Baldwin drew his hand over his eyes to simulate laying a blindfold over them. With a laugh, he announced, "I was blind!"

"That's quite a skill, the fool that fools while acting the fool himself."

"A skill." The squire clutched his leather purse and squeezed the contents. A reassuring gesture. "But no more."

"Why the change of heart?"

"For as much as I relied on the scarf to blind the fools to my dupe, it did not serve to blind me. I began to notice the lost hope, the tragedy in the eyes circling Melmoth's stage. Their eyes were wide with the hopes of a magical cure to end all their woes, their pains. They were so much like the orphan boy that stood before them on the stage. And I was selling them snake oil. Abbe Belloc reassured me that dedicating my life to God was a noble effort."

"Indeed, it is. If you are prepared for such sacrifice."

"I am. Maybe. Hell…" He sighed, riffled his fingers through his this-way-and-that hair. "I'm working on it." He gave his purse another squeeze. "I'm not yet ready to give up the bones."

"Bones?"

Baldwin shrugged. "I bartered in bones as well. No longer. But I do have some excellent treasures." He dug in the leather purse at his hip. "See here, St. Miranda's finger bone. 'Tis an excellent charm against mud slides and natural disasters. And here!" He displayed a thin white bone before his glittering eyes. "The finger bone of St. Jude the Obscure, patron saint of Hopeless Causes—" he cast a glance Sera's way "—which could certainly be put to use in our endeavors."

Sera shook her head.

"Well, St. Eustache's toe bone really does work!" Baldwin insisted. "I rubbed it both nights you rode into battle."

"I see," she said. "And so I suppose they do work, for I am yet all of one piece."

Baldwin gave an exacting nod.

Sera reneged her challenge with a deftly concealed smirk behind her hand. The man needed some faith to cling to. And until he was ready to accept his own courage—for he did possess courage—he would need the false reassurance the bones offered him.

"And what of you?"

Sera lifted her chin at Dominique's query. No mistaking he had addressed her.

"You lost your family. A tragedy. Was there also…a husband?"

The smirk grew wider, and Sera had to dip her head to keep San Juste from seeing the mirth she knew glittered in her eyes. The mercenary's question came across as more personal than the man might like it to sound. Did he have an interest in her beyond his mission? She who slaughtered men, and stomped about in armor, and was more in resemblance to a man than a woman with long beautiful hair and a delicate step beneath flowing skirts?

Her heart warmed to think such. She could not fight the damsel's desire for love. Much as she had chosen to deny her tattered heart that emotion, she knew it was needed.

But it was not required for healing. Only avenging her family could provide that.

"I was to be married on the first day of the New Year." She regarded Dominique for his reaction. A raised brow. The warmth in his eyes contrasted acutely with his sharp features; she wasn't sure whether to trust this man or slit his throat.

She raked her fingers through her spiked coif and scratched. With a splay of her hand she said, "Despite outer appearances, I am marriageable. My father had land on the coast he wished me to have, so he found a husband. Someone who would not interfere with my desire to control the holdings."

"In cther words," Dominique figured, "a man malleable to your desires?"

"In a sense. I am not a cruel person, San Juste. Nor was my father. It was simply the only way I could own land. Henri agreed."

"Your husband?"

"Henri of Lisieux. He hadn't any land to inherit after a brush fire, courtesy of Mastema de Morte, razed his father's holdings. Lisieux was an interesting man…"

"Sera! You'd best run a comb through your hair and tidy up. Father has already declared the festivities begin."

Sera stood up from brushing under Gryphon's belly and pushed a long strand of hair from her eyelashes. Antoine slapped Gryphon's flank, then chucked his sister under the chin, pointing out the smudge of dirt there.

Since when had he been overconcerned with her appearance?

Ah. She found the answer in her brother's bright-eyed smirk. "He is here?"

"Father outdid himself with this one. Truly, you must see the man to believe it."

"That hideous to look upon?" Sera handed Antoine the brush and jerked her rucked-up sleeves to her wrists. The red damask kirtle was clean, though hay clung to the hem, and certainly the odor of stable would cling for the day.

"No, no, Father would not be so cruel to his only daughter." He slid an arm around her shoulder. "I still find it troubling that you allowed Father to choose your husband for you."

"Fathers choose their daughters' husbands every day, Antoine. Why should that disturb you so?"

"You are not like most women, Seraphim. Do you not desire... well, love?"

She shrugged, shooed away a metallic green hover fly from near her brother's face. "What woman does not?"

"There is still time to make your own choice. Do you not care for any of Father's knights?"

"Ha! They are adept idiots, the lot of them."

"I will remind you that I am a knight, dear sister."

"You are not stupid, Antoine. The knights that practice in the lists are adept at but one thing, and that is being men. Boisterous, unclean, single-minded, sword-swinging, idiot men. They reign on the battle-field, and I know they choose to reign in the bed chamber, as well. I cannot live with a man who will seek to reign over me, Antoine, you know that."

"Indeed, I do understand. So you must go then, look upon the man

Father has chosen. But be cautious you don't frighten the mouse away with your overwhelming Amazon presence."

Sera left Gryphon to Antoine's care and strode out into the courtyard, destined for the great hall, where she felt sure to find amidst revelry and celebration her future husband.

So Father had done as she had requested. Just a proxy for her holdings; she and Father had agreed. Not a man who had designs on her future, let alone his own future. Someone compliant, simple, and agreeable. Though not meek. She did not wish a milksop to have to protect should her holdings ever be challenged. He must command a sword as well as a gentle tongue.

She would be no man's chattel.

Offering a good day to the laundress who hung wet sheets to dry on the line, Sera marched inside the castle and followed the gay melody of lutes and harp-strings to the rush-strewn keep. Baldwin Ortolano, the abbe's newest postulant, bowed and offered a "Good day, my lady."

A gray-bellied dove swooped down from the rafters, flittering a breeze across Sera's face. At the far end of the great hall Father and Mother were seated upon the dais. 'Twas a rare occasion that saw Mother out of her solar. She held her simply coiffed head regally, though her curled fingers were clutched tight to her stomach.

Mother's lady-in-waiting stood with a hand cupped over her mouth. The object of her stifled glee stood on the floor before the dais, a maroon velvet liricap spilling from his head onto narrow shoulders. His doublet, belted in gold about his waist, did not so much hang from his shoulders, as drip. Two long sticks for legs were capped off by long pointed leather shoes. Not so much comical, as pitiful.

Had this man ever touched sharpened steel in defense?

Sera halted but three strides before the man. Behind her, surprising winter sun beamed through the windows set high upon the wall, lighting her figure in worship. She had planned her position thusly.

Placing arms akimbo, and raising her chin assertively, Sera spoke with a certain discernment, "My lord Henri, I presume?"

The man's jaw dropped. He pointed a long finger then, thinking better, dropped the hand to his side. He stuttered on the first syllable, then finally spat out, "My—my lady Seraphim?"

"I told you she was a fine piece of woman," Marcil d'Ange bellowed from his throne. "Wine! We celebrate from this moment until the stroke of midnight, when the New Year comes marching in. Let the First Foot bring blessings for us all!"

A lute player plucked an arpeggio of notes and the flute joined in. Serving maids rushed in with pitchers of wine and silver goblets, and the merriment of the hall resumed. But Sera remained, hands on hips, a smile curving her lips, as she studied Henri's nervous gaze. Gold eyes rimmed with thick blond lashes dodged here and there. He dared not look upon any one part of her for too long, yet his gaze could not help but stride over her face, shoulders, and body.

He surely thought, What the hell have I gotten myself into?

"I do not bite," Sera said, and offered her hand.

Henri stepped forward, bowed to one bony knee, and kissed the back of her hand. A sweet gesture. One that startled Sera. Amidst the stir of music and dance and drink, this man had just promised something to her. His faith, his trust, his acceptance. Such a simple victory. But hardly a triumph over one so...malleable.

"Forgive me if I stare, my lady." Henri's voice no longer stuttered, but he had to shout to be heard above the din of revelry. "You are quite remarkable."

"My father claims the d'Anges come from hearty Amazonian stock."

"No doubt. Er, but it is your beauty I remark upon." He hastily removed his cap, exposing stick-straight blond hair cut in a fashionable circle that rimmed just above each ear. "I feel quite a shrew next to your bright shining star. I hope I can be everything you expect in a husband."

She smiled at his humble confession. "You already are, Henri."

Her father had chosen well.

Sera, deciding to walk alongside Henri, allowed him to take the first step up to the dais and lead her to the seat next to her father. For the evening she allowed the romance of marriage and gaining a man to claim her land to overtake reality. When it neared the midnight hour she was drunk, tired, and quite pleased with the circumstances of her life.

"If you'll excuse me, my lord Henri," she whispered in his ear. "I must retire."

"You'll not stay and ring in the New Year?"

"I was up before dawn, and have been busy in the stables and the garden and the larder all the day. The festivities have brought me to the peak of exhaustion. I wish to sleep, repair for the new day, which will find me a blushing bride at your side."

Henri afforded an embarrassed smile. Sera couldn't be sure if it was that, or perhaps excessive drink that colored his cheeks. Sweet man. He would be easy enough to ignore. Or perhaps, grow to love.

She pressed a palm to his cheek. "Good eve, Henri. May the First Foot bring happiness to our lives."

"The First Foot?" Dominique asked. A blaze of sparks burst skyward at the poke of his stick. Somewhere above the encampment an owl hooted.

"The first man who crosses the threshold after the midnight hour," Baldwin explained, his gaze fixed to the flickering flames, "holds the futures of all the family members within."

"It is said a man with dark hair and a dark complexion is most favorable," Sera offered, as blandly as the squire had. "He did have dark hair."

Dominique looked to Baldwin for explanation. The squire muttered the name, "De Morte."

"Did not the wardcorne announce his arrival from the battlements?" Dominique wondered.

"I found him with an arrow to the brain," Baldwin said. "Lucifer's entire army appeared as if bats rising up from hell. There were so many of them…"

A chill silence held the threesome. Had the flames voice they would have cackled wicked taunts at Sera's tale.

Had her family been punished for the sanguine choosing of Henri de Lisieux as her proxy? No. Maybe? No. Father had been to arms against Lucifer de Morte for weeks. Lucifer demanded payment for the surplus wheat d'Ange lands had produced over the past three years. The new methods of agriculture her father had been testing had proven fruitful beyond imagination. Father had given the surplus to the needy villagers.

She could still hear the deafening roar of her father's voice as he'd set Lucifer's messenger to right. "You tell de Morte I'll see him in hell before I bow to an English king. And the surplus has been given away!"

"Ah! But what of you, San Juste?" Sera chased away the haunting echoes by averting attention from herself. "Have you family? Tell us about them and lift this sudden darkness that has fallen over our heads."

"My family." Dominique stirred a branch in the snow at his feet, designing a circle. "My parents are both dead. 'Twas the plague brought over by the English a few years back."

"I'm sorry." She remembered that horrible summer. The plague had reduced the numbers in France by a quarter. Elizabeth, the young girl who had tended the d'Ange sheep, had been stricken. She had suffered two weeks of agony before finally surrendering to death. "Have you a wife? Children?"

"Neither a wife nor child."

"That you know of," Sera said with a hint of mirth. Anything to lift the spirits of this dismal trio.

Dominique rose. His expression showed no clue that he'd

caught the mirthful mood. "I have no children, my lady. And believe me, I would have a care to know if I did."

"Honorable words, uttered by many a man," she said lightly.

"I know women believe men lust after any wench who should cross their paths, but that is not the case with me. My lady——" he gazed down upon her with fire-glinting eyes "——when I love, I love deeply. And I do not take the act of carnal relations lightly. Yes, there may be occasion when a wench will serve, but she will be treated with respect and dignity, as one should only expect. Unlike some people I have come to know, who bully others about with commands and choose the most amiable of matches to lord over in their marital bliss."

He then turned and marched off into the forest, destination unknown. His exit left the encampment a cold hollow shivering amongst the cage of winter-raped trees.

Snapping out of the icy hold of Dominique's words, Sera looked to Baldwin, who nodded effusively in response to her unspoken question. "He was speaking directly to you."

"Hmph. I had no intention of *lording over* Lisieux." She toed a stray piece of bark into the fire. "Why do you always side with San Juste?"

He shrugged. "He is different from most. Not your normal boisterous, demanding male."

She lifted a brow at Baldwin's stunning insight.

"And he has an eye for you."

"Ridiculous."

"As you wish," came Baldwin's reply, smothered by the wrap of his cape as he settled himself back into a cocoon. "He is good for the both of us, Sera. I pray you grant him the chance to prove it."

"I have denied him nothing," she said, and allowed her body

to fall back against the elm trunk. A heavy sigh spumed a thick puff of frost before her face.

When I love, I love deeply. I do not take the act of carnal relations lightly.

"Indeed," Sera whispered. "What fortune a woman should reap, to be loved by Dominique San Juste."

SIX

So it had arrived. Dawn.

Dominique stood alone at the edge of the forest, his face turned to absorb the amber rays of sun as they widened and stretched the horizon in a dance of majesty. An incredible sight to behold. One he'd not missed for as long as he could recall.

Always the rising sun called to him. Much the way the moon beckoned he worship her luminescent glow.

But the sun's lure was not a favorable calling. For with the dawn came the darkness. At this time of day the evil thoughts, that dark roil of *something else,* burned deep within Dominique's being.

They did not want you. You are evil, not right!

Seraphim's voice wavered in the depths of his mind, blending with the other dark whispers. *Faeries are evil, malicious creatures...*

Curse them all!

He clenched his fists as tight as his jaw, then stretched out his fingers in alternate moves. Like a beast preparing for the lunge, working its talons in anticipation of the kill.

"What *is* this?" he asked now in a low hiss. As he would always ask.

An answer did not come. As it never did.

And so he replied to the silence. "Is this what it is that made them reject me? This anger within? The unexplainable darkness? Has it to do with my appearance, my dark hair and eyes? Or is it the evil that clutches my heart with every sunrise?"

Yes, the evil. It had been this very darkness that had possessed him yesterday morn, and had spurred him to challenge Seraphim. A necessary challenge, yes. But one he would not have issued to a woman had he not been cajoled by the dawn.

He was different because of his connection to the dawn. But why?

For decades Dominique had questioned his inner cache of unconscious memories, hoping to recall a preternatural image of his birth mother's face. Had she looked upon him, for one sweet moment, with love in her heart?

The image was impossible to fathom, to put into any real form. He'd been rejected and traded for something else. A more desirable—yet lesser—being.

Changeling was the word he'd learned to hate. Something...not right. Different. Unwanted. Cast out of Faery with no hope of re-entrance. He knew it was there—Faery. The Other Realm shimmered and moved all about him. Always so unreachable. All attempts to connect, to *become,* had been fruitless.

Dominique's wool cloak fluttered out from his body, flowing like a shadow dancing upon the slight morning breeze. The muscles between his shoulder blades tightened and flexed.

He would never possess the freedom to just *be.* But he prayed that with the answer to his greatest desire he could finally learn to accept. And with acceptance would come a certain freedom from the darkness.

In the distance, the sing of steel reverberating through the crisp morning air coaxed Dominique's thoughts from the past and all he could not become because of its elusivity.

Pulling his cloak securely about his shoulders and slipping off a glove to push stray hairs away from his face, he blew out a heavy exhale. Again the song of steel slicing winter air sounded. Drawn by curiosity, Dominique trod across the field of thick snow, crusted with an ice-crystal top layer. He landed a rise on the ground where Seraphim worked her blade with surprising skill.

Here in the long-stretching shadows of the forest the sword she wielded caught no sunlight to gleam or sparkle. But the motion of sharp, swift steel, and alluring female curves worked an orchestration of power, fire and beauty. What this woman lacked in physical strength was made up for with stealthiness. Feline prowess moved long legs—bent at the knee, her feet planted—to direct the sword's path. Chain mail and armor shrouded any feminine charm she might possess. But the notion that there, beneath the silver mesh, lay temptation, planted itself in Dominique's mind and clung like a burr to wool.

This warrior, this self-proclaimed Amazon, was not a woman to be wasted on such feebleness as the ill-fated Henri de Lisieux. Seraphim d'Ange was fire, and feral wickedness, and bright pride.

Fierce concentration kept her attention from his approach, until he was within distance to challenge. Her figure drew a graceful line through the icy air.

A few more steps, close enough to wound with a swift lunge…

"You're up rather early, San Juste." She expelled a controlled breath and swung her blade around to face him. The tip of her sword skimmed one of the hematite stones sewn onto his cloak. "I could have your head if I wish." A lift of her dark brow spoke defiance.

Perhaps being a woman was not a disadvantage after all. What man could concentrate on protecting his own hide when looking upon such a stunning opponent?

Every tilt of her head showered new light upon the different angles of her face. Cheekbones Dominique had once assumed sickly and gaunt were really quite fascinating in their elegance. Dark, narrow brows arced in a language of challenge and warning—and then allure. A smirk pursed thick, pink lips into a curious moue.

Surely, Seraphim would carry such advantage into Abaddon's castle. The Demon of the North's weakness was women. Luscious, brazen, beautiful women intent on serving him as their sexual master. Or so the Oracle had reported with blasé disinterest.

Dominique wondered now if Sera's appearance could be enhanced, made a bit more feminine. While intent observation most certainly found the beauty in her movement, the grace of her delicately sculpted visage; a glance, or a mere summation would see but the shaved hair, armor, and tattered men's clothing.

A man should desire to run his fingers through long luxurious waves of silken tresses. As would Abaddon. Sallow complexion from lack of food, and those dark circles under her eyes—hmm—how to improve her chances of success?

"You're dead, San Juste. I've just severed your head." She twisted her wrist, glancing the sword-tip under his chin. Dominique jerked his head away from the shaving steel. "What is it, man? Do you walk in your sleep yet?"

Dominique tried to shake away the distraction of Sera's feral attraction. But fierce interest plunged back upon him with sight of her heaving chest. Exertion. Energy. Power. *Female.* Beneath the chain mail lay a lush, full bosom that any man would desire to lay his head upon. To feast upon such delights—why, it had been months since he had suckled at the breast of a voluptuous woman. And he was no man to deny himself the pleasures of the flesh. Even if he must use glamour to mask his true identity.

Caught up in the beguiling rapture of such a fantasy, Dominique's feet suddenly left the ground. A hard force bent his knees. With one startled yelp, he lay on his back, staring up into the lightening morning sky.

And there was that face. Darkly arced brows, elegant cheekbones, and an ear-to-ear grin that revealed sparkling white teeth and a spot of glee set into each of her pale blue eyes.

"I can only hope that Abaddon is as dull-witted as you in the morning." She made a show of carefully drawing her sword across his neck, but not touching flesh, before backing away. "Perhaps that is the plan, we strike at dawn, before the Demon of the North has risen from his bed of iniquity?"

Embarrassed that he'd been taken down while his thoughts had been captivated by the unremarkable curves and motions of a woman who preferred man's dress, Dominique jumped to his feet, and brushed hard crystals of snow from his knees and the backs of his arms.

"I am not at my best at dawn," he remarked and, having had quite enough, turned to march back to the fire.

But some force would not allow him to retreat. It fixed his boots in the snow and stiffened his knees. *He had to know.* The fantasy certainly warranted the question.

Reneging his stiff stance to a more genial smoothness, Dominique turned and asked, "Did you ever have occasion to behave as a woman, my lady? Perhaps before Lucifer de Morte decided to irrevocably alter your life?"

Sera stabbed her sword into the snow and, arms akimbo, marched up to him. A grin affixed to her face and glittered in her eyes, akin to that of a highwayman before he stripped one bare of coin and clothes. "Aye, I did once have a care to my appearance. I used to wear a gown, and curtsey and bow to my betters in the most ladylike manner. I was chatelaine of my father's home for over a decade. Besides practicing in the lists with my brother, I daily tended the larder, took accounts, and supervised the salting of meat and preserving of vegetables. I pressed my fingers into dough to knead it for evening meal. I scrubbed walls and swept rushes. I lowered my gaze when I deemed it appropriate for visiting lords and ladies."

She bowed her head then swept her gaze up to meet his. Challenge glinted in icy-blue hardness. Winter-pale lips smirked. "Why do you ask, San Juste? Are you in the market for a wife?"

"Perhaps."

His comment shook the challenge from her hard visage— but for a moment. She swung her blade up to rest casually against her armored shoulder. "And what would you do with a wife, who, when she is not kneading bread, is beheading villains?" The raspy tone of her voice possessed an unmistakable trace of seduction.

"Perhaps sleep a bit more peacefully. A man cannot do all the work."

No answer to that one.

Pleased that his reply had hit its mark Dominique strolled off. She was a tough nut; or so, she had mastered the mask. But he wouldn't mind pulling the hard, armor mask away from all that she hid. Maybe even—no, no, no! He'd set his mind to be her protector, not her lover. Besides, he much valued his ballocks. And that woman's eyes flashed "emasculation" beneath every alluring arc of those deadly, dangerous brows.

"And don't forget it," he muttered to his mutinous subconscious.

Baldwin had risen to stir the embers and warm his hands. Dominique stopped and lifted his sword belt from the concave nest in the snow where he had slept through the night.

A glance back over his tracks found Seraphim had resumed practicing her maneuvers. Those long arms and broad shoulders delivered a swift blow. A man must be on his guard when approaching her, whether with challenge in mind, or seduction.

No, certainly not her lover. Not…yet.

"Squire, tell me what the two of you did the morning after Lucifer had annihilated the d'Ange family?"

Baldwin rubbed his hands together in an attempt to bring warmth to his palms. Two forceful blows into his fingers distributed heat through his flesh. "We buried her family."

What any grieving woman would do. But…

"Did Seraphim shed tears?"

"Not a one."

Dominique nodded and sat before the fire. "I thought as much."

"He is Master of the Seven Hells," Dominique explained as the threesome, mounted, journeyed cautiously down a well-traversed stretch of road. Still-warm horse droppings—tested by Dominique—gave clue whoever had passed before them was not far off. The party was quite large to judge from the wideness of the trail. "Which translates to seven booby traps surrounding Abaddon's person. The first of which, being boiling water."

"No oil?" Baldwin wondered, as he rubbed his hands briskly together and thrust them under his armpits.

"Too expensive," Dominique called back. "Abaddon prefers to spend his coin on the finer luxuries such as food, scent, and woman-flesh."

"Not entirely foolish," Baldwin added with a glance to Sera, who admonished with a look. He flinched, and lowered his head, then muttered as he clutched his bag of bones, "I know I've got a bone in here for the mongoose eye. Somewhere…"

"And where is this boiling water?" Sera wondered.

"It is released from the battlements upon a stranger's approach. There is a fine lacing of machiolations surrounding the entirety of the castle. But never is a guard seen. Some believe the Demon of the North to dabble in the black arts. His castle is a living beast, acting against intruders by its own volition."

"What are the others?" Sera urged. "If we make it past the scalding water." She sat ramrod straight upon Gryphon, but her eyes peeked out from under her hood. She had wrapped her cloak about her body from mouth to toes.

"There is a tunnel that leads to the main bailey. The walls of Abaddon's castle are twenty feet thick. You pass under a tunnel that is lined with murder holes. Rumor has it a man must keep his eyes shut up tight, for the moment the whites of his eyes are revealed, a poison arrow shoots out from a murder hole and strikes him dead."

Baldwin drew in a breath. He clutched his heart, and shook his head. "I've no bones for that."

"Easy enough," Sera commented, much to the squire's stunned jerk of head. "To traverse a tunnel blind. What of the third hell?"

"Ah, well that is rather interesting," Dominique explained. "They say the inner bailey is cursed with swirling winds so fierce they will pluck up a fully armored man and toss him as if a doll of rags against the castle wall."

"Ouch," Baldwin said on a shudder.

"And if we pass that?" Sera prompted.

Dominique turned on Tor's back and eyed the stone-faced angel. Did she have no fear, or was she more foolish than he dared suspect?

"The door to Abaddon's castle is protected by a force of spears on a spring mechanism—a porcupine. One touches the door to open it, the springs are released, and the man is skewered from head to toe with hundreds of iron stakes."

"How do you know so much about Abaddon's castle?" Baldwin wondered. "Have you been there before?"

"I have not. The Oracle provides me the information I need."

"Yet this oracle did not inform you that the knight you sought was a woman."

Seraphim's raised brow worked an odd twist in Dominique's gut. 'Twas as if a fire sprite leapt from her triumphant gaze and burrowed deep inside his body. The sprite pushed aside the darkness of his past, kicked aside the insistent pining for answers with a flaming toe, and planted herself with a satisfactory smack of her palms. She had gotten under his skin. And he wasn't sure if he wanted to scratch that itch, or let it settle, allowing it to spread throughout his body like the plague.

"Why do you stare at me so, San Juste?"

Still considering the fire sprite, Dominique inclined his head. No, he would not evict the mischievous entity. He rather liked the way it made him feel.

Baldwin muttered, "You've bewitched the poor soul."

A snicker from behind him averted Dominique's thoughts. "She's done nothing of the sort." In a flurry of kicked-up snow and clinking mail, Dominique pressed Tor ahead of the trio.

"You've explained but four of the seven hells," Sera rasped out in that scratchy voice that was becoming less and less irritating to Dominique's ears. He'd noticed the scabbed line of a wound peeking out from her cloak. If Lucifer had left her for dead, most likely she bore that bastard's brand upon her neck. "What happens after we gain Abaddon's door?"

"I know naught of the interior of the North Demon's castle. But if we are not bloodied and beaten by then, I wager we just might have a chance."

At Sera's sudden straightening, Dominique swung around to scan the horizon. She had spied a band of travelers. A caterpillar of bobbling lights marched slowly through the gray velvet night.

"Mummers," Baldwin whispered. "Most likely stopping at the next village. Which would be Creil."

"Our ticket inside Abaddon's walls," Sera said with a decisive nod. "We blend in with the caravan and slip in unnoticed."

"Indeed." Dominique said. "Perhaps we shall make a few new friends this eve."

Dominique led the trio in amongst the conglomeration of covered wagons and horses. Sera took notice that the mercenary seemed to win the trust of the mummers with a mere glance. The stones surrounding his hood *clacked* with each congenial nod of his head, alerting those that had not seen him to the dark stranger who could charm with his eyes. Following Baldwin's long strides, Sera kept her head down and her hood pulled over her cheeks.

They quickly learned that the mummers had stopped just outside the village to eat and rest through the night. They would not stop in Creil, for they feared the occult reach of the Demon of the North. Although the only way through the village was a

narrow passage sandwiched between a treacherous granite out-
crop and Abaddon's castle wall. 'Twas a perilous journey that
must be contemplated before attempting.

The mummers acted like a colony of well-organized bees.
Each person had a duty, such as gathering firewood, starting the
fire, or preparing food. A cursory scan of the snow-glittered encampment marked out three dozen men and women thriving
in the rags and filth that a life on the road pressed upon them.
Hair hung in clumps around dirty faces. Fingers and feet were
bound by soiled cloth to keep back the cold. But everywhere,
spirits remained light.

The mood grew magical as a great bonfire exploded to life
and salted meat was passed from hand to hand. Watered ale and
stale bread served the dancers, musicians, and self-proclaimed
artists their midnight meal.

Accepting a chunk of meat from a dwarf with bells jingling
around his felt cap and a ferret peeking out from the neck of
his tunic, Sera thanked him, then separated herself from the
bevy of women that now crowded around Baldwin.

She took great joy in the meat this time, for Baldwin's speech
in Pontoise still resonated.

No one bothered her overmuch as she moved around the
perimeter of the camp. 'Twas fine, for she did not make for good
conversation, and had always felt uncomfortable around a mass
of strangers. Women especially. She had never really fit in
around the castle. Be it with her mother's ladies, who would sit
and tend needlework and listen to the minstrel's romantic tales,
or with the serving women who most often avoided her for fear
she would assign them yet another task.

'Twas her father's knights, and their conversation, that had
always drawn her. Talk of battle skill and boasting, and of cam-
paign long and arduous, yet satisfying in victory. Even a bawdy

line or two about a fetching wench who worked in the laundry or scullery had served most interesting.

Certainly Sera had learned much about the carnal relations from such snippets of conversation. Enough to know the pain she had felt the night Lucifer had violated her was not normal, or right. As for pleasure, now that was a man's right. The woman merely served as a means to release.

No, that's not right, the damsel whispered. *A woman can know pleasure if the man cares to make it so.*

Sera knew as much, for her father had been gentle and doting with her mother. All Sera's life she had witnessed her parents' lingering caresses and breathtaking glances, even up to the night of her wedding celebration. A true knight of chivalry, her father.

But chivalrous knights were few and far between. Certainly Sera might never be so fortunate as to capture the eye of a kind and caring soul. She had always been different, set apart from others. Perhaps because of her size, which certainly frightened off more men than it did attract them.

Perhaps, as well, she was different due to her forthright manner and unwillingness to be but a mere woman. Nothing wrong with that. She'd never once felt lonely. No, never lonely when ensconced within the loving reach of her family's arms.

And now you have no family.

A dry, awkward swallow forced the final chunk of meat down Sera's tender throat. She needed ale to chase the hideous taste to her stomach.

A glance around the encampment to sight liquid rescue spied Dominique. He had slipped to the edge of the disembarked cavalcade of wagons, and now conversed with a pretty young girl clad in turquoise wool and glittering silver bells. She couldn't be any more than ten and six, Sera figured. Much too young for the man. Yet she batted her lashes with the stealthiness of a pouncing tiger. Not too young to tempt.

It was when Dominique slid an ungloved hand along the girl's arm, and slipped his fingers beneath her wool cloak that Sera inhaled sharply. Did the man think to serve his pleasures this eve while she and Baldwin stood by waiting? No wonder he had been so eager to join with the mummers! That certainly explained the lustful looks he'd been giving her lately. The man was randy. And, obviously, sought a cure to that lustful state.

Trust him? Ha! Trust? When he had more thought to swive wenches than in the task he'd set to himself of protecting her hide?

Sera scanned the crowd and found Baldwin engulfed by women. "All the men in my employ are but slackards," she huffed. "Damn them both! I can see to Abaddon de Morte myself."

Dominique had held Sera in sight, had felt sure she'd chosen a spot to sit and rest for the night. But now the ground before the branch-stripped willow was bare, the ax-abraded trunk unblocked by a tall, mysterious black knight. 'Twas a good thing the mummers had come from the North; they'd not yet heard of the legend. Not that it should matter. But Dominique liked to keep the odds in his favor.

Stuffing his well-earned prize up under his jerkin and tucking it in the waist of his braies, Dominique then stepped carefully over logs laid around the fire and bodies engaged in settling for the evening beneath blankets and thick sheep's wool wraps. The sweat that had begun to run from his scalp froze as Dominique stepped farther away from the fire. It had been quite warm in the wenches' covered wagon with the candles and two other women and all the many yards of fabric and pillows. A virtual harem.

A bit of renegade coruscation hadn't been noticed by any as he'd climbed inside to view their wares. Everything had been granted a bit of glitter for the candle glow and relaxed inhibitions.

But now he was cold. And worried.

Where had Sera gotten herself to?

While he felt confident that none of the men had had time to determine the lean young knight in hood and mail was not a man, Dominique could not be sure Sera hadn't scouted out trouble.

Baldwin was useless. The squire, surrounded by women, had been escorted to a wagon with a tankard of ale in one hand and a wench's hindquarters in the other. Seeking vows, eh? Difficult to imagine the lanky young man in robe and tonsure. But he could not dispute the man for sowing his oats. Baldwin did not strike him as overly pious. Bone bartering and toad swallowing? Pray there are no toads in the women's wagon, Dominique thought with a smile.

The sweet scent of burning ash filled the encampment and lingered in the frozen air. His spurs muffled by packed snow, Dominique spied movement behind the first wagon heading the mummers' train. He paused, listened to determine if it might be a man standing guard or—

"Seraphim!" Dominique sprang out, and jumped before the woman who marched from the encampment. "Where the hell do you think you are going? And by yourself?"

"On to Abaddon's," she huffed. "It is but half a league away. Gryphon is tied up two wagons down—he'll not serve me inside the man's lair."

"You speak insanity." He gripped her wrist, but she pulled from his fingers. "We planned to enter the castle as a trio. Why do you march off?"

A haughty jut of her chin turned her sapphire-hard eyes on his. "Because you've nothing in mind but swiving wenches."

"Swive— Ah!" She must have watched him work his best seduction upon the dancing girl. Then to see him climb inside her covered wagon?

A smile curled Dominique's lips. He pressed a gloved finger over his mouth to hide his mirth. "And would that bother you overmuch if, indeed, I had more amorous intentions this evening? Surely a man must be allowed to tend his needs."

"Needs? I—I've no concern for your love affairs, I assure you that."

Oh, didn't she? Dominique quickened his steps to match her own, then swung around to block her path. "Then why mention it?"

"I—bloody hell, San Juste!" She stepped to the side, but he followed her motions. Twice now they had danced. He enjoyed this round thoroughly. "When you would much prefer swiving over the task at hand—"

He gripped her shoulder, stifling her foolish rampage. "We agreed to follow the mummers' train to Abaddon's castle tomorrow morn before the sun rises. Remember? We enter under cover of a crowd?"

"Mayhap cover of midnight's bleak darkness would serve a lone intruder just as well."

"Seraphim."

"Very well! I shall wait until morn." With a jerk, she detached herself from his touch, and clamped her arms across her chest. Her gauntlets scraped shrilly across the thick chest plate she wore. "Return to your swiving and leave me be."

"If you must know, I've no desire to swive anyone tonight."

"Make me believe that after all the hungry looks you've been giving me lately."

"You noticed?"

She gave a shrug. "I should have to be blind not to."

Dominique followed her turning body with a deft step. He bent to catch her gaze, and when he found it, he would not release it. "And did I act upon these hungry looks?"

She stared hard at him. Something was going on behind those fixed blue gems, but he could not determine exactly what. Although—he braced himself—emasculation wasn't a pretty sight.

Finally she said, "You are too offended by my appearance. Worry not, mercenary, I understand, you had to wait until you found more feminine fodder for your lust."

His lust? Who was she to speak of things she could never know!

This time he gripped both her shoulders, forcing her to meet his gaze. "I am on a mission, and cannot concern myself with amorous temptations, so you may set your worries aside, my lady of the stolen armor. I desire no woman."

"Not anyone?"

Her eyes were not cold, not indescribable in color anymore. They were blue. A deep, rich, creamy blue that had been plucked from the sky on a warm summer's eve.

"No, er...no," he said, more softly. *Not really sure of that answer, eh, San Juste?* Did *anyone* also include a mail-garbed angel? "I was merely on a mission—"

"Ha!" Her breath spumed out in clouds. A hard frost glazed over the softness in her eyes. "A mission which involved running your hands over the body of a pretty young woman."

"She wasn't so pretty," Dominique said. "Oh, damn it all—here!" He reached up under his jerkin, then thrust the bundle he'd seduced off the wench on the ground at Sera's feet. "I thought this would aid you to insinuate yourself into Abaddon's chambers. I did not remove it from any woman's body, nor did I have to remove any of *my* clothing to obtain such. As it seems to trouble you fiercely that I might have. Good eve to you, d'Ange."

He turned to stomp away—but figured he better check before he left. "Can I trust that you will remain through the night for departure at dawn?"

"Aye," she said, very softly, as she stared at the red damask splayed on the ground.

With that agreement Dominique spun and tromped back to the fire. He would find a cozy blanket—sans woman—and hunker down for the night.

Sera bent and drew her fingers over the glossy swash of arabesqued silk. It slipped over her gauntlets like blood from a rose. Dominique had somehow gotten a gown for her. *I did not remove it from any woman's body.* He'd had no intention of enjoying that woman; he'd only been thinking of her.

Abaddon de Morte's weakness is women.

She would need this dress.

I desire no one...

A sudden twinge compressed inside Sera's chest, squeezing, then releasing her heart. For some reason, the idea of Dominique San Juste *not* desiring her hurt. And she couldn't begin to reason why it should.

SEVEN

"That's not going to work," Dominique commented, as he slipped a hand up under Sera's arm and began to undo the leather buckles that secured the pauldron to the breastplate she wore.

"Unhand me!" Sera twisted away, eliciting a bite of anger from Dominique as the armor pinched his winter-iced flesh. "I'll not take kindly to such intimacy, San Juste."

"Intimacy?"

It was dawn. He was testy. He could not allow that comment to go unchallenged. Gripping Sera's arm, Dominique pulled the fiery vixen against his body in a swift movement that took her by surprise. A rarity, he felt sure.

"My lady, I vow to you, should I press an intimate touch upon your person, you will certainly know it when it happens."

Her icy-blue eyes flared wide as she processed that remark. But she did not back down from her arrogant stance, holding her chin firmly thrust and her shoulders squared.

"Feisty piece of chain mail," Dominique muttered. He released her in a chitter of mail rings and armor plate. "This attire is not in any way a boon to your mission. You cannot wear the black armor that has made you infamous in the ears of the de Mortes. Every castle guard will be on the lookout for such."

"You said there were no guards."

"That I know of. Do you want to risk that chance?"

No reply. She had difficulty in answering to him when he challenged her authority. He would not press. This time.

"Now come, let me help you out of this. Your mail and leather tunic will serve until you stand before Abaddon."

"I must wear the cuirass."

He afforded a lingering glance over the curved breast plate she tapped. It expertly disguised any hint of what might be a very generous bosom. *Yes, she is voluptuous beneath the hard armor. A full lush body to complement her brazen take-charge persona.* He prayed it.

"Yes, that would be wise."

"Have *you* no armor?"

She dropped her stubborn guard and looked over his plain clothing of cloak, jerkin, and laced leather boots. A thin vest of mail slipped out from under his leather jerkin. He did not wear it for protection. It provided the weight he required to keep from suddenly floating up from the ground. But she must not know that.

"That mail will not stop a spring-loaded spear. And your head, man, where's your helmet?"

"I shall survive," Dominique said. He knew he would. Perhaps a spear to the brain would do serious damage, but he wouldn't move slowly enough to catch steel with his head. "Besides, I can only follow you so far. Once the seven hells have been overcome and there remains but Abaddon, it is in your hands to fell the demon. I have merely been sent to guide and protect."

"Some protection. You would leave me alone with this man?"

A stutter in Sera's heartbeats preceded a vision of horned shadows upon her chamber wall, and the stinging pain of entry as Lucifer de Morte debauched her. Damaged her soul.

She would make it right, fit back together the pieces of her soul.

"You know the plan. Abaddon's weakness is women. Not a woman accompanied by a mercenary. With this sword at your hip, and if you follow the plan carefully, de Morte won't have a chance to spring. Remember, gain access and strike immediately. Don't give him time to think. You are the One, the only one with the connection."

"Connection?"

Dominique regarded her coolly. "There is but one who walks the earth who can end the de Morte reign."

"That's news to me, San Juste. Is this more of your Oracle's doing?"

"There is but One who is connected to the villains in some way I am not privy to. The Oracle provides only the information I need."

"And you are *sure* it is me?"

"You've murdered two de Mortes thus far."

The word murder sent an icy chill up Sera's spine. She did not like to consider herself involved in such. *If you do not take down the de Mortes, then who will?*

Indeed. Sera tightened her jaw.

She had embarked upon this revenge quest knowing there was some force pushing her forward, an unnamable, yet powerful urge to see justice. Perhaps that force was this connection San Juste spoke of. It made little sense to her. But if she were to stand back and look upon her life at this very moment 'twould make little sense as well.

She, the one with this mysterious connection?

So be it.

Sera let out a hefty sigh as Dominique knelt on the ground and unfastened the curved metal greaves from her legs. His movements were light and brisk, far from the intimacy she expected a man's touch to harbor. Hell, what was she thinking?

She gripped her sword and slithed it up and down inside the steel scabbard at her hip. For some reason this man toyed with her concentration. She knew why. He was in her life for more reason than to protect. He was here to tempt. Though were she at home with her family—had de Morte not murdered them—San Juste's presence would serve a temptation no longer. Without this quest to allay her attentions, she could have allowed herself to feel, to admire, to…desire. *The damsel might have had her moonlight knight.*

As it was, she must commit to the task.

No armor? Very well. It would create too much of a clatter. Her mail chausses would protect until the very last moment. But wield this large blade? Surely her disguise would be given up when sporting a sword outside a fanciful damask gown. She would fasten the kris dagger around her ankle and, hidden by fabric, it would serve when the time came. It would have to. She just prayed it would serve the *coup de grâce* when needed.

The first two de Mortes had been felled upon battleground. Sera had been surrounded by men, enemy and ally, each distracted from her progress by their own objectives—like staying alive. Confidence had surged through her system as she'd ridden in upon Gryphon's mighty back and had swung her sword. A mindless act, spurred on by the calamity that had surrounded.

But to face one single man in a room without any other, save perhaps a servant who could also be counted as her enemy?

"Seraphim?"

She flashed her eyes open to find the deep crushed-violet depths of Dominique's eyes fixed to her gaze. Every wobble of the mummers' torches, moving around behind them, sparked another layer of color in the orbs that had begun to fascinate in ways difficult to resist. *Erie* was the state of enchantment the peasants attributed to a gaze the faery could fix upon a hapless soul. Fallen into enchantment. Captured by the unknown. Compelled to seek, to surrender.

Sera snapped her head to the left and blinked. She returned a more cautious look to the mercenary. Had she just been thinking him a faery?

'Twas those violet eyes. Certainly any man or woman who should glance at Dominique would think his eyes black. But she knew better. To look, to really see, told a different tale. Dominique's eyes possessed a rich satin shade of violet fit only for royalty.

No, not of the enchanted realm. He did neither glimmer nor fly about. But this man was special, she knew it. However, why he had put himself in her life was still a beguiling mystery.

"Seraphim, what is wrong?"

He stood so close that his lips brushed her earlobe when he spoke. The sensation zinged a sensual shiver down her spine. *Feed the damsel. Don't let her die!*

"Have you second thoughts? We can succeed, but you must trust me."

Before she even thought the reply through, she found herself saying, "I do."

And she *did* trust him. For reasons still unfathomable to her. Perhaps those reasons were as mysterious as Dominique himself. Trust had taken on the color of violet satin, a rare but elegant shade.

With a final check over her sleek garb—mail tunic, the gown tucked into her chausses, gauntlets, swords and chest plate—Sera decided it would serve. "I will march into Abaddon's chambers and slay him. I can, and I will."

"Good." Dominique slapped her across the shoulder, as a man would offer encouragement to another. The action set her off balance and ripped her out of the lull of confidence she'd fallen into. "Sorry." He offered a sheepish grin. "I forget you are but a woman."

In a stunningly swift move, Sera gripped his wrist. The violet orbs studied her own, but she offered no challenge, only bold pride. "Why must it always be *but* a woman? Can it not be simply, a woman?"

The tip of his tongue glanced out to moisten his lower lip. His eyes dashed from her left to her right. Then a smile grew upon the sharp-boned visage of this stranger who would stand at her side as protector. "Indeed. A woman. Seraphim d'Ange, a woman to be reckoned with."

The mummers' train slipped around the high limestone walls of Abaddon de Morte's castle like a centipede slowly traversing the smooth curve of a shore-ridden river stone. The Seine bordered the castle northwest to northeast, leaving but a single entry point at the south. High above, a night-flying kestrel followed the wobbling trail of rush lights. 'Twas early yet, the dawn embraced the horizon in a narrow line of blush.

Sera clung to the cold surface of the outer bailey wall, becoming a shadow with the flattening of her body, arms spread out to the side, and feet pointed outward. Frost crystals skittered over her gloves and bruised her chin.

Overhead, Abaddon's crested banners whipped in the chilling breeze. White salamanders *rampant gardant,* on red background. The animal represented fire, and the beast's curled talons and toothy snarl made it more a dragon than a small slithering nuisance.

Baldwin, a nervous ball of energy an arm's reach away, clung to the wall as well. Sera could feel the vibrations of his terror as a palpable shudder down the back of her neck. They had sighted no guards upon approaching the castle. But thick white columns of smoke steaming up from behind the crenellated battlements had given clue to the cauldrons of boiling water that awaited one false move from below.

The only available trail made them hug the outer walls below the gaping machiolations that promised death by boiling should they become suspect. No plans to enter this forbidden realm; the covered wagons would pass quickly, quietly, thankful to be ignored. When questioned by an unseen voice through the tightly latticed portcullis, the mummers explained they were but passing by and hastened onward, eager to clear the frightening walls of the North Demon's lair.

Dominique, his head tilted to catch the rising sun's wink upon his cheekbones, surveyed the battlements that set a jagtoothed run around four imposing towers stretched to corner a long rectangular base.

The trio of avengers had to move quickly, while there was still diversion to keep the wall guards occupied—if there were guards—and while the shadows still darkened this side of the castle. With a flip of his hand, Dominique signaled Sera and Baldwin to follow. They slipped inside the cold darkness of the entry tunnel.

"Is any one here?" Dominique called, quietly, but not without command.

Sera eyeballed the glint of Dominique's dagger, held behind his back. She fingered her sword hilt.

"Who goes there?" came a muffled voice from an indeterminable location.

Dominique scanned the oily blackness. When he gripped Sera's arm and pulled her close, she almost let out a shriek, but stayed herself. "My lord Abaddon expects this wench from the mummers."

"I've not been told such."

With a jerk of his head to the right Dominique pinpointed the vicinity of the voice.

"Neither have I," Sera growled.

"Silence," he reprimanded her, then, "Aye, but she's a fine morsel of flesh."

"Let me see her!"

"Raise the gates and I'll shove her inside," Dominique answered.

"What—" Sera began, but the mercenary silenced her with a nudge of his elbow to her side.

"Ready yourself," he whispered, as the portcullis rose on silent pulleys. "Baldwin?"

Sera saw the squire had already bent in preparation to dart under the gates. At least someone had been availed of the mercenary's plan. If it was a plan. Dominique pushed her forward and down, and she felt him follow.

"Not all of you—" the guardsman started, but the sudden gurgle of death ended his plea.

Feeling the heavy gate plunge back in place behind her, Sera assumed Dominique had just displayed his expert skills to her. Not out of vanity, but necessity. Certainly he had moved swiftly. He had just been behind her...

Alas, there was no time to consider logistics. They were inside. The scent of blood was but a fleeting whiff as the chill air overwhelmed.

"Keep your eyes shut," Dominique hissed.

A wide hand firmly clamped Sera's hand. She in turn, reached for the squire's hand, but he beat her to the clutch with a tight grip.

"That was too close for comfort," Baldwin said, as he drew close to Sera.

"You have not been scalded, and we've easily gained access," she whispered. "Let us now see if you can walk a blind man's steps."

Taking the lead, with Baldwin in the middle, Sera closed her eyes and began to traverse the twenty-foot tunnel that would lead them to yet another hell. The air was chill and heavy. The mummers' din, the turning of wooden wheels upon the snow and the intermittent *ting* of jester's bells, grew distant. Beyond the thud of Baldwin's footsteps—for Dominique trod lightly upon the earth—lingered but the eerie silence of darkness and fear.

No— "Not fear," she whispered. *Always faith.*

Sera pressed one foot before the other upon the ground. The urge to open her eyes, to look about, spy the murder holes that waited just that action, was overwhelming. There could not be many. Could there? How would she know what danger really lurked unless she looked?

"I'm going to stumble."

She reached back, touching Baldwin's arm. "You will not. Don't let go of my hand. Keep your eyes closed."

"Silence." Dominique's voice wavered up from behind.

Like a wraith from her past, the mercenary haunted and clung, not touching, but never leaving. She had not asked for this kind of protection. And, at the moment, it did not feel as if his presence offered safety. She was on her own. As she had always been.

Wrong, her conscience chided. *Just knowing he is near gives you strength immeasurable.* His presence reached beyond that of the squire's friendly companionship. Dominique San Juste offered Sera the presence of a man. A man of her equal. But as an equal, she did not fear Dominique as she would a man who was stronger or more commanding than she.

Now to learn to accept his overwhelming male presence without falling victim to the damsel's desires.

Just ahead the icy hiss of winter's arctic breath beckoned. The end of the tunnel lay a few footsteps away. Fighting her need to rush forth and out of the tunnel so she might turn and look upon the darkness she had just traversed, Sera tugged Baldwin's hand and squeezed. He sensed her urgency, and with a few more steps the twosome stepped out into daylight.

Before Sera could congratulate the squire on their success-ful accomplishment, a gust of sand-spattering wind lifted the man from his feet and twirled him high into the air above Sera's and Dominique's heads.

EIGHT

Dominique gripped Sera by the arm and pulled her to him. He flattened his back against the inner bailey wall. The tornado that enveloped Baldwin muffled the squire's shrieks and spun his flailing limbs around and around. "Unreal."

"'Tis as if the faeries have lifted him into a mad dance," Sera said, wisely remaining at the wall, but unknowingly clinging to Dominique's body.

"This is not faery magick," Dominique snarled. "'Tis the work of banshees."

He drew a hand up before Sera's face to protect her from the dirt and sand pebbles that spit out from the wind tunnel. Then he spied the entrance across the bailey-court. Not another moment must be lost to macabre fascination.

"The door to Abaddon's castle is just ahead. We must use this chance."

"Aye!"

She dashed across the courtyard—surprising Dominique—arms braced up to block her head from flying debris. He had expected she might plead for the rescue of her squire. Like any woman with half a mind to compassion. But she was not any woman.

Dominique found himself smiling once again in the discovery of Seraphim d'Ange. Such strength behind those glittering sapphire eyes. Power that attracted in ways he was finding more difficult to resist.

With a dash across the bailey, he clutched Sera about the waist, and carried her across the remainder in half the time she could have done it. They bounded up seven wide stone stairs, completely ignored by the gusts of wind that ribboned through the courtyard, and seemed to be attracted only to the hapless squire. Together they slammed into the stone wall framing the door.

"You move so fast!"

Dominique spun and answered in calm breaths that did not huff as Sera's. "I do not wear so much armor as you to weigh down my steps." Nor did he subscribe to the mortal way of lumbering upon this earth.

"He will die," she said, as they observed the relentless oddity of nature that had imprisoned Baldwin's defenseless limbs. 'Twas funnel shaped, and black, and whistled like a wild she-cat. "He is being twisted about. Will be ripped to shreds!"

"We cannot afford rescue when Abaddon awaits. He is a strong young man, Sera. Put him out of your mind, and think on how we will pass through that door without being skewered."

The door to the Demon of the North's lair stood but five feet away, set into a recessed wall that was lined with oak beams. Between each of the beams grew a void, black and foreboding, for within those spaces waited the porcupine of spears that would pierce their bodies from head to ankle as soon as they touched the door. Or so the Oracle had foretold.

"I cannot listen." Sera pressed her face to the stone wall near Dominique's head. The first emotional reaction to her squire's pain that Dominique had seen. He turned to spy a hand had punched out from the sandy tornado, which acted as a door for Baldwin's maniacal screams.

"I have to think," he muttered.

As he pressed his thoughts to scheme out the situation of entering the castle without becoming a pincushion, Dominique drew his hand up Sera's back, smoothing, reassuring. His foster mother had done much the same many a time when he was a child. He did not think about the action, it was a natural reaction to Sera's surprising fear. She needed him to be strong for her now, even in her show of false strength.

"He's been so kind to me, San Juste. Do something!"

There was no question; they had to rescue the squire. "Maybe we could—"

At that moment a great explosion of sand and rocks scattered wide across the courtyard, spewing Baldwin upon the ground. A tangle of limbs collapsed without display at the base of the steps. The squire, crumpled and heaving, but remarkably alert, managed to lift up his head.

Sera moved to rush to him, but Dominique caught her around the waist. "Do not go out there. The winds could pick up in an instant and whisk you away. He must come to us."

"Mercy," Baldwin muttered. His hand clenched around a smooth fist-sized stone that had come to rest on his knee, debris stirred up in the tornado. Rivulets of blood trickled down his face and shoulders and stained the brown hosen wrapping his legs. Wide boggled eyes fixed on no single spot for more than a moment.

Finally, with an explosion of grunts, he stood, wobbled, and swayed to the left, his feet double-stepping to counteract gravity. But he did not fall.

He eased the heel of his palm over his bruised forehead, then raised his other hand and gawked at the stone in his fist. "Damn rocks!" He thrust the stone at the door.

Steel gears spun upon greased axles, releasing the cage of spears in a blinding rush of speed and power. A fine mist of dust sifted out from the center where the spear-tips met in a connection of sure death.

Dominique, seeing their chance, gripped Sera by the hips and pushed her to the bars of steel. "It will recoil, and we can run through. Get ready. Come, squire!"

Baldwin, his feet crissing and crossing with each wobbly step, accomplished two strides as the steel bars parted and slowly began to wind back into their fittings.

With the first aisle of space, Dominique pushed Sera ahead and the twosome lunged through the open door.

"He'll never make it!" she cried.

For as much as Dominique tried to pull her in and away from the spears, she clung all the more to the door. As soon as the mechanism had recoiled he suspected it would again release. Until the door was closed.

"Quickly, Baldwin!"

The squire paused upon the top step. A begroggled smile twisted across his blood- and dirt-smeared face. "You really do know my name."

"Aye, 'tis Baldwin. Now run!" Sera pleaded.

Dominique braced himself with one foot against the wall, his arms around Sera's waist. He expected she would run out to rescue the stone-boggled squire, giving no care for her own safety. Much as he should be the one to do just that, it was the black knight he had been assigned to protect. He could not risk trying to save the squire if his inattention might endanger Seraphim.

"The spears are almost recoiled. Quickly, Baldwin," he coached. "Yes! Just a few more steps—"

The smart zing of springs releasing registered in Dominique's blood like the icy chill of a man buried in snow for days. Still clinging to Sera, he looked away as the porcupine shot out from the wall. Sera's body did not slacken in his arms. As the spears locked into place, he felt in his arms the tension that stiffened her torso. She did not scream—

Dominique looked over Sera's shoulder. "Morgana's blood!" He was still alive. How did the man do it?

The spears had run around either side of the lank squire. His legs and gut were pressed like a fillet between steel bars, both arms straight to his side. One spear traveled under his chin, another cut across the bridge of his nose. He bled, but the pointed steel had not cut deep. He'd been packed in like a magician's dummy stuffed in the sword-box.

"Hold still," Sera cautioned, her voice rough with past pain and the dust that fogged around them. "They'll retract in seconds." She reached carefully between the iron rods and gripped Baldwin by his sand-tattered tunic. "I'll pull you in."

"I...I want...to go home," Baldwin managed on tear-filled gasps. "But I don't...have a home, Sera."

"Of course you do," she gently reassured.

The spears had not yet moved to recoil. Dominique found he grit his jaw so tight his teeth scraped shrilly across one another.

"You have a home with me, Baldwin, always."

"I do?"

"I swear it to you."

"But you don't have a home either!"

A creak, and the grind of gears started the recoil. The tip of steel that dragged across Baldwin's nose opened a larger gash. Blood poured like tears down his cheeks. Sera pulled the bedraggled squire inside and Dominique closed the door behind them.

When he turned he found Baldwin curled on the floor, arms clutched around his ankles, and Sera's body draped over him. She hugged and cooed and whispered so sweetly...for the moment, Dominique forgot all about that other woman, that hard, determined black knight of a woman.

Yes, there lived a loving, caring woman beneath the armored exterior. A woman capable of emotion and kindness. Dominique pressed a hand to his pounding heart. 'Twas not exertion that quickened the pace so. Indeed, 'twas Seraphim d'Ange.

She glanced to Dominique, gave him a reassuring wink. And his heart surrendered to the damsel hidden beneath the armor.

She was like no other. Little thought went for herself. She tended the squire as if a brother. Family. One of her own. Her only reason for this insane quest was for the love of family...and the countless families that would be saved from suffering should she be successful.

Yes, she would see her quest to the end, for Dominique would have it no other way. Countless thousands would benefit from the extinction of the de Morte clan. As well, Seraphim d'Ange must live to have a better life. A carefree life. A life free of the horrors she was now trying to extinguish.

And Dominique would not rest until she had that life.

It took a while for Baldwin to come around. He wanted to leave, Sera knew, to flee this nightmare she'd led him into, but with a few brave sniffles and a straightening of his shoulders, he pushed her away and pulled himself up by the wall. The gash on his nose no longer bled. A crusted trail of maroon painted down his left cheek and slipped under his jaw. Sera saw now one of the spears had pierced his hip, but again nothing more than a surface abrasion. He had survived. And though he stood a bit wobbly, he managed a smile.

"So what comes next, roasting the squire on a spit?" Baldwin didn't wait for a reply, instead he walked to the edge of the wide foyer they stood in and scanned down the dark hallway that turned into oblivion, his back to them.

Sera knew he could not show emotion, just as she would do the very same. Hide. Baldwin needed his blindfold to protect him from the fear that had resurfaced. Resurfaced? Hell, it had been forced out of him by a screaming wind tunnel and a mesh of sharp spikes.

"Perhaps we should leave him here," Dominique suggested in quiet tones. "I'm sure we'll need to pass through this way on our return."

"No, he comes along." Sera marched to Baldwin and laid a firm hand on his shoulder. "The black knight needs her faithful squire, bruises and all."

"You needn't talk me up," Baldwin offered, a shudder still clinging to his voice. He held his arms clamped across his chest. "I agreed to accompany you from the start, I'll not back down now. Hell, I've survived tornadoes and skewers…what could be worse?"

"Shall we venture onward and see?"

At Dominique's ominous invitation, Sera followed in Baldwin's brave footsteps and the trio marched down the rushlighted hall of limestone. The hall did neither sway down nor incline. They remained on ground level, so should escape be necessary, one might not have to jump from a three-story window. If there were windows in this dark labyrinth.

"Sera?" Baldwin wondered as they walked onward.

"Yes, squire?"

"I—I think I saw *Him* when I was trapped in that tornado."

"Who?"

"Him, Sera. Him. And he smiled at me."

"Do you take that as a good sign?"

"Well, that, or he was laughing because I'm finally getting just reward for my past crimes."

"Then it was not Him, Baldwin. For he would not be so cruel as to laugh at your pain."

"You think so?"

"I know it."

As they continued onward, Sera couldn't help wonder why she had said that, or how she knew such a thing. Only that she did. With all her heart.

"What of the disturbance outside the gates?" Abaddon requested of the messenger quivering in his chamber doorway.

"Mummers, my lord. We currently await word from the gate keeper regarding their passage."

The woman nestled between Abaddon's legs made such loud slurping noises, he wondered should he end it all right now. What he must endure for a few seconds of bliss!

Trying best to ignore the obnoxious sound and draw himself back into the moment, Abaddon flicked the messenger away with his fingers. "They will not enter. They have passed many times before. Leave them on their way."

"Good eve, my lord." The messenger backed from the room.

Abaddon threaded his fingers through the woman's long, greasy black hair and worked her rhythm faster by pumping against her forehead. "Darling?"

The wench did not cease.

"Dearest, you test my patience. Can you bring the insidious racket down to an appealing whisper?"

She did not appear to comprehend anything he said, she remained so intent on her task. Hell. Enough already. As he released, Abaddon made a mental note to become more discerning of his selections in the future.

Only one thing in this world made Sera cringe. A furry-legged spider.

The long-legged beasts had crept all over her father's home, often nesting above her bed or in the stone embrasures. Sometimes they literally fell from out of nowhere to land and skitter across her shoulder. She could be standing in the middle of a razed plot of soil and have a creepy critter land upon her shoulder. It was remarkable how such a small thing could upset her so. Sera had pleaded with her father many a time to sweep them all away, but her mother would always say that the insects served their purpose. They kept the flies out of the castle, and most especially the kitchen.

But nestled at the foot of her bed and beneath the sheets?

No good purpose in this life, Sera thought now, as she looked over the seething nest of arachnids the threesome had come upon. They clung to the floor, walls, and ceiling for a distance of about the length of two men laid head to toe. Masses of skittering, sticky-legged, beady-eyed beasts. And such a cacophony. 'Twas demonic the clicking, chittering, and thrushing.

A touch to her elbow walloped Sera's heart up to her throat. She jumped around and punched the offender in the gut. "Damn you, Benwick!"

Doubled over and clutching the wall, the squire could only

choke out a feeble, "Have mercy, my lady, I am already wounded."

"You fear spiders?" Dominique drew out his sword and tapped one of the fat-bellied creatures. It fell from a netting of silken web to the mass writhing upon the floor.

"Don't do that," Sera pleaded. "They seem to be in such a...nice...little conglomeration. I wouldn't want them to think they could spread out. Th-this way."

"But we must pass through," Dominique offered with utterly sanguine calm. "There is no other route. We've already tried the other two halls. Dead ends."

"If we must pass through, that also means we'll have to re-turn this way to escape," she said in utter horror. "I cannot do—stand up!" she commanded Baldwin.

"Yes, *my lord*." He straightened, winced as he clutched his gut. But for all his bruises, he put up a good front. Dominique's ca-sual bravery forced the squire to appear equally aloof. "We could make a run for it."

"Unless you've a better plan, squire, close your mouth."

"There is no better plan."

Dominique's hand on her shoulder might have been meant to offer courage, but it only reminded Sera of their differences. Male. Female. Brave. She, acting the coward.

They were but lowly insects. The hairy-legged creepers did not wield swords, nor armor. They were but the size of her fist, for mercy's sake.

Aye, but that was the problem. They were the size of her fist!

"I'll carry you through," Dominique whispered in her ear. Sera turned to peer into the violet salvation on Dominique's face. "If you would allow it?"

Where had this man been when Lucifer had attacked her fa-ther's home? This knight sent to rescue a damsel in distress thought only of her. She knew not the final payment he would receive for his task, but she certainly hoped whoever had hired him had agreed to pay him well.

"I am too heavy in mail and arms," she offered, with a lackluster glance to the side.

"Never," came the whispered reply to her fears.

Airborne, her sword clicking against the wall, Sera had only time to close her eyes and clasp her hands over her mouth before they entered the seething mass of crawling insects.

Heavy clods of something—the infernal hairy beasts!—dropped on her head and shoulders and legs. Each contact was followed by the tickle of fine hairs or the pinch of long appendages. The entire mass of insects increased in sound and motion. But Sera did not pry open her eyelids. She sensed Dominique's footsteps slow—he slipped; thick spider parts were crushed under his heel—but he pressed onward.

Behind her, Baldwin yelped as, Sera assumed, he rushed blindly forth, his eyes closed as well.

When they cleared the spiders, Dominique plunged forward, releasing Sera most ungracefully in a heap near the wall beneath a flaming rush light. With a peek out of one eye Sera saw him stumble back to the skittering insects and brush off hordes of clinging beasts from his arms, legs, and head. Baldwin did the same.

A scan of her own person found her limbs remarkably insect-free. Not a single crawly beast on her legs. She pushed up against the wall and checked her arms, the top of her head, her face. Not a— "Yeooww!"

The tickle of eight hairy spider legs across her breasts set Sera's heartbeats to a frantic pace. Frantic? Hell, the beating organ exploded. She bounced and pulled at her jerkin and the chain mail, which only dislodged the beast from her breasts and dumped it upon her stomach. How had it managed to breach the tight shell of her armor?

She unbuckled the leather straps and released the cuirass. "Get it out!"

"My lady?" Baldwin, twitching, and still flicking away his own tormentors, couldn't figure the reason for her animated dance.

"Where is it?" Dominique gripped her by the shoulders. "Down your tunic?"

At her nod—for she hadn't realized he would take it as leave to literally answer her plea to help—Dominique plunged his hand down behind her clothing. Cool male flesh brushed her breasts. Dominique's fingers landed immediately on the mass of insect and coiled. As he pulled it out, his wrist skimmed her nipple, setting it harder than her fear could ever freeze it. With a toss, the spider was relegated to the mass whence it came.

Clutching her hands to her chest, Sera gasped. Heavy breaths worked to calm, but not erase the scintillating force of that unwarranted touch. He'd touched her...her bare flesh... *Mon Dieu,* but her heart raced to a beat that was not fear, but desire!

Dominique pressed a hand to the wall behind her head and leaned in close to her face. Though his lips remained straight, solemn, glee danced in his eyes. "Any more?"

More? More reason to allow this man of the beguiling eyes to stroke his fingers over her naked breasts? To stir her body to such a frenzy of confused sensations that she could naught for words? Well...if he gave her a moment...

How his touch stirred the hidden desires within. Oh! But the damsel coiled in delight. To be touched in such a way!

"Sera?"

Unfortunately that was the last of the creatures. Sera stared at the pulsing muscle in Dominique's jaw as he waited her response. For a moment she fell into the *erie* of enchantment. This close proximity certainly left nothing to be misconstrued. And everything to be desired.

She had not before noticed the scent that surrounded him. Almost like a perfume, but not of any fragrance or flower she had ever known. It was crisp, masculine, woodsy. The fine shadow of mustache that burnished his upper lip glistened with perspiration, drawing attention to the thickness of his lips, the sensual curves that up until now, had been disguised by his aloof manner. A lift of his brow spoke volumes.

"There are no more," she finally said, forcing herself to abandon the silly thoughts of romance that stirred inside her head. Romance? No, 'twas naught but fear confused into apprehension. "Thank you. For the extraction, that is."

He inclined his head closer, so close she thought he might kiss her. "Forgive my impropriety."

Before even thinking the reply through she said in a hush, "Never."

An arch of his left brow teased her sense of modesty. "Never?"

"Er, I mean…aye, certainly, San Juste. You were only doing as I requested. 'Tis nary a problem." She tugged at her leather tunic, inadvertently sliding the silken gown across her tightened nipple. "So it is on to the next hell then?"

"Indeed," Baldwin called from behind.

Sera had forgotten they were three. At sight of the lank squire, standing legs planted and arms akimbo, a teasingly bewildered grin affixed to his tornado-ravaged face, Sera released her sword from the scabbard at her hip and swung it at him.

"What the——" He ducked, but she did not miss her target.

The squat black arachnid that had been sitting upon Baldwin's head severed in twain in the air before the squire's wide eyes, and sailed against the wall in a splat of spider innards and blood.

"Mother," Baldwin muttered. His knees bent and he fainted.

NINE

"The keep must be just ahead," Sera instructed, as she pressed forward, leaving behind all thought of spiders skittering down her stomach.

"I hear music," Baldwin declared from the tail of the group. "Can it be that Abaddon celebrates in the wake of his brothers' deaths?"

"Every minute of every hour of every day is a festive celebration to Abaddon de Morte," Dominique solemnly explained, as the threesome drew upon the entrance to the keep.

Double blackened-oak doors towered above their heads, arcing into a sharp point two stories up the wall. All down the doors, gilt arabesques curled and formed into—upon closer inspection—naked bodies, both male and female, twisted into all sorts of acts, both festive and repulsive.

Sera looked to Dominique, at an utter lack to comment on the ornamented doors.

"I did mention Abaddon's fetish for the carnal pleasures," Dominique said.

"Information from your Oracle?"

"Yes. You, er——" he splayed a hand up and down the explicit carvings "——favor any in particular?"

Sera felt her jaw drop. But at Dominique's twinkling grin she quickly recovered. "Mayhaps all." And with that, she turned and pressed a hand against a pair of twined bodies, intent on entering the keep. "Shall we?"

"Indeed," she heard San Juste say. The tenor of his voice gave her pleasure immeasurable. But the squire's squeak jerked her back to reality.

"Is there another option?"

"If you favor spiders, spears, and tornadoes, there is," Sera said, and she stepped through the open doors ahead of Dominique.

The squire offered no answer to her remark. Dominique followed close behind. And Sera cursed the damsel's brazen flirtations. Now was no time to go soft just because a handsome knight flanked her side.

Indeed. Find your head, woman.

Clutching her sword at the ready, she gasped at the vision that filled the stone keep. The rafters were as a mews, decorated with pigeons and hawks and white doves that sparkled with myriad colors of glitter, as if a faery had sneezed upon their wings.

Indeed, a faery had exploded upon the entire room. From the grand mouth of a hearth that blazed a blue-red fire at the opposite end of the keep, to the hundreds of dancers that skipped and clapped and made merry to the song of a lute player that spun about in dizzying circles.

Food was offered along the walls; long banquets of roasted meat, jeweled and candied fruit, and myriad variety of breads and cheeses cut into stars and hearts and spades. Pale white wine flowed from a great stone fountain decorated with male and female bodies to match the obscene positions on the entrance doors. Without missing a step, dancers swung by the fountain, dipped their goblets into the flow of spirits, then spun back into dance.

Everyone danced. And if they were not dancing their bodies moved in rhythm to the melody piped from the musicians' gilded instruments.

A bit of homesick-memory for her father's great fêtes twanged at Sera's legs, causing her to bounce to the beat and infecting her with just a little mirth.

But beneath the glitter and gaiety dwelled something unspeakable. She could not put a finger to it, or name its shape, but she felt sure it would birth upon her troubled mind when she least wished it.

"There." Dominique nudged Sera's arm and pointed across the merry-making crowd to the far wall where a gaping darkness gave clue to their destination. "The only other exit that I can see. We must cross and continue onward."

"What if Abaddon is in here?" She scanned the bobbing heads and laughing eyes. Veiled faces, bejeweled hair and ears and eyes glittered everywhere. Mouths curved in merriment and opened wide in celebration. Pauper to prince peopled the keep in all forms of dress, from threadbare tunic to gold-threaded doublet. A surprising mixture.

"I do not see him. Yonder throne is empty."

Sera spied the gilded travesty. Throne indeed. Should it be melted down the gold used to ornament such a thing would feed half of France's peasants for a lifetime. Were those rubies pressed up and down the legs of the opulent piece?

"He could be dancing," Baldwin observed. "Making merry

with a fine wench. Do you even know what he looks like, San Juste?"

He cornered a look on Baldwin. "I haven't a notion to his appearance." Sera noticed the sanguine smile that briefly attacked Dominique's lips. "As for a wench, if rumor have truth, that would be exactly what the man is doing. But I know he is not in the hall. I can feel it."

"Have you a mental bond to the man? What say you?" Sera pressed, suddenly aggravated. He always seemed to have a grasp on what was going on, to know a little more than he should. He hid something from her, she sensed it. "You *are* in league with Abaddon, I knew it."

"I am not."

In a swift movement, she bent, lifted her foot to her hand, and unsheathed her dagger from the ankle belt. But Baldwin laid a hand over hers, stopping her midthreat before Dominique's chest. "Sera, don't do it. Look around, the mood is light, everyone is making merry. We will be suspect."

"But he has led us right to the Demon of the North's hands." She narrowed her eyes on the calm mercenary. Did he never react with anger? An affronted expression? Infuriating. And she had even thought to place him in her mind romantically. To flirt with him! "No wonder he knew so much about the castle traps."

"Are you quite through?"

She bristled at Dominique's calm remark, but did not see fit to respond. A lift of her chin spoke her distemper. The evil eye would serve no use when he did not look directly at her.

"I've told you once before, I receive all my information from the Oracle. I have never in my entire life met Abaddon de Morte. And much as I'd like to keep it so, I swear to you upon my mother's life—"he lifted a stone bound around his neck with a leather cord "—that I speak the truth. I am here only for you, Seraphim."

It was the first time she had seen the amulet dangling from the cord that had, up until now, been hidden beneath his leather jerkin. A brilliant red stone—not a ruby, nor a garnet, for the cloudiness, but sharp. *I swear to you upon my mother's life...*

'Twas the first time the mercenary had invoked his family in such a way. But wait—he'd said his mother was dead. How could he possibly use her life in such a way now? The liar!

"Fine." Sera sheathed her dagger. They had work to do. To think on Dominique's deceptions would tax valuable time better spent working toward her goal. "But I'm keeping an eye on you, San Juste."

"If it pleases, my lady, so shall it please me."

Her double-take served Sera a bawdy wink from her mercenary. That, and a subtle quiver inside her chest. The damsel so wanted release.

Not yet.

But...soon.

Disregarding her toiling conscience, Sera strode out into the bustle of merry-making, intent on the opposite door, and distancing her heart from San Juste's grasp.

Ten strides into the crowd, and she was swept into rhythm of the dance by those surrounding her. Initially reluctant, second thought decided that to join with the festivities would be a boon. Certainly mail and arms did not blend with the extravagant costume of the crowd. She could allay suspicion and dance to the door without question from anyone.

A scan of the jewel-bangled silk hennens and soft velvet caps and dove-glittered hair spied Baldwin already swept into a jig by a trio of silk-clad women. Young and pretty, the women's lips were red as strawberries, their gowns sewn tightly to expose a veritable field of bosom. The squire certainly had a knack for picking out the lovelies.

Baldwin caught Sera's mongoose eye and made a gesture toward the far door.

Very well, he had had the same idea of blending in.

Drawing in a deep breath stirred the scent of hickory smoke and berry wine and roasted meat on Sera's tongue. A hop-skip step loosened her legs and her mood. Glitter sifted down from the rafters, dotting her arms and fingers. She was spun in a circle by a conglomeration of hands, momentarily confusing her navigation toward the door.

"Wine, my lady?" A pewter goblet was pressed against her palm before she could refuse the voice that did not seem to come from any mouth she looked upon.

Mumbling thanks, she decided not to drink. She'd passed through enough dangerous traps to know better. The wine could be drugged. With a spin, Sera bowed to a wool-clad peasant sporting wrinkled gray brows and a mouth void of teeth, then handed him her goblet and spun onward.

Many a time she had danced in the keep of her family's home. So simple to seduce a wide-eyed knight with but a commanding smile and a crook of her finger. And just as easy to remove his lecherous touch from her hip with a well-placed knee to the man's delicates.

Dance was to be enjoyed, a freeing of one's worries, it was not a prelude to carnal pleasures. Though—Sera glanced about, but did not spy Dominique—perhaps to dance with a man who had already beguiled might awaken the desire to continue the match elsewhere, such as in a darkened corner, or sprawled across a nest of plush velvet pillows.

The fantasy intrigued; slipping into Sera's subconscious with a whisper and a caress, it took hold of her heart. 'Twas the damsel that now danced joyously beneath the rain of glitter and merriment. Engaged in a high-stepping beat, she tilted her head back and closed her eyes. The music carried her this way and that, as her thoughts swayed hither and yon. The mood enthralled. The hiss of satin seduced.

The damsel let out a giggle.

And the armored avenger did not even notice the harsh rasp that tainted such merriment.

"My lady?"

Spinning toward the sound of the beguiling male voice, the damsel's hands were taken up in a loose clasp. 'Twas not her moonlight knight. A tall, dark-haired man with silver-threaded lace flowing over his wrists and silver studs dotting his black leather tunic, coaxed her into a slow rhythm that defied the gaiety of the room. Lulled by the languorous pace, the damsel offered him a warm smile. He sparkled like a gilded doll. But as she looked upon his face the happy arc on her lips slipped like ink from a quill.

"F-father?"

Marcil d'Ange's kind old eyes smiled down at the damsel. Though the hair was still long and black, and the figure much slimmer than her father's broad shoulders and strong carriage, the face was undeniably that of her father's. A broad nose, flattened at the tip, and thick lips that had always granted her the best eyelid-kisses. Heavy black brows lorded over his wide-set eyes; hard, indigo eyes that mastered his face.

"This is not real." The damsel tried to twist her grasp free of the man's fingers. Though he did not bend them to hold her, the loose grasp was unshakable. "Father? But you are— Is it really…oh…Father. I've missed you so."

Surrounding their intimate clutch, the dancing faces no longer smiled, but instead wore moues of sadness. But the damsel did not notice. This man even smelled like her father, like sweet hickory smoke and soft, tilled earth.

"Father, if it is you, speak to me," she pleaded with the face that had, in her memories, been painted a horrid gray pallor with deep blue bruises tracing his jaw and forehead. A head lying at the base of the keep stairs, severed from his body by Lucifer de Morte.

Mon Dieu. Her father.

Dead.

She should have been awake! If only she'd had known de Morte had plans to attack that night she would not have retired early. She would not have imbibed so freely in the celebration wine. Instead, she would have stood alongside her father and brother, raised her sword against the enemy…

Sera wakened from her walking slumber and shoved the damsel back into the shadows where she belonged.

"No!" She twisted free.

The vision was gone. The damsel had retreated. No sign of a tall male anywhere near her.

Sera turned this way and that, trying to make order of the crazed excitement around her. Glitter fell upon her face, tickling her nose. Where had he gone? "Father?"

The full, gorgeous warmth in her belly chilled and deflated. It had been an illusion. A trick conjured by the erratic mood, the innocuous noise, the drink—no, she had not drunk of the wine.

And she…she had, for a moment, ransomed her hard exterior to the damsel's desires. No more warmth. No giddy joy. Only solitude, bare and black in her gut.

"Stay alert," she whispered to herself now. "Don't dance. Yes, 'twas the dance that made me forget my mission."

Tracking her progress, Sera, on tip-toes, surveyed the keep. The exit door was again at the opposite end of the hall. Her dance with the mysterious stranger had brought her back to where she had begun!

She pushed a giggling woman in a silver leaf-dagged gown aside and stepped frantically. For as fast as she swung her legs, each stride seemed to move at a snail's pace. Sound flattened and stretched out. The melody of mirth stretched and distorted. Everything worked at a lugubrious pace. What was happening? 'Twas as if she were soused from a most wicked ale. She looked up to the rafters. Every flutter of the doves' wings showered a burst of glitter upon the heads of the revelers.

"Seraphim!"

A familiar voice pierced the distorted revelry. Jerking out of her lethargic observation of the mews, Sera turned to find Dominique's hand waving her to the edge of the mad dancing. Joggled and pushed and roughly twirled, she made the perimeter of the crowd, and was virtually spat out into Dominique's arms.

"I saw my father," she gasped, her breaths heaving and irregular. She watched her fingers clench into the soft leather of Dominique's jerkin, interpreted the move as desperation, a child's plea for safety, but could not address it as such. "I danced with him!"

"There is something suspect about this party," he said, and drew her close, until she stood with her cheek pressed aside his neck. Warm life beat against her flesh. Scent of man, powerful and stoic, flushed her senses. Another piece of her heart surrendered to his allure.

But was it the damsel's heart or her own?

"I have tried three times now to gain the door," he said. "Each time I end up back where I began. And Baldwin, there, do you see? He is headed back this way, as well." He touched her cheek, wiped away the glitter, and rubbed it between his fingers to study. "There is a charm of sorts fallen upon the room."

"Witchcraft?"

"I cannot be sure." He blew the dust from his fingertips. "But I have a plan."

"Damnation!" Spat out from the dancers, Baldwin barged into Dominique and Sera, severing their intimate connection. "This is the second time I've returned to this entrance. I cannot broach yonder exit. And no one is normal, have you noticed? They've all a glazed look upon their faces, like lacquered masks."

"There is a spell upon the room." Sera released her body from its pleading hold upon San Juste and drew straight. It had felt good those few moments when she'd stood in his arms, breathed in his brute scent, relaxed her weary bones against his broad chest. *Forgotten the pain.* He wielded a dangerous allure. Dangerous because his presence coaxed her to let down her guard and allow the damsel full rein. She must hold firmly to her convictions in the future.

"What is your plan, San Juste?"

"We dance," he said. "Together."

Dominique could only guess that the masque had been under a spell of enchantment. Not of the faery-kind, he knew as much; but he was not familiar with its source. He just wasn't knowledgeable of Faery. Much as he should be.

Sera's confession that she had seen her father was no surprise. Dominique had seen the face of his slender, young dance partner transform before his very eyes to that of a rosy-cheeked woman, with vivid violet eyes and long silvery hair that flowed over her shoulders.

His mother? The desire to grasp that wonder had been so strong. He'd wanted the moment to last forever. He'd even blurted out the question that had taunted him for years. "Why?"

She had only smiled and inclined her head in a servile gesture. When she'd looked up the vision was gone, and the blonde spouted a giggle that had only sickened Dominique. Disheartened, he'd turned and found himself back at the ballroom entrance.

They gained the opposite door by clasping hands, the three of them, and dancing through the crowd. Without worry of joining with an enchanted dance partner their trip across the great hall was swift and successful.

And now they stood at yet another fork in the long and winding hallway that seemed to snake in and out, and back and forth, but never coming upon doors or even an arrow-slit window or embrasure. Yet certainly there were torches every ten strides or so.

A clench of his fingers near his sword-hilt worked the tension up and down his arm. Dominique did not like this castle and its mysterious enchantments. It was as wrong as the heavy snows that blanketed the soil outside. The world was askew. Heaven and earth and hell were asunder. All was not right.

Even his own heart had been set to an unfamiliar pace by the compelling presence of a female warrior.

"I count six," Baldwin said. "Boiling water, tunnel of spears, tornadoes, skewered squire—" he paused, touched a finger to the crusted wound on his nose "—spiders, and endless enchanted dancing."

"One hell remains," Sera said, as she wandered ahead and disappeared around another corner.

"What next?" Baldwin muttered as he followed Sera. "A plague of locusts?"

Much as he did not even want to guess, Dominique felt the time had come. Abaddon was close. Sera must proceed by herself. He had been hired only to protect, not to aid in the destruction of the de Mortes. He knew Sera possessed the strength. And she was a woman. The only person right for this particular job.

But in this case, he also knew she would need a little *exterior* help.

"From here you'll have to go alone."

"I know." Sera pulled the front of her mail tunic away from her stomach and indicated to Baldwin to lift it from her shoulders. "One more hell to go, and then it is dinner and romance with a demon."

Her light comment betrayed the ambivalence Dominique sensed. He was sending a mere child to battle the Demon of the North. A mere—no, she did not like to be referred to as a mere woman. *Definitely not a mere woman.* But it could be no other way. The Oracle had specifically required he protect, not interfere. For only the One with the connection held killing power over the de Morte demons.

But how the de Mortes and Sera were joined in this connection was beyond him.

He would not question. He trusted the Oracle implicitly.

Baldwin laid the mail on the floor, silently, so as not to alert. A fall of crimson damask wisped from Sera's shoulder to her stomach where a sash of vivid cerulean cut the skirt of her gown in a river of ice. Baldwin fastened her sword belt around her waist, the heavy weapon clinking against the wall behind them. A dead giveaway, but a necessity. If she acted quickly, Abaddon wouldn't have a moment to consider why a supposed dancing wench was wearing such. A wide border of blue damask squared around her neck. Pretty, but its coverage would heed her task.

"If you would allow, my lady." Dominique displayed his dagger and touched it to the damask trim. "A slight adjustment is needed."

"Don't tell me you've dress-making skills?"

"Nay."

"Then watch where you slice. I should like to preserve what lies beneath."

"So should I," he said with a wink. He cut through the trim and ripped it from the gown. Sera's breasts were exposed to the rosy cusp of nipple. She stood proudly, unaware of the sensual mounds that loudly proclaimed her as a woman. So much more than a *mere* woman.

"Perfect," he commented.

"Indeed," Baldwin said, his attention riveted to her bosom.

"Men," Sera muttered, with a roll of her eyeballs. "If my breasts are all that are needed to defeat this enemy, this shall be a simple task."

"They will certainly not impede," Dominique said, admiration lightening his tone.

"I can see that." She swatted Baldwin's chin.

"Ow!"

"You've had enough, squire, remember your vows."

"Forgive me, my lady, it's—"

"Aye, well don't claim it has been a long time. I saw you with a fine bevy of wenches last eve. And you did no look worse for wear dancing with the trio of Aphrodites in the masque."

Baldwin shrugged, a sheepish grin stretching to his eyes. "I cannot help that I am so attractive to the female sex."

"*Sangdieu,*" Dominique muttered.

Sera pressed a hand to her shorn locks. Subconscious, Dominique now noted. For the first time he understood she was more than just a puppet wearing armor and acting out a revenge play. She was a woman who cared about the way the world viewed her. A silken damsel who had been debauched by a demon. He saw so much of that damsel now permeate the hardened exterior of the warrior.

He had to reassure. She needed the strength. As he needed the subtle interaction of companionship.

"Abaddon will not be put off," he offered. "You look lovely."

A flicker of hope sparked in her pale eyes as Sera's gaze latched onto Dominique's for a tumid moment. His breath caught behind his tongue. Heartbeats accelerated. If he could just reach out and touch, smooth his hand along her soft rose-dusted cheek...

"Seduce," he whispered, echoing his own thoughts. "Keep the North Demon's gaze in your eyes and you will succeed."

"And if not my eyes, a bit lower, eh?"

Dominique felt a blush heat his cheeks. He simply nodded, unafraid that Sera would see inside to his true desires.

But she made no note of his discomfort. A facade of hard vengeance washed over Sera's softened features, gifting the pale baubles of sight with a sheer armor of hate, and tightening her lips into a determined clench. "I will return the victor," she said. Accepting the torch Dominique held, she then marched down the narrow hallway.

Now. The realization sparked in Dominique's being like a candle taking light in a smothering dark cave. The time to use his powers to aid her success had come.

Dominique stretched out his arm, following Sera's retreat with his digits. He closed his eyes and concentrated. The surrounding air grew light. He fell into a moment of catatonic darkness as his magick shimmered toward Sera and enveloped her without perceptible touch or sound.

She would not sense his interference. Nor would Abaddon; save that which Dominique wished the demon to see. A few sparks of iridescent energy flashed through his every nerve-ending. And it was done.

Baldwin spun on Dominique, thrust his finger in Sera's wake. "What—was that?"

Dominique regarded the glittering mist that quickly subsided to a few particles of coruscation. "Glamour," he said decisively, for he could not speak a lie with the truth shimmering in the air. "She will need it."

Clothed in the flowing damask, Sera's legs felt impossibly light, as did her shoulders and head. It had been weeks that she'd worn the heavy mail and armor, day and night. The finely crafted steel had become her prison of revenge. Now she had broken free. But though the chain links were gone, she was still a captive to the vengeance that must be answered for her soul to shine anew.

Leery with every step, she slowly approached the massive iron-hinged door that sat in the heart of Abaddon's castle. His chambers, Dominique knew. *How* he knew still bothered her. She wasn't yet ready to completely trust the violet-eyed mercenary. Though the urge to trust him was oddly tormenting. But 'twas a different part of her mind San Juste's presence taunted. Mayhaps, not even her mind, but her heart.

That rebellious, intrusive heart of hers. She could not afford it further attention while embarked on this quest. It would be suicidal to do so. The damsel must be kept in the shadows.

Sera jerked as an odd sensation swept across her shoulders. A shimmer of cool air. The fine tickle of...something.

She pressed her hand to her head. Eyes shifting to study the empty darkness behind her, she patted the short juts of hair that sprang from her scalp. She shook her head again. Turned her chin from side to side. It felt as though—her long hair were slithering across her back!

Clamping a hand to her neck, she reassured that indeed the

midnight locks she had once spent frustrated mornings braiding to keep from her face were no longer there.

Again a toss of her head produced the sensation of something sliding across her shoulders.

Sera pressed her back to the cold wall. Above, set into an iron bracket laced with spider webs, a torch blazed. She tilted her head forward, but her chin would not lower any more than a hand's breadth, for her hair was pressed between the wall and her back— No!

Sera leapt from the wall and spun to see what was not there.

"I am going insane," she whispered. To feel as if her hair had grown back? "I have been on the road too long. Starved my body of the proper food and my mind of sleep. Please God, help me through this night."

Resigned to ignore the odd sensation Sera stepped onward. It would not do to let down her guard. If Dominique's information were correct, there was still the seventh hell to overcome. What could possibly stand between she and Abaddon's chamber? The foreboding black door was but two horselengths from where she stood.

Her thumb glanced across the hilt of her sword. She had worn the heavy weapon to put Baldwin and Dominique's worries aside.

Remember, he'd said, *gain access, strike immediately.*

Aye, but she knew it would be suicide to step inside her enemy's chamber with such a weapon to hand. Abaddon would immediately know she had not come with mere pleasure in mind.

Unfastening the leather hip-belt, Sera then carefully set the blade against the wall. Her father had given it to her on her sixteenth birthday after many years of pleading on her part. The hilt, enrobed in plain pounded leather with decorative silver stitching, caught the torch fire and glinted.

She felt at her ankle for the dagger secured beneath her skirts. Feeble defense at best, but it would have to serve.

A high-pitched creak set Sera on edge. She swung around, her hand at her ankle in preparation to attack, but settled upon realizing the source of the noise.

There on the stone floor before Abaddon's door sat a lonely cricket. She bent to study the insect. 'Twas no cricket, this was a locust.

A plague of locusts, Baldwin had said.

"Damn." Holding her position, half bent before the door, Sera searched her periphery for an oncoming swarm. She studied the ceiling. The walls. Not a single crack in the chalky plaster to allow one locust passage, let alone a swarm.

She had survived the crawl of spiders over her flesh; but locusts, these creatures could fly as well as skitter.

"It cannot be. It *will* not be."

Sera remained in her bent position, listening, praying, eyeballing the single jade locust sitting unmindfully before her. Once she thought she heard the echo of Baldwin's voice, then realized it might be the dancers' gaiety carrying up from the keep. Nothing happened. A swarm did not buzz overhead to overtake her feeble flesh.

Releasing a breath, Sera almost chuckled, but cautioned her relief against the nearness of her enemy—just on the other side of the door.

"So it is just you then, eh?" The squire will love to hear this one when she returned, Sera mused. The seventh hell was a plague of one locust.

"See you in hell," she whispered, and pressed her bare foot upon the crisp-winged creature.

TEN

With Seraphim gone ahead to rout out Abaddon, Dominique had to work quickly to prepare for the inevitable.

"I believe I will venture down this final passageway in search of an escape route," Dominique called to the squire, as he strode away. "Will you fare on your own?"

No answer. Dominique paused in his strides, and gripped the stone wall. "Baldwin?" Still no answer.

Odd. He'd left the squire sitting against the wall, the heel of his hand pressed to his swollen eye. The boy needed a few moments of rest after defeating death twice over, then coming so close to literally being frightened to death by Sera's swing at the spider sitting upon his head. Perhaps he'd fallen asleep? Passed out from exhaustion? Pain?

"Baldwin?"

An eerie foreboding liquefied the bones in Dominique's shoulders. Dashing back around the corner where he had left the squire, he found the lanky teen standing rigid and staring.

He quickened his pace to the man's side. When he touched his arm, Baldwin let out a squeak.

Then Dominique heard the buzzing. 'Twas thick and hideous, like a swarm of bloodthirsty insects.

"Here c-comes the plague," Baldwin managed on a shriek. He lunged behind Dominique, using him as a shield. "Don't let them get me!"

Though he did not see the swarm, the buzzing grew louder. The cacophony worked Dominique's heart to a frenzied pace. Even as he tried to brush off Baldwin's clinging hands from his shoulders, he unsheathed his sword.

"A sword?" Baldwin bawled. "What good is that going to do?"

"Unless you have a bone to ward off locusts?"

"I don't think—Mother of Mercy, they're huge!"

Dominique felt Baldwin drop in a dead faint at his ankles. At the same time the swarm rounded the corner and flew into view. A swarm of three locusts, to be precise.

Locusts the size of field oxen.

"A sword will definitely serve," Dominique reassured, and swung at the flurry of jade wings that approached.

The buzzing, accompanied by the slither of metallic wings across hardened jade bodies, pounded inside his head. Sharpened wings, they were. 'Twas as if the beasts wore armor and wielded wide, glinting blades on their backs.

Another swing of his sword connected with the steel fabric of a jade wing. The locust blocked the blow with a snap of its front tarsus, which sent Dominique plunging back against the wall.

He shook off the jarring blackness created by stone wall catching skull, and spied the lead locust creeping over Baldwin's inert body. A needle-pointed proboscis extended from its mouth and scratched a bloody tear across the squire's forehead.

Dominique pushed from the floor and, his body not using the ground, in a lightning-fast motion soared forward. He hammered his sword across the leader's head, severing it from its thorax. Jade blood oozed over Baldwin's chest, startling the man awake and into maniacal screams.

"Stay there!" Dominique commanded. "There are but two more."

An agile swing of his body, and he brought his leg up, heeling one of the beasts right in the eye. The multi-faceted compound eye shattered like glass. The beast drew its proboscis across Dominique's leg. No pain. His leather braies protected.

"San Juste!"

Alerted by Baldwin's cry, Dominique spun around to see the third locust had passed them up and now moved slowly down the passage in Sera's wake.

With one beast still swinging its proboscis at him, Dominique bent low and slid beneath its belly. Reaching up, he grasped the proboscis—icy steel blades cut through his flesh—and snapped it off. Dominique thrust the needle of steel after the retreating locust. Direct hit! It speared the insect in the belly, perhaps the heart. It dropped with a thud to the floor, shaking and spurting jade blood.

Giving his wounded hand a good shake did not disperse red sprays of blood across the floor. Dominique did not bother to inspect the wound. 'Twould be healed before he remembered the injury.

The sharp grinding of wings across one another reminded of the final locust. Not that he needed reminding. The acrid scent of the beast's breath trickled down the back of Dominique's neck. He turned in a quarter spin, brought up his leg—this time the kick lodged his boot-toe in the belly of the insect.

Dominique struggled for release. The locust's gnawing

mandibles worked near his ear in a hideous sawing scream. Everywhere, the air glittered with the residue of his exertions. But he could not work a glamour on these beasts, for they had already been enchanted by a dark evil.

The shrill buzz of wings increased. The locust's body lifted into the air. In that moment Dominique let go his hold on the insect's neck, allowed his body to swing free—his foot remained lodged in the insect's gut. He unsheathed his dagger, and plunged it into the locust's heart.

"No!" Baldwin cried, as the insect fell from flight and crushed Dominique between its dead weight and the floor. "Dominique?"

As he lay beneath the massive insect body, a piercing pain pulsed between Dominique's shoulder blades. He'd broken something. *No.* Mayhaps he was but wounded. He prayed as much, for he could not seek aid from any mortal.

"Dominique!"

With much grunting and heaving, Baldwin finally rolled away the locust from Dominique's body. The squire plunged to the floor and lifted his head. "Speak to me, man!" His words chittered from locust-blood-coated lips. Thick green droplets spattered Dominique's face. "Tell me you're alive!"

He pressed his face right next to Dominique's, his eyes scanning frantically. Frantic breaths puffed over Dominique's eyelids.

"I live," Dominique managed. A splat of jade blood oozed over his nose. "But if you get any closer, I'll presume you've a notion to take me as your intended."

"You better believe it!" Baldwin planted a slimy kiss on Dominique's forehead. With a smack of his hands, and a swipe of his wrist across his goopy face, he declared, "I thought you were dead for sure. Damn! Look at those things!"

Dominique touched the slippery spot where he'd been kissed, studied his fingers, then closed his eyes and released the tension from his muscles. "I think we just saved Sera from the seventh hell."

This one he had never before seen. Abaddon could not recall seeing the looming seductress in the enchanted masque. Though, she wore no feathers or gild over her face now, so he might have missed her earlier.

But to have overlooked such exquisite form? Tall and broad shouldered, yet sinuous and lithe. Red damask clung worshipfully to long legs and slender hips. A wide blue sash emphasized her narrow waist and drew attention to the voluptuous breasts that peaked beneath the low-cut fabric. The creamy rose circles surrounding those hard nubbles of flesh swelled in half disks above the red fabric.

Beads of sweat glittered on her flesh, in the curve of her neck, at the pulse of her temples, and in the soft indentation crowning her upper lip. She seemed to twinkle all over in a surreal vision of beauty, temptation, and sex.

And surrounding all, a luscious wash of obsidian hair. It streamed from her head, over alabaster shoulders, and undulated like the ocean's waves around her hands and waist. Hair as black as hell, and just as inviting. Oh, to tangle his fingers in that, and pull her down on top of his body, drowning himself in the liquid black tresses.

Abaddon sat up on his bed, plumped with satin pillows and velvet throws. At sight of this exotic creature with pouting lips and downcast indigo eyes, he gave a kick to the form lying beside him. A glance to the floor verified his previous lover, her arms sprawled over her head, and wide black eyes staring blankly at the ceiling. Blood spiraled from her parted lips.

"Women are so terribly delicate," Abaddon mused.

He allowed a vicious smile to overtake his sex-flushed face. Without another thought for his victim, he stretched out an arm and gestured this new woman approach. As his fingers moved to coax, the muscles in his tawny, tightened arms flexed and bulged.

How fine a body this is, he thought, with a glee that fired his lust and his appetite for blood all at once.

"Come, my statuesque Aphrodite," he beckoned.

One sweep of his hand across his lap removed two layers of gossamer bed linens to reveal his entire body, lying in repose after his last climax. But certainly ready to be mounted again.

The rusted portcullis bent and finally cracked with the weight of Dominique's hip pushing against it. After they'd moved the dead locusts around the corner (to prevent Sera from seeing them) he'd then left Baldwin to guard outside Abaddon's door, while he ventured to check the one narrow passageway they'd yet to traverse. It was a quick exit that led outside the walls of the castle. Surrounded by trees and stacked firewood, this entrance would provide fine escape after Seraphim had completed her task.

"Damn it!" Dominique kicked the inner wall of the passageway and beat a fist into his palm. He had left Seraphim alone to face the Demon of the North. He'd been so busy poking giant bugs, he'd forgotten all about what was of real importance.

"She is alone."

A woman all alone in Abaddon's lair. What had he been thinking? "I've got to return."

His boots crushed life-drained leaves and rubble as he took the stairs, but three steps up the glowing chimera of the Oracle stopped him.

"Out of my way," Dominique growled. He placed a hand to

his sword, but knew it would serve naught against a figment. "You wanted me to see the black knight to the final de Morte? Well, I cannot leave her to Abaddon's cruelty and allow him to end this quest just as it has begun."

Dominique pressed forward, but found he could not broach the next step. 'Twas as if the Oracle wore an invisible shield around him.

"Let me pass!"

"You are exactly where you should be right now," the boy whispered. His figure glimmered in a vibrant indigo shade. "Trust me."

"Trust?" He'd done so blindly since the inception of this quest. Why now was he questioning the Oracle's wisdom? Perhaps because, as Sera had implied, he knew little of this child, where he had come from, what his purpose was. "She will die."

"I sense there is more reason beyond the mere completion of this mission in your sudden worry for the black knight's safety."

"The black knight is a woman. Her name is Seraphim d'Ange. Do not use the legend to gift her with more power than she is capable. She needs me," he pleaded.

"And you promised there was no reason to fear your alliances will waver."

"Waver? They are stronger than ever. I am that woman's protector—"

"Really?"

Dominique took a step down from the Oracle's unwavering frown. He sighed, feeling his staunch bravery flow out with his breath. He eased a hand over his shoulder, but it did not stretch to the ache on his back. No, nothing broken. But the fall from the locust had jarred his bones something fierce.

Ah, but Seraphim. What protection *did* he provide? Certainly Sera had proven her mettle. Could it be that he wanted to be at her side for more than just protection?

She was a lovely woman. He could not deny he'd had thoughts about her. Lustful thoughts. The remembered feel of her nipple skimming the back of his hand rushed to the fore. Indeed, there did lie softness beneath the armor. Voluptuous softness.

What made this woman so different from any other?

Well, that was easy. He could feel her energy to the very core of his being. She did never but stand and simply fill space. She was everywhere, near, far, and so very, very close. Her energy pinged, here and there, touching him even when she was not aware. And that touch teased him, coaxed him, tempted, and at the same time, defied him.

Did he wish her success for the good of the mission, or his own boon?

"You see," the Oracle said, "you know the answers already."

Yes, but the question had more than one answer.

"Very well." Dominique pressed his back to the wall and toed a small stone off the edge of the step. It landed with a *tink* in the pile of leaves at the base of the stairwell. Another heavy sigh puffed a cloud of cold air before him. "You must know something I do not. Of course, Seraphim will be successful. I must concentrate on—"

But when he turned to the Oracle, the boy was no longer there.

"One of these days," Dominique muttered, as he stepped down to finish his clearing of the bars from the exit, "I will learn to do that."

Gain access, strike immediately.

Easier said than done.

At sight of the naked man lying on the bed, Sera's left foot did not step upon the marble floor at the moment she expected. Thinking it in place, she moved her right foot, which caused her a momentary stumble—but she quickly righted herself without having to grip the nearby table for support. Spilled water from the waiting silver ewer would not a fine entrance make.

A brush of the hair-like sensation that had tormented her in the hallway caressed her bare arm. Much like a soft summer breeze tickling her flesh—but she could not think on that.

Focus, she coached inwardly. *He lies bared before me. He has no weapon in his hands.* Hands which were wide, the fingers long and surprisingly muscled. Abaddon's entire body rippled with taut muscle and masculine brawn. Walnut hair flowed over bronzed shoulders and down his chest. The redness circling his nipples matched his red parted lips. Though he bore little resemblance to his slain brothers; he was a handsome man. A massive man, all corded muscle and sweat-glimmering flesh. A fine challenge to any woman's heart.

"Fool," Sera whispered to herself. Those attractive muscles could prove effective weapons against her weak physical-combat skills.

He has murdered hundreds of men, violated tens of hundreds more women. He is the enemy.

Drawing her shoulders back and straight, Sera inhaled a breath of bravery and approached the edge of the luxuriously draped bed.

Heartbeats jittered out of control. Her breathing, threatening to become as rapid as her heart, must be slowed. *Calm. He is the enemy. Those hands can snap your neck before you can reach for the dagger at your ankle.*

An immediate strike was impossible. This was not like battle. No darkness, no mud and snow, not even the myriad shouts of clashing soldiers to confuse. No noise to mask her frantic heartbeats. One on one. Seraphim d'Ange and the Demon of the North.

She recalled Dominique's last minute wisdom. *Seduce…*

"My lord Abaddon," she said in a whisper, knowing that to raise her voice would release the frog-tones forged by her wound. She managed a curtsey, but did not lower her eyes. *Keep him in your eyes.* "I am here for your pleasure."

"Indeed, you are." He pushed up on his elbows, but Sera stopped his further movement with a hand thrust before her.

"No. You mustn't lift a finger in your pursuit of pleasure. Not yet."

Greedy hunger, not so much demonic as demented, sparkled in the dark voids set in close proximity upon Abaddon's face. Predatory eyes.

"Allow me to do it all, my lord. You need only lay back and enjoy."

"A fine wench who knows her place." A wicked growl curdled in Abaddon's throat as he let his head sink into a pile of velvet pillows. "Come serve me, wench. Draw my lust into your throat. Feast upon Abaddon de Morte!"

Sera bit her lip so hard she could hear the flesh split.

Not this woman.

Her fingers flexed at her thighs as she looked over her enemy, blatantly bared before her. *No sword at my side.* Sera knew she must close the distance. The illusion of compliance must be created. She would have to put herself into the salamander's grip in order to place the killing blow.

A mist of scent curled in graceful arabesques from the marble table to Abaddon's right, dancing a seductive finger of perfume over his shoulder and across the bed to draw Sera closer. Crawling onto the bed that sat upon a high damask-draped dais, Sera then placed a knee to either side of Abaddon's ankles. The heat of his body permeated the fabric covering her legs in a most evil way. 'Twas Hell's steam seeking a corruptible innocent.

She had already been corrupted by one de Morte. Such catastrophe would not again occur.

A glance to the left of the bed spied the woman Abaddon had unceremoniously shoved from his side. Her head lay twisted upon her shoulders. Long strands of golden hair splayed artfully over her face, but remained clear of her wide brown eyes. Dead.

A scream broke in Sera's gut. She clamped her mouth tight, wincing at the pain in her wounded lip. She looked away, closing her eyes to the woman's dead gaze, to Abaddon's greedy stare, and to that horrid body part that jutted straight from the base of his abdomen.

"She will not interfere," Abaddon commented, his hand gesturing to the floor, then sweeping back to capture Sera's hair in his fingers. "So fine." His fingers dug into her scalp, coaxing her farther up along his legs until her face hovered over his rigid phallus. "You are hungry?"

"As—as a newborn infant, my lord." She swallowed and drew up her knees, positioning herself higher, but remaining on the alert. "But for the wine upon your lips."

Hungry eyes studied her face. He could sense her trepidation—or not? So intent he was in the pursuit of his own pleasures. Sera felt she might have a chance against this man. Blinded by desire. *Yes.* A rigid cock did not make for a rigid mind. Aye, an easy mark.

Lowering her head, she pressed her lips to his. A greedy tongue swept out and lapped at her broken flesh, stabbing her tongue in a hideous danse macabre. The action horrified, yet Sera concentrated only on the slide of her fingers down her right leg. The only rigid part she was intent on touching was the hard column of her dagger. One perfect move, and—

The weapon avoided her grip as Abaddon's fingers slid over

her breasts. Hard, groping, merciless caresses stirred animal moans up from his throat and spilled into her mouth.

"My lord, you were to but lie back——"

"You are here to serve me? I require your naked body. Right now. On your back, wench."

"No!" Her cry stopped him cold. His hands still gripping her breasts, Abaddon's brow crimped into question. "I——I mean. No, I shall mount you, my lord."

"Ahh..." Pleased with her suggestion, and with a pinch to her nipples, he slipped his hands from her body and crossed his arms behind his head. "Then ride me well, wench. For if you do not, it shall be your last."

Her hips hovering precariously above the siege perilous, Sera slid her hand down her ankle and grasped upon the hard leather-wrapped hilt of her dagger. The weapon was hot against her palm as she carefully drew it out.

Abaddon's mindless gyrations increased in intensity. His hips pumped against her thighs, his hands gripping the black bed linens in tight puckers. His face screwed in what looked like a painful grimace. She'd yet to lower herself onto his shaft, but he took pleasure in rubbing it against her thigh. So blinded he was to all but satisfying his lust.

Time to strike.

In one smooth motion, Sera raised the dagger above her head, gripped its handle in both hands, and plunged the tempered steel into Abaddon's chest. It slid perfectly between rib-bones. She felt but a moment's hesitation as the blade cut through tough heart muscle. Blood gushed around her fisted grip on the blade.

She could not be sure, but the pulsing moan that poured from Abaddon's mouth might have been that of pleasure. It was the most bizarre death cry Sera had ever heard. His eyelids stretched wide and the dark circles of his eyes rolled back, exposing red vein-lined orbs in a hideous death mask.

Frozen in a state of marvel, disgust, and fear, Sera still worked the dagger handle. She pressed hard, wanting to ensure death. One final plunge relaxed Abaddon's body beneath her. His head lolled in surrender to life. Black blood sluiced from his mouth.

Sure of her success, with a yank, Sera pulled the dagger out of bone and muscle. She pushed back and slid from his legs to stand and look over the destruction she had wrought.

But the crack of Abaddon's neck bones, bringing his head on center with his shoulders, startled her to her knees.

ELEVEN

Eyes rolled back into his head—yet apparently dead, to judge from the crimson life spewing from his chest—Abaddon's body seemed to work at the will of a puppet master. His mouth snapped wide, and wider…and…wider, until Sera heard the *crack* of his jaw bones separating, and the leathery tear of his flesh as his skull cleaved open to release a ball of fire.

Brimstone suffused the air with a hideous stench of the underworld. An impact of unnatural strength blasted Sera's chest. Her feet left the bed. Propelled backward, her spine connected with the tapestry-hung wall to the right of the door.

A fireball hovered before her, sizzling and crackling like a bonfire. Flames licked at her face like a swarm of hungry bees. Stunned and unable to move, for the pain of her landing tingled in her legs and back, Sera raised her dagger and slashed blindly before her.

The fire began to form into a recognizable shape, taking on Abaddon's ridged brow and smirking lips. Fine threads of flame swayed like hair upon the skull of amber-red heat. Lips formed of fire opened into a hollow bellow and blasted her with a wind of hot flame.

Sera's screams were lost in the fire beast's roar of triumph. She slashed and stabbed and kicked, but the creature was able to dodge with the agility of a flame caught on the wind.

Losing hold on her position, Sera could feel her body slide down the wall—when a thought occurred. Answering gravity's relentless pull, Sera slid down, until she found herself horizontal beneath the beast's belly. With one great thrust, she slashed her dagger across the neck. No effect!

Another violent breath of flame licked at her cheek and crackled in her hair. Behind her she could hear a muffled shout. Someone had entered the bed chamber. Another wench for Abaddon's midnight meal?

Licks of liquid suddenly splashed Sera's face. Cool, redeeming water tinged with rose-scent. The brunt of the water rained over the fire beast. In a spray of flame, and a great howl of demon-rage, the beast dispersed, and fire sprites scattered to all corners of the room. The bedclothes burst into flame, igniting the damask curtains and Abaddon's fleshy body.

Behind her Baldwin dropped the silver ewer. "What—" he heaved, and expelled a monumental breath "—the hell—was that?"

"Damned if I know." On her knees, Sera scrambled to the door. With Baldwin's aid she was able to stand and stumble out into the dark hallway. She panted and heaved, feeling the fire singe in her throat.

Baldwin patted her hair to diffuse a flame. "That couldn't have been the seventh hell, because Dominique and I—"

"That was Abaddon!" she rasped, as stunned as the squire at

what she had just witnessed. "A demon birthed from his mouth…after I stabbed him."

Cold, wet, shaking, and boiling all at the same time, she gripped Baldwin's wrist. "Where is San Juste?"

"Just outside, keeping watch. He discovered a back exit."

"Let's be off." Sera retrieved her sword propped by the wall. "San Juste seems to know so much about the de Mortes." She allowed the squire to brace his arm around her waist, and they fled down the hallway. "I think he forgot to mention one small detail."

"I didn't mention it because I thought you already knew."

"Knew?" Aware that her silk vestments had been singed to mere shreds that barely covered her body, Sera accepted the wool cloak Baldwin wrapped around her shoulders. Then she rounded on the overconfident mercenary. "Knew what?"

"That the de Mortes are demons. True demons." No matter what form Dominique shaped with his gesticulating fingers before Sera's face, he could not convey what he attempted. Finally he clutched the air and spouted, "Demons! The immortal kind that can only be exterminated by the severing of their heads. I assumed you knew this because both Satanas and Mastema were beheaded."

"You assumed? Ah! Assumptions!" she declared in a bold rasp. "Nay, I did not know they were immortal. The first two just happened to be in a position to lose their heads. You knew I was going in there with but my dagger—"

"You had your sword," Dominique insisted, without allowing his voice a slice of rage. "What happened to it?"

"I would have been a fool to wear it inside. Abaddon would have known from the start I was there with ill intentions. Real demons? Immortal?"

"Mother of Mercy," Baldwin punctuated Sera's tirade.

Sera slumped against a narrow birch that grew at a forty-five-degree angle from the outside of the battlement walls. The movement shook a clump of snow from the winter-raped branches to land on her knees. She could not even feel chilled for her lack of clothing; her rage burned like an inner furnace. 'Twas as if *she* bore a fireball in her belly. "I'm fighting *real* demons?"

Dominique nodded. Baldwin had taken to kneeling before her, trying to coax her legs into the mail chausses he'd dug from the saddlebags. One of them had retrieved the horses in the short while she'd been in Abaddon's lair. Most likely the mercenary. Dominique had so little regard for her safety. And with this new information, it was even more obvious.

"I thought their titles just nicknames," she said. "The Demon of the North, Demon of the South. Not real demons. Just mean, violent *mortal* men."

"Forgive me, Seraphim, I thought you knew."

"Well, I didn't." She allowed the squire to pull the chausses up her legs and truss up the points. The mail was lined with cambric, which provided a welcome bit of warmth. He followed with her boots.

"Now you do know," Dominique offered.

"So I do."

"So will you end this quest for revenge?"

After tasting death? Twice over? Sera pounded a bruised fist into her palm. "Never."

"Good."

"Have I no say in the matter?" Baldwin sprang up, and poked Dominique in the chest with one of Sera's scaled gauntlets. "Look at her! She almost died inside that demon's chambers. And had she not died she would have been roasted as a fowl upon the spit, then consumed at Abaddon's pleasure. Look at her! She is hideous with bruises and burns!"

Sera lowered her gaze to the slush-moistened ground. Baldwin's words extinguished the fire that had carried her through Abaddon's lair. Her belly was empty. Not a single ember burned there. Now the silk-gowned damsel reemerged, only to be brought to her knees by an awareness of her outer appearance.

"How the man was ever convinced to allow her into his bed is beyond me." Baldwin slapped Sera's gauntlets against his thigh, then wandered away to stand near Gryphon.

Dominique knelt next to Sera and lifted her chin. "You are not hideous." He touched her cheek, perhaps just under her eye. Her face was numb; she could not judge whether he touched her flesh or merely drew close. Until she saw her own tear glisten on the tip of his forefinger.

She didn't know what to say. Words of anger, of vengeance or valor, would not birth on her tongue. The fire had been drained from inside. She felt defeated and weak. So, so alone.

Had she known that within Abaddon de Morte lived such a beast, she might have turned and run days ago. Oh, God, she wanted to burrow beneath the snow and hide. This was not her place. She was not meant for such a life.

How could she be here?

Dominique's caress felt odd, intrusive. She began to struggle as he wrapped his arms around her shoulders, but his whisper, "You are cold," stayed her.

Instead of fighting the contact, Sera settled into Dominique's embrace and released. Her muscles unclenched, her bones relaxing against the hard exterior of his body. She could not think that tears were a sign of weakness or defeat. Only, she surrendered to their cleansing power and let loose against Dominique's neck.

"I am here." His whispers permeated her tormented mind on a sweet wave of salvation. "I will hold you for as long as you need. And then some. No more talk of violence, of blood or fire or demons."

"I'm the only one," she muttered against his shoulder. "I must stop the de Mortes. I just want it to end."

"It will. Soon enough. But not without peace of mind. You need to clear yourself of the evil that has taken hold of your heart. There is no victory in revenge, Seraphim. Triumph comes through honor and integrity. I will bring you to my cottage in the Valois Wood, and there you will rest and return to yourself. Restoration, Sera, you need to escape."

"I cannot. I've no time. There is too much to be done. Demons to be extinguished—"

He pressed a finger to her mouth, silencing the fearful child within. "It will happen. But for a few days?"

Yes, the damsel pleaded. *Take me away from all this death!*

Violet salvation, flashing warmly in Dominique's eyes, coaxed the battle-ravaged black knight to side with the damsel's pleas.

"Very well," Sera spoke. "One day."

The side of her scalp scalded—her convictions singed as well—Sera had been able to do little more than nod at Dominique's suggestion they detour from their next destination of Sammael's castle, and retreat to his home in the Valois Wood. A day of rest and reconnaissance before they rode on to face their next foe.

A foe greater than the last three.

Now with the horrible knowledge that she fought real demons, Sera didn't know what to think. What to do. It all seemed so unreal. Though she believed in the supernatural—

her sister's abduction had fortified that belief—she'd never had tangible evidence of its existence. Demons were a manifestation of evil born in malicious humans. Witches were no more supernatural than the earthbound herbs used to brew their mysterious concoctions. Faeries, well, their kind were cruel, and not to be given a second thought.

But the assumption that the supernatural did not exist unless it could be seen could no longer be held. What had become of Abaddon de Morte after his mortal body had released its final breath was certainly nothing of this earthly realm.

You must sever their heads to ensure final death of the demon within.

Dominique had suspected she knew such a thing?

The man who had been sent by some oracle to protect her surely might have discussed the slaying of true demons before allowing her to enter Abaddon's chamber alone. That Satanas's and Mastema's deaths had occurred in such a manner had been fluke!

But he knew you had your sword at your side.

He had insisted she take it along. Sera recalled now, Dominique's strange look when she'd initially thought to leave it behind. He had believed then that she knew she fought real demons.

How now would this knowledge affect her quest?

A shudder traced Sera's spine and settled in her breast, like a fist-sized snowflake that would never melt, only radiate spikes of chill throughout her being. She had thought she was hunting flesh and blood men. Men who were vulnerable, men who could be tricked, challenged, *killed* with a sword to the heart.

How could she possibly defeat the next demon?

She was but mortal. A visceral being that walked the earth on two legs and swung her arms with muscle and might. A human who possessed emotion and pain and joy…and tears.

Sera jerked her head up and stiffened her jaw. *Fool woman, what are you thinking? You can do this. You* must *do this! In your family's name the de Mortes must fall. And for all future victims to come!*

Tonight Abaddon had fallen in her mother's memory. There were but two villains left.

Dominique's insistence that revenge would not bring triumph was wrong. She would triumph through revenge. It fueled the fire that blazed in her breast and pushed her onward when all seemed futile. She could not function without that blaze.

Could she?

The snowfall picked up as the trio ascended a slope in the thick woods. A clearing rose in the eerie, moon-drenched illumination of winter. There in the center of the clearing grew a petite square cottage, topped with graying reed thatch. Heavy stones, bound by twine and used to weight down the thatch, gleamed with caps of snow. The chimney wore a white beard of the same. A short, round door might allow no more than a troll entrance; Sera knew the countryfolk fashioned them so to prevent intruders from entering. A thief in search of coin should not wish to bend and cross the threshold when such a vulnerable position heightened the risk of losing his head.

Sera urged Gryphon ahead with a heel to his belly. The horse's hooves *shushed* through the thick, powdery diamond-glittered snow.

"It is a faery cottage," Baldwin whispered loudly from behind her.

Dominique rode up alongside the squire, the brilliant white stallion's breath frosting in thick clouds. "Why say you such a thing, squire?"

"There is enchantment here," Baldwin said.

Sera smirked and drew in a deep breath that iced her throat.

Enchantment, indeed. Certainly her perception of the world and its many wonders must change after her encounter with the fire demon. But enchantment? She recalled the strange state of *erie* she had felt when looking deep into Dominique's eyes.

Perhaps. But of nature's hand.

She removed her hood to let the snow salve her sore flesh. The fire demon had singed the left side of her head. It was a good chill that soothed the pulsing ache on her scalp. "Aye, enchantment. I can feel it in every snowflake," she muttered, to no one but herself. "I think I will sleep well tonight."

Dominique eased Tor past Sera and Gryphon. "There is a stable around back. Enough room for the three of our horses. Come."

"How do you fare?" Baldwin said, as he rode alongside Sera in the trail of Dominique's wake. "Does your head pain you?"

She shook her head and offered a smile. An easily summoned gesture, feeling as she did right now. As if she'd ridden into a world set apart whence she had come.

Indeed, a world of certain enchantment.

"It will heal. Though I wager my coif is quite laughable, eh?"

"It did fry the hairs down to your scalp," Baldwin offered. "In a streak over your ear. You're looking rather, hmm…"

"Hideous?" she offered to the squire's struggle for something kind to say.

"Forgive me, I was angry earlier. A bit tattered, is all. You've been through seven hells and overcome three immortal demons in but a fortnight. 'Twas fine you agreed to come here, Seraphim. You need the peace, a respite."

"You forget your own struggles, squire. We both need this rest. But for a day." She hitched a heel into Gryphon's flanks. "One night, then on to Sammael's lair."

For if she allowed herself to soften, to even begin to believe there was something beyond this fierce, ugly life she had embraced, it would never end. And then she would know true evil really did exist.

"Indeed," Baldwin's voice said from behind, "battling giant locusts tends to tire a man."

"Giant locusts? Ha!" Sera cast the squire the mongoose eye. "Have you barn owls nesting up in yonder skull, squire?"

Dominique swung Tor back around and rode up between the two of them. The black cape flared out behind him in billows of soft mystery. "What bothers you, squire?"

"Not a thing. I was just telling Sera about the locusts—"

"What locusts?" Dominique cut him off abruptly.

Baldwin shook his head in amazement. "Huh?"

"There were no locusts," the mercenary said.

"I did see one," Sera said. "I stepped on it. Figured that was the seventh hell." With that, Sera hitched a heel to Gryphon's flank and rode ahead.

"Stepped on it?" Baldwin gaped. He jerked a look from Sera's retreating back to Dominique's calm expression. "What is with you, San Juste? No locusts?"

"The events that occurred inside Abaddon's castle are now in the past," Dominique explained in a low hiss. "There is no need to frighten Sera over something that no longer exists."

"Ah hell!" Baldwin fisted the air with a lackluster punch. "She kills the baby, and we get stuck with the mother and father. And one hell of a pissed-off big brother."

"Baldwin," Dominique cautioned. He sported a surprisingly-honed evil eye, himself.

The squire slumped upon the saddle. "Who's lying now?"

"Some lies are necessary," the mercenary said in a low tone. "To protect those we care about."

At that, Baldwin pricked his ears. "Care?"

But Tor had already cantered off, leaving Baldwin to contemplate the idea that someone might actually care for him, and the notion that some lies were necessary. Then there was the pain in his backside that surpassed even all his bruises, cuts, and wounds. He wasn't cut out for riding. This whole squire business certainly didn't pay enough to compensate for all he had been through in the past few weeks.

And he definitely would not have agreed to join Seraphim had he known it was real demons they sought.

"Ah hell." Baldwin urged his mount around the side of the cottage. "Of course I would have done as much."

Because the only other option, remaining behind and seeking out room and coin on his own, just didn't appeal as much as accompanying a legend.

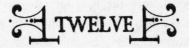

TWELVE

Sera was the last to come in from the stable. Baldwin had helped Dominique start a fire in the hearth. The two men had decided to trek to the freshwater stream behind the cottage to bring in water to wash.

"Let me take a look at that before we venture to the creek." Dominique slid a hand down Sera's arm, directing her tired footsteps away from his rope trundle bed and toward the trestle table. Her body collapsed with little display on the short bench hewn from a single chestnut branch, but she held her back straight. Too proud to admit she was tired.

"It is nothing to be overconcerned." She drew in a sharp inhale as Dominique touched the burned flesh. Fire had worked nasty blisters to her scalp, scorching away the hair in a crescent over and behind the tender shell of her ear.

"I've some salve that will cool," he said, and went to retrieve the pot of his mother's healing elixir from the cupboard. Mixed with catmint and lanolin, she had always brought it out whenever Dominique would come running in with a skinned knee or bruised elbow. Which had been often. Now he knew the cream did only but soothe, not heal. 'Twas his mother's kiss that had done the real healing. "Hold still."

Sera remained a statue, half asleep already, as he pressed a thick wodge of the fragrant ivory cream against her scalp. Not a peep, not a flinch. So brave.

Baldwin paced before the fire, his attention taking in the walls of verdant wattle and moss, and the ceiling shrouded with the same. "There are flowers," he said in an amazed whisper, at the floral display that dotted the walls.

"Pansies," Dominique offered. "My mother's favorite. Amazingly they grow all the year through."

"I told you there was enchantment here," Baldwin directed at Sera's swaying figure. "Now, if you'd just believe in giant—"

"There is a clean shirt in the chest at the end of the bed," Dominique directed sternly. "Bring it to me, will you, Baldwin?"

With a grumbling pace, the squire did, and Dominique instructed him to rip a wide portion from the hem so he could press it over Sera's wound.

"Have you more?" she wondered drowsily, her eyes fixed to the hot flames.

"Cream?"

"Shirts."

"Nay, but the one on my back, and now this shorter one."

"I am not worth such sacrifice."

"You are worth far more than a mere strip of fabric, my lady." He carefully wrapped the cloth around her head once and secured it with a tucked knot. "And until you come to realize that, you will still be fighting fueled by revenge instead of honor."

"I'm tired, San Juste. Are you almost finished?"

Dominique lifted the cloth he'd pressed to her scalp. The

burns were red and oozing. Short tufts of hair sprouted here and there. A hideous sight. But he could do something about that.

Glancing aside, Dominique checked Baldwin standing near the fire; the squire's gaze was lost in the dance of flames. Everyone was numb and tired.

Quickly Dominique rubbed his fingers together, dispersing the right amount of coruscation over Sera's wound. It spewed from his fingertips and glittered like snowfall over the bubbled flesh. He pressed the cloth to her head just as Baldwin turned.

Casting the wide-eyed squire a wink, Dominique then offered Sera his bed. She tottered to the pallet, and rolled from a standing position into a dead sleep in a single graceful movement.

Baldwin followed Dominique's long strides around the thatched stable. The mercenary had to be as exhausted as he and Sera, but he showed little more than the occasional short stride or audible huff. Baldwin found the soft clicking of the stones set around the man's collar worked like a tune that lured him to follow. A beguiling piper coaxing him into danger. But not really danger. For as much as he wondered about him, Baldwin also trusted Dominique.

No locusts?

On the other hand, the man was too humble for his own good. Though he *had* defeated all three beasts. And Sera did not need another thing to worry about. Aye, very well, Baldwin felt safe in Dominique's presence.

Though that presence was different from most. The man must be very light, for his strides barely pressed imprints into the snow. Odd. Baldwin's steps sank many inches in the surface.

Prepared to duck and examine the imperceptible trail, Baldwin suddenly bounded upright as he sensed the mercenary turn to see if he followed. Baldwin offered a genial wave of his hand. "Right behind you."

His gaze fell immediately to the trail as Dominique turned back around. The man's steps did no more than disturb the upper layer of fresh-fallen snow. Why, San Juste would have to weigh less than a fox to leave such curious footsteps.

It was when the mysterious mercenary dodged a low-hanging sessile oak branch, and scuffed his boot against a snow-buried tree root, that Baldwin saw the same glitter of iridescent particles he'd seen surround Sera before she'd ventured into Abaddon's chamber. A small puff expelled from Dominique's heel, like horse breath in the chill weather. And maybe a little from his elbow, as well?

As this happened the mercenary—still measuring a good stride—again turned and eyeballed Baldwin. *Do not question,* he silently said with those dark, flat eyes that lodged a thick gulp in Baldwin's throat.

When Dominique turned to resume his stride, Baldwin bent to study the snow where the sparkly dust had seemed to spray out from the man's very foot. It dazzled more than usual, like diamond dust in the illumination of torch glow. Yet the moon was hidden behind dark clouds at the moment. Hmm… He drew his finger through the snow, his glovetips tunneling a trench far deeper than the impression of Dominique's footprint.

"Coming?"

Snapping upright at the man's call, Baldwin knocked his head on the same branch Dominique had just dodged. Untangling his gawky limbs, he then took a step, but the mercenary stood—right there—at his side. When he should have been— Baldwin turned and scanned the trail ahead of them, no tracks. What was going on?

"You were just——" He pointed to where the man should have been.

"Going to fetch water from the stream?" Wide innocence colored the man's eyes a certain shade of violet. Curious.

What had he just asked? Water?

Without a single logical explanation on his tongue, Baldwin turned from Dominique to the trackless trail where he'd been sure the man had been leading—not there—then finally shrugged. "Indeed."

Dominique's words, spoken as Sera had left to conquer Abaddon, revisited Baldwin's thoughts. *It's just a glamour. She may need it.*

Glamour? Wasn't that for…faeries? And just now…the man had moved so swiftly. Without sound, or perceptible motion. Baldwin was sure of it. Dominique had been in front of him. And then he was not.

Baldwin cast another glance to the back of the swinging black cloak. There was something very peculiar about Dominique San Juste.

Wide and shallow, the stream bubbled crisply, slicing a shimmery silver line through the thick Valois Wood. Heavy snowfall had bracketed the stream in a wide lacing. Dominique stepped carefully, judging his weight against the strength of the dense, wet snow. He did not want to sink to water level and risk wet boots and an icy trip back to the cottage. But the snow packed under his step and easily held his fey weight, so he bent and dipped his bucket into the frigid waters.

Baldwin did the same, following his careful measuring of safety before bending to draw up clean water.

He had seen. Dominique had sensed the squire had bent to study the surface of the snow to find the evidence in his wake.

He knew there would be none but a glimmer. And that could easily be construed as snow-shine. But the squire had also witnessed his casting of glamour in Abaddon's castle. Much as Dominique trusted Baldwin would not question him, he wondered now if he would tell Sera.

Should *he* tell her? Not that it mattered. She must know sooner or later.

You believe only in what you can see?

I do believe in faeries and demons…they are evil creatures.

Dominique preferred later.

He lifted the bucket to his lips, pressed his chin to the time-smoothened wood, and gulped down the liquid. Much-needed refreshment iced against the back of his throat.

Sera had not known the de Mortes were true demons. How was that possible? No mortal man could be so cruel. While many came close—or even for a brief stint in battle, matched the level of the de Mortes's tyranny—none could ever sustain a reign of terror as had the de Mortes. The five brothers had been born into this world to serve no other master than evil. And they had succeeded. Tremendously.

Of course, Dominique realized that mortals such as Sera, while brought up on faery stories and demon tales whispered by the flickering firelight, could not truly believe such creatures walked the earth. There were the superstitious and the wary, but true believers in pure and vicious evil? Only those who were then considered lunatic.

Though Sera had come to believe easily enough after her battle with Abaddon's fire demon. Poor woman, she had been nearly burned alive. He should have been there, should not have heeded the Oracle's warning. He had not belonged down by the portcullis.

He should have cast a stronger glamour upon Seraphim,

placed a spell of protection around her being. But to go through the machinations to do such would have given him away in her eyes that same moment.

Why keep his faery nature a secret? Should he not be proud of his heritage?

Yet what heritage? Dominique knew nothing of his lineage, his nature, the ways of his kind. He had been raised amongst mortals who could no more know his ways than a horse could know the ways of a cat.

He was a changeling—looked upon with horror by his own kind. He did no more belong in the mortal realm than he could rejoin the realm of Faery. For he could not enter that realm, though he knew it was all around and everywhere.

His birth parents had punished him by making him a changeling. Why?

After decades of fruitless wondering, he would have that answer.

After Sera felled the final de Morte.

"I wager Sera will be sleeping like a corpse when we return."

Dominique smiled and stirred the bottom of the bucket in the stream. Metallic waves *schussed* out from the entry point, and glimmered to blend with the purling waters. The flutter of wings preceded the reddish brown body of a hawfinch; it landed on Dominique's shoulder and settled to a wing-tucked peace. Dominique paid the visitor no mind. "Seraphim is brave and determined. Not an idle bone in that fine body. Will you tell me what it is that has put the fire in her heart?"

After regarding the bird for a curious moment, Baldwin then lifted his bucket and peered into the depths. No man could miss the painful squint that drew his brows to center and creased his forehead.

"It will only serve my own endeavor to assist if I can learn the source of your Seraphim's power."

"Source of power?" Baldwin smirked. "She is a mere mortal, San Juste."

"I know."

"But you are not." The squire cast him a look. A look of belief, of *wanting* to believe. An accusation too loud for voice.

"We are talking about Seraphim d'Ange, not me."

"Will we ever discuss..." Baldwin glanced back to the spot Dominique knew—the tree with the raised root. Then he whispered incredulously, "You are of the fair folk, aren't you?"

"Is it so important to know when you can already believe?"

The squire wrinkled his brows as he thought about that one. The crystal movement of the water harmonized with the rhythm of their heavy breaths into a quiet night symphony.

"I will tell all when it is necessary. When I know Sera can accept..."

"You mustn't tell her—" Baldwin abruptly halted his own words, then quickly added, "She's not...ready to accept. Faeries, that is. Best you keep it to yourself a while longer."

Dominique, surprised at the man's honesty—for his eyes had not bulged in evidence of a lie—nodded. He was accustomed to keeping secrets. Though, this time he was more willing to expose them than usual. He wanted Seraphim to trust him, and he knew complete trust could only come with complete truth.

"Sera may be young, and I had once thought her delicate, as you do. She is not." Baldwin readjusted his stance and pressed his palms to the edges of the bucket for balance. "Since her mother's illness she was forced to take over her duties, as well as the entire household. Seraphim is quiet strength. Delicate, but unbendable. But it was Lucifer de Morte who took that unshakable strength and forged it into steel mettle."

"All members of the d'Ange family were murdered? Including both brothers?"

"There was but the one brother. That was merely a lie I concocted to protect her identity."

"But Sera is alive. Why would the demon spare her?"

Decisive, Baldwin propped his elbows on the rim of the bucket, and pressed his forehead against his arced fingers. "I can only reason that de Morte must believe her dead. He left her there— She was so near death. I'm sure the man cannot have any clue who the black knight is."

"I don't think any man would accept the black knight as a woman. Not even Lucifer de Morte."

"She was supposed to die."

The sound of Baldwin's swallow echoed in Dominique's head. Human sorrow reached inside his own heart and gripped. He hadn't been able to stand by and watch as Sera had bravely fought against her tears outside Abaddon's castle. She had needed comfort. It had been easy to offer. And for a moment, she had comforted him. A desire he hadn't known he'd needed filling until he'd closed his eyes and lost himself in her arms.

The finch's wing-feathers brushed his ears. So soft, the touch. Unconditional, and uncompromising.

How long had it been since he'd steeled himself to avoid contact? Even when he'd taken a wench to serve his needs, he would cast a glamour so she could not truly see him—his real appearance. Sex would be quick, clinical, and he would feel no more than the satisfaction of release. It had to be that way. For his own protection. For he needed to hide. Always.

"I...I found her that night," Baldwin started. "It was the first morning of this New Year. We've told you about First Foot. They say the first man to cross the threshold after the clock chimes midnight casts a portent over the fate of the entire household."

"Lucifer de Morte. Hell of a portent."

"Everything happened so quickly. The castle flamed all around me. Cries of wounded and the dying spun in my head, making me sick to my stomach. I had just found Elsbeth, the lady of the manor. She had but one breath left in her dagger-torn heart. She said to find her children. I knew that Antoine had been felled out front in the inner bailey. I didn't tell Lady d'Ange though."

Dominique listened with care as the man told of the horrifying events he'd witnessed. He would not question how the squire had made it through the attack unscathed. He could guess. Young, rangy, and fearful of the sword, surely he had found a cubby and tucked himself away. But he would not judge. This man had done what was necessary to survive. As had he.

"I passed Henri de Lisieux on the way up the tower stairs. His heart had been gutted from his chest, but he still shivered and moaned. He lived yet!" Baldwin pressed both hands to his face. Dominique could see the tension wrinkle his forehead and the impressions his fingertips made in his flesh. "When I reached the tower room, I saw Sera's legs stretched across the floor. The blood...I knew she had been violated," he said in a quiet voice.

"As soon as she saw me, she released hold on her neck and revealed the gush of life. Lucifer had slashed her throat and left her to die. But the devil, if that woman wasn't determined to live! She tried to speak. The names of her family members gurgled up in spatters of blood as I bandaged her throat. I did not believe she would make it through the night, let alone this far."

"The jugular must not have been cut," Dominique commented, finding it odd that Lucifer could have been so careless. The man's profession demanded accuracy. He did not toy with life and death; he merely chose death. Always.

"I know nothing of jugulars, or surgery, for that matter. The wound should have been sown up. It's terribly scarred. I am sure my ineptness is the reason for Sera's damaged voice."

"You could have done no better. She speaks, and that is reason to give thanks. Hell, man, she lives!"

"Aye." He considered that, as though it were not thought of before. Nodded. "I sat there the remainder of the night praying like I have never before prayed. 'Twas the following afternoon that Sera blinked open her eyes and begged to see her mother.

"She insisted I escort her through the castle to look over the dead. Ninety percent fell under Lucifer's rage. If only Marcil d'Ange would have relented and handed over the estate. He had other properties."

"The one he'd promised to Sera?"

"Aye, and others spread throughout France. I suppose he wanted to keep the castle for his son. Ah! De Morte had no right to d'Ange land. 'Tis worth far more than the surplus crops he demanded payment for."

"De Morte cares not," Dominique said. "Charles VII is cowed by his presence. Lucifer collects land and holdings like a shepherdess plucks flowers from the meadow, without care, and with a smile on his face."

"It was a hideous sight that morning." Baldwin, his brown eyes fixed to the stream, swallowed, and continued. "We gathered the shuddering few who had survived, and set immediately to burying Sera's family. Henri's heart…it was not to be found. I couldn't bear to watch her frantic search for that organ. She insisted he be buried whole. Finally I pulled her away from her mad quest and we stood over the graves. Not a tear was shed, save a promise over their graves that the d'Ange family would be avenged.

"Two days before that I tell you the light in Seraphim's eyes was pure heaven. I knew the Lord had put the birth name

Seraphim on Elsbeth and Marcil d'Ange's lips for that very purpose. Because she truly was an angel in every way. She would
glide through the keep in her long red skirts, bright and ethereal. Always a 'Good day', and 'God grant you good eve.' Even
practicing in the lists at her brother's side, the beauty of her
standing with sword raised over her head...like the avenging
angel Michael, I tell you.

"But standing over the fresh graves of her loved ones, I looked
up to find heaven had fallen from her eyes. A dull horror cast
over the pale blue."

Baldwin gripped Dominique's sleeve. "I want to see the
heaven in her eyes again. It is not right! She should not be expected to ride this insane revenge."

"She chose to make this journey."

"It must stop, before it is too late! You say you have come to
help her achieve her goal? It is impossible! Sera had no idea the
men she would choose to hunt down are demons. We will all
die for an impossible quest."

"It seems your struggle for faith has made you fearful."

"Hell yes! I will always choose fear over faith."

"You choose the easy route."

"In a heartbeat."

Dominique lifted both buckets, intent on returning to the
cottage. But the squire's rage needed venting. He halted at the
pull on the corner of his cloak. The pressure of fabric against
his back rebirthed the ache between his shoulder blades.
Reaching back, he ripped the black wool from Baldwin's
greedy grasp.

"You have magick, don't you? You can ensure Sera lives
through this? Better still, you can cast a glamour over her, convince her there is no reason to continue this trek. Make her want
to put on a dress and set her fancy upon a rich husband some-

where far away from all this blood and evil. Italy! Aye! Send her on her way there."

"With you at her side?"

"Aye—er, well, I should like to be away from this hell—"

"If she does not exterminate the de Mortes, then who will?"

"Someone else!"

"She'll not survive if the remaining de Mortes are left to plunder the whole of France."

Baldwin spun on Dominique. The unspoken knowledge of truth flashed in his eyes. "He will come for Sera?"

"It is not a question, but a fact."

"But he doesn't know she is the black knight!"

"It won't be long before he does." With that Dominique stood and, hefting a full bucket in one hand, followed Baldwin's deep footprints back to the cottage.

They stepped inside the cozy one-room cottage and secured the door for the night. Baldwin shrugged off his cape and tiptoed over to the fire.

Dominique placed the bucket on the table and strode over to his bed. "She's asleep."

"Didn't I tell you? She sleeps like the dead. Mayhap that is the reason she was able to sleep through the attack upon her family's home." Baldwin set his bucket before the blaze and shrugged off his hood, gloves and boots. He rubbed his hands before the fire.

Sera lay peacefully, still clad in the shredded gown that topped mail chausses. The squire had trussed the points to thin shreds of the gown. Dominique observed the rising and falling chest of the enigmatic black knight. Soft, yet so strong.

That she had brought so much destruction to the de Mortes thus far was truly amazing. Determination wore the face of an angel and the mask of a mysterious knight.

But Sammael de Morte would provide an insurmountable challenge. The youngest de Morte dabbled in poison.

And if Sera got past him, would Lucifer allow her the final victory?

THIRTEEN

Smells permeated the fine veil of dream-sleep that teased Sera's mind. Her body rolled onto her back, centering itself on the straw-rope trundle bed. Her mind banished dreams, images of the deceased—faces of those she had known since she was a child, and the one man so new to her, yet quickly cherished, Henri de Lisieux—to the shadows of her memory. Her nose drew in the scent of roasting meat, dry, soil walls, and musty fire-scent. And somewhere, close by, the faint aroma of spring. Pansies.

Cinder snaps exploded her easy reverie and she opened her eyes. Above, the tidy ceiling beams harbored ribbon-tied bundles of dried lavender, sage, rape, and a few other crinkled flowers she could not name, though she had seen them in the fields surrounding her father's home. Not a spider's web, not a morsel of dust. And here and there, sprouting happily from the dirt walls, were patches of deep violet pansies. The petals were dark and velvet, like Dominique's eyes. 'Twas as if the world had been turned upon its head and she floated over it all.

"Hungry?"

Sera turned to the silken voice that had called from near the hearth. Dominique knelt before a spit, turning what might be the carcass of a rabbit, golden brown and sizzling. He'd discarded the heavily riveted jerkin for a plain woolen that hung to his knees. Soft black hose caressed well-muscled legs. He still wore the cloak—strange, though he might be chilled. He looked less dangerous, peasantlike, were it not for the regal bone structure and concerned eyes that sought out her attention.

Dominique smiled in question.

She nodded. Indeed, hunger bellowed within. She could eat all of a dozen rabbits if laid before her. And oh, for a bite of mother's sweet pastries, the kind she had made with the honey and almonds. As a child, Sera had been the one to sample mother's treats early in the morning when the castle was just beginning to stir.

"Have you any honey pastries?" Sera mumbled, as she pushed up and sat, her back melding to the moss-frosted clay wall behind her. A delicate pansy petal tickled her cheek.

"Afraid not," Dominique said, with another of those interesting smiles. 'Twas as if he startled himself with his mirth. His lips would not allow the surprise smile retreat. And so the rest of his visage must conform to the expression. "Rabbit and raspberry wine to break our fast. If it will serve?"

"Raspberry wine? Aye, how lovely." A hand to her chest felt exposed skin. Tugging her cape from under her legs, she pulled it around her shoulders. She would have to dig the quilted gambeson and mail tunic out of the squire's saddlebags. But not until she had filled her aching gut.

"Where is Bertram?" She rose and walked to the fireside, where Dominique loosened their meal from the spit.

"Out feeding the horses. A leg or the belly?" he asked, as he laid the rabbit on a wood platter. With a few deft strokes of his dagger he separated the juicy meat into portions.

"Both," Sera said, not realizing her hunger spoke more quickly than her manners.

Dominique's laughter shook her from her drooling gaze over the hot meat. "Then the lady shall have both." He sectioned the rabbit in three equal piles upon the platter, and gestured to her portion.

Her manners had given up the ghost since she'd taken on the quest. Fine lady she had become when all it took was mere weeks to lose the training and refinement her mother had instilled in her since childhood.

To hell with manners, she was hungry.

"Do you think you can drink very much wine?" he wondered. "I've many bottles in storage close to spoiling. I'd hate for them to go to waste."

Her mouth already filled with the scalding meat, Sera could only nod as she fought the need to slow down and let her food cool.

"Eat your fill."

The sudden heat of flesh to flesh startled Sera as Dominique's touch accompanied his words. She looked up from her vociferous gnawing and felt the spear of his violet gaze plunder her aura. He did not remove his finger from her cheek. "I want you to get back the woman you once were. And the only way to do that is to succumb to a little rest, a lot of food, and maybe even play."

"Play?"

"Yes, play."

With that, he bent close—the scent of his lips teased of the raspberry wine Sera had yet to sip—and pressed a lingering kiss to her forehead.

An unchewed hunk of rabbit nearly gagged her at Sera's graceless swallow. Dominique's touch seared like the fire in the hearth.

Sera tugged the cape tightly to her breasts. Keeping the damsel at bay would not be easy if this man's intentions included more kisses and the mysteriously intriguing…play.

Sera drew a curry comb along Gryphon's sleek coat. The beast bristled in gratitude, and nuzzled its nose into the mound of hay she'd forked down from the rafters. The scent of hay and horseflesh, and the quiet of the day caused her mind to drift from the present to this morning when she'd broken her fast.

He'd touched her so boldly. So…intimately. And yet, she hadn't even moved to reciprocate the touch.

If only he had kissed her on the mouth.

Resting her arms upon Gryphon's withers, Sera trailed a fingertip across her lips. They had regained their plumpness, still a little dry, but the insides were moist and soft. Such an intimate and personal place, far more personal than her loins. There she had been touched by Lucifer. Never so kindly as Dominique might. But she could no longer equate that region with intimacy.

With a sigh, she realized it was the coalescing of souls by touching lips, an intimate bonding together, that she craved. But she feared this craving as well as desiring it. To allow herself to succumb to the mercenary's presence would serve dangerous implications. She would be as a naked babe bared to the world should she allow this new desire to overtake. How then would she sustain the fire that raged for revenge?

A kiss would soften, change her. She would be less, not the hardened blade horror and injustice had forged of her soul. Surely to kiss Dominique would bring her to her knees before the enemy. An easy target.

The damsel's desires would be her downfall.

"Good day to you, my lady."

Sera swung around at the honey-smooth voice. Dominique's eyes glittered with the fire of new dawn. He stood in the opened stable door, gold rays of the rising sun lighting him from behind. The effect gave him a supernatural appearance. A tall, mighty knight, glowing from all about like a religious icon immortalized in oil paints.

"I plan to brush down Tor next." Sera looked away from the tempting sight as Dominique stepped inside and closed the door. She patted Gryphon's flanks, then smoothed her palm across Tor's suede-soft nose. "He is beautiful," she commented on the white horse whose mane flowed to its knees. "What is this patch here?" She studied the oval on its forehead, bare of the white hairs, 'twas pink, and appeared tender.

"Don't touch it," Dominique said, gently. "He's rather fussy about that spot."

"Is it a wound?"

"Of a sort. It has healed. When I first came upon this mighty beast, I found he had been wounded. He followed me home, perhaps sensing I could offer him solace—"

"And respite?" Sera wondered. Tor's feathery mane fluttered under her absent strokes. "Do you often bring strays home, San Juste?"

"You are but the second."

She smiled, liking the reference for reasons she could not fathom. Indeed he had brought her home. "I imagine Tor might fit out a king all garbed in royal livery and shining silver armor."

"A king I am not," Dominique said, as he coaxed the brush from Sera's hand and took to Tor's flanks. He stood in close proximity—so close, his breath warmed her cheek. Sera did not move away. "Nor do I consider myself Tor's master. Merely one of his many thankful partners."

"A partner? That's very odd. It is almost as if the horse owns you."

"Indeed."

"And the name, Tor, is it the name of a great Greek warrior?"

Dominique smoothed his hand over Tor's mane, ruffling playful fingers up and down the horse's neck, which produced an agreeable shake from Tor's head. "Tor is short for Vercingatorix, the last Gael chieftain to surrender before Caesar. He was a great man who stood for his beliefs and would not surrender until all was lost."

"Such as yourself?"

"Me?" He shook his head. "Nay. If there is any who should be compared to the chieftain it is you."

"I am no leader of battles, San Juste. I am one lone rider set on a ridiculous quest."

"It is not ridiculous."

"No." She scratched lazily across Tor's flank. "It's not, is it?"

"You are a remarkable woman, Seraphim. Perhaps someday your name will be spoken with the same reverence given Vercingatorix."

"I seek no fame, only satisfaction at seeing de Morte blood run down my blade."

He raised a brow. She could not have startled him with that statement. He knew her mettle. Though, she sensed his curiosity for her softer side. Especially in his touches. For it was those touches that sparked equal curiosity in her.

"I don't wish to speak of my reality. Save…this morning." She placed a hand on his arm, halting his attentions to Tor. "Dominique, I must know. You touched me. In that one moment we shared…so much."

He pressed his elbow to Tor's withers, resting his forehead on a palm for but a moment before turning and gifting her with complete attention. "I did touch you."

"You do not seem to regret it."

"I regret nothing I do." His gaze did not waver from hers. The *erie* took hold. "I do nothing that I will regret."

"Then...tell me, what does it mean? The two of us..."

"It is simple. I allowed myself to express my feelings toward you this morning. If you would rather I not—"

"So you favor me?"

"Of course I do." His words were hushed. "In but a very short time I have seen such remarkable courage and bravery emanate from your body as to reduce me to awe."

"I don't wish you on your knees before me, only here." She threaded her fingers through his. "By my side."

"You don't fear losing your edge? That hard blade that you must balance to find success?"

"I do. But I don't." She turned and paced away. Her chausses *chinged* with every careful step across the mounded hay. A shake of her head sifted sense over nonsense. What had she just said? She wanted San Juste close by her side? Ah! but the damsel had again snuck up without warning.

"Oh!" Sera fisted her fingers, then spread them wide before her. But she could not grasp the unknown. "I don't know! Dominique, I sense something has begun to form between the two of us. Something...irreversible. And good. Something I would be a fool to turn away from."

"But you must, to keep your edge?"

"Must I?"

Such struggle on her visage. Dominique had not seen the like, even when she had been preparing to march on Abaddon all by herself.

"What about you?" she said in the soft, unnatural rasp he had come to favor. "I know little about you, Dominique, save that you live alone in an enchanted cottage. I suddenly want to know what thoughts rush about inside your head. When you think of me, is it a good thought, or nay?"

Dominique allowed the brush to slide from his fingers and land softly in the forked up hay behind him. He approached Sera slowly, but did not break with her brightly curious gaze. Or was it confusion that lit those precious blue gems?

"When I think of you, it is as last eve outside Abaddon's castle when your body trembled in my arms." He reached to touch her cheek. She did not flinch away, and so he smoothed the back of his hand over her cool flesh. "You did not think to cling to your edge last eve. You simply released. Surrendered. It was then I saw the real Seraphim. That is how I feel inside when I touch you."

With a twist of her head, she broke their contact. "It cannot be a good thing."

"But it is, my lady."

"We should fight it."

That had certainly been more question than statement. But a question that did not desire agreement. "I will do as my lady commands."

"Why must you leave it to me? Why can you not just sweep me into your arms and have done with it?"

"Because you are not a mere woman."

"Ah. Aye, I suppose I am not what most men first think of when deciding to sweep someone into their arms." With a shrug and a sigh, she smoothed a hand over Tor's nose. "I...should be going...to...check on Baldwin. Um...yes."

With that Sera marched out of the stables.

He should have followed, should have negated her self-effacing statement. But he was too caught up in his own troubling thoughts. Dominique had never questioned his feelings until now.

Why *not* take the lovely Seraphim d'Ange into his arms and love her forever?

Besides the obvious? That she did not like his kind. That even if she had no prejudice against him, she might never learn to accept his differences. Because he wasn't sure if she would be around for much longer. Her future looked bleak. And his future would be, unfortunately, far longer than her mortal forever.

Cruel man, why not love her while you've the chance? Damn the differences! Give her a reason to love you. Give her the love she needs right now.

So much thought on this emotion called love!

No. Part of Dominique felt Sera needed her edge as well. To love her would only weaken her, coax her back to the woman she had once been, and condemn her to die at the hands of the demon de Mortes.

Some protection you offer. You do love her. You know you already do.

Dominique squinted his eyes shut at the battle of emotions that raged inside his brain. Was that it? *Did* he really love Seraphim?

Hell! If the black knight had been any other—man—then Dominique would not be having such thoughts now. But the fact remained, she was not a man. She was a woman. An amazing woman...who had captured his heart.

Like it or not.

So now he must accept those feelings, and get on with it. He wasn't a man to deny the truth. Though, he did sense he must be as cautious with this new realization as he was with his identity. Sera was one confused woman. He did not wish to push her off the edge she so precariously balanced.

But he could not deny his own feelings any longer.

Dominique coaxed Tor from the hay he fed upon, then loosened Gryphon's reins from the iron hitch. The day was bright and calm. Despite his caution, he wasn't finished with Seraphim d'Ange. Not in any way, shape, or form.

Play beckoned.

They rode out into the open field that bordered the Valois Wood. Dominique kept to the rear, for he did not want Sera to notice how he gazed upon her features. He relished this secret observation in surprising ways. Again, he noticed that from different angles her face could appear either delicate and feminine, or hard and determined. Graceful, elegant, yet deadly in her deceptive beauty.

Seraphim d'Ange deserved the world. And should she for but a moment possess it, she could certainly control it with a commanding word and a swing of her mighty blade. Not to mention, the undeniable power of the mongoose eye.

He no longer feared emasculation. Dominique had found his niche in the world that Seraphim d'Ange occupied. He had figured out when it was best to challenge, and when it was better to concede. He'd stymied her with that kiss to her forehead this morning.

He liked that he could do as much.

Dominique had to smile at the conflicting attributes that made this woman so appealing. Certainly, she was a formidable match to any mortal man. But should that mortal man wish her as his partner? What would be the point? Too much competition. Sera did not strike Dominique as the sort who would meekly bow to her husband's demands for food, servitude, and sex. As she'd said, she would be no man's chattel.

As for himself, Dominique found Sera's fiery spirit such a

great lure that he would gladly forgo some of his inherent male control to match with her. Hell, he didn't need control. Only trust. She was near to his equal. She certainly held reign over the emotional aspects of their relationship, whether or not she realized as much.

Tor slowed at a hawthorn tree. Gryphon followed Tor's hunger, and both animals halted at the edge of the forest. Sera dismounted, slapped Gryphon across the flanks, and walked out into the smooth swath of glistening snow that blanketed the stretch of field. Here and there spikes of foxtail jutted out of the surface, looking as lone hairs on a bald man's pate.

The sun beamed upon Sera's hooded crown, her eyes closed against the cool brightness of the day. For a moment Dominique imagined a brilliant half-disk halo surrounded her face, as in a Gozzoli painting depicting an angel. As Baldwin had so perfectly stated, Seraphim truly was an angel, in face and soul.

Hmm...thinking of angels...

The moment struck him. Dominique rushed up behind Sera and nudged her arm. "Come," he coaxed, backing across the clean, smooth snow. "Have you ever made a snow angel?"

Sera quirked a brow at Dominique's playful suggestion. He had become animated so suddenly, that it struck her hard just how much she still did not know about him. But every glimpse into his life only heartened the need to press onward. She wanted to learn everything about him. She would not be satisfied with mere costume and outer details.

"Snow angel?" A hand to her brow to block the sun's glare, she plodded through the heavy snow.

"Don't tell me your mother didn't show you how to make angels in the snow?"

Sera shrugged. "There was never so much snow inside my father's bailey as there is this year. It is unnatural all this snow. And yet the sun shines so brightly. 'Tis as if nature is betwixt and atween. So, show me."

"All you've to do is relax." Dominique lifted his arms up from his sides and fell backward. A graceful landing stirred up whiffs of the diamond-glittered snow around his body. "Then, sweep your arms and legs out like this. Go on, fall next to me. But not too close, or you'll clip my wings."

A tentative nibble to her lower lip spiked up pain and remembrance of how Sera had come by the wound. In Abaddon's lair of sex, and death, and fire.

Don't think about it. Fall into the snow and trace angels to the tune of Dominique's seductive laughter.

Aye, forget it all. Laugh for but a moment.

And so she did. The fluffy snow captured Sera's spread limbs with a compacting crunch and a kiss of scattered flakes. She drew her arms up high over her head, then swept them down to her sides, leveling smooth arcs in the surface. But she found she could not concentrate and move both arms and legs at the same time.

"A trifle uncoordinated, are we?"

She scooped up a handful of powdery snow and flung it at Dominique's face.

"What do you expect? I am no angel, San Juste." She shushed her legs back and forth, then sat up to look over her creation. Dominique's angel stood aside hers. Their wings touched, almost as if holding hands.

"Do you suppose that the true angels have no idea of their nature?" Dominique wondered as he knelt and looked over the twin snow angels. "Those come to earth, I mean, to serve a higher purpose. Guardian angels, if you will. Such a burden that would be to bear, knowing they are heavenly creatures and no longer reside in the heavens, but our cruel, hard earth."

"Perhaps..."

Looking over the wings, Sera let her mind, for a moment, grasp the notion of being a heavenly creature. Hadn't He sent down his warrior angels to battle against evil? Exactly as she was doing. But He had also banished the wicked angels from his heavens. Perhaps those fallen creatures were the true evil that walked this earth. And here she stood, Seraphim d'Ange, mock angel, fighting her own demons.

She glanced to Dominique, who was busy poking his finger deep within the head of his snow angel. Creating eyes and a smile. He possessed such whimsy. She hadn't noticed such before. She'd been too busy planning the best possible way to bring down Abaddon de Morte.

"Of course," he said, looking up from his creation, "if you do not believe in demons, and despise faeries, then I imagine the concept of a heavenly being with wings and halo to be quite out of grasp."

"Angels are real. This I know."

"Indeed?"

"Aye, and I do believe in demons. Now." Certainly, she had not been given a choice in that matter. "As for faeries, they are an evil breed."

He slapped his palms together to clean off the melting snow and sat back on his haunches. "Why say you such? Have you ever seen a faery?"

"I've not yet witnessed a faery come fluttering into my sight, though I do remember—"

"They flutter?" He cocked her a sideways look. A swath of dark hair fell over one eye, hiding the mischievous glint that matched his exposed eye.

"I don't know," Sera said, wanting to drop the whole conversation about the evil creatures who would steal an inno-

cent child and leave behind a changeling. But Dominique's
mood was so light, so beguiling, she could not help but want
to know more. To learn all she could of him. Even if it meant
speaking of the hideous creatures. "You tell me what *you* believe them to be like."

"Very well." He drew his fingers up under hers, raised them
to his lips, and kissed the back of her hand. "I shall tell you about
faeries."

Coaching herself to remain calm, Sera nodded, and kept her
mouth shut. But her attention remained fierce on their seem-
ingly casual contact.

"To the untrained eye faeries are as any mortal man. Tall and
lithe…and always fair of flesh and beauty."

Difficult to believe. The creature that had stolen her baby sister could not have been beautiful. She would never forget the
ugly mewling creature lying in Gossamer's cradle. The
changeling had been hideous and sickly. Nor would she ever get
the sound of her mother's piercing screams from her head.

"There is an old wives' tale that the Faery are actually angel
messengers. A liaison between the worlds of heaven and earth
who speak for the angels, and can actually determine Fate.
Though I don't believe as much." He bent and traced a halo
above his angel's head. "They are said to possess violet eyes that
can see into a man's soul, and with a wink, can cast a glamour
over any mortal to blind him from the truth."

"Violet, you say?" Sera afforded her curiosity a long and
preening trip into the fathomless depths of his eyes. "How curious. So I stand in the presence of a faery?"

Dominique lost the whimsical cast to his visage. Utter horror crossed his eyes. He pushed away her hand, as if touched by
a steel-tipped whip. "Why do you say such a thing?"

She shrugged. "Your eyes are violet."

"Nonsense." He stood, and tramped through his snow angel to Tor's side. "We should be getting back. I'm sure Baldwin worries of our overlong absence."

"Fine." She didn't question his reaction. Perhaps he felt as ill toward the faeries as did she. And angel liaisons? Ridiculous!

But Sera could not erase the eerie feeling that she had just tread upon a piece of Dominique San Juste's soul. She had dipped her toe within the depths of his being, and now teetered on the edge of diving in and losing herself.

And every moment she wished she could just take that dive.

"Are you coming?"

Not yet, the damsel pleaded. *Just a bit more time alone with the moonlight knight.*

Sera stretched her legs straight before her. The mail chausses were filled with powdery snow. A secret smile tickled her lips. "I need help up!"

With a huff and a forced expression of exasperation, Dominique trod back to her side, but did not offer a hand. "You would have me believe that my lord Demon Fighter has trouble standing up in less than a foot of snow?"

She shrugged, sensed the lightening of his mood. Inside, the damsel clapped her hands together expectantly.

Sera extended a hand, which Dominique clasped with his own de-gloved fingers. When her thighs left the ground and she could stand with but a bend of her knees, she tugged, and brought him down. In a deft move, Sera slid on top of her wary prey and pinned his shoulders into the left wing of her angel. "You are not so quick on the sneak attack, mercenary."

"Ah, but what of your reaction to *my* sneak attack?"

"Your— Foolish man, you expect I shall succumb to—"

Her words were stolen by a hot, snow-melting kiss. Pulled to Dominique's chest, Sera pressed her hands into the snow, prepared to make a quick escape—but found her body would not listen. 'Twas her heart that vied to be heard this moment. And the silk-clad damsel that desired beauty, and peace, and the rugged presence of a man.

Falling into the mastery of Dominique's sneak attack, Sera allowed him to turn her onto her back. He became the master of this deadly move. A move that shot cupid's arrow through her heart, where the iron branded a new scar onto her soul.

"Forgive me, my lady," Dominique muttered into her mouth, his lips burnishing heat like no forest fire ever could. "I could no longer bear standing so far from you. The fire that blazes within you and pushes you on your quest, is the same fire that compels me to you now. You are a mighty force, Seraphim."

"Oh, Dominique, this is not right. It cannot be. But…it feels right."

"You are thinking of the hard edge you must balance in order to complete your quest?"

She nodded.

"I promised I would help erase the vengeance from your soul. Trust me, Sera, you need a pure heart to complete your journey. Vengeance will only weaken you."

"Your kisses give me a new kind of strength. But I wonder, is it a deceptive strength? What will I do when I must face Sammael and it is the heat of your kiss which intrudes upon my thoughts? I mustn't do this!"

"I've gone beyond my intentions," he admitted. Dominique pushed up, but she caught him by the wrist.

"What *did* you intend?"

"Only that we should spend time alone, in quiet and harmony. But I push you too quickly."

"You did." She glanced to the ground. Half of Dominique's snow angel had been crushed beneath their embrace. 'Twas almost as if the angel were his shadow… "I'm just…not ready. Not prepared. I cannot—"

"Say no more." He gave her a quick kiss. Too brief. "I said what I meant. No regrets. Just, know you can trust me?"

"I do, Dominique, I do."

"So tell me of Sammael de Morte," Sera said. "What horrid hell does he lord over?"

Swiping his forearm across his lips, then swigging back the remains of his raspberry wine, Dominique first glanced to the squire, whose reaction Sera didn't look for.

With a push of his tankard to clear the table before him, Dominique began. "This man I have once seen in Paris. Sammael de Morte is small of stature and weak of countenance. The man is a rat. No, a mere mouse that one might easily crush with but a loud shriek or a well-placed sword. But…"

The slick taste of rabbit remained on Sera's fingers, which she cleaned with care. She halted at Dominique's *but*.

"The Demon of the East is known to some as the Master of Poison."

Baldwin stopped chewing. "Oh joy."

Dominique inclined an agreeing nod. "Rumor has it the man has no need of servants or guards, for the castle itself is a weapon against all who would enter without Sammael's knowing."

"Just like Abaddon's castle?"

"Yes, and no. They say poison seeps from the battlements and creeps down the walls like a fine perspiration. The air even, if one can believe such, is so vile that to breathe it will bring certain, yet slow death."

"How then can anyone enter, friend or foe?" Sera wondered.

"I'm not sure."

"Not sure? But you know all about the de Mortes. Were you not sent to ensure my success?"

"I was."

"And yet you know not how I will gain this demon's lair without breathing myself to sure death? Has your Oracle abandoned you?"

"Never. He but tells me what I need to know."

"And how to avoid dying is not a need to know?"

Well, when she put it that way. "There must be a way. There *are* ways," Dominique insisted. "We just need to think on it."

"How does Sammael survive in a poison-bleeding castle?" Baldwin wondered.

Sera scuffed the squire playfully across the back of his head. "You should know that, toad-eater."

"Ah!" Baldwin raised a rabbit leg, the bones bare of meat. "He has conditioned himself. No doubt the man consumes poison in small amounts, builds up an immunity."

"Indeed," Dominique said. "There are rumors his own brothers fear the man for his presence may bring death to all he passes. Though I wonder should the man be reduced to dementia for surely to consume poison, no matter what small amounts, must wreak havoc upon the mind as well as body."

Baldwin's rabbit bone hit the table with a *clank*. "Are you implying what I think?"

"You've not dropped dead at our feet yet, man." Dominique clamped Baldwin heartily across the shoulders. "In fact, you might just be our resident expert."

"So I must consume poison to match this man? Oh no." Sera stood and paced before the glowing hearth. She pressed a hand to the bandage over her ear and studied the flesh beneath. "Perhaps if we wear masks? Aren't there antidotes one can prepare?

Soak a mask in a potion of herbs and such that will block the poison?"

"It is a thought."

"Why do his brothers fear him?" Sera asked. "If these men are demons, immortals as you have explained, are they not immune to death?"

"They become immortal only upon the release of their inner demon. If slain correctly, as you have done twice over, they perish as a mere mortal."

"What of Abaddon? He was slain with an ewer of water?"

"Water is a force against fire."

"That's just too odd to figure. It boggles my brain." With a sigh and a slug of wine, Baldwin's interest transferred to the rabbit leg that sat untouched on Sera's wooden plate.

She shoved it toward the squire with an encouraging nod of her head.

Pensive in his own muddlings, Dominique's gaze did not leave the corner of the trestle table where knife marks serrated the edge in a decorative design. Carved during long talks with Father while Mother would tend the mending. They had spoken of honor, challenge, and of a world more expansive than a single man could ever comprehend. Dominique's mortal father had always the desire to sail the seas. He never got farther than the Valois Wood, though.

"We could concoct some sort of antidote, or protective coating," he said, "but how long will that serve? If it is sure you can get in there and get out immediately…perhaps—"

"You will not accompany me inside?"

Sera's eyes glimmered with firelight and an uncertain fear that had been present since she'd defeated Abaddon last night. A fear that, though she denied it, lurked deep within, just waiting for the most inopportune moment to strike, possibly to bring her down. How he desired to wipe away such fear with a magick that he knew he did not possess. Though they had shared a certain magick this afternoon. But a simple kiss did no more than stir up pleasure, it could not defeat fear.

"I have been warned against interference," he said. "Much as I wish I could, I cannot upset the balance of what must be."

"Of course, I should expect nothing more."

Sera's sigh rifled through Dominique's body, twanging at his already tightened nerves. What was he, a man or a follower? He could not allow a woman to face this demon alone. Just let the Oracle try to stop him this time. "Although…"

"This is my quest. I started it, and so I must see it through. You've provided much assistance thus far."

"Morgana's blood, I will go inside Sammael's lair with you, Sera. I would not see you into the mouth of hell alone, and would have you safe!"

"But your promise?" Baldwin prompted.

"Damn my promise. And you will accompany us as well, squire, we may need your expertise on poison."

"I am no expert. Of course, if you really do need me?"

"You said you agreed to see me to the end of this quest in return for something?" Sera touched Dominique's shoulder. "You are being paid well, I hope?"

"'Tis not coin I seek, but information."

She tilted her head, her silence beckoning louder than words.

"It is not important," he said, then gestured that Sera turn her head. "I want to check the dressings. Turn around, let me look."

He gently loosened the bandages and prodded the flesh. A bit of coruscation wisped away to nothingness at first contact to the air. "That does not pain you?"

"Nay."

"Amazing," Baldwin gasped, from his observation over Dominique's shoulder. "It is entirely healed. The flesh is pink and your hair—Sera, the fire did not singe away your hair, after all."

"But I felt it, my flesh was hot and bubbled and—" She ran her finger over the cool, unabraded flesh. "How?"

Dominique had taken to wrapping her bandages in a coil. He tossed them in the fire. A spray of sparks sizzled up around the offering, fine and golden as they fizzled up in thanks. How was not a question he was willing to answer just yet.

"It's a bloody miracle," Baldwin announced, rabbit leg held high to the heavens. "Break out another bottle of wine, I'm in a mood to celebrate!"

"And I—" Dominique eyed Sera "—am in a mood to spa. Shall we?"

FOURTEEN

Sera followed Dominique through heavy pillows of snow. When they set off for Meaux on the morrow, the horses would have a tough go of it, for the snow reached to just under Sera's knee. And still it snowed tumescent, gentle flakes that packed like goose down on a bed, thick and frothy, making it difficult to gain purchase. 'Twas like a veil of newness laid over their tracks, at once concealing, then urging forgiveness and absence of mind.

They crossed a stream at a point where a wide log had been cleaved in two and smoothed flat—forged by Dominique's father, he called back to her.

She realized now they shared a common bond. Both so young—or at least Dominique appeared young; he could be a few years older than she—and without family. His parents might have died of old age, but it was doubtful. She then remembered he'd said the plague had taken them. Strange luck, for the majority of deaths in the area ruled by the de Mortes were attributed to the demons. If not directly by their hand, then by their influence. The English, as well, had taken more than their share of lives over the past century.

So much death, Sera thought now as she stepped upon rough granite rocks that surrounded a snow-capped hill. *My life is filled with death.* It had become death, too, for with every swing of her sword she felled yet another.

If she had been told a fortnight ago that here is where she would be standing this very moment in time, Seraphim d'Ange would have certainly tossed aside her long braid and laughed the bold laughter of a woman unconvinced.

Nothing so delicate would ever leave her scarred throat again. It no longer hurt to swallow. But the pain lived. Along with death came unbelievable pain. Pain she had never before in her life felt. So raw and open and real. It was not the burned flesh or the violated soul that pained her. 'Twas the deep pain of loss, of utter abandonment. *Mother and Father.* No longer would she kneel before her mother's chair and lay her head upon her soft velvet-draped lap. Elsbeth d'Ange could but move her arms to nudge the back of her wrist against Sera's cheek, never caress with those curled-in fingers. It mattered not; Sera knew her mother would hold her if she but could.

To never again know her mother's touch... She was all alone in this world.

What would she do after the final de Morte had been felled? If she got that far. The d'Ange castle was gutted, destroyed by fire and a hail of boulders rocketed from de Morte's trebuchet. As for the coastal holdings, she would have to prove her father's intentions to the English king to take them into hand. Would she be successful? Did she desire going back to the huge, empty castle where nightmares lived, trapped in the new webbing of spiders?

You are all alone.

Alone and filled with a bitter revenge. But a se'nnight earlier she had trod the smoky remains of the castle d'Ange. The few carcasses so badly burned, mere ash had been left when burying the dead. The great keep was but a carapace. Bits of armor and weaponry could be picked out amidst the charred beams and debris of stone.

Sera had spied the damaged shield bearing the d'Ange crest and motto—Honor, Valor, Truth. The word "honor" had been sheared from the corner of the shield. How her father had lived by those words. It was not right! That such a valiant soul had been taken down by evil.

So many valiant souls.

Kicking aside a burnt timber Sera had bent to retrieve a blackened broadsword. The shield leaning against the wall upon which the hearth had once stood, she thrust hard with the sword. The tip cleaved through the dented shield and fixed into the charred wood wall.

Reeling with anger, Sera had scooped up a chunk of charcoal. In place of the missing word she scrawled "vengeance." And whipping the charcoal through the air she let out a cry of rage.

The de Mortes would not rest from this day forth....

No more afternoons spent in the lists, mimicking her brother's every move. Father's boisterous laughter was but an echo in memory. But she had danced with him...one last time in Abaddon's keep. It had been a cruel enchantment that had made her believe such, but she planned to hold to that memory as if it had been real.

And now you are alone. Alone...

That harsh realization weakened Sera's knees. She felt her body answer gravity, could not fight the heavy release of sorrow. Winter iced around her thighs as she landed, bent-kneed, and caught her face in her hands.

"All...by myself...now," she gasped, fighting against all torments the tears that beaded at the corners of her eyes. A heavy inhalation was riddled with stuttering gasps.

"Sera!" Dominique rushed to her side, bent, and smoothed a hand across her forehead, pushing away a long strand of hair that had avoided Baldwin's stylistic skills. "What is it?"

She shook her head, wishing away the horrific visions of New Year's morn—but with their banishment came the visions of her future. A cold, bleak future. Alone, so alone. No more family. No hugs, no tender words of comfort. No safety.

"I am the last d'Ange," she managed to say. A loud sniff kept tears from plunging down her cheeks, betraying her strength. "I am..."

No, do not say it. For to speak the word would only give it more power. And she was averse to giving up her power. Not now. Not when she needed the mask.

Pull on the mask of bravery. Push down the damsel's pleas for mercy. *Yes.* "Ah!" She shook her head and forced a brave front. "What is it with all this damned snow, anyway?"

"It is unnatural, to be sure." The heat of Dominique's ungloved finger touching the corner of her eye startled. Sera knew he'd caught a renegade tear. But he did not speak of it. "The world is not right, Seraphim. You must continue to have faith, though."

"It becomes difficult at times."

"I have faith in you."

She allowed a weak smile to curve her lips. Dominique's presence did indeed give her courage, and hope.

With a swallow, she regarded her feeble position. It was becoming more difficult to fight the damsel's weakening influence. Though she knew it had not been her inner woman, the damsel, who had just been felled by the memories of family.

'Twas her, Seraphim d'Ange. The bold warrior—who would remain so.

"We should continue," she said, standing.

Continue on with life, to perhaps avoid the loneliness that waited?

"Just ahead?"

"Yes, hold my hand, it's a tricky descent."

Expelling her troubled thoughts to the darkness of yesterday, Sera stepped upon a massive, flat rock and stood beside Dominique. A gaping hole, no larger than an ale keg, led into a dark mountain cavern. Thick scallops of snow draped across the arced entrance.

She gripped Dominique's outstretched hand and stared at their clasped hands, their thick leather gauntlets disguising gender, strength. Even while granting courage, this man challenged her convictions. He offered himself without request for a return favor.

Or at least, he had not requested as such from *her*.

Someone had promised him information of such importance he would risk his own life to help a stranger complete an impossible quest. The mystery of Dominique San Juste only deepened. And while the depths of his person grew darker, Sera felt compelled to lean over and peer inside, hoping for a glimpse of the bottom, the prize that was hidden in the darkness.

It kept her thoughts from her own pain.

Would this man ever request a favor of her? Could she request one of him? *I don't want to be alone!* the damsel cried.

They passed through the mouth of the cave with difficulty. Snow-slicked rock made purchase awkward until they had pressed a horse-length inward. Dominique moved slowly along a wall of stone. The darkness, he explained, would be brief, for he kept a rush light in the inner chamber.

"What *do* you want in return?" Sera asked, as she drew a hand along the wall to guide her.

"For my assistance?" His words sounded hollow within the cave, though they did not echo. "I ask only that you are pleased with your success."

"Why should I not be pleased with pressing the de Mortes into extinction? For ridding the earth of those diabolical demons. But will you not ask for coin, or land, or...favors?"

"I have no need for anything you could offer me, my lady. As you have seen, my world is rich in that I've a home and horse. I desire no material possession beyond the sword at my side. I'm going to release your hand now so I can light the torch. Stand still or you'll fall in."

Fall in? Clinging to the warm rocks behind her that sweated a fine moisture, Sera listened as steel scraped across flint.

He asks nothing? What an odd man. And he'd not taken the bait at her mention of favors. But the damsel, ever vigilant lately, had to know. "Can I not even entice you with the offer of my body?"

The torch took to light with a spitting blaze of flame and a blue-white tendril of sulfur. Sera flinched, recall of Abaddon's fire demon making her do so. But the scent of hell had been much stronger, more defined back in Abaddon's chamber. Brimstone. She felt sure if she wandered the entire earth she might never again smell such a wicked stench.

The flame flickered in Dominique's eyes as he stood silently, considering her question.

Offering her body? A bold suggestion, she knew. Was she even prepared to honor such an offer?

"Your body—along with your spirit—has already enticed me, Seraphim."

"You would not have me?"

"I would." Stepping closer, his eyes glinted in the amber glow of light. Royal violets. Peaceful, yet seductive. How could he possibly think them black? "But it must not be a request, but a mutual agreement. I would have it no other way."

She recalled his bold declaration made by their first campfire. *When I love, I love deeply. I do not take the act of carnal relations lightly.* How the damsel yearned for such a love.

"It is all right." He gripped her hand and beckoned she look around. "See there."

A pool of indigo rippled in silver flashes under the play of torchlight. An exotic treasure hidden here within this nondescript hill.

"About as deep as here." He pressed his hand to his waist. "There are natural shelves all around beneath the surface, so a person can sit and relax."

The blue water resembled that of a gemstone Sera's father had worn on his sword-belt, lucid and icy in its beauty. "It must be terrible cold."

"Not at all. It is a hot spring. They are all over beneath the grounds of France. This is the very reason my father chose to build on this site. I bathed here often as a child, and have spent many a day more steeping my soul."

She afforded a cautious summation of the colorful ripples. "How does one steep their soul?"

"By closing your eyes, drawing in calm breaths, and just…releasing."

Dominique's soul was a bright violet light, Sera mused now, as she looked up into his glittering eyes.

Pulling off her gloves and abandoning them without a care near the wall, she knelt and dipped her hand in the water. Deliciously warm. A zinging sensation scurried through her blood and flushed her cheeks with the desire to plunge in fully clothed.

"I'll return in an hour?" he asked.

"No." Sera spoke before she reasoned the consequences of that one small word. The last time she had been alone Lucifer had snuck into her room. While the pool was inviting, the silence of solitude could prove threatening to her agitated conscious. "Don't leave me. Please? I don't want to be alone."

"But you should wish to bathe?"

"I do." Steam rose from the lucid surface to caress and curl about her face and head, and seep beneath her tunic and into the scarred flesh on her throat. Resistance was now an impossibility. But to bathe alone? "Could you please just turn your back while I undress?"

"My lady—"

"Are you not bound to protect me?"

"I…am."

"Then I should not be left alone."

He sighed heavily. "As you wish."

Sera waited as he pulled his hood up over his glossy black hair and turned away. The wide swath of wool hood blocked his peripheral vision. Thoughtful of him. Though nothing prevented him from swinging his head around for a glance at her naked body, she knew he would not. She felt Dominique's integrity permeate her very bones. Integrity forged of truth, honesty, and determination. The same qualities she strove to uphold. They were two alike.

And yet, two so very far apart.

Ah, but she would reason out their differences later. The urge to surrender to the warm pool did not relent.

Tunic, and boots, and chausses were moulted like a ground snake's useless skin. Stepping carefully into the hot water, Sera sank down to her chin. The sensation of warmth rippling over her flesh and hugging her delivered a welcome that must never be refused, and always be cherished. Her skin tingled and she felt the pores open wide and breathe. Buoyant in the water, she floated for a moment before plunging forward, submerging completely. Sweet, cleansing water. It had been weeks since she had bathed. And such warmth! Never had her baths, taken in the privacy of her mother's solar, been more than tepid.

When she could not hold her breath for one more moment she surfaced with a grand, "Ahhh."

"How do you fare?" Dominique called from over his shoulder.

Spitting out the water and slipping her hands over her pebbled nipples, Sera sank beneath the surface until the water kissed her chin. "This is a heaven fallen to earth!"

His soft laughter, as welcome as the warm waves sloshing around her shoulders, caressed Sera's heart. She *shushed* her fingers over the tender flesh above her ear. Indeed, the hair had not been burned away, as Baldwin had been so joyous to discover. And she felt no scar. Amazing, considering she'd taken a direct hit from Abaddon's fire demon. 'Twas nothing there now but slick, short hair. Shorter than most men wore their hair.

Once again the damsel emerged, for but a moment of sadness. Sera considered just how long it might take for her hair to grow past her shoulders. Ages, surely. Had it been a sacrifice well worth it? It was too soon to determine. Only triumph would bring meaning to the sacrifices she had made. *Besides,* the warrior insisted, *worry over regaining your beauty in order to attract suitors is too foolish to comprehend.*

For the only man she even dreamed to have court her sat but a few feet away, fully clothed, while she was stripped bare.

When I love, I love deeply.

Never had she felt so vulnerable. And yet...powerful.

"You may turn around," she called to Dominique's back.

"I shouldn't wish to compromise you, my lady."

"I cannot hold conversation with you looking the other way. I am submerged." She peered through the rippling water. It was so clear she could see her breasts and thighs and toes even when they touched the bottom of the pool. Though, they were slightly distorted by the ripples. "I do not fear such exposure."

"Very well." Dominique turned and rested his arms across the ridge of stone that separated the pool room from the long dark pathway they had traversed. A shrug of his hand over his head released the hood to his shoulders.

"That's a lovely cape," she commented, without drawing her eyes up from the pool's surface. Tracing her fingers over the ripples blurred view of that beneath the surface.

"My mother sewed it and my father polished the stones. They are hematite, a charm for the blood."

"The dark stones hold a brilliance, like stars set in a velvet sky. Very unusual."

"That is much what my father said. A grand cape for an unusual young man."

"He thought you unusual?"

"In the most caring of ways. He knew I was not like most. My father was a good, honest man. As my mother honored the simple life with hard work and prayer."

"You speak grandly of your parents. They must have been very proud of their son."

The silence that answered her question was quite unexpected.

How quickly she forgot he was a mercenary. There was no pride in taking coin to serve in battle. Her father had hired many a mercenary over the years. Indeed, she did recall her brother's snide comments about the homeless knights. Of course, she had always thought that if the men had not a home of their own, they had every right to travel from castle to castle in search of work.

Sera lifted her chin and met Dominique's dark, violet eyes. Always seeing more than she could ever know herself.

Surely she could no more tempt a man in her bedraggled condition than a mouse could lead a horse to cliff's edge. She had seen the horror of her own appearance in Baldwin's cringe. Now she remembered the thick scar across her neck.

Sera rushed a hand to cover the vicious wound, so blatantly exposed. "I have always been too prideful of my body," she whispered. "But as you can see, now there is nothing to pride myself on."

"Hair grows back," he said. No revulsion in that comment.

His eyes held hers. Perhaps out of respect for her nakedness, Sera knew not—he did not glance lower. She could feel compassion drift from him. The emotion was palpable, almost as if she might reach out and clasp it to her breast, then force it through flesh and bone to her heart.

With absent regard she traced the raised flesh on her neck. The scab had been worn away by her mail coif, though here and there, the wound felt as if it would open and bleed anew if she stretched. The skin, new and tight, possessed a silken texture. But were not fine dresses and newborns the only things that should be silken and soft?

"That scar is not so remarkable," Dominique offered. "Surely a battle prize to be compared with others. But to *win* the comparison?"

She smiled now to recall the many times she'd happened upon Antoine and other of her father's knights comparing scars received in battle. Tunics were rucked up, thick hosen pulled down to expose the havoc incurred during siege. The longest and widest scar always won the prize. Pity the man who dared compare a mere sword slice to that of a mace gouge, or a rut hewn into a shoulder by a halberd.

"It makes my voice so horrible," she rasped. "I used to...to sound like a woman."

"You are a woman, Sera. Your voice is nothing but a means to convey words and sounds. Your true feminine spirit comes through those dazzling blue eyes."

Dazzling? She blinked, flickered her gaze to the surface of the water. She'd always thought her luxurious hair her most prized possession, had never studied her eyes—dazzling?

The smile that tickled her lips appeared so suddenly it embarrassed. Sera looked away from Dominique's beguiling gaze. "Thank you. You have a way of most unexpectantly putting a person at ease. Of—" Enchanting them, she thought. "You are a kind man."

"I am a mercenary, Sera. Do not mistake courtesy for honor. I kill for my coin. Let no man befriend me on Monday, for Friday may bring a new purse and his death."

"But you haven't killed lately."

"You speak of things you cannot possibly know."

"I can see it in your eyes. And I can sense it in your nature. When you have killed, it has been only those deserving. Criminals, murderers, torturers. We all do what we must." She ran her fingers across the water, stirring bewitching ripples upon the surface. Silver waves glimmered upon the blur of her pale thighs. "I—I don't like killing people, you know."

"The de Mortes are not people. They are demons. Never forget that."

"I don't believe I can." A chill shudder traced Sera's spine. So difficult to put behind her all that she now knew. "Had I known they were immortal creatures..."

"You were spared from death, and perhaps from complete knowledge of your enemy's true identity in order to carry out this brave expedition."

"'Tis not as brave as you might think. It is merely revenge I seek. Cold, selfish revenge."

"I believe not."

"What else is there?"

"For every de Morte you bring down, hundreds, perhaps even thousands of people, will be saved. Families will not have to suffer the death of loved ones because there is one less de Morte to toy with them. Mayhap soon—with Lucifer's influence abolished—the English will renege control on Paris and France will finally be whole. You know very well that is the reason you are doing this."

"Returning Paris to French control is a rather lofty ambition."

"What of gifting the French with peace of mind knowing the de Mortes are dead?"

"That, I can accomplish. But it is not the most important reason. It is the faces of my parents, and Antoine and Henri, that live in my mind as the rage pushes me from one de Morte to the next."

"You must use whatever works. But will you be able to close the door on those faces when all is done?"

"I hope so. I wish to. But Dominique, there is something more. I have felt since the very day I set out on this quest that there is something more. Some internal voice pushing me, beckoning me onward, even in the face of sure defeat. I cannot explain what it is. Only that I must answer its call."

"A subconscious call to correct that which has been skewed. You only wish to make things right. There is no shame in that."

"I fear though, that my life has been changed, so irrevocably. Perhaps I will always be haunted by such images. Do you know, Henri de Lisieux—his heart..." She closed her eyes, wishing away the horrid memory. "But so be it, it is a hell I must pay for the souls of my family. When faced with fear or faith, I choose faith. Always."

"You speak a martyr's words."

"Oh no, I am not. I am no witch in pursuit of battle in the name of God. As I've said, this is a selfish desire, not divine communiqué as d'Arc claimed."

"Can you be so sure?"

She gave a little chuckle and shrugged. "I have not spoken to angels, Dominique. Would you even believe such blasphemy?"

"Ah yes, the nonbeliever. I forget you rely on the material world—what you cannot see cannot be real. So indeed you've not been recruited by a higher power."

"What of you? Whence does your Oracle hail? Mayhap he is an angel that planted you in my path?"

"Unlikely."

"You've never asked?"

"I've...never thought to."

"How long has he been appearing to you, sending you on precarious missions?"

"For some years now. Appearing, that is. I choose my own missions. This is my last."

"Mine, as well. Dominique, would you like to join me? You're starting to shiver."

"My lady speaks of bold compromise."

"I am bold." She felt an erotic heat prickle across her chest, hardening her nipples. "And trust me, it is too late for any such thing. This body has suffered enough compromise and humiliation for a dozen women."

"I know."

She jerked her head up to find Dominique's response lingering in his eyes. His shoulder lifted in a shrug. "Baldwin told me. Do not be angry with the man, I pressed him. I was curious as to who lit the fire in your quest."

Sera's heartbeats worked frantically behind her breast. She

wasn't sure what to say. Why hadn't he asked her? Not that she would have revealed the reason for her insane quest, but still. She felt betrayed that he'd gone to the squire for answers. And yet, not. For it made things easier not to have to voice the horrors of that night.

"My father always said I possess a certain fire."

"I wagered as much. Baldwin also told me how you'd assumed your mother's responsibilities after an illness made her too weak."

"Aye, she took ill after my sister's…disappearance." The pain of memory was chased away with a swallow. "You know so much about me, mercenary," she said in careful tones. "And I know little about you."

"You are here at my home, you've slept in my bed, supped at my table. You know my parents are long dead and I've but Tor as companion. What more is there to know?"

What makes your heart sing, she wanted to ask. *Can it be me? Could you ever consider?* No. Most likely not. But he *had* nearly confessed love…

"Why don't you come in?" she asked again. "Just keep to one side of the pool. You needn't be shy, I'll turn my head."

She listened as he remained silent for a moment. Vacillating. Was she that hideous to look upon?

"If your squire should find out that I have shared a bath with you—"

"I won't tell," she rushed in. The lucent blue depths of the water wavered over her body. So exposed. And so willing to be exposed. For she felt safe in Dominique's presence. And she craved, oh did she crave, closeness.

"I…mustn't. Not yet."

"I understand." Safe, but still not trusted. "Do you think we can defeat the remaining two?"

He cocked open an eyelid and regarded her for a time. Then closed the lid. "Anything is possible."

"They are immortal creatures."

"It was easy enough for you to bring down the first three. You're over halfway through, Sera. Why now this doubt?"

She floated back to her original position; arms spread wide upon the surface, and played her palm across the hot ripples. "Perhaps knowledge is not always the best weapon. Before I did not know what I was challenging. I just want this to be over." She gripped a fist before her. "To start anew and put this hell behind me."

"It will be, soon enough." He stood now, and took a few steps until he was poolside. Considering? No, he merely sat and regarded her with those dark eyes that caught the torchlight and gleamed in perfect violet. "If you were clothed I would reach over and hold you close, to make you feel safe, protected. Confident."

"I do feel protected by you. But confidence is so fickle atimes." She wrinkled her nose and snapped the water's surface with a forefinger.

"Ha! You've more confidence in the tip of your nose than an entire army of mercenaries. Look how far you have come, Seraphim."

"It might not have happened without you."

She floated her hand on the surface and Dominique reached to touch her finger with his. Odd as it should have been to think such, Sera felt a surge of power stream from his forefinger through hers. It rushed up her arm and suffused her neck and face with a boldness that straightened her spine and reminded her that, yes, she was capable. "Do you feel that?"

"I feel something." He glanced away, his jaw pulsing with a tension that belied his relaxation.

With a move to the right, Sera caught Dominique's hand in hers. "Tell me what it is you feel. This hot rush, the need for...something."

"It is desire, Sera. At least, that is what *I* feel."

She gripped his wrist as he made to move away from the pool. Not sure what she really wanted him to do—stay or leave— but knowing she must answer this urge of wanting. Sera pressed her eyelids tight and bit her lip. "You are right, it is desire. And I think...I just...need to feel it. To...to lose myself in it."

"In hopes of blocking out the pain of the past weeks?"

She slumped to rest her chin on the moist cave floor. "You see how selfish I am? Always thinking of myself, of ways to enhance my experience, or of losing my pain at the expense of another."

He bent down near her head and touched the crown of her hair, so lightly. She felt drops of water disperse across her shoulders as he toyed with the cropped strands. The promise in his violet eyes was mysterious. She did not know what he granted, but she would allow it.

"You are a survivor, Seraphim d'Ange." He drew a finger along her chin, down her jaw and to the scar. The sensation of his touch sparked a shiver up the back of her neck, but she did not flinch away. "Does it pain you?"

"Not so much, save when I shout. Which I always forget pains me until it is too late."

He kissed her throat, pressed his lips to the aching red flesh of the hideous scar.

Hot tears slipped from Sera's eyes. She spread her hands through Dominique's hair, pulling his head down to hers, and closed her eyes to the bittersweet bliss of his cleansing kisses. It was as though with every press of his mouth to her tormented flesh he wiped away a little of the horror Lucifer de Morte had branded into her soul.

Here, take it all, she wanted to say. But was content to release just a portion into this man's kiss.

If only he were in the pool. She might wrap her legs around his hips and hold him close, no promise of sex, only companionship, closeness, visceral contact.

The nuzzle of his forehead against her earlobe suddenly thrilled. Desire overwhelmed pain and sadness. She wanted to give herself to him, but the notion that she might only wish such to erase the path Lucifer had forged, stayed her from speaking her desires.

Instead she tilted her head back. The water cradled her shorn scalp with a gentle lull, and Dominique supported the back of her head with a hand. One more kiss to her scar and he pressed his cheek to hers, caressing, hugging, coddling her into a womb of calm.

"Your beauty shines through the tortures your body has endured, Sera. I can feel it radiating from inside you. You've such strength. A fire," he said, his voice growing hush in the flicker of torch glow and ripples of silver water. "Don't ever forget that when all seems lost and you wish to give up, Strength resides within." He touched her forehead, signaling he spoke of her thoughts, her mind, her common sense. "Triumph is not measured in the swing of a sword or the grunt of a killing blow."

"I've felt it since the siege Mastema laid upon Poissy, and before that I rode through the ranks to find the Demon of the South. I don't know where it comes from, but I'll not question it."

"You are wise to react to instinct. Don't worry overmuch," Dominique coached, his lips tracing her ear in soft glances. Surrender loomed so close. "Just feel, and follow your inner wisdom."

"Thank you for bringing me here. I did need this," she admitted. This hour of quiet and companionship with a kind soul. Of release, and relaxation. "But we ride for Sammael—"

He pressed a finger to her lips. "No more talk of business. This pool is sacred, I'll not allow you to contaminate the peace with talk of battle. Agreed?"

"Agreed."

"I should leave you to relax in peace now."

Sera turned in the water and reached up to grip the hem of his cape. She slid her knees upon the shelf meant for sitting, lifting her shoulders and breasts out of the water. Dominique's study of her naked body ignited the desire in his eyes.

"You tempt me, my lady," he said. He knelt again and touched her lips, her chin, the scar on her neck.

"Just a few more moments of your touch," she whispered. "I need it." Sera closed her eyes. "Please."

Dominique wanted to dive in and take this woman, right now. But he'd avoided undressing for a reason. And he would not press a glamour upon Sera now. That would be betrayal. He wished to be honest with her.

But he still was not prepared to reveal all. And so, as he knelt before the pool, exploring her neck, her lips, he prayed this contact would suffice for now.

A kiss to each knuckle elicited surprisingly delicate whimpers from his battle-scarred angel. Dominique bent Sera's hand and pressed his mouth to her palm, then to her wrist. He studied the water-wrinkled lines that darted here and there upon her palm, wondering at the meaning, but not knowing. Fate carved its path in every man's hand; to try to solve the puzzle would only bring frustration.

When he traced the lines braceleted around her wrist, he saw the small blue symbol permanently impressed into the flesh.

'Twas far from random, the design. It curved into an arabesque that symbolized an age-old meaning.

Releasing her wrist with a startled cry, Dominique stood.

"What is it?" Sera asked through lazy eyes.

"Hmm? Oh, er…mayhap I've overstepped—"

"You forget, I am beyond compromise."

"All the same, I should not treat you any differently than one who is unaccustomed to compromise. Besides, there are… things I need to do. Tor…has not been fed. You wish to linger?"

"Only in your arms." She reached for his cape, but he moved swiftly away. "I've offended you, haven't I? I am so—"

"Don't say it, Sera. You are beautiful, so, so…perfect. I just can't…"

"You are not ready?"

"Not yet. Maybe another time."

There was nothing he could say. Nothing he could do. He had seen the symbol. He knew exactly what it meant.

And he could not believe it.

FIFTEEN

"He requests an audience with you, sire."

"Send him in," Lucifer said, with a dismissive gesture toward the iron-studded door separating his private solar from a labyrinth of underground tunnels. "But inform him he must remain on the opposite side of the table. And he mustn't touch anything."

With a nervous nod, the guard backed from the room, leaving the hot glow of the blazing fire to his master.

Lucifer allowed a frown to temporarily crimp his visage. Sammael here, in his fortress? Damn, but the man would not respect his wishes to keep away. The foul bit of arsenic and wolfsbane!

Of course, he had expected as much. Word of Abaddon's death had reached Lucifer's ears just this morning. There had been nothing left of his brother's body. His bedchambers were—oddly, the messenger had reported—scorched from floor to ceiling. The only remains were charred bones. Had the head been severed from the body? No, it appeared not.

Burned to char? Now that was a remarkable death. Also

strange, quite unbefitting of the legendary black knight. He'd obviously had Abaddon trapped in his own chambers, without guards or weapons to hand. It would have been so easy just to sever—

"Aggghhh!" Ice-sharp pain rippled over Lucifer's scalp. It felled him to his knees beneath the blood-red stare of the stuffed eagle.

The sting of impact, fragile mortal bone to hard marble floor, did not overcome the sudden wrenching grip to his brain. Just beneath the skin, a band of sharp-edged prickles raced back and forth from one temple to the next, scurrying on wicked feet like thousands of insects. Lucifer's vision blackened—only to be thwarted with flashing colors, bright, and loud, and tormenting.

He'd never experienced such. Could not comprehend how or where it had— Oh, the agony!

The sharp intrusion of pain, initially red, suddenly burst to a whiteness so pure and beautiful, Lucifer actually smiled amidst his terror.

Remember.

Still on his knees, he lifted his trembling shoulders and raised his hands upward, clutching for the blinding light he saw only behind his closed eyelids, but never grasping anything solid.

Flashes of memory, of the past, perhaps...the future, zinged through his thoughts.

Pure blue light...

...covetous desire...

*...mortal man, possessed of the will to take that which he desires...
So fortunate, to possess this free will. But there is another option...*

Comprehension was difficult, save to touch the corner of an image.

...naked female flesh...gold glittering upon fingers and neck...the blue, curved design of a symbol, so familiar, like a delicate arabesque...

—or to jerk away at the sight of what could only be the future—

...tattered black appendages...wings.

The other option is... Rebellion.

And he Remembered.

All.

Fallen, he was. As were Satanas, Mastema, Abaddon, and Sammael. Brothers bonded not by blood, but by the rebellious desire to become of the earth, to indulge in mortal pleasure.

Remembrance flashed through Lucifer's skull, bits here and there. Something flickered in the corner of comprehension, solid, yet weightless... *Wings?* Perhaps. And again, the blue symbol. He knew it. It was impressed upon the underside of his wrist. He'd puzzled about it for years...

And then emotion took hold. *Grace and melancholy. Yearning.* Yes, the deep, wounding yearning that worked at his heart like acid to steel. And, too, utter boredom.

Such pining and desire contained within the images of his past, his other life. But anger as well. Or rather, envy. Must know the earthly delights. Must indulge in the sins of the flesh. Must taste, touch, and smell the flow of mortal blood. Must...consume.

There is only the One who can release you from this mortal punishment. Only one...

With a shriek—and a burst of blue light under Lucifer's clenched eyelids—the pain subsided. All was as it was before.

Still on his knees, his knuckles stroking the floor, Lucifer swayed back and forth. As the final remnants of Remembrance fluttered away he snatched the image of his Fate, gripped it tight with an imperceptible fist, and stashed it deep into the folds of knowledge.

An audible sigh released the last filaments of memory. But it was too late, he'd preserved the moment.

"Christ's blood," he murmured. A violent shake of his head spattered sweat droplets about the room. He heaved, fighting to regain control of his breath.

He turned his wrist over. There, the blue symbol tattooed upon his flesh. "Seraphim," he whispered the title, sweet triumph tightening his jaw. "Of the highest order."

Pulling himself up to stand, a satisfied grin overtook his tight lips. He understood so much now. The black knight had released Abaddon's fire demon. A creature that lived within all his brothers, as well as himself. The ultimate prize to those who Fall and can then Remember. He had not been aware of his Fall, had not Remembered.

Until now.

He was of the seraphim, the highest order of angels. The symbol on his wrist proved such.

And now that he knew this, his own future would change.

Satanas and Mastema had been assassinated quickly. And—he now knew—correctly. No chance for immortality. They had never even known what glory awaited should their fire demon be released.

But this slip with Abaddon— Could it be that the black knight hadn't a clue with whom he was dealing? Of course not! Not even Lucifer had been aware of the stakes until this very moment.

Lucifer settled in a chair. He leaned forward in his leather-and brass-studded throne and stretched his arms before him on the trestle table, seeking the appearance of calm. Beneath the clean white damask cloth he could feel the knife-pocks, set there by dining, war-play, and anger. Anger worked a delicious brew in his blood. It had served him for decades. And would continue to serve when finally he ruled.

That had been the original plan for Falling—to rule. Only now did he realize such.

So Abaddon had not survived the release. Perhaps the black knight had been prepared, knowing fully what to expect when the fire demon was released upon the mortal realm. Impossible to know for sure. There had been no witnesses to the actual event. The black knight had broached all of Abaddon's traps. Iron-clad enchantment of traps laid down by a particularly nasty witch with whom Abaddon had once had an affair.

Who was this man who had reduced the de Morte blood by more than half? Why, he must be immortal himself to achieve such a goal.

A goal. Indeed, the black knight had a goal. His next stop, if he followed the compass, Meaux. Sammael's domain.

And then Paris.

Now there was no question, the mercenary he had hired must not kill this enemy, but instead, see the black knight to Paris.

Hmm…there was but one man who would have such a desire, let alone the strength, to challenge the de Morte clan—to bring down their fount of power. And, as Lucifer could only now know, that man must be connected to the de Mortes by blood. Only One, as the Remembrance had told. Whether by marriage or parentage, though, this new knowledge did not specify.

No mortal that walked this earth possessed such a connection. Surely thousands had spilled blood at the de Morte brothers' blades. But they had never married, did not even keep a woman for reasons that had been unknown to Lucifer until now.

As for their parents, the brothers five had assassinated their mortal mother and father when they were very young. Not out of insight to their Fate, but pure experiment, evil, and boredom. Lucifer had but lived a mere mortal nine years when the urge to take upon the world by himself had struck.

Yes, an urge; part of a more deeply buried memory. And now, he'd finally Remembered his very reason for walking this earth.

But what was the connection between the de Mortes and the One?

A knock on his chamber door jerked Lucifer back to the moment, the here, the now, the current struggle toward Fate.

Damn Sammael. Did *he* know? Had his remaining Brother of the Fall had a flash of Remembrance? He prayed not.

Time to rid his lair of rats—and himself of the competition.

Wood slammed against the limestone wall. Sammael de Morte flung himself into the heat-festered chamber. Short and feeble, surely the weakest of the brothers physically, but not in his deadly expertise. He stood before the table, clutching his head, heaving and fighting against his breaths as though he'd raced up a hill with an angry crowd to heel.

Brother indeed, Lucifer thought now. But not by mortal standards. Still, he mustn't become sanguine with this new knowledge. There were precautions he must take in Sammael's presence. For they were both still mortal.

Lucifer pressed his shoulders against the back of his chair and moved his leg out from under the table and to the side in preparation to dart. "Stand back, Sammael! I no more crave your vile breath upon my person than I need a quick beheading. What hell froze over and allowed you to believe you would be welcome in my home?"

The simpering man lifted his head from his shoulder, though still it tilted west, as if the brains inside had been joggled and come to rest there. Wide gray eyes, bulging in their sockets as they normally did, pleaded above a spittle-moistened mouth. "I am your brother!"

"And I love you as only a brother can," Lucifer barked. "But

I am not so much in a swoon over you that I do not value my own life. One breath of your poisoned air is all it will take to reduce me to fits."

Although...immortality was just one more severed head away. Ah! To have lived so long and to but learn the truth now.

Sammael, twisting his fists together, and with a sheepish smile to his sniveling countenance, rose to his full, short, tilted-head height. "I am clean for you, brother. I swear upon the moon witch's undead child."

Yes, yes, some blather about his latest conquest, no doubt. "All the same, state your business and be gone."

"You know why I am come," he sniveled. Took a step closer. A drop of sweat quivered at the tip of his nose.

At sight of the poisonous bead, Lucifer sprang from his chair and stepped back before the hearth. He stroked the dagger strapped at his side.

"Fine." Sammael made a staying gesture at sight of the glinting blade. As if he would simply stand there before the table. But Lucifer remained on guard. "Abaddon is dead."

"I know this."

"Then you also know that I am next!" Sammael pounded the table with a fist, and followed with his skull. He pressed his forehead to the clean damask, imbuing it with his tears and soil. And his poisoned sweat. "He is coming for me," he whined, as he gripped and clung to the cloth. "I don't want to die, brother."

"So you seek refuge with me? The very next place the black knight will ride should he find your home empty?"

"I was frightened. I know not what to do."

"You will return home and wait out the black knight like the grown man you are. That wicked bastard won't get farther than your bailey with the plethora of poisonous traps that await." Yes, by all means, allow the illusion of strength. "Now be gone with you, before I must set this room to flame and smoke you out!"

"You cannot put me out!" Sammael lunged around the table and gripped Lucifer's wrists.

Reacting as if he'd been singed by the very flames he so worshipped, Lucifer thrust a steel-spiked boot-toe into his brother's hip and shoved him away. Sammael's body hit the wall near the mounted saddle. His moans splattered the floor with blood-tainted spittle.

Lucifer dashed to the ewer of water a servant had freshened but an hour ago. He plunged his hands in to the wrists, scrubbed at the flesh and leather sleeve Sammael had touched, then flung the full ewer against the wall. Fine Corsican porcelain shattered and showered the floor in geometrics of razor-edged snow.

"Damn you!" Lucifer shook his wrists out before him. No tingling, nor the telltale fire that Sammael's poisons always held. Perhaps he *had* come clean. Impossible. Now, more than ever, Lucifer could not risk his own mortal death. Only one could take him down *and* release the demon. "Look at your blood, everywhere. I shall have to have this chamber burned!"

Sammael clutched at the gaping wound on his hip. He stared up at Lucifer, actually had the nerve to cast him a pitiful pout. "Look what *you've* done! My blood stains the floor because of you, brother."

"You leave now. It is your turn!" Lucifer raged. "You must stand against the black knight, as did our brothers. Entomb yourself within a poisonous cocoon if you must—" he fisted a clench of fingers before him "—but stand brave and fight as the de Morte name demands."

Sammael pressed the palm of his hand to his cheek and smeared away the tears, leaving a wide trail of blood. "This knight that stalks us is immortal, I know it. He has powers! No one has ever been able to defeat us, brother. I fear the first tread he makes upon my land shall bring the first of my final breaths."

Lucifer pressed his hands to his forehead, mining for the vein in his temple that betrayed the promise of immortality with each pulse of life. He tired of this prison of flesh and blood and bone. Bring on the black knight! He would let no man take his head from this body. But he would allow a sword to this feeble heart, or a dagger twisted up inside his gut. He was prepared to die a mortal death for the reward of everlasting immortal reign. Anything to release the demon within.

Sammael sniffed, probed the wound on his hip with a finger, then smeared the blood across his nose as he swiped at the humors dripping from his nostrils. "Sorry, brother, I merely sought a bit of reassurance."

"So you have it."

Lucifer eyed the sweat mark that had formed a crescent stain on the tablecloth. He ripped the damask from the table, upsetting a goblet of wine, and flung the entirety into the hearth.

"I trust the black knight shall meet his match in Sammael, Master of Poison," he said, pacing apprehensively before the fire. "Abaddon was blinded by his lust. Mastema could not see past his bloodthirst. And we both know Satanas's brain was nothing but rot after years of drinking that damned champagne. You, Sammael, are well-informed, and shall be prepared. There's not a concoction you can't brew that won't bring the black knight to his knees, begging you to kill him mercifully."

"This is true."

"You've plenty of guards."

"Well…"

"Not that you need them. That damned castle is a festering pit. I dare say the black knight should expire upon first breath of your foul air."

"You think so?"

"I know so." Lucifer fingered the warm hilt of his *espadon,* propped by the hearth. Forcing the scowl from his face, he turned and gave Sammael his most genial smile. "Are you happy now?"

Taken by a sudden shrill of joy, Sammael rose and bowed profusely before Lucifer. "Forgive my intrusion. I'll take myself back to Meaux and do as you say. A cocoon of poison. Just the thing. Ha! Good day to you, brother."

As the simpering fool backed out of his chamber, Lucifer followed, sword in hand, careful to avoid the crimson blood splats that trailed hither and there behind his brother's retreat.

"Hire a peasant to come clean this up," he informed the outer guard. "No sense in sacrificing one of my own to scrub up Sammael's poison-laced blood."

Turning back to the fire, Lucifer watched, hypnotized, as the final threads of the white damask were flamed to ash amidst a great roar of amber flame.

One more brother, and then it would be his turn. The black knight did have an imposing opponent in Sammael. There was even the chance he might not succeed, so infested with poison Sammael's home was. His brother was immune to the stuff himself, for he breathed and tasted poison daily as a newborn taking in air.

He drew up his sword and pressed the flat blade against his forehead as he thought. How to ensure the black knight survived the poison master's lair? For if this legendary knight truly was the One, Lucifer wanted to meet him, blade to blade, and finally be released.

Ah yes, the mercenary he'd hired to track and kill the black knight. 'Twas obvious he'd yet to succeed in his task. Fortuitous, though.

* * *

The mixture of chamomile and meadowsweet that Dominique crushed in his mother's mortar smelled too fragrant to lend possibility to its power of repelling poison. But his mother's carefully written notes, found in her book of receipts and spells, stated as much. "To stave off poison." She'd never fancied herself a witch, only a purveyor of herbal cures and restoratives.

No, not a witch, but a loving, kind woman, who had overcome much and raised her son in the manner of goodness and honor. Much as her changeling son had not been what she had expected, she'd never once given Dominique reason to wonder did she love him. For she had. With all her wide and giving heart.

The question that had haunted him for years had been stifled and set aside in a dark corner of his soul for that very reason. Dominique could no more disrespect his mortal parents by seeking the truth of his parentage than he could fly to the sun.

So he had honored Phillipe and Rosemary San Juste in life, and following their deaths, he remembered their spirits with every tread upon these clean cottage floors. Every time he mixed up one of his mother's restoratives. And every time he crossed the stream on his father's bridge. Good people, the San Justes had been. They had given him respect, home, and family. A place to belong.

He had needed nothing more.

Until his family had died, leaving his buried questions to surface in the darkness of his soul.

His own search for information proved that he did need more. Closure to the insistent wondering. And when he did have the answers, what then would he do? He'd already decided this would be his last mission for remuneration. Coin was not necessary to live a peaceful and prosperous life here within the abundant Valois Wood. And to think that he'd once been so greedy as to consider siding with the English. Ah, but money had once led him astray!

Nevermore.

But what would he do after Sera had felled Lucifer de Morte and the world continued to breathe and laugh and sigh and cry? And Sera…Dominique suspected one thing—that when the final de Morte ceased to walk this land, she would then return whence she had come.

He recalled now seeing the blue symbol emblazoned on her inner wrist. Delicately carved, the arabesque, but quite clear in its meaning. Seraphim d'Ange did not belong to this earth.

Dominique glanced across the table. Sera eyed his motions with bright interest; a pansy plucked from the wall by the door, flickered in her twisting fingers. Baldwin was out feeding the horses.

"What will you do when all is done?" he wondered aloud, slowing the crush of the pestle to quiet turns. "Where will you go? Does your father's castle yet stand?"

"The d'Ange castle was decimated. De Morte's trebuchet launched huge boulders at the bailey walls. It can be rebuilt, but I believe I'll leave it to the king."

"Does not your father serve a lord?"

"Lord Lucifer de Morte."

"Ah."

"But that bastard's life is to be cut short very soon, so my father's lands will revert to the king. The English king. I can abide giving our damaged home to the English, but unless I can find proof of Father's intentions to leave the coastal property to me that land, as well, will go to the enemy. Or rather, I must prove his plans to leave the land to Henri de Lisieux. Which will then leave me in a bind."

"I'm not sure I understand."

"The fact remains, if I am to claim land I am still in need of a husband."

The mortar slipped from Dominique's grip and lolled back and forth on the table. He groped for the heavy stone bowl, but Sera reacted as quickly. They both touched the bowl at the same time, her hand sliding over the back of his, and staying.

Her eyes held a perfect blue heaven captive. "If I do not marry, I cannot claim the land my father had set aside for me. Henri and I had not said vows. I do want to receive the land set by the sea, it overlooks Mont St. Michel. The surrounding heather fields draw a deep violet band across the emerald meadows. 'Tis captivating...like your eyes."

Dominique blinked. He turned his wrist and clasped Sera's fingers in his. Drawing her hand across the table, he leaned forward and kissed each of her knuckles. Her flesh was tender from the constant wear of gloves, and possessed a sweet taint from the pansy petals.

When he flipped her fingers up to kiss her palm, he again saw the symbol emblazoned on her wrist. Sera would not have her happily-ever-after on some distant seaside manor. She could not, for her fate had already been set in the deep blue lines that curled upon her wrist.

But did she know as much?

"Tell me about this." He turned up her wrist and laid her hand on the table. Reluctant at first to touch the blue marking, Dominique finally lowered his finger and traced the curls and lines that formed a telltale design. "Have you had it always?"

"My devil's mark."

Stunned at that declaration, Dominique hid his doubt by keeping his head low, his eyes focused on her wrist.

"That is what Father called it," she offered. "When I was but six or seven I spilled a kettle of boiling water and received a burn right here on my wrist. The skin bubbled and formed a scab. When the scab fell away this mark lay beneath. It's very curious. Father immediately took to teasing me that the devil had bitten me in my sleep, and I should not show a single soul or they would curse and tease me. Mother, being more practical, assumed 'twas simply the woad dye that had been in the water. It had been laundry day, you see. The dye seeped beneath the damaged flesh, and when new skin grew over all, the color remained."

"Hmm, perhaps so." He made show of being curious. The design was too perfectly crafted to be a random dye mark. And he did know this mark, for Father's catechism had displayed beautiful illuminations of the angels' symbols. 'Twas not the symbol of her namesake, the seraphim, but of a Power, one of the nine echelons of angels. Though, he could remember little more than that.

"Certainly if the devil had bitten you, you might have remembered, eh?"

Sera pressed a hand to the scar on her throat and shrugged, offering but a sheepish smile.

Dominique read the unspoken horror in that action. Of course, the devil had bitten her. He'd slashed his blade across her throat and left her for dead. And it had nothing to do with the mark on her wrist.

Dominique bent to study the design more closely, but Sera pulled away. "So, you did not reply to my statement that I am in need of a husband."

"Do you need a response from me? Very well—I shall marry you and give you the lands that should be yours. Though I cannot promise I shall be as malleable as you desire."

Her shoulders sagged and a hefty sigh escaped her lips. With a frustrated pound of her fist into her opposite palm, Sera stood and paced to the fire.

Not the excited reaction Dominique had expected a newly engaged woman should have. What had he said? "Do you not wish to marry me?"

Firelight sparkled on her shiny black hair, crowning her spiky coif with an amber halo. Like that of— *No. Don't even start to think like that.*

"My heart has changed over the past few weeks," she said. "I've been looking at life differently. Now...well, now I wish to marry for love. Not because a union will grant me a stretch of flowered land."

"But it was you that proposed to me."

"I know. I just thought...it would be more—" she splayed her hands out before her as if to catch...something, then dropped them "—romantic. Between us." She rubbed her palms up and down her arms and strode to the door. "I should see to Baldwin—he's been out for a time. We leave tomorrow morn?"

"Yes," Dominique answered, but the slam of the door muffled his reply.

I just thought it would be more romantic.

Dominique pressed his fingertips to his forehead and squinted his eyes tightly. The antidote forgotten, he shook his head. Romance? He could not give Sera what he did not know. Even if he could perform some act of mock romanticism, what good would it serve? She could not be his.

For the mark on her wrist claimed her for an ineffable fate.

"Of all the idiotic—" Sera slammed a fist into the stable door, then followed the creaking plank inside. Her flat-soled boots crunched across newly spiked hay. Her appearance startled Baldwin, but Gryphon merely gave her a snort.

"What has set your fire ablaze, my lady?"

"Oh!" She gripped the wide wood beam that separated the stalls and punched it. Again, and again. "I cannot believe I said that to him!"

"Said what to who? Why are you beating on helpless wood? Sera?"

Too frenzied to stand still, she paced before Baldwin, fisting her hands at her hips and working furiously at her lower lip with her teeth. "I told San Juste I needed a husband. Oh! Such a swooning fool I have become. I've lost my edge, Benedict. This rest and restoration was not so very wise. Whose idea was it anyway?"

"I believe—"

"Toss me Gryphon's reins. I need to ride, to scream at the top of my lungs, so the world will know my frustration."

As she mounted, the squire scrambled to clear his tools out of Gryphon's path. "You asked Dominique to marry you?"

"And he agreed!" she barked, already turning Gryphon to the door. "That bastard agreed, damn him."

"Aye, well—hmm..." Baldwin scratched his tousle of hair. He squinted one eye shut at the bright sun that split through the stable door and raised an inquiring finger. "He agreed? Isn't that the point of asking in the first place?"

"I do not wish him to agree out of sympathy for my plight."

Gryphon, sensing his mistress's discontent, stamped the ground and reared up on his hind legs. Sera easily handled the gelding's fire.

"I want a man who will whisk me up in his arms and promise me true love forever. For no other reason than that his heart demands as much. Clear out!"

Baldwin shuffled out of Gryphon's way, as Sera heeled the beast's flanks and flew from the stables in a tirade of odd anger. In their wake, glitter of broken hay sifted slowly through the slash of sunlight.

So she had come to trust the mercenary so much she'd asked him to marry her? Baldwin flipped the wire grooming brush around his forefinger. The two had become much closer than he'd suspected. Course, they had spent the entire day together yesterday.

"Where is Seraphim off to like the devil riding the dawn?"

Baldwin spun on Dominique, pressed the curry comb into the man's chest, and sharpened his voice to an accusing tone. "So, you brought her here to seduce her, eh?"

"Squire, you try your place—"

"Damn my bloody place! I will not bow to an untitled man, nor one that chooses to toy with my Sera's heart."

"She is *your* Sera then?"

"I—" Baldwin retrieved the brush from the center of Dominique's chest with a snap. He smoothed his thumb over the impression the wire tip had made in the man's black leather jerkin. "She is no man's woman, mercenary. Even should she marry, she will be but wife in name. Never in soul."

"I know that."

Baldwin spumed at him, "You broke her heart! Just moments ago she was raging about your acceptance of her proposal."

"It is what I thought she wanted. How could I possibly have broken—"

"Don't you see? She does not want what you *think* she needs."

"That makes no sense."

"Ah! Does anything a woman should do make sense?"

"I suppose you would know."

The man did know a fine rogue when he saw one. Baldwin

straightened. "You better believe it. Sera wants you, San Juste. Just you, your heart and soul, and everything else."

"Isn't that what I granted her?"

"No, you gave the easy answer. It was you that should have brought up marriage, not her."

"I would if I could, but…it cannot be." The mercenary paced to Tor's stall, and smoothed his glove over the beast's pink-marbled nose.

Baldwin tucked the brush under his opposite arm and spread his legs to a defiant stance. "What the hell makes you think she'd marry a damn faery anyway?"

The remark hit target. Dominique visibly stiffened, then wrapped his arms about his ribs, lowering his head. Baldwin hadn't meant to shame the man, only make him face up to the secret.

"Are you ever going to tell her?"

"You told me she would not like to hear such."

"Well, maybe I was wrong. Her hatred for faeries goes way back. But that was then, this is now. She favors you, San Juste. But she likes what she can see—she's no idea of what lies beneath the pretty face and the mysterious manner. And if you don't think it's necessary to tell her all when already you've offered her your hand in marriage, you've got another think coming."

"What has she against faeries?"

Baldwin toed a bucket of spring water set down for the horses. "It is something about her sister. She was stolen when she was but a babe and a changeling was left in her place. But I don't think Sera would hold that against you."

"A changeling?"

"Aye. But are you listening, San Juste? She needs to know. Everything. Maybe I should tell her?"

"It would serve no purpose."

"To hell it wouldn't. Knowledge that you are immortal might give Sera the confidence she needs."

"It is not confidence she needs."

"Oh, really? She just flew out of here cursing her romantic heart. She needs to know you will be there for her."

"Seraphim d'Ange needs no one. Her fate has been destined since birth. Have you no seen the mark branded upon her right wrist?"

"What mark?"

"The mark of an angel," Dominique said. "One of the Powers, the only celestial order that is allowed to come to earth and work right against wrongs. I can only imagine she is destined to battle Lucifer."

"Destined? An—an angel? You speak madness! Seraphim is no angel. It might be a fine name—"

Dominique gripped Baldwin's tunic. For three seconds, the squire's feet left the ground until Dominique set him gently down. A glimmer of coruscation surrounded the twosome, but Baldwin could not worry of that when he was still thinking of being so easily lifted.

"I know what I saw, squire. Look for yourself when she returns. It is a sacred mark branded deep into her flesh. She may have been born of mortal parents, but before that symbolic birth she lived in the heavens. She Fell, Baldwin. Seraphim d'Ange is a fallen angel come to annihilate the de Mortes. And when she's found success, I can only guess that she will be returned whence she came."

"To...heaven?" Baldwin gasped.

Dominique merely nodded. Once. A final, chilling answer to a devastatingly eerie statement.

"Why then would she need you?" Baldwin double-stepped to

catch up to Dominique as he made way for the door. The brightness of the noon sun blinded him momentarily as they crunched out onto crystal-frosted snow. "Shouldn't she know that she's a real angel?"

"And what would that knowledge serve Sera but to further torment? To know she had once lived in heaven and now walks this hideous, cruel earth in mortal form?"

"You lie!" Baldwin called.

The mercenary rounded quickly. In a flash, he stood before Baldwin. The hush of the man's breath played across Baldwin's nose. The urgency in his voice bade him mark his words. "You may look for the mark on her wrist, but you mustn't repeat to Sera any of what we have discussed. Do you understand?"

"No, I don't—"

"She will not believe you. As far as I can determine she has no memory of being an angel. Why, I do not know. Promise you will keep our silence, squire."

"Or what?"

"Or I shall feed you to Sammael de Morte myself. Poison toads have little over that demon's monstrous methods of torture. I wager you'll hold your tongue if you wish to avoid such a cruel death."

Baldwin held the faery's dark, foreboding gaze for as long as he dared, then flashed his attention to the trail Gryphon's hooves had beat through the snow.

Angels and faeries and demons? Mother of Mayhem, he should have stuck with eating toads.

·❦ SIXTEEN ❦·

A thick frosting of gray clouds muted the light of a new day. Lucifer allowed a sigh to overcome his strong shoulders. It was rare that he succumbed to such base actions. But the winter months were a disappointment. The Dragon of the Dawn needed the light, the pink stretches of heat across the horizon to ensure, strengthen, and challenge.

But the dull, sunless sky did not decrease the strength that teemed inside his muscles, twisting into tight coils of energy that, when released, packed the preternatural strength of a man tenfold. Always he regarded the dawn as giver of his power. His peace. His foresight. And now…his Fate.

But on this morning he could not grasp the glimmer of vibration that would tell him if the black knight was on the move. The knight could not yet have broached Sammael's lair. For the ride from his brother's home to Paris was but half a day. Lucifer would have known by now. Would have sensed the release of shared power. Or, if Sammael's demon had been released, Lucifer would have felt his own strength wane. Just a bit, as he had for the few brief moments Abaddon's fire beast had escaped his feeble mortal shell.

This unknowing frustrated beyond measure. Though, 'twas not entirely vexing. Lucifer enjoyed a good siege, laid out for days, weeks, even months by the finest knights in hopes of conquering their enemies. So inspiring it was to watch the mortals scramble about the de Morte lands in attempts to bring them to death. And always they would fail. Oh, such sweet, simple victory!

But this victory would be the sweetest by far. To face the One. The one who held an inexplicable connection to the de Mortes.

And to triumph.

Lucifer inclined his head down and surveyed the bustle on the Paris streets. This is what had seduced him to Fall decades ago. From high in his tower room he overlooked a panoramic view of the vast city, seething with iniquity and temptation. He greeted all mornings here in the lofty heights that touched so close to the fickle heaven he'd come to care so little about. Below, bakers and fishmongers pushed carts and strode on boot and wooden patten. Washerwomen skittered from well to well in search of space to do their laundering. The king's guard heeled royal horse flesh in anticipation of yet another day, another coin in their purse. Whether by trick or trade earned—yet another day of life.

Life. Such a common word on the mortal tongue. But for one of the Fallen consigned within mortal flesh, it merely slid like poisoned blood down the blue face of a day-old corpse. Not an entirely undesirable scenario, Lucifer mused. But tiring all the same.

Lifting his head, he sensed another had arrived. Minute vibrations moved the air around him, altering the temperature by a few degrees. Fresh taint of…spring, lingered near his nostrils. Fellow brethren; not Fallen, but Sent. It was strangely satisfying to now realize the relationship he held to this one that had served him for years.

Without turning away from the sun's struggle to push through the thick wadding of clouds, Lucifer wondered, "How fares my mercenary?"

"Rather well, I must say," came the dulcet, boyish voice.

"He has attached himself to the black knight?"

"Indeed."

"Yet he has not slain him, as requested."

"He bides his time."

Indeed? Could this figment, this creature of another realm possibly lie to him? He'd never had reason to disbelieve…until now. "Well enough. But there has been a change of plan. The mercenary will ensure that idiot knight's quest is not cut short."

"You wish the black knight success?"

"I do," Lucifer answered, delightedly pleased with his own change of heart.

"The mercenary remains close and is determined to see the black knight's quest to the end. Which…is not your original intention."

"My intentions have altered. Though, I am discomfited to learn you are aware of the mercenary's path. Did you not order he *kill* the black knight?"

"My methods are of no concern to you."

Not a lie. Merely playing by his own set of rules. The insolent.

"Always so irritatingly impartial." Lucifer ground his jaw. Ah! But he would no longer have need for this one's assistance after he had been released from the mortal coil. "I approve of the mercenary's position as protector. You are paying him well for this, I trust?"

"The coin you provided me was not necessary, as I initially stated." A clink of coin, muffled inside a velvet purse, *chinked* as it landed at Lucifer's feet. "If a man wishes faith from his servants he must know how to compensate. I will pay the mercenary with his greatest desire."

"Ah, yes, the easiest way to win a soul. Temptation." Turning to look upon the young face of the fading image, Lucifer's lips curled into a wicked grin. "You have served me well, Leviticus."

"I serve neither good, nor evil," the boy replied. "Only keep the balance of nature."

"Yes, yes, do see that this mercenary escorts the black knight through my brother Sammael's lair. It will be a nasty trek, but should they triumph the reward will certainly outweigh the danger."

The boy inclined his head in an accepting manner, then shivered into nothingness.

A flutter of wings sounded right at Lucifer's ear. For a moment, he felt the regret. Alone upon the stone ramparts of the tower he stood. No wings. Not the ethereal knowing of peace. Not ever again. Alone—and so ready to be alone. No false brothers to share and sap his power.

Only one.

The black knight would bring him this crown of power with one misplaced strike of his sword.

Sammael's lair was but a day's journey that drew the compass tip from the Valois Wood to the east. Baldwin took up the lead, his speckled roan plowing a trail through the loose, glittering snow.

Dominique had started in the middle, though occasionally he would pull out of line, fall behind Sera for an hour or so, then ride back up in the middle. As he passed her on the left for a third time, intent to fall onto the tail of their mini caravan, Sera nodded, smiled, and cast her face forward. She wore cloak and mail-coif, and a long woolen scarf wrapped around her head to conceal as much of her face as possible from the rude bite of the season.

The winter air flattened the usual smells of nature: of the horses' sweating hides, the brew of mustard seed and lavender just lingering beneath the surface soil, waiting for spring's rousing call. The foul tang of animal droppings was even muted by the icy briskness of this unseasonable snowfall.

And then there was her traveling mate's scent. Sera wished for a summer breeze to swirl up from behind, sift through Dominique's loose, dark hair, and carry his manly essence to her nose. She had smelled it in the steaming bath deep in the underground cave. Feral and musky. A man scent without a doubt. Not tainted with the usual foulness that the men who had flickered in and out of her life had worn, such as sweat, filth, and lust. There was something different and pure about Dominique San Juste. He was of another realm.

Perhaps?

Certainly not from the demon realm whence her enemies had risen, she thought with a grimace. But most certainly someplace—else.

When Dominique had stood up from the snow angel they'd made yesterday afternoon, she had studied the impression in the snow for a moment, thinking the winged design could have been his shadow. But real angels did not come to earth in mortal form. Did they?

Sera tilted her head back and blew out a puff of frosted air. If there were ever a time when she might give credence to having a guardian angel that time was now. Dominique had appeared from out of nowhere, and had attached himself to her as protector. But he didn't have his script right. He'd said he would marry her.

Or maybe it was she that did not follow the script.

Had she been too demanding to wish romance? To expect something more?

Her frenzied ride up and down the forest edge this morning had worked to clear the rage from her head. But it had not pressed down her pining for Dominique. And now, destined for her most challenging enemy yet, Sera could not sort out her confusion of thoughts. The worry that she might not succeed. And the nervous pining for a man who defied her need for freedom, her need to control her own destiny.

"Deep thoughts?"

Sera startled to find Dominique at her side, the liquid depths of his black-violet eyes focused on the slit in her head wrappings that revealed but her eyes and nose.

"Just wonderings," she said through the scarf.

With his nod, he then winked and fell behind her on the trail. He wore nothing on his head, for the hematite-decorated hood had slipped to his shoulders hours ago.

She turned and called back. "Are you not chilled?"

"I sure as hell am!" Baldwin called from the lead. With that, he turned his mount and stopped Sera and Dominique in their tracks. "Might we stop at the next village? I fear for my toes. I cannot feel them!"

Sera looked to Dominique; his face showed no sign of chill or of turning white—as Baldwin's nose-tip did.

"Soilly is three leagues off."

Baldwin groaned.

"Meaux is but another five," Dominique offered, spurring Tor into motion and taking up the lead. "I think we should ride straight through. Sera?"

"I can still feel my toes," she offered, wiggling the appendages in question to be sure. "But I shouldn't wish my squire stumbling about like a drunkard if he loses his to the cold."

"He will not," Dominique answered confidently. "Just think warm thoughts. Great bonfires and hot August days."

"If I wasn't an icicle I'd knock you from your horse," Baldwin snapped from between chattering teeth. "I cannot conjure a single warm image to my bechilled brain. My bonfires are frozen over, and my Augusts are rainy and gray."

"Ha!" Dominique heeled Tor's flank, then gave a shove to Baldwin's shoulder as he passed him by. "Ride on, the two of you."

With a reluctant groan and a string of blue oaths, Baldwin eased his horse toward the east. Sera road alongside him for a while, hoping her company, maybe conversation, would keep the squire's mind from the numbing sensation in his boots. She was beginning to feel the tip of her nose do much the same.

Bringing up the rear, Dominique slipped a hand from his glove and smoothed it across Tor's neck, pausing to scratch that one particular spot at the base of his mane that he so enjoyed having itched.

"Shall I grant them a reprieve?" he asked the stunning white beast. "I suppose lady Sera is right, 'twould not serve to have a stumble-toed squire in her service."

Stretching out his hand, he closed his eyes, and drew up the warmth from his body. A jolt to his system set him rigid upon Tor's back. Coruscation gushed from his fingers and enveloped the duo riding before him. Neither noticed the exotic iridescence that surrounded them, briefly, before permeating their woolen cloaks, steel armor, and seeping into their flesh.

It was another four hours that the trio rode on through Soilly and finally landed Meaux. And not a single complaint about the cold. In fact, Baldwin did a little jig as he dismounted before the Sign of the Blue Moon, and Sera, too, was all smiles.

There was naught but a barren stall available for the night in yonder stable out back of the Sign of the Blue Moon. But, oddly, the threesome did not so much mind. For all the time she'd spent on Gryphon's back facing the elements today, Sera was feeling rather toasty. An enclosed building, be it a fire-warmed tavern or a horse-warmed stable would serve well enough.

Baldwin prodded up his portion of hay and made himself a nest before settling in, grandly wiggling his hips to further root out a comfortable position, then smacked his hands together. "So, what are the plans for taking the poison master's lair? Anyone?"

"I figure," Dominique said, as he leaned against the stall, waiting for Sera to make her own nest, "there is but one option."

"Which is?" She settled close to Baldwin and looked over his meticulous inventory of supplies he normally kept tied around his waist.

"We do have an expert in poisons…" Dominique suggested.

"Ah, we do." Sera flashed the mongoose eye Baldwin's way. "What say you, squire?"

Baldwin paused from picking through his bone bag, lifted his head to find the look Sera gave him, and dropped his jaw. "What? Me? You want *me* to go in after a demon? I don't think so!"

"We need you to lead us in," Dominique said, kneeling before Sera's boots and plucking up a shard of hay. "With your immunity to poison, it would be wisest. Will you be our guide?"

"So in other words, send in the most expendable man first?"

"You are not expendable," Sera said, meaning every word of it. "But Dominique is right, it would be wise to take precautions. If you sense out an impenetrable passageway, we will not take it. Come, Bertrand, I have faith in your expertise."

"You do?"

She nodded then gestured to his leather pouch. "Mayhaps you've a bone in there that will serve your safety?"

"I do!" he suddenly declared, then dug about and produced a short white relic. He displayed it before the three of them, as if a single gold coin rooted out from a beggar's soiled shoe. "St. Benedict's toe bone. He's the patron saint of poison victims."

"Let me see that," Sera said.

"No." Baldwin clutched the bone to his chest. He eyeballed Sera and Dominique uneasily. "I'm afraid I cannot let you touch it. I must, er...protect the magick."

"Ah, I see." She cast a wry look Dominique's way, then offered slyly, "Me thinks it looks like a rooster bone."

Baldwin gasped, affronted.

Sera matched Dominique's breathy chuckle. "Very well, it could possibly be some dead saint's bone. Certainly I must allow you that." She stretched back and nestled her head into the pillow of hay she'd plumped up behind her. "We've all our own secrets to protect. Isn't that so, San Juste?"

At that surprising conversational twist, Dominique lifted a bewildered stare to Sera.

She shrugged, feeling a bit of mischief coming on. Wasn't difficult after the long, tiring day. She leveled the mongoose eye upon the mercenary with utmost precision. "What have *you* to protect?"

"What makes you think the man has anything to protect?" Baldwin rushed in.

Sera regarded the squire—strange that he would defend the mercenary—then flashed a more serious look back at San Juste. "Since when do you allow Benwick to speak for you?"

"It is Baldwin!" the squire declared with a surprisingly irritated shriek. He gathered his bones into his purse and pulled the leather drawstrings as taut as his jaw. "Baldwin, my lady. Bald-win." He forced the words through gritted teeth. "Why can you not get that simple name into your brain?"

"Mayhaps, I just do not care for it—"

"But it is *my* name!" He thrummed his chest with a fist. "A name given me by my parents. About the only thing they ever gave me without then taking it back, or mutilating it, or destroying it with ignorance. So I shall ask you to be respectful of it and use it well."

With that, Baldwin pushed to his feet and strode out of the stall in a symphony of *tinks* and rattling bones.

"Hell." Sera pushed up, prepared to run after the man, but Dominique pressed himself between her and the stall.

"Let him go," he said.

"But I've upset him. And he was right." She pressed the back of her hand to her cheek, shook her head at her cruelties. "I show him so little respect. He deserves so much more."

The grip Dominique held on her arm loosened, and he relented with a nod. "Indeed. For as much as we believe we are his friends, he is but alone in this world. I can see his craving for stability. A home. A family to call him—"

"Baldwin," Sera finished, and pressed a kiss to Dominique's forehead. "You love him as much as I do?"

Dominique nodded.

"I'd best hurry after him."

The Sign of the Blue Moon rumbled with hearty male laughter and the clang of pewter tankards, along with the occasional shriek from a manhandled wench. Ignoring the mirth of the men inside, Sera rounded the tavern and found the squire leaning against the outer wall, his head pressed to the wattle and daub, his eyes searching the velvet night sky. Stale gray thatching hung but inches from his nose. He tapped at the frayed ends with a finger.

Dominique's observations were so wise. Indeed, this man—her reluctant squire—was still but a boy in need of family. Of stability and love. Of someplace to belong—as Sera so desperately needed.

Might the church have filled that void for the man? It was difficult to know. Mayhap, just the presence of others, of those who care—her family—had been exactly what Baldwin Ortolano needed most. And now they were both alone.

But they did have each other.

Pacing purposely toward him, Sera stopped but a foot from his lanky frame and fell to one knee before him.

"Sera, what are you—"

"I've come to beg your forgiveness, Baldwin."

"This is—" He bent, lifted on her arm, but she would not relent her position. "This is nonsense," he whispered, as if in church and expecting to be reprimanded for making noise. "You should not be kneeling before me like a common—stand up! Please?"

"Nay." She granted him her eyes, and in his she saw the tears put there by her own cruel teasing. If there were ever a time to allow the damsel free reign, it was now. "I do this correctly, or not at all. You mean the world to me, squire. I should not have spoken so lightly of your name. I have a tendency to find myself a comfortable tease, without thinking afore it is used. You are right, every man's name is a gift that deserves respect."

Baldwin knelt before her in the slushy snow. He towered over her by a head, so long and agile his torso was. He would prove a mighty force should he seek his spurs.

"Thank you, Seraphim. But I should apologize for raging at you in the stable. I just—"

She pressed a finger to his lips, cold, soft, and quivering. She wished he could have memories of a loving touch from his mother. "No apologies. You have served me well, Baldwin, and I respect your right to speak your mind. As you should, always. You've been exceedingly brave thus far."

"I haven't had much of a choice." He touched the scabbed wound on the bridge of his nose. "Though I can't say it hasn't been an adventure."

"Now, we look only to the future. We will successfully take Sammael's castle, and kill the bastard. I know it."

Baldwin untied his purse from his hip and rummaged inside, producing St. Benedict's toe bone—or possibly, as Sera had guessed, a rooster leg pawned off as a holy relic. "You will need this."

"Me?" Sera studied the bleached bone. Looked to be more fowl than human. But she would not set a challenge to Baldwin's convictions this day. "It is you that will venture first into Sammael's lair."

"I've an immunity you do not possess. At least, I hope I do." His Adam's apple bobbed at a deep swallow. "I've never encountered an entire castle dripping with poison."

"You and me both."

"Here." He offered the bone. "Take it."

"I cannot." She reached to touch the white appendage, but drew back when she recalled Baldwin's earlier statement. "I'll spoil the magick."

"No. There is magick immeasurable inside you, Seraphim. If this rotting old bone does possess a bit of charm your holding it will only increase its strength."

He believed in her. In ways she could not fathom.

"Thank you, Baldwin." She clasped her hand around his, for the moment feeding his chill flesh with her warmth. "Where shall I keep it?"

"Have you no pockets? What about, hmm...stand up."

He tucked it behind the criss-cross laces on her left boot. "It should be secure there. Pray to St. Benedict he sees you through the Poison Master's realm unscathed."

She leaned forward and kissed Baldwin's cheek. He caught up her hand and kissed her knuckle, then held it in his so her wrist was exposed. He dipped his head to study the devil's mark, an obvious reaction, as she had observed many do upon first noticing the design.

"That's very...pretty," he managed to say.

"I've never thought of it that way. Indeed, it is." Leave it to this man to see something that could be so evil in a unique and utterly different manner. Sera gripped his shoulder and squeezed, reassuring.

As they both stood, Baldwin gave a half bow and spread a hand over his chest. "Thank you, my lady, for putting up with me."

"Thank you, Baldwin, for renewing my faith."

SEVENTEEN

Sammael's lair sat upon what looked like a man-made protuberance, the base very narrow, and growing more slender as it fused with the ash-coated castle walls and worked to a fine spike in the sky. Like something out of nightmares, a devil's horn thrust up from hell, spiked once on either side with a turret that glowed a jaundiced yellow from the illumination within.

"Imposing," Dominique commented. Mounted upon Tor, he worked a fist inside his opposite palm. He actually smiled when addressing Sera. "Want to turn back?"

In a heartbeat.

"Never." Sera led Gryphon by the reins, her mail chinking softly, as she found a narrow dirt path that appeared to twist and wind like an embroidered arabesque across the mountain of black velvet before them. "I've come this far, no runt of a demon is going to chase me off. Even if he breathes poison. I'll die severing his head from his body."

"You won't die," her companion said softly; not meant to be overheard. "You cannot."

The unspoken emotion in that simple statement touched Sera. No, she couldn't die, because there was someone who cared whether she lived or died. Actually there were two some-ones who gave a care. And she would have a care to breathe yet another day, as well.

Sera rounded on Baldwin, who stood fixed in the spot he had landed upon dismounting. "So you're off then, squire."

Baldwin pulled himself from the jaw-gaping stare he'd held on the castle. "M-me?" He pressed his eyelids shut, scrunched his entire face in what looked a rather painful pose to Sera. "I've been doing some thinking. Why do *I* have to go in first?" He spread his hands before him imploringly. "I am no knight."

Dominique swung around and slapped the squire across the cheek.

The startled man stumbled backward, clutched his face, and blabbered out, "Wha-what the hell?"

"I dub thee a knight," Dominique casually offered. He then cast Sera a gleeful twinkle of eye, though he kept his expression a study of seriousness.

"Oh—oh!" Baldwin fought with his own tongue. He eased a fist over his stinging cheek. He blabbered some more "ohs," and then, "Fine! Just—" He stomped the ground and flung a hand curtly before him. "Fine! This is what I get for fooling fools. A fool's death!"

"Come now, Sir Baldwin," Dominique said, "we've discussed that you will be first to enter the Poison Master's lair. You are the most qualified to sniff out danger."

"*Sir* Baldwin?" The man's countenance brightened. "You called me sir?"

"Indeed. Granted, the ceremony was a bit primitive, but all the same, you are now a knight."

A kaleidoscope of emotions wrestled on Baldwin's smack-flushed face as he considered Dominique's declaration. Finally, mirth won out. But as he opened his mouth to rejoice, a bushy brown brow crooked and a frown dashed back into place. "But I have no sword. So!" He smacked his palms together in a satisfying ring. "I still cannot go on ahead."

Dominique drew out his dagger from the sheath strapped at his side. He turned the glinting steel before him, displaying it to the squire. Inlaid with damascened gold, 'twas a valuable piece of steel, crafted by his own father. He could not send an unarmed man into Sammael's lair. He offered it to Baldwin, handle-first.

Baldwin performed much the same ceremony of holding the impressive weapon before him, gazing upon the fine, sharpened blade—and then his brow crooked again. "This is too damn short!"

Dominique now regarded him with his own version of the evil eye. "But minutes you are a knight and already you complain like an old hen. You should not refuse such a gift, squire."

"Ah, ah," Baldwin waved an admonishing finger between he and the mercenary. "Knight."

"Yes, yes, *Sir* Baldwin," Dominique corrected.

Sera chucked Baldwin on the shoulder with a tender fist. He was being brave. She suspected it wasn't as difficult to mine that bravery as the man thought. He was noble in his own unique way. "Onward, Baldwin."

Baldwin paused after two paces and turned to Sera. Before he even opened his mouth to correct her, she threw in, "*Sir* Baldwin."

He smiled a truly happy smile, tapped the air with the dagger in an accepting movement, then turned to blaze a path into the poisonous lair of the Demon of the East.

"Bam, you're a knight!" Baldwin hissed and cursed his way down the narrow passageways that slowly winded themselves up and around inside the intestines of de Morte's evil lair. 'Twas like drilling upward from hell to reach the lord who reigned, he decided.

"Did anyone ask me if *I* had an opinion about this knight business? I think not. San Juste just needed a reason to lay me out." He rubbed his aching jaw. "Damn hard slap, too, if you ask me. Which, we all know, no one *did* ask me."

Another step took him around and into a much narrower passage. The walls seeped with…something. The pearlescent white slime smelled of animal waste—and then, flowers, like a full meadow overcrowded with luscious white blooms.

Baldwin's curses dissipated in fear as his senses began to react. Most likely poison purled down the walls. He was so busy with his fate that he hadn't been paying attention.

Time to get serious. He pulled the torn cloth each of the trio had designed as protection up over his nose to keep from inhaling noxious fumes. A tug to the lower portion of the cloth secured it over his mouth and chin.

"If I get out of this alive," he whispered, calming his need to turn and dash for safety, "I'll tell Sera everything. That her damned savior is a faery—her least favorite kind of being— and that he thinks she's an angel. An angel? Of all things! I must have a bone for that—something to ward off maniacal faeries who see visions of angels. Ha!"

Although, he had seen the mark on Sera's wrist that Dominique claimed was of the angels. He'd not known what to say as he'd held Sera's hand. Pretty? Not if it meant what the faery said it did. It couldn't mean as much. It didn't. Baldwin did not believe in angels come to earth to rescue mankind. Why, the very notion was ridiculous. Where were her wings? Her flaming sword? A halo?

And if she really was an angel, he most certainly would not be where he was right now. Deep in the bowels of this poisonous lair.

Ahead lie a forked turn. Decision time. Baldwin paused, listened for Dominique's and Sera's footsteps. The mercenary had said they would follow close behind as Baldwin would rout out any poisonous traps. He could hear nothing but the trickle of liquid running down the walls. And the clatter of bones inside his purse, for he shook like a willow in the wind.

Should have kept St. Benedict's toe bone for himself. Sera wouldn't have known had he given her the finger bone of St. Matthew, patron saint of tax collectors.

Another turn into yet another seeping passageway. Baldwin stepped carefully—still, his long legs moved him far more quickly than he desired. With one hand clenched tightly about Dominique's dagger, he afforded the other hand a journey down to the bag of bones at his hip. With all the holiness contained within, he should glean some protection.

A squeeze of the leather bag discovered the ovular piece of spine bone once belonging to Jude Thaddaeus. "Patron saint of desperate situations," Baldwin muttered. "Yes, indeed."

The flash of a rush light caught his attention. Slipping the bone remnant around his thumb, Baldwin then stepped forward and lunged around yet another corner.

'Twas not flaming rushes that lit the small rest-chamber like a bright summer day, but thick white candles, as wide as a man's head, set upon rusted iron bases. Globs of white tallow spilled to the floor and froze in liquid motion. It was almost serene, the atmosphere.

Baldwin lowered his dagger hand and released hold of the bone bag. He closed his eyes, and felt the heat of myriad flames warm him. The scent of flame and soft tallow tempted him to walk to the center of the sanctuary.

This was peaceful, alluring. Rich in the promise of safety.

He smiled, absently smoothing the porous spine bone across his thigh. "This is nice," he whispered. "Here be no poisonous monsters."

Behind him, there came a sound that did not blend with the flicker of flame. It scraped, slowly, heavily. Foreboding rappled up Baldwin's spine with icy talons. Pining to remain a statue in the center of salvation, Baldwin's curiosity finally got the better of him. He turned to investigate the noise—and looked upon the fattest, longest snake he had ever seen. The hooded cowl of the beast was very near the size of Baldwin's own head!

And it was poised to strike.

"Mother of Murder," he managed in choked gasps, knowing the short little dagger, barely contained in his sweaty palm, would serve him no favor.

With a hiss, and a flick of pink tongue, the snake struck.

EIGHTEEN

His entire body had conformed to a cringe, knees bent, one leg pulled to his gut, arms snapped to chest. But the pain that should have come—a bite to his ankle, thigh, or arm—did not.

Baldwin pried open a tightly squeezed eyelid and glanced down. The shimmer of a long steel blade, thrust before the one leg he balanced on, glinted in the candlelight. And sliding down the blade, the snake—mouth spread wide and fangs dripping clear poison—until it collapsed in a loose coil on the ground.

Dominique's blade. The breaths hushing over Baldwin's shoulder were that of the mercenary's as well. One moment later and Baldwin would have been snake supper.

He expelled a hefty lung-full of air and set his foot on the ground. "That's some fine steel, San Juste."

Dominique pulled back his sword and turned it over and thus before Baldwin in a casual manner. "Folded sixteen times by blind Mongolian monks who lived in silence for three decades in the Alpacian mountains."

"Can we get the hell out of here?"

"Why?" A lift of his sword hefted the snake body up between the two men. "Snakes bother you?"

Baldwin dodged to avoid the taunt of Dominique's sanguine teasing. "Hell, San Juste, do you have to be so calm about everything? You just saved my miserable hide."

"You'd have done the same for me."

"You think?" He shrugged. "Perhaps. Course, I'm not so sure I wouldn't have turned and run had our positions been reversed."

"What if Sera had been in your position, and you in mine?"

"That's easy, Sera would have cast the beast the evil eye and sent it slithering out of sight."

"She does have a way about her." Dominique chuckled, and tilted his sword, allowing the snake to slide off in a heap at his feet. "Let's be off, Sir Baldwin. You've proven bravery against opposition. Now, to sniff out Sammael's hiding spot."

The air inside the thin limestone walls was humid and thick. Though her mouth and nose were covered by the herb-soaked cloth Dominique had prepared for this mission, Sera sensed were she to pull it away and draw in a deep breath she could bite off a chunk of air, so heavy it hung upon her shoulders.

She glanced to Dominique, who offered a nod that they press onward. Baldwin had been elected to guard the opening to this, the final passageway. After hearing about his narrow escape from the snake, Sera was more than willing to allow him to sit this round out. Relief had been evident in the man's hefty sigh.

Ahead, she picked up the dim sound of gurgling, much like bubbles boiling upon a stewpot. She couldn't be positive for the fine veil of music that carried over all, a complement to the eerie sounds of the castle, and yet, not. A stringed instrument, its notes boxy and metallic, paired with a pan-pipe. Very faint, yet mystically alluring as the sharp notes sang a haunting lullaby that tempted, while at the same time mourned.

She moved in anxious steps. The urge to rush forward and discover the source of the intriguing melody was strong, but it did not overpower her caution. They had encountered no guards, not a single booby trap since following Baldwin's lead into Sammael's lair. Which could either prove fortuitous, or so very, very bad.

An easy entry into an inescapable tomb of poison?

She prayed not.

The hallway was dark, for there were but few torches spaced so distant as to not share their fuzzy globes of light. Stepping into the thin glow of another torch, Sera spied a short, rounded door set into the wall just ahead. The first door she had come upon. It was barred with a thick black beam of wood and rose to a height but a head shorter than her nose.

Reaching to lift the wood bar, Sera stifled a gasp as, from behind, Dominique lunged to grip her extended hand.

"Must I continually remind you of the danger?" His eyes blazoned none of the rich royal violet as he beamed the seriousness of their task into her own gaze.

"No." A bitter tear glossed Sera's eye. Her heartbeats charged toward a cliff. *Yes,* she then thought. She had been out of her head just now. Stirred by the alluring music and myriad thoughts of what her outcome would prove; she hadn't been in the present moment.

She touched Dominique's cheek, just above the black cloth that he wore over mouth and nose. "Thank you."

"Just performing the task I've been sent to do," he said.

"And don't forget it," she muttered to herself.

Dominique lifted his knee and toed the barring-block with

his boot. Carefully he inched the heavy lock to the side, until the door creaked and opened. Before Sera could nudge the door open with an elbow she found herself in Dominique's embrace.

The black cloth pressed in and out from his lips as he whispered, "Question your every move before you make it." He pressed his gaze deep into her own, branding her with an urgency that she could not place. "Promise me you'll stay alert?"

She nodded. *Warrior,* she thought to herself. *Do not look into his eyes or you will lose the edge you must balance upon. It is but his mission that concerns the mercenary.*

"I'm going to follow you from a distance. Keep out of sight, yet within rushing length. By your leave?"

"Aye." She knew the plan. It was only by her blade that Sammael would fall. Dominique would stay close enough to protect, but not obstruct. Baldwin would remain outside, prepared to lead the way to escape with torch and some sainted bone in hand. "But how will I know it is him? I've not been given a description beyond that he is a rat."

"I'll keep watch, alert you as soon as I can. Now go, before our new knight expires from fear."

She glanced to Baldwin's shuddering figure. Silhouetted by torch-glow, he flickered his gaze from ceiling, to wall, and down the blackened passageway they had traversed. Fear or faith?

Perhaps a bit of fear was advantageous. Keeps one on their toes. But a little reassurance wouldn't hurt either.

"Kiss me—" Before Sera could finish the damsel's surprising and foolish request, Dominique pulled down her mask and pressed his warm lips to hers.

Much as she should have pushed him away, drawn her sword and marched boldly into danger, resistance was unthinkable.

This kiss tightened the push and pull her heart had been fighting. Marry him, desire him; defy him, resist him.

Just experience it, her heart pleaded. *Give me the passion I desire. Feast on the love he offers. For tomorrow may never come. Damn the edge, this power can be used as well!*

Yes, the power of love. For indeed, she had come to love this man. That was the only word she could put to the feeling his presence stirred in her. If Dominique San Juste were to step aside, to disappear from her life at this moment, Sera felt sure an ache would grow in her belly. And it would bleed and quiver until Dominique returned to her side. No, this feeling did not live in her belly, but her heart. How full and perfect her heart felt standing next to this man, holding him and sharing his kiss.

Yes, love, the damsel whispered. *This is right…*

Dominique broke the kiss. "Enough. Are you prepared for this, Seraphim?"

She tugged at his cape, drawing him closer. "Never enough."

"There's always tomorrow."

He was far more optimistic than she.

He squeezed her arm; the mail links pinched, reminding of the imminent pain that could be more real than her passions. For she would suffer pain unending should she fail this task. A monumental task, now that she held the knowledge she fought fire demons.

"How does one prepare to meet with a demon?"

Dominique lifted her hand, pushed back the soft suede underside of her glove and kissed her wrist. Right over the curious blue devil's mark. "You have prepared for this since before your birth."

"Before my—"

"You will not fail. Remember— *Can* you remember?"

She searched his pleading gaze. "I don't understand?"

Hope glistened in his eyes, but for a moment. He released a sigh, as though he were bidding farewell to a longtime friend. "Forgive me, I speak nonsense. Just…know that I love you. I love the fire that blazes in your breast, the ice that shimmers in your eyes, and the challenge in your kiss." He touched her cheek with a gentle press of steel gauntlet. "I also love the fierce warrior that refuses to back down until all is right with this world. You will be successful, Seraphim. Now go."

He directed her to a bend and Sera passed through the short, curved entry. On the other side of the door grew a luscious, exotic greenhouse. 'Twas as if she'd stepped through a portal of time and into a verdant summer forest. Green leaves and bright flowers blossomed over all. The ceiling was a complex checkerboard of glass and lead partitions to allow in the daylight, perhaps even the few rays of sun that graced the French sky.

Sera drew in a breath, but only smelled the sweet floral herbs that Dominique had soaked into her mask.

"How magical." She turned about before an aisle that stretched a great distance between thick crops of flora. "In the dead of winter, there is such life."

Dominique stepped inside the humid planetarium as Sera rushed toward the main aisle. "Don't touch anything!"

At his hissing remark she drew back a hand from an innocent blue columbine.

Dominique was at her side in less than a blink. "Not a thing," he reprimanded. "This is Sammael's garden of death. Surely all these flowers are poisonous."

"But I don't think columbine—"

"Sera! These flowers were grown by a master of poison. If you should so much as brush along a stem and snap it, it may be the last flower you ever admire."

Sera drew the corner of her lip in between her teeth, her gaze switching from Dominique, to the flower, and back. He certainly did not know how to put a soft spin on things.

"There." He pointed ahead where a small door with a crescent peep stood at the far end of the garden. Thick vines wove up the fieldstone wall surrounding it and twined in a loose braid over the door. "Most likely Sammael brews his deadly concoctions close by. If we are to find the man, surely it will be in preparation to meet the black knight."

"Brewing up poison?"

"Are you sure you can do this?"

A flick of her tongue across her lips renewed memory to the sweeter things in life. The taste of Dominique's kiss brewed courage in her heart. "I can."

He nodded and slipped away behind a great ruffled fern that curled and fluttered out across the aisle. Sera blinked and completely lost sight of him. Though she could see to the wall opposite, there was no sign of her protector. He had a way of moving so quickly atimes. It did not seem natural.

With a sigh, she turned to face her task.

Alone now. But not alone.

"But I feel as much," she whispered.

Turning to face the aisle that led to yonder door, Sera surmised that if she turned sideways she might traverse the narrow path without coming in contact with the blossoms that greedily waited for her touch. Checking over her body she assured that no flesh, beyond her eyes, showed. What she wouldn't have given for a bascinet with visor and a narrow eye strip.

She had walked one dark alley blinded for fear of getting an arrow to the head. She could do the same here. Just turn to the side and walk straight down the aisle. Dominique would protect. Somehow. Though, she would feel much better if the man wielded a crossbow.

And so she turned and slowly traversed the long aisle. The melody playing in the background formed a macabre duet with her pattering heartbeats. Light and carefree segued with heavy and pendulous. At one point she heard the small snap of a fragile green stem, but as she cringed and froze to gauge her next move, she knew she could not dare to open her eyes. *Move on. Quickly.*

When she felt she'd broached the end of the aisle, she opened her eyes to find a patio with stone benches and a round marble-topped table laid before her. A latticed curling of vines and flowers shaded the court from the dull daylight threatening to brighten its aura. Half a dozen thick white candles flickered madly as the wind of her arrival stirred them.

A garden solar meant for quiet lunches amidst the deadly flora? How morbidly unappealing.

Releasing a heavy breath—perhaps the very same one she had started with at the beginning of the path—Sera stepped onto the stone patio.

She now knew Baldwin's fear upon setting first foot in this castle. A lift of her left foot verified St. Benedict's toe bone was still tucked safely behind her boot laces. If ever a trinket were to possess supernatural power, she prayed for that now.

Just knowing her enemy held immortality on his side vexed her. But no—Sammael could have immortality only with the misplaced sweep of her sword.

She held all the power.

That realization filled Sera's lungs with a breath of bravery. Enough fear. She would not grant the prize of immortality to any de Morte this day. Time to strike down another villain. This one was for the memory of her father, Marcil d'Ange.

From behind, she heard the squeak of door hinges and spun quickly, her armor-scaled glove moving to the sword at her hip.

"A visitor?" A short, yet wiry man with sweating brow and long, sticky black hair wobbled across the stone tiles. His hands clasped before his chin, and his head seeming at a permanent tilt upon his neck, he eyed Sera with mismatched baubles of dark and pure white. The flesh on his face was at once greasy and flaking. A condition of illness, perhaps disease. Or...prolonged exposure to poison.

Sera took a step back as he slithered close to examine her. To turn and scan the garden in search of Dominique would only raise suspicion. But without Dominique's signal how would she know if this was the man she sought?

Hell. Nothing had changed. She was on her own. Again. She was a lone woman on a quest for the restoration of her soul, for her family's peace—for retribution.

Yes, take it all back from the hands of the de Mortes. In your family's memory.

With a snap of her neck, Sera straightened and assumed battle mode. "Are you Sammael de Morte?"

"Who asks such of a mere servant?" The man's voice slurped from his lips on saliva-riddled hisses. "If you do not know my master, then I shall question your presence in his home."

His master? Not her prey. She hadn't expected as much. This man was no threat to the people of France, no leader of mayhem and destruction. Though, Dominique had described him as weak and small. And he did bear a remarkable resemblance to a sewer rat. "I come with a message for your master."

"I shall relay it. Speak, I beseech you." He tapped the side of his head, tilted his face up. When he smiled the cracked flesh edging his mouth widened and began to seep. "Tell, tell!"

"It is only for your master's ears." She made sure he saw her hand play meaningfully across her sword hilt.

"Why should I admit you to my master's chambers? Eh? Who are you that you come in disguise and without introduction?"

"This mask is nothing more than protection against your master's foul trade. And would there had been guards at the gate, an introduction would have been granted."

"We've had a bit of a revolt lately." The foul miscreant rubbed his hands together in evil design. "Difficult to find employees who will serve in such a...delicate environment."

"As it is, I have come this far, you will now reward my efforts with an audience to Sammael de Morte."

"I will not."

She gripped her sword, but did not release it from its sheath of leather.

"You challenge me, stranger?"

She dodged, thrusting her right shoulder back to avoid the spittle that flew with each word this sorry rat uttered. "I come with word of the black knight. And I will thank you to keep your...bodily fluids...to yourself."

The man's brows rose, his smirk wobbled into a frown. A pustule split open near his eye and rank liquid oozed down his cheek.

"I know who the black knight is. I can describe him to your master."

"Indeed?" His body hunched, and his stringy hair dripping near his knees, the servant tilted his face up to study Sera. "You say so? Hmm..." He hobbled around, gifting her with his back, and muttered in a genial tone, "But where are my manners? Indeed I shall inform my master of your arrival. And I shall bring you tea while you wait."

"No—" Sera tried to protest any sort of liquid that might harbor her death, but the disgusting servant was out of sight before she even had a thought to see him move. Yet another person who could move with a swiftness unnatural.

Sera turned and scanned the rows of deadly plants, hoping to spy Dominique's deep violet eyes peering from between meshed fronds, even to see him wave reassurance.

Nothing.

Her heart sank to her queasy gut. Where was her protector?

"I thought I told you not to touch anything."

"Would you cease with impersonating the mother that never cared?" Baldwin snapped. "I'm dying here, San Juste." He grimaced as Dominique jerked his hand up to study the bubbling flesh.

"What did you do?"

"I was leaning against the wall, then remembered that wasn't such a wise thing. Oww!"

"Why weren't you wearing gloves?"

"I had an itch. Damn! Watch it, San Juste."

"You'll not die. Maybe lose the flesh padding your fingertips, but you should survive." He prodded the blisters mercilessly. "It appears to be flesh-eating, the poison, but it is not fast-acting. I've no clean water."

"The antidote you mixed up? Will this mask help? Ah! The pain, it really is eating my flesh. Bloody saints, why did I give St. Benedict's bone to Sera—San Juste!"

A swift fist to the squire's jaw provided much needed silence and calm. With Baldwin out, Dominique could tend the man's burns without struggle.

He slid a hand inside his jerkin and pulled out the leather bag containing the herbal antidote. He had to act fast. And not just to save the man, but to get back to Sera. She was all alone in a poisonous jungle.

The rattle of a wooden push-cart startled Sera from her jungle search. The boil- and spit-riddled servant pushed the makeshift roller up to her. She stumbled and landed on the stone bench right behind her calves.

The mismatched set of one black eye and one a milky white perused her with a greedy once-over as he poured dark liquid from a porcelain pot into a delicate white cup.

"You are familiar with tea?"

She shook her head. It mattered not what he poured; she had no intention of allowing one drop of that poison to cross her lips.

"It is imported from China. All the rage in Paris, I'm sure you know. King Henri favors it during his ritual bleedings. Go on, drink. Take down that silly mask you wear and drink!"

She'd be damned if she removed the mask. Sera leaned over the cup, but not too far. *Don't inhale any fumes,* Dominique had cautioned. Dark and still, the liquid sat in the cup. Didn't appear dangerous. Of course, what could prove harmful when ensconced in delicate bone china and decorated with painted blue cornflowers?

It had been a day since she'd put food to belly—no! The man had claimed the English Henri VI as his king; he was most definitely the enemy.

Sera pushed the cup away. "It is too hot. I shall wait for it to cool."

The servant tilted his head; quite a feat, considering he had to shift his shoulders and rearrange his entire spine to move his head from one side of his neck to the other. "You have not heard of tea. As well you are not aware of its restorative qualities."

"Have you informed your master I am come?"

"Do you know what one sip of this delightful drink can do?" He lifted her cup and sipped down a swallow. When he pulled the cup away a glisten of the dark liquid sparkled on his cracked lips. "It smoothes away the rough edges," he hissed in a strangely alluring tone that burrowed right through the steel cuirass Sera wore and worked its way to her heart. "What was once damaged, becomes new again."

What was once damaged…

Sera lifted a gloved fingertip to her throat. The edge of a steel scale scraped across the tightly-linked coif of hand-forged rings. Beneath the leather and mail she knew the thick scar glistened silver. No longer painful. But never again would the flesh be beautiful. Could this hideous excuse for a man possibly know that she had been damaged?

"Indeed," the servant snarled in snake-charming slowness. "Such a lovely voice you once possessed, my lady."

Sera jerked her hand away from her neck and speared the hideous freak with the evil eye. "How did you know——"

"You move with a grace that belies your disguise, woman."

She stood and reached to grip the obnoxious thing of blisters and boils, but just as her finger glanced over his leather jerkin, Sera wisely recoiled. "Bring me to your master! I tire of this silly entertainment."

"Yes, yes, all in precious time! Such ugliness in your raging voice. I will return, mistress. Such ugliness!"

He disappeared again without, it seemed, even opening the door behind him. He moved much the same as Dominique, stealthy and soundless. Preternatural in its eerie design.

Straining her vision, Sera peered through the moon-peep set into the door. No movement, not a trace of light in the darkened shadows that filled the crescent.

Pressing her palms to the cart, Sera cocked her head, listening, but could not judge any sound beyond the lilt of the music and the flutter of plant leaves. Were there musicians tucked in and about the foliage? Was the master's chamber just beyond that door, the dark inner rooms peopled with instruments to please him with sound, as only sex could have pleased Abaddon?

The liquid in the cup below her stopped wavering. Sera found her reflection staring up from the brown depths of steaming liquid. *It smoothes away the rough edges... Such ugliness!*

If that were true...

"He lies," came a voice from within the surrounding plants. Dominique. Unseen, but so close. His voice worked like a firm grip on Sera's shoulders.

"I know," she replied. Then she muttered to herself, "But there is nothing wrong with dreaming."

"Keep sharp."

"Where have you been?"

"Baldwin had a...situation. No worry, he is...er, resting. Concentrate, Sera. Fear or faith? Choose now."

Without hesitation she whispered, "Faith."

In a flurry of frenzied motion the servant was suddenly before her again. He moved with lightning speed to the edge of the patio, his heavy head barely lifting from his shoulder as he strained to peer over the vast jungle of destructive plants. "Who do you speak to?"

"Hmm—oh, myself. I was remarking on the beautiful plants."

With a graceful spin, he inclined a curious raise of brow on her.

Sera could only shrug and pray the man was not aware of Dominique's presence.

"The master will not see you."

"Impossible."

"You are foul. He wishes—"

"*I* am foul," Sera raged. "And yet he allows such an atrocity to serve him? He is just beyond that door, no? Move aside."

In another flash of ungauged motion, the servant stood with

a plucked rose, the stem oozing a clear substance down his wrist as he held it with the sweet reverence of a child who has brought home a posy for his mother. The poison did no more foul the man's flesh than—

"It is you!" Sera gasped. "You are Sammael de Morte."

He shrugged. "Tell me of the black knight and I might consider your safe passage from my home." He closed one eye and angled the open white eye on her. "Tell me lies, and this rose shall be your death."

Sera pressed the herb-soaked cloth against her mouth and nose. She thought to step back, but something would not allow it. Pride. Stupid audacity. The knowing that she was but one swing of her blade closer to ending this whole nightmare.

But she was not close enough to strike. And should he even see her move to her sword he could dash away with untold swiftness.

"He wears black armor," she said.

"If that is all you have, you die now." Sammael lifted the flower to reveal the liquid that seeped from its stem now flowed steadily, dripping from his elbow to splat at his feet. A narrow river had begun to trickle toward Sera's boots.

"He rides a black stallion and is but an hour from your home."

"Continue."

"Perhaps it is less than an hour."

"Does he ride alone?"

"Of course."

"You lie." His voice became hard and solid. All business now. "There are two others close by. I can *smell* them. Come out, frightened mice. You would allow a mere woman to face me alone?"

As Dominique rose from amidst the fern fronds, Sera bristled at the announcement that she was a mere woman. Did all men think alike? Damn them all! This one would suffer for his idiotic declaration.

She took a step, but the sound of bone clattering upon stone alerted her to the ground.

As she sensed Dominique's arrival behind her, Sera looked up to observe Sammael's observance of Baldwin's gift.

"What is that?" the poison master squealed.

"St. Benedict's toe bone," Sera said, a smirk irrepressible.

"The patron saint of poison victims?"

"Aye," she said, as she swept forward to retrieve the icon, "but I am not a victim—"

"Yet!" Sammael was much quicker. He claimed the prize with a victorious bark of power. "This relic will only serve once you've been poisoned, my sweet."

"Time to die," Dominique growled from behind Sera, and lunged forward. His sword did not even move the air before Sammael for the little man dashed away. But the mercenary had captured the man's attention.

"Who are you?" Sammael yelled from his new position atop the bench. No weapons glistened at his hip. He spat, but Dominique flung his arm up to block the deadly saliva from his face. "You've come to die this day, as well? You are both trapped within a cocoon of poison. There is no escape!"

"If there is an entrance," Dominique said, "there is escape."

Suddenly aware that she but stood there, observing the odd exchange between the two men, Sera kicked into action. Her sword was soundlessly released. She lifted her arms overhead and swung. St. Benedict's toe bone sailed past her ear, flicking her hair, as Sammael's death squeak ended as abruptly as his life.

With no mail to hinder her sword's path, de Morte's head was easily severed. Dominique dodged to avoid the flying skull. But Sera, still following the swing of her sword, was not quick enough. Spray of brilliant crimson coated her chest plate, mail coif, and neck. The sting of poison sizzled just below her jaw.

The last thing she heard as her body swayed and collapsed, was Dominique's cry, "No!"

❧ NINETEEN ❧

"She is wounded!" Dominique yelled, as the brisk outside air slammed into his face. "Hurry, we must extract the poison! Sammael's blood, it seeps through her flesh. Here, right next to the largest vein."

Baldwin, who had swiftly led them to safety, scrambled to Dominique's side. Both men knew the blood was poisoned. That it would do nothing less than kill Sera. She could have anywhere from hours to mere minutes. Already her lips were blue and her eyelids fluttered. Chill trembles shook her shoulders and knees and worked her jaw in a frantic chatter.

Baldwin plunged to his knees and touched Sera's boot. "Where is it? She has lost St. Benedict's toe bone! She is doomed!"

"Get water. Snow. Run!" Dominique barked, knowing it would serve Sera no good to have the merchant of doom wailing over her.

Baldwin's flat-soled leather boots slipped in the snow as he scrambled away, muttering oath after blue oath.

Dominique bowed his head and pressed it to Sera's forehead. She was hot, burning with fever. "I can't lose you, I can't!"

Her lips quivered against his cheek. "Dom-Dominique?"

"Do not tax your body. Every movement you make pushes the poison through your system. Remain still. I will not let you die."

He carefully removed the mail coif from her head and tossed it aside. *Chink.* His heartbeats pounded against his rib cage. *Boom, boom, boom.* The sound of tragedy was deafening. But he would not give up that easily. He would not let this woman die.

Because he loved her.

"Is—is he dead?"

"You killed him," he said. "Correctly."

Closing his eyes, Dominique drew on the inner glow that undulated within. Born of his ancestors and forged by his parents. It had been mere accident that he'd ever discovered the power of his glamour. 'Twas ignited by nothing more than wish.

He had never drawn so much from this cache until now. Feeling the power rise from his gut and envelop his being, Dominique ripped the padded wool jerkin away from Sera's shoulder and bent to press his mouth to her neck. But there was no wound, no tear in the flesh.

He reached for his dagger; not there. Baldwin had it.

Drawing out his sword, he gripped the blade and pressed the tip to Sera's flesh. Blood oozed down the blood-groove. He hated causing her more harm, but this was a necessary evil.

Blood and poison and anxiety slipped over his lips as Dominique worked upon Sera's flesh. He sucked out her tainted blood, drawing deeply, mining for the first threads of poison that he sensed already journeyed down her arm and the side of her torso. When his mouth filled with taint, he turned his head to the side and spat. An angry blossom of angel blood and demonic poison flowered the hoof-trampled snow.

He resumed his ministrations. Surrounding his and Sera's limp figure, he could feel the Faery power coruscate, gifting him with healing, curative saliva. It shimmered in his peripheral view, swirled before his face in a beguiling fog, and blinded him so that he had to close his eyes. Never before had he used his power in such a way.

He felt Sera's body jerk beneath his legs. Her arm snapped up to hold his head. The steel claws of her gauntlet spiked into the back of his scalp, but Dominique persisted. She clung as though the desire for life was there, whether or not she knew it.

He spat again, but this time did not taste the sulfuric taint of poison in the blood. Once more, to be sure.

"Dom…" she muttered. "What…where—it is gone." Heavy gasps for air, to breathe back in the life that had begun to leave.

Draw back in life, yes, don't stop.

"The poison. No more. I can feel—what are…what are you doing? Dominique!"

He pulled away, brushed a hand through the shimmer of dust that hovered in the winter-frosted air between them, but it was too late.

Wide-eyed and openmouthed, Sera had seen.

She pushed to her elbows. The wound on her neck was but a narrow slice, clean and poison-free.

"W-what is this?" She lifted a weary hand, pointed a finger through the coruscation. "*Mon Dieu,* Dominique, what are you?"

The final remnants of faery iridescence glistened and dissipated as condensation on a frigid eve.

"The poison is gone," he offered, ignoring her question—but knowing she knew. *Perhaps she has always known.* "I feared you would not make it."

"Thank you," she hastily snapped.

Then she gripped his cloak and pulled herself to her knees before him. Gone were all signs of weakness, of Sammael's violent touch. The angel warrior had emerged, unscathed, renewed, for the glimmer of Fate Dominique read in her eyes.

"What did I just see? That cloud of shimmering particles. It came from you, I know it did. Dominique?"

"You are up!" Baldwin dropped an armful of snow in a *splat* at Dominique's side and rushed to Sera. He pulled aside Sera's jerkin to check the wound. "He did it. You saved her," he said to Dominique. "I thought surely we had lost you. By God's good grace you are alive!"

As she brushed aside Baldwin's caring gestures, Sera did not break her gaze with Dominique. "Yes, but *how* did he do it? Have you seen this man work a strange magick before, Baldwin? Did you see the dust…the…the faery dust?" She tilted her head as she looked at Dominique in a new way. That of utter horror. A perfect frown drew upon her pale, winter-chilled lips. "Are you… Aye, you are." She pressed cold hands between the two of them, palms out as if to block, push away. "The violet eyes. Your movements…so fast, I— Why didn't you tell me you're a damned faery!"

Damned faery.

Indeed.

Dominique pushed up and walked away from the duo, intent on distancing himself from Sammael's nightmare castle and the accusing words of the most beguiling woman he'd ever met.

Now he was completely revealed. He felt naked, vulnerable.

And so, so lost to the one woman he could never possess.

No sooner had the closemouthed mercenary mounted and fixed Tor to a trail, than had three armored guards come charging out of Sammael's lair. Baldwin saw before anyone else. He scooped his hands under Sera's armpits, literally dragging her up from the ground, and pushed her toward Gryphon. "Can you ride?"

"I can." Sera pulled herself up onto the saddle. With a heel to Gryphon's flanks she galloped off behind Baldwin in a flurry of hoof-stirred snow. No pain whatsoever in her shoulder. But certain pain should they slow and allow Sammael's henchmen to lay a hand—or one of those glinting steel halberds—upon her head.

⚜ TWENTY ⚜

So Sammael had guards after all. Where had they been when their master had needed them most? Why did Sera care? 'Twas fortunate they had not shown until now. Or rather, fortune was not the word, but some sort of strange fate.

By the time they gained Dominique he had seen their pursuers and gestured toward an open field that bore but a single tree. "Take shelter!"

A huge plane tree, stripped of its summer finery, dominated the field. 'Twas massive. Where its branches became heavy with age, they dipped to the ground, tracing the circumference of the tree. Where those branches touched ground, new trees grew up in a fence of tenderlings. It was large enough for a mounted rider to pass beneath, but hardly a viable shelter, for the latticework of branches concealed nothing.

Sera opened her mouth to protest such feeble escape. In that instant, as Dominique looked back to see she would follow, she saw confidence flash in his eyes. *I will protect you.*

But for as urgent as she must act, and for as much as her heart-beats deafened her senses, she heard her conscience scream loud and clear. *What did you just witness? He is the very thing you most hate. A faery. Evil and wicked. Cruel mischief is his weapon. His kind destroyed your mother's happiness.*

No, another voice deep inside her argued. It came from her heart, and spoke in the damsel's gentle pleas. *There is no time to doubt, you may question him later. You do trust him.*

Indeed, there was no time to vacillate. She would sort out her conflicting emotions later.

Snow rimmed the circumference of the tree. Gryphon's steps slowed. The beast trampled through the fluffy new snowfall and under the bare branches that formed a lacing over the area of the tree. Sera ducked her head and slid off as Baldwin's mount paralleled hers. She gripped the reins of his horse.

Dwarfed inside the umbrella of this massive, ancient tree, she could only sigh in wonder. 'Twas exquisite shelter. But if they had entered, so then would their enemies.

"What now?" she called to Dominique, who dismounted with the grace of an eagle landing a nest. "They are but five hundred paces off. They can see us!"

"Not for long."

Dominique marched to the edge of the cleared ground and jammed his toes into the ridge of snow surrounding their makeshift shelter. He did not have to look to the approaching band of henchmen to know they would be on them in less than a minute. Urgency gushed through his veins as he raised his arms over his head and looked up through the network of branches that crissed and crossed and grew up to the sky all around them. When dressed in spring finery, this tree might resemble a huge green ball, so wide and expansive. Perfect.

From the very depths of his soul he whispered, "Shelter."

Dominique closed his eyes tight, gritted his jaw, and braced himself against the force of coruscation that shimmered out from his body.

Outside the skeletal canopy of branches the wind picked up and a flurry of side-sleeting snow whipped into a tornadic swirl.

Sera, for the moment transfixed on Dominique's actions, now snapped out of her frozen state and raced to the edge of the tree shelter. Every branch twinkled inside the swirl of blizzard that had suddenly curled up around their hiding spot. She could see the three riders, the powerful hind legs of their mounts pumping faster as they shot by. The scent of their malice was palpable, poisonous should she draw in a breath.

They did not see! Sammael's henchmen rode past the tree without a glance to the massive structure.

The wall of snow that circled the tree grew as the blizzard raged and the wind whistled in shrill screams. Sera reached out beyond the network of branches—but instantly pulled back. Her hand had been pummeled by the force of the blizzard. Yet here inside...

Sera turned to find Baldwin stood next to her, doing the same thing, testing the outer limits of their growing shelter. "Is it faery magick?"

"'Tis not of the sort I've seen."

She jerked a glance to the teen. He had *seen* faery magick at work? Exactly how much did the squire know about the mercenary?

Her anger re-igniting, Sera turned to find Dominique wrench out of his masterful pose. His knees buckled and the elegant knight collapsed, a shimmering veil of faery dust sifting up around him. 'Twas a beautiful moment, in a soul-clutching sort of way. But at the same time...

He is the enemy.

No! Sera released a tight fist. *You do not believe that. You cannot.*

Pumping her way to his side, Sera plunged into the tender blanket of snow and faery dust surrounding Dominique.

Behind her, Baldwin noticed, "It's covering the entire tree. We'll need light soon!"

Indeed the blizzard that swirled outside was building a wall up around the tree. The dome over the skeleton of branches was almost complete.

"Build a fire." Dominique snapped his eyes open and stretched an arm toward the massive trunk. "Break off some lower branches. Quickly!"

Baldwin jumped to do just that.

"It'll melt the walls." But Sera could no more concern herself with the shelter. 'Twas this man she worried for. He heaved and gasped to breathe normally. "Dominique? Are you…"

"Just a little drained. Sammael's men, have they passed?"

"Aye, but might they turn back when they realize they've missed us?"

"I should expect so, but we will be safe. They'll not see beyond the walls of glamour. Have you kindling?" he called to Baldwin.

Dominique turned on the ground, lifted up on his elbows, and spied the makeshift pile of branches Baldwin had snapped off just as the last disk of sky was closed out by the blizzard. Eerie illumination grayed their shelter, for the snow walls appeared not so much thick as strong.

"Stand back," Dominique commanded of the squire. With a flick of his fingers, he sent a spark to the kindling and a great blaze roared up, the tips of the flames licking at the lower branches, before settling to a calm fire. It provided light and warmth.

And further mystery.

Sera looked to Dominique. The mongoose eye was not appropriate; but neither could she summon the evil eye. The mercenary matched her wondering stare with his silent violet eyes. A brush of his hand over his forehead laid his hair away from his face.

With a nod, he promised her answers.

The horses, remarkably, hadn't been troubled by the strange happenings. Dominique had kicked up the snow to reveal a large patch of grass on the opposite side of the tree. It was brown and dry, but the beasts did not question the much-needed feast.

Baldwin, after again testing the snow wall of their shelter with a fist—and finding that the wall sealed up as quickly as he could retract—settled to a fetal ball on his wool cape before the fire and drifted to Nod within minutes.

The day had been long with their travel and adventures inside Sammael's lair; Sera would have been surprised had Baldwin lingered awake any longer. He had served the trio well, the newly dubbed knight who had ventured first into the poison master's death trap.

As had Dominique. He'd saved her from death. Sera drew a finger under her chin, trying to locate the imperceptible sword wound. She had felt the icy tendrils of poison flow from her neck, down, through her upper arm...and it had began to trail the opposite way, toward her heart. She'd felt the chilling hand of death, and had been defenseless, completely at the mercy of Sammael's posthumous power. Had Dominique not acted quickly, Sera did not want to consider the results.

She owed Dominique her life.

Feeling her fist tense into a ball, she corrected her thoughts. She owed this faery her life.

As Dominique settled beside her on the blanket she had laid out and stretched beyond her legs, Sera pulled the hood of her cloak close together before her throat. It was more difficult than she had hoped to finally mutter, "Thank you."

"You should cover up with the wool blanket in Baldwin's pack."

"I'm not cold," clattered out between her teeth. "And Baldwin is sitting on his pack. I think it keeps his backside warm."

"It is only you I am concerned for," Dominique said. "If you should take ill—"

"I would be but a single locust crouched before the mighty Lucifer," she offered with a short burst of false-humor. Anything to cover the dark confusion of emotions struggling inside.

"Indeed." He regarded her with a look that jettied past outer gazes and straight to her inner being. Gauging, testing that all was indeed as well as she claimed. Which it was not.

His face was red with cold, his eyelashes laced with delicate ice-spittle. She dared not ask about what had just happened. Dared not speak the title, faery, when its invocation could only dredge painful memories to the surface.

Too late for that, they had already surfaced. Now, to avoid them.

"When we arrive in Paris I shall purchase a room for a week," he offered.

"A week? We've got to strike now, while Lucifer has yet to hear of his brother's demise."

"You actually think the Dragon of the Dawn has not been preparing for your arrival since Satanas's death? He is not a fool, Seraphim." His gaze fixed to the bewitching flames, Dominique eased his hand absently along his thigh. "He will be prepared for you tonight, tomorrow, and for all the days to come."

"Then I haven't a chance."

The four de Mortes' deaths no longer held significance, only the remaining challenge of the final de Morte. The most powerful. The one man—demon—who had a personal stake in keeping her at bay. She leaned forward and caught her forehead in her palms. "I know Lucifer's power. Demon or not, he holds too much over me."

"The night of your family's death?"

She looked into the deep violet depths of Dominique's eyes, and fell, down, down, into the darkness. He knew so much about her, and she, still so little about him.

"I should have died at his hands that night."

"But you did not."

"He won't allow such mishap a second time."

"You won't give him a chance."

"I cannot do this myself, San Juste! I am but one woman. One cold and tired woman, who should, by right, be dead and buried alongside my family. Why did it have to be me?"

"I thought we were to keep it as a woman, not *but* a woman. Simply, a woman, beautiful and strong."

The press of Dominique's hand on her shoulder claimed her in an odd way. The wound on her neck did not pain her. She could not tell she'd even been poisoned. She had felt the burn of Dominique's blade as he'd cut her, but at the time, could do little but trust him.

I love you, Seraphim. He'd said that to her. A *faery* loved her!

He bit the middle finger of his glove and yanked it off, then pressed the backs of his fingers to her fire-burnished cheek. She flinched at the contact, but decided it would not do to turn away and dredge up the questions that just lingered at the edge of her tongue.

"You are almost there," he whispered. "You've come this far, overcome insurmountable challenges. Sera, Lucifer can be no stronger than you will allow him to be."

He smoothed a finger over a lock of her hair that had escaped the mail coif. For some odd reason the hair that had been singed from her head by Abaddon's fire beast had grown back with surprising rapidity. He was able to curl it once completely around his finger.

"If you give him your fear, your sorrow over what happened that night at your father's castle, then he will defeat you. But if you release it, release all the anger, the need for revenge—"

"What is left without revenge? I will never release the desire to sever that man's head from his neck. As he did to every member of my family. And the fear—"

"The fear will bring you down. I thought you chose faith?"

"Fear has chosen me. Much as I speak a brave front—" She swallowed—but the words would be spoken. "I *am* frightened, Dominique." She clasped her hands before her and blew out a heavy breath. "At first sight of Lucifer I shall recall him hovering over me, the sound of his evil laughter as he laid himself between my legs. How can I release the little girl that was shivering in the clutches of that demon?"

"Know that you fight for more than that little girl. You fight for all of France, every little child that has ever lost a parent by the cut of Lucifer's blade. Every woman who has been violated by him, every man who has been felled all in the name of that bastard's sick obsession."

"It is too much."

She pressed the heels of her palms hard against her closed eyes. The heat of the fire did not warm so much as remind now of the New Year's morn her life had so irrevocably been changed. Fire had consumed the castle d'Ange. Everywhere she had been within the past fortnight there had been fire. Fire destroying her home. Fire blazing in her enemy's chambers. Fire demons trying to kill her. She'd had enough!

The click of hematite alerted her that Dominique moved around in front of her. He touched her hands, beckoned them into his own. "What of the damsel?"

Sera met his eyes in a moment of stunned knowing. Inside the damsel fluttered and screamed, *Yes!*

How could he possibly know of that secret part she'd tried so desperately to hide?

"Does she not pine for release?" he wondered. "She wishes for salvation, I know it, as I know my own heart. Set her free, Seraphim. Return to innocence."

"Impossible. Once lost, innocence cannot be regained."

"Innocence is a language of the heart, Sera, not a thing that can be taken away. It can be damaged, but never stolen."

Aye, the damaged damsel did plead for release. She had been pleading since that first eve Sera had risen from her chamber floor and set upon locating her murdered family members. She had suppressed the damsel's voice then, stifled her insistent cries by playing the warrior. By hiding beneath mail and armor and the power of a well-thrust sword.

Only Dominique had touched the traces of her damsel's pleas. But what the damsel wanted from Dominique, and what Sera needed to do to repair her soul, were two very different things.

Maybe?

She nodded, sacrificed her fears to necessity. "I do need you to complete this quest. You must stand at my side. Please, Dominique, I beg your help."

"You will have me by your side. I just don't..."

"What is it? You accompanied me into Sammael's castle."

"But I could not swing the killing blow. *You* must carry this quest from beginning to end. You are the One with the connection."

"What connection can that possibly be? You said it was a blood connection. There is no relation between the d'Anges and the de Mortes."

"Maybe it is as simple that d'Ange blood flowed at Lucifer's blade."

"You don't believe that. If it were so, then hundreds in France would possess the same connection."

"True." Still kneeling before her, he bounced tentatively upon his toes. Deep thoughts kept his gaze from hers. "You have never encountered this man before that night?"

"Never." She touched his lips. The damsel quivered with longing. But the black knight cautioned against the new knowledge of Dominique's kind. What had he said about faeries being angel messengers? "Have you ever considered it might be you?"

"I was not there for Satanas and Mastema. Besides, it is impossible."

"I don't understand. Dominique, tell me all. I must know who you are, where you have come from. Who is this higher power that has sent you? Does it have anything to do with my accomplishing this mission alone?"

"You ask very much, Sera." He pressed his forehead to hers, the caress of his breath upon her nose a ridiculous sensual delight. She wanted to breathe in his warmth, draw it over her body and forget all about the hell that waited. "But you have given too much for me to deny you anything you should ask."

"You are a faery?"

"I am."

Those two simple words dropped Sera's heart to her gut. Her throat tightened and her fingers curled into fists. Then a heavy sigh rippled the tension from her body. It might have been mere exhaustion that made it so easy to relax, or just finally *knowing*.

A faery.

That explained the glitter of iridescent particles that had surrounded Dominique and herself as he'd sucked the poison from her body. Faery magick working to draw out the taint; and in turn keep him safe from its mortal effects. Simple enough to accept now, after she had battled four demons.

But acceptance did not change the fact that he was the enemy.

"Baldwin told me of your sister."

She tilted her head, worked her jaw in a hard grind. How easily the squire had gifted the enemy with her secrets.

But he would know her pain. "They stole Gossamer when she was in the cradle but one month. My mother was devastated."

"Not all faeries are so cruel."

At Dominique's noticeable wince, Sera had to question his sincerity. Was his truth a lie? It had to be. For she knew faeries to be malicious. And she would have this man know her heart now. They could not continue without complete truth.

"Cruelty can be measured in many forms. The faeries that stole my sister left a changeling in the cradle," she whispered, the fire drawing her gaze to stare upon the liquid amber motion. "It was a sickly, hideous creature."

Dominique's heavy intake of breath preceded an even heavier sigh. "Sera—"

"It died but three days later," she continued. "I've despised faeries since."

"And so the entire Faery race should take blame for that event? Sera, that is like saying all men are cruel because the de Mortes favor torture."

"The de Mortes are not men, they are demons. You said so yourself." She let out a hefty sight. "Perhaps you are right, though. I must not blame *all* faeries. But the changeling is an ugly, cruel thing. I can't imagine such a beast ever possessing kindness."

"Sera—"

"So you are not mortal…" she said, as she figured this out in her thoughts. "You have always been a faery?"

"Since…birth."

"You falter. What is it, Dominique?"

He pressed a hand to his forehead, squeezed his eyelids tight, then let out a sigh. "I am a changeling, Sera."

She could not disguise her rasping intake of breath.

"That same sort of hideous creature that was laid in your sister's cradle."

Changeling. A word whispered in horrified tones by women who had just given birth. Great rituals were performed for the months following the birth of a new infant to prevent losing the precious child to mischievous and spiteful faeries. Rowan branches were woven into the cradle and red ribbons worn about the infant's chest. Elsbeth and Marcil d'Ange had never given credence to the myth.

Had they but known…

Dominique continued. "My parents chose a mortal child over myself, so disgusted they were by my apparent horrid features."

"Horrid?" Did the man not possess a mirror? "Dominique, you are a beautiful man."

He flinched as she touched his face, but she did not relent. He was perfect in bone and flesh, not a scar, nor aberration to ever cause a turned eye. A handsome knight to be romanced in minstrel's song. And beyond the surface beauty lived an immense and loyal heart.

Indeed.

That she could have ever, for a moment, considered him cruel, even her enemy, was unthinkable now.

But he, a changeling? It was difficult to grasp.

"What could possibly have given your parents leave to reject you? Is there something you are not telling me? Have you a missing foot or an extra finger?"

He smirked, but couldn't help smile at her innocent inquiry.

"I was raised by mortals, Sera. Everything I know about the faery race has been gleaned from folklore and happenstance. I can only guess at the reason my faery parents had for placing me in a crib and dashing off with a mortal infant to raise as their own."

"My sister," she whispered.

"Indeed. I have nothing but sincerest compassion for your own parents. Though my mother's eyes were filled with love when she looked upon me, there was always that hidden fear, the lost longing. I imagine she never forgot her true child. Never…stopped wondering."

"My mother was never the same," Sera said. "She literally curled up into herself after Gossamer's abduction. I did never see happiness in her eyes after that. But your situation was very different from my family's. You survived, Dominique. I cannot believe you to be the same as the creature that was abandoned in my sister's place. You are not the same."

"But I am. Changeling is my name, shame and unknowing have been my constant companions for decades."

"Your faery parents could not have known you would be affected so. Aye, there must have been some reasonable explanation for them to abandon you."

"I have always assumed it my appearance, my dark hair and complexion."

"Your—your hair? That sounds too silly to comprehend."

"One thing I have learned over the years, faeries favor beauty above all. As I've said before, they are fair of face and hair. Blond tresses, the color of fresh wheat waving beneath a hot bright sun. Pale, moon-washed flesh, that of snow upon the silver waves of a pond."

"I guess I don't know a thing about faery lore…beyond the despicable."

"And my eyes," he offered. "All faeries have violet eyes that luminesce with an unnatural glow."

"But you've violet eyes!"

He turned to study her screwed up features. She looked directly into his eyes. Still she thought them anything but black? "They are black."

"They are violet. A deep, deep——"

"They are black as hell, no mistaking."

"Have you not looked in a mirror?"

"They are violet," offered a drowsy voice from the ground before the fire. Sera and Dominique both looked to Baldwin, who glanced up, shrugged a shoulder, then snuggled his head back against his chest. "Perhaps he cannot see what he does not wish to see."

"Nonsense." Dominique sat up, his knees bent and his elbows pointing his thighs. He spread his fingers to embrace the fire glow. "I have studied my eyes many a time in the hot springs behind my home."

Sera tilted Dominique's chin around to face her. "You would trust a pool of water over the word of me and my squire?"

"Knight!" Baldwin reminded from his cocoon.

"It is there, Dominique. I saw it the first time I laid eyes on you as you stood beneath the full moon worshipping its wide white splendor. A violet glow so deep and true one could not mistake it for black."

"Indeed?"

She nodded. His flesh, so warm and smooth, transferred a rush of heat through her fingers, arrowed right for her heart. That she could have for one moment considered him in measure with the cruel faeries who stole her sister shamed her now.

He spread his hands up over his face, and raked them back through his hair. "But they are so dark as to be nearly black."

She could not argue that. "Aye."

"Which is the only reason I can fathom that my parents should trade me for a mortal child. Why? Why else would my mother and father do such a thing? Abandon me to live amongst the mortals? To struggle to learn, hither and there, bits and pieces of my very nature?"

"Perhaps they expected you would die quickly, as did..." She must not speak of the horrors of her sister's abduction. It would not serve to improve the conditions of Dominique's own tortured heart.

"One thing I have learned," he said in fire-mesmerized whispers, "to the Faery, the mortal realm is lesser. And yet, my faery parents chose a mortal infant to be their own." He gripped a fist before him and lowered his head to his knees.

Sera sensed the struggle in Dominique's heart. Orphaned by his own kind for that which the faeries must consider an inferior race. Forced to learn of his heritage through what—faery tales and stories whispered by the spark of the midnight fire? But Dominique was perfect in every way imaginable. And it was not just his outer appearance. Sera had seen inside to the honorable, proud man—or rather, faery.

No matter what their reason, Dominique's parents had given up a true gift.

And she would not look upon him with the hatred she had carried in her heart for years. Damn, had she been so wrong all this time? To despise an entire race over one misfortunate happening?

"I'm sorry, Dominique," she whispered. "I'm just...very sorry."

"There is nothing to forgive. You have only reacted to expectations ingrained in you since you were very young. Children hold the memory of pain far longer than an adult. I know, the pain of my abandonment has fixed itself in my heart since I was but a child. And that is the reason I agreed to protect you." A heavy sigh lowered his shoulders. "I promised the Oracle to guide you through your quest, to protect you—though at the time I had no idea you were a woman—in exchange for the names and location of my real parents."

"Oh, Dominique." Sera slipped her fingers through his and pulled them to her breast. With her other hand she traced a strand of glitter-sparkled hair from his eye. "Then we must succeed. I should wish your greatest desire be granted you. You deserve as much."

"You are not angry with me?"

"Whatever for?"

"I am using your quest to gain information. This is but a self-serving mission."

"You think my quest is not? As you've said, you knew not who I was when you agreed to this. Even now, you hold no fealty to me."

"Don't say that, Sera. I pledge myself heart and soul to you." Fingers as warm as her heart slid up through her hair. The violet depths of his eyes sought out hers. Compassion and love burst from the colored orbs.

No, not cruel, this man, but a fine match to the damsel's heart.

"My original desires have changed," he said. "If serving my own wishes requires putting you in danger, it no longer matters that I learn the secret of my past. I don't think we should ride on to Paris."

"But Lucifer—"

"Let him rot in his lair, lying in wait for a fictional black knight that will never come."

"Are you having second thoughts about our ability to defeat Lucifer?"

"Mayhap." He pulled her hand to his lips and pressed a kiss to the back of her palm. A warm, thick kiss, possessive and needy. So, so right. "It is only because I can no longer fathom you risking your life. I almost lost you to Sammael's poison. I don't want to imagine a day spent without you, Sera."

He turned her wrist over, traced his finger along the blue symbol. A heavy sigh formed a cloud before him, even with the heat of the fire warming the air. "On the other hand, there are some things even I should not question."

"Dominique, what are you saying?"

He tapped the design on her wrist, formed a decisive moue with his lips. "Only this. I cannot lose you to a demon. I would forgo the knowledge I seek to keep you safe. Forever grounded on this earth."

He would give up so much, all he had ever pined for in his lifetime. "But it will not keep me safe. You said yourself, Lucifer will not rest until he sees me dead."

He fell back into the cushion of snow and wool cloak. Sparks snapped and flames flickered. Still the snow walls remained, unmelting against the skeleton of branches that braced the curved walls. "I should have prevented you from this insane quest the moment I discovered you had no knowledge the de Mortes are true demons."

"You could not have stopped me." Sera turned and lay on her side next to him. Her mail tunic *chinked* as she shuffled to lay close, drawing warmth from Dominique's body. "You're just lucky I did not kill you when I thought you to be Lucifer's mercenary."

"You certainly tried…"

"But would you have died with a slash of my sword? Are you immortal?"

"Not in the sense that I shall live forever. Perhaps centuries. I'm just not sure. I never had faery parents to teach me the ways of our kind."

Sera drew a finger along the side of Dominique's face, and traced the smudge of beard that stubbled his chin. "They must be very beautiful."

"Who?"

"Your faery parents."

He quirked a brow.

"You've the glamour of a knight errant, yet the eloquent darkness of a fallen angel."

Ah, yes, the darkness. Not so eloquent. Always it churned just out of reach. Until dawn. But the only angel fallen to earth this day was not even aware of her origins.

"You are the angel, Seraphim d'Ange."

She smiled. "You know, there are days that I feel so out of place. As if I had indeed fallen from—somewhere—and this earth is just so new. But when I am with you, like this, so quiet and peaceful, I feel right. Like this is my place and this is where I belong." She pressed a hand to his chest. "With you."

"You could love a faery?"

"I already do."

How bittersweet to hear her confession of love. For much as he returned the love, he knew it could never be more than fantasy. Happily ever after just wasn't possible.

"Tell me what it was you said about faeries," she said softly now.

"I don't recall."

"When we were making snow angels. You told me faeries were fair of face and hair, and that they did not flutter."

"Ah, yes," he said on a chuckle. "Something about them being angel messengers."

"Yes, that was it."

"Myth tells that the Faery are a liaison between the worlds of heaven and earth…" He startled himself with the words he'd spoken once before. But knowing what he knew now—

Sera's sleepy voice fluttered in his ear. "That sounds so romantic, the faeries leading the angels on an earthly quest."

Indeed. He'd not given the myth credence before. Could it possibly be truth?

A thought suddenly occurred to Dominique. If he really was a liaison of sorts, perhaps he could keep Sera from riding on to Lucifer? He could keep her forever by his side. The angel's mission would not be complete. She would not return to the heavens.

Yes?

Hell, what was he thinking? She had been born onto this earth for one purpose. Should she not complete her quest, countless thousands would continue to suffer under the de Morte reign of terror. That fact blazed strongly in Dominique's heart. And for as much as he wished to dowse that angry blaze, he knew control was completely out of his hands. He was just the liaison. Fate held all the cards.

Sera snuggled closer and said in a tender, lulled voice, "I do love you, Dominique."

Much as those words should have gratified, Dominique felt the pain of heartbreak tear through his heart and form a heavy stone right in the center. The fire sprite that had taken up residence days ago kicked and prodded and fought for victory—but he knew the final victory would find he and Seraphim's love for one another sacrificed for the good of France.

For now, he must simply enjoy Sera. While he could.

"I love you, too. And I feel much the same. That I belong with you." He leaned in and kissed her, spread his fingers over her leather hood, and released it from her head. Sera cringed as his fingertips ran over the flesh on the side of her head. "It has healed," he reassured, tracing a finger around the graceful shell of her ear. Not a hint of torment or scar. "The hair has even started to grow back. Rather quickly."

"Might I attribute that to faery magick?"

"Perhaps a little sprinkle."

"*Mon Dieu,* but it was you in Abaddon's castle. Did you cast a glamour upon me—my hair?"

He shrugged. "I saw the fear in your eyes, that mayhap you might not look the part. I wanted there to be no reason for Abaddon to refuse you. But your hair, it means nothing beyond outer decoration. You are beautiful to me, Sera. For it is here—" he pressed his open palm to her breast "—that the true beauty lies. You've a huge heart and strong will. It overwhelms me atimes."

"I'm sorry."

"No. You should not be. I like the feeling of being unable to judge, to contain, to determine just exactly what your next move shall be."

"You would be the first that will ever say such a thing."

"You fear finding someone else to love you?"

"Why must I seek someone else? Can I not have you?"

"I thought my acceptance of your proposal angered you? I am no man for romance, Sera. I just...don't know how to summon enchanting moments that will delight and beguile you." He nuzzled his nose against her throat, drawing his lips along her scar. He drew his mouth up to her ear and whispered, "All I can offer is this. I love you, Seraphim."

"But—but—"

"What? That cannot be?" he answered lightly. "Why? Because

you've a butcher for a barber and a penchant for beheading demons? Ha! That may be the very reason I love you so much. Or perhaps, it is this burning desire inside me. It is so new. But I know it was put there by your hand." A kiss to her lips, and he opened her mouth to speak softly against her breath. "Let's turn back. We can ride for England, Italy, China—somewhere far away where Lucifer will never find us."

"But I love France. It is my home."

"You no longer have a home. Save, the one in my heart."

"Oh, Dominique, and you say you don't know romance."

Her kiss was hot with the flames that burned beside them. As she pressed herself upon his body, Dominique followed Sera's movements and lay back in the snow. She straddled him without breaking their contact.

Sweet mighty enchantress of the black armor and pixy-fire hair. Her tunic chinked against his hard leather jerkin. But even through the armor and clothing he could perceive the need in her body. It shimmered and wavered and pulsed in rhythm to his own wants.

If Baldwin did not lie but a leap away he might strip the mail and underclothes from her limbs and join with her right here inside this snow-glittered faery tree.

"You know I would have you as my husband in an instant."

"But?"

"I can give you a week," she muttered as her kisses glanced his lips, sucked his lower lip, then opened his mouth wide.

A week? For what? Them? Did she know that this earth was not to be her final home?

"Lucifer lies in wait. We will make plans when we arrive in Paris, and then move in for the attack. After he is defeated, we discuss *us*. Can we do that?"

Dominique shook his head to separate his confused senses.

She was kissing him and planning battle tactics at the same time. How this woman's mind worked!

"Whatever my lady wishes. You are the commander on this mission. I am merely a mercenary hired to protect—"

"You are my partner, San Juste, eye for eye, and sword for sword, we are equals. Do you agree?"

Had Charles VII had Seraphim d'Ange on his muster the French would have defeated the English years ago.

"I agree. We take Lucifer down together, side by side. And then…"

She kissed his lips, greedily eyed his mouth. "And then?"

To spend forever, he wanted to say. Instead, he offered, "And then the world will see to putting all where they rightfully belong."

"I know where my place is."

"Indeed?"

"The first thing I want to do after Lucifer de Morte has been felled is to dive into your hot spring and lose this persistent chill from my soul. Wash away all the evil that has sluiced over my body."

"Then we've a bargain," he whispered into her mouth. "We ride at dawn."

"How will we know when it is dawn? The snow walls…"

"I always know the dawn," he said, feeling an unbidden frown pull the smile from his face. "It is an inner darkness that calls to me each day."

"Why darkness? The dawn is beautiful and light."

"I'm not sure why, Sera, only that it is. Midnight is the time of the faeries. But much as the dawn frightens me, I am compelled to greet it each day. That can only be another of the many reasons my parents chose to leave me to the mortal realm. I am not right—"

"You are right by me." She plunged against his mouth, kissing him hard, and ending all protest for the night. "Hold me until dawn then, beautiful knight of mine. And wake me with a kiss and your violet gaze."

❧TWENTY-ONE❧

He could sense the dawn birthing on the other side of the semilucent walls of snow braced against the withered branches of the plane tree. The closer Dominique rode to Paris the stronger the red burn roiled in his gut. The fire of dawn; a dark, evil hiss that voiced from his soul.

He released the clench tightening his jaw. A difficult action to control, the tension. Something out there waited in the mystery of the new day. It called to him.

It threatened to push him to the edge.

Behind and to the other side of their igloo, a rather unpleasant sound propelled him to seek Sera and Baldwin. As Dominique rounded the main trunk and spied Sera bent over at the edge of their sanctuary, Baldwin rushed over and skirted him back a few steps so they stood out of her peripheral view.

"Just a touch of the dog that bit her," Baldwin said. "Remnants of the poison to be sure. She'd rather you didn't see her this way. Give her some time alone, eh?"

"Of course, the poison—but I—"

Dominique had sucked every drop of poison from her system last eve. He knew it as he knew the alteration in nature was not aright. Had he not removed all the poison, Sera might not breathe this morn.

"There is no poison in her body now," he muttered to himself, as he stepped under a low branch and over to her side.

Had she taken ill from the cold? There was no cause for her sickness. A woman did not expel the contents of her stomach, unless...

Awareness delivered an invisible smack to Dominique's face. Could it be? But he hadn't—well, he'd considered it—but he had not.

Sera stood up from her knees, shakily, then smoothed a hand over her sweat-riddled hair. When she spied Dominique she swiped the back of her hand over her lips. Her tired blue eyes flittered this way and there, defying him to match her gaze. "Didn't Baldwin ask you to keep away?"

"You are not well?"

Ignoring her body language—the forced stiffness and dodging glances pleaded for him to keep his distance—Dominique walked right up to her. The hard glitter in her eye had been replaced by a murky tiredness and she smelled of sweet sweat.

He slipped a hand over her stomach, steadying her stance, yet at the same time, serving his own needs—delving. Immediately the answer to his curiosity became known. Beneath the mail minute vibrations of light echoed out from her belly. Dominique winced. Unmistakable in their rhythm, their meaning. Why hadn't he suspected before?

"Seraphim, you're—"

She pulled from him and crossed her arms over her chest,

but did not walk away. "Doesn't one always toss the cat after they've been poisoned?"

This new knowledge shook Dominique to the very core. Realizing she was a Power was one thing, but now this? Morgana's blood, in what sort of strange dream did he travel?

He must remain calm for Sera's sake. She did not know. Or perhaps she did, and chose not to tell him?

No, it was too early. It had been what—but a fortnight? Sera was still blessedly innocent of this knowledge.

"Indeed. Yes, it was just…remnants of the poison."

He allowed her to wander to Gryphon where the black steed nudged its nose into her cupped palm. Sera drew her hand over the gelding's neck, then laid her head aside the braided midnight mane. She turned and smiled at Dominique, a weak gesture. She yet did not feel well.

Without a doubt, Dominique knew poison had no hand in her weakness. And he sensed Seraphim hadn't a clue as to why she'd been sick this morning.

Now the only question was, did Lucifer know?

The travel-wearied trio passed through the eastern gates to Paris just as the city guards were preparing to bar the outside world from the entrails of the city. English guards. But, with offer of coin, they offered little resistance to allowing the threesome entrance.

The streets were calm and dark. The moon, high in the sky and half-waning, formed a silver scythe of light. It illumined the wet mud crushed into half-disk craters beneath their horses' hooves. Even filth could touch beauty under the glamorous eye of the moon.

Sera recalled the first night she had met Dominique as he'd stood romancing the full moon. To measure the size of the glowing orb this eve, a week had passed since then. Impossible to fathom when the passage of time seemed no more than a few nights.

Tonight Dominique rode with calm and veneration beneath the moon's watch, frequently looking up to bask in its glow. "The time of the faeries grows near," he commented, as their mounts clopped over the sloppy cobbles.

"Midnight?" Sera wondered.

"Yes. It is a time in which I feel my greatest strength."

Sera reached out and Dominique joined hands with her. Together they took the Rue du Vincennes with careful measure. Baldwin followed, Jude Thaddaeus's spine bone clutched in tight fingers. The eerie emptiness of the streets did not bode well in Sera's heart. Something was not aright this evening.

When the flutter of a charcoal-dark crow skimmed close by her face, Gryphon startled and reared up on his back legs. Sera felt her body answer gravity, and quickly tightened her thighs against the horse's muscled girth. Baldwin's shriek matched her own silent scream.

Gryphon's brief spell discomfited Sera. "Do you feel it?"

Dominique nodded, then whispered, "There is evil afoot." His eyes scanned the wall of a limestone building to their right; and to their left, the ink-silver surface of the Seine, her waters flowed quietly, holding tight to the trapped secrets she had captured from centuries of tortured souls. "But you see there." He pointed out a lone hawker pushing his covered cart, and there, a pair of mounted guards passed by the trio with a nod of their red-plumed hats. "Mayhap we are merely spooked."

"Spooked, haunted..." Baldwin rode between Dominique and Sera, turning his mount to face the two. Behind him the twin spires of Nôtre Dame speared the sky in devilish design. "My bones won't cease the shakes until I'm settled in a tavern with food in my belly and wine spilling over my lips."

"And a wench to warm your bed?"

He regarded Sera's knowing comment with a smirk and tapped the air with the bone. "You know it."

"There is a fine inn on the main isle," Dominique said, as he led the trio toward the Pont Nôtre Dame, a bridge at the far end of the island sandwiched between the left and right banks. "My father and I would stay there on our infrequent trips to the city to gather supplies. It's close to the cathedral."

The joy and warmth with which the bearded old tavern keeper welcomed Dominique into his closed inn re-ignited the fire in Sera's chilled heart. So normal and loved, he was. A faery. But not evil in her mind. And no different from she in his need for love and companionship.

The innkeeper introduced himself to Sera and Baldwin with a tilt of his bald head and a clap of his wide, clean hands. "You'll be hungry?"

Baldwin did not afford the time for an answer as he swept up the mug and trencher from the innkeeper's wife's hands and planted himself on the neatly swept floor before a smoldering hearth fire. Sera, feeling much better than she had this morning, also managed to consume all that was laid before her.

There was but the one room available. After an entire day on horseback, Sera would not allow either Baldwin or Dominique to play the martyr and sleep outside with the horses. The threesome would share the room.

That plan also tamped down the damsel's insistent longings. With an extra body close by, Sera knew she could resist Dominique's irresistible allure.

She won the straw pallet by mere proof of her gender, which she decided not to argue, for she was tired, and with a full belly,

the call of sleep pleaded strongly. Nôtre Dame's choir of feminine bells chimed the threesome to a weary quiet. Jacqueline,
Sera knew the largest bell to be named; her music, a gentle reassurance that though evil reigned, it would not for long. For
strength bore a feminine name and a proud, resonant voice.

As she closed her eyes and chased the swift dance of her
dreams, Sera was barely aware of the soft kiss that fell upon her
lips, and the whisper that bid her sweet dreams.

Soft crimson damask skimmed her bare legs and caressed her
breasts as she swirled about a sea of yellow coltsfoot behind her
father's castle. 'Twas not yet bright day, for the dawn had just
commenced upon the horizon.

A spin, her head tossed back and her long black hair kiting
out around her, found her facing a man clad in silver-studded
leather. The enigmatic figure smiled at her from under a fall of
wavy obsidian hair. Violet eyes glistened, and with an otherworldly glow the royal-tinted orbs spoke to her in whispered
tones.

"You mustn't celebrate the dawn, 'tis the midnight moon, the
time of the faeries, that beckons you. Only there will you be
safe."

Taken by this man's statement, Sera stopped spinning.

But she favored the sunrise. It gleamed upon the tree-jagged
horizon at this moment, thick golden beams washing over the
black line of treetops and valleys. 'Twas warm and bright, like
flame. 'Twas the color of heaven, a place long lost to her.

"I cannot protect you now," the faery-being whispered with
his eyes. He vanished in a dazzle of brilliant coruscation.

"I need no such protection!" Sera laughed in dulcet, blithe
tones. She hadn't a care! Protection? Nonsense.

As for the midnight, it was an entire day away. She skipped, and with a swipe of her hand through the tall plants, drew up fingers full of coltsfoot petals. "Bring the warm light of dawn upon me," she called to the lightening sky. "I desire the sun to brighten my day!"

And it seemed the rising sun crackled audibly as it rose in the sky. Sera saw a massive form fly overhead. Shadowed by the brilliant entrance of morning, its great wings spread in a glide as it circled. A graceful creature of scale and exquisite emerald color. With a pull down of its long neck, it plunged toward the color-saturated meadow.

'Twas a dragon that landed with a *thump* before her. The ground shook, loosening the petals from Sera's fingers. An exhalation of fragrant steam puffed from its wide nostrils.

She couldn't think to be frightened.

"What are you? You've come from the sun," she marveled, as the dragon breathed flame and glitter out from its emerald-rimmed nostrils.

"I," the beast declared in deep, heated tones, as it drew its torso up to reveal the pearl-scaled underbelly and the finely-veined underside of its webbed wings, "am the Dragon of the Dawn. Bringer of Light, the dark, beautiful, Fallen One."

It snapped its head down to Sera's level. The red eyes were as large as her head, slashed through the center from top to bottom by a narrow black pupil. It drew its wide, saliva-rimmed jaw back to reveal sharp, pointed rows of teeth. "I've come for you, black knight."

"B-black knight?" She stumbled backward, wasn't sure what the creature meant by invoking such a curious title. "I am b-but a woman. Be gone with you!"

"Ah, but I cannot leave my brethren."

"Your brethren?"

"We are connected." The dragon's drool splat upon the verdant ground, a hiss of steam spiraling up in its wake. "Do you not remember your own Fall? We are two of the same. With the sacrifice of your quest we shall then wed, and you will rule the dawn by my side."

"My—my fall?" Fragile stalks of coltsfoot snapped under the weight of Sera's skirts. Beneath her bare feet the ground began to tremble.

"You can never go back—fall up, so to speak. Content yourself with this earthly realm, black knight. And surrender your trust to my hands. Soon a new race shall begin, and we will take back our place as rulers. Leave heaven to Him. We desire this cruel, feeble, mortal realm."

"But, I am mortal—"

"Of a sort."

"No! Be gone with you, foul thing!"

"I cannot," the beast hissed, with a blink of its blood-red eye. "I am a part of you now, Seraphim. We will always be joined by a bond, throughout eternity…"

Sera startled awake. The hard, wood pallet pressed merciless numbness into her hips and shoulders. Her eyes slowly adjusted to the darkness. She lay in the room above the tavern. Close by, soft breaths reminded of her bunk-mates.

She blinked, drew the small window high upon the wall into focus. There loomed no emerald beast in the square of gray sky she could see outside. No flowers. Her attire *chinked* when she moved; no soft, flowing damask.

It had been a dream. Only a dream.

She closed her eyes and lay back, twining her fingers upon her stomach. The dragon had burst up from the dawn as if born of the light. She recognized the name it had given her now. 'Twas the moniker given to the final de Morte. Lucifer, Dragon of the Dawn, one of the Fallen Ones, the most beautiful angel in heaven. Tempted by the earthly delights of sin, he'd purposely fallen.

Fallen?

What had the term meant in her dream? The dragon had said *she* was one of the Fallen Ones?

Ah! She was tired, hallucinating horrid creatures. This quest had taxed her to the ends of her sensibilities.

The final challenge lie close at hand. And with that, she would answer her damaged soul's desire for cleansing.

Dragon or not, Lucifer de Morte's head would be hers.

Sera slept peacefully as Dominique and Baldwin wakened at the same time. They rose from the hard floor, eased the kinks from their aching muscles, and scruffed fingers through their hair.

With a dull nod of his head, Baldwin signaled he was going down to scavenge some food. "I'll see to the horses, as well." The reluctant knight closed the door behind him with a squeak.

Wiggling his toes into his boots, Dominique stretched his head back and across his shoulders. He'd not lain on his back. Ever since his battle with the giant locusts the muscles between his shoulder blades ached. He needed to be free of companions for but a moment to release and stretch.

Behind him the first rays of morning poked through the bubble-riddled aqua glass set into the window. Too damn early for any creature, he thought to himself. Curse the day the dawn decided to ride him. Just once he would like to sleep past the rising of the sun. He wasn't sure if it was possible, but what a dream that would be.

A glance to Sera's figure, sprawled on the pallet, made him smile. Now this woman could sleep through dawn, dinner, and a full-out assault, so dead to the world she became upon surrender to sleep.

Of course, he recalled Baldwin's account of finding Sera in her room after Lucifer had struck the castle d'Ange. She had slept through that attack. 'Twas good she had not been awake to witness the deaths of her family members.

But might she have averted Lucifer had she been armed and prepared? Had it been a part of the master plan? Certainly she was skilled enough to face such a challenge.

Dominique had to wonder. Sera had proven her mettle ten times over in the past week. But had she battled Lucifer, might she have unknowingly released the demon that night?

What he now knew of Sera and her condition made him glad she had slept until the last moment. Had she no memory whatsoever of her celestial life? What good would it serve her quest to allow her to wander the earth without clue to her true power? Could she possibly know? Was she expected to master the memory, or to triumph through mortal ways?

So many unanswered questions, not in the least, his own. Had Sera agreed to leave France, flee Lucifer's hand, he would have easily sacrificed the desire to have the answer he pined for. For the trade-off—Sera—would have been infinitely more valuable.

Shifting to his knees, Dominique crawled over to the side of the pallet where she lay. The hay was wilted and gray, but Sera hadn't given it any mind last eve when she'd plopped down and plunged to Nod.

She lay on her back, one leg bent, her arms splayed carelessly out from her sides. Though fully armed with dagger and sword, she was in no way prepared to lunge up and put an end to an attacker's strike. Dominique could not determine if her death-sleep was more a boon or a bother.

Himself, he slept with one eye open. One never knew what

lurked in the dark of night. What he wouldn't give for a peaceful sleep. Just once, to sleep past dawn. To possess Sera's knack for deep restorative sleep. Was that so much to ask for?

He smirked at his own folly, and leaned over her. Her lips were parted to allow the soft purr of sleep escape. Her belly rose and fell with every breath. An angel at rest, fire and vigor stirring in her gut, building and preparing, ready for challenge.

And now there was a new spark.

Placing his hand just over her stomach—but not touching—Dominique closed his eyes and drew himself out of the mortal clutch of his body to fuse his senses directly with Sera's. He could feel her breath moving in and out of her lungs, sliding easily up and down from chest to nose, tickling the new scar inside her throat with every trip.

And there was another.

Another heartbeat.

Mail *chinked*.

Dominique withdrew his hand to his gut as Sera turned to her side. She must have sensed his presence, for a smile curled her lips, and she whispered, "Dominique?"

"I was just watching you sleep. Are you warm enough?"

"Almost," she muttered, the smile still there. Her eyes remained closed, as if she would fight the dawn for as long as she could. "Such horrid—" *yawn* "—dreams, I've had. Hold me."

Hold me. The words shivered through Dominique's skull, echoing and reverberating like large stones cast about in a tornado. Tempting with each hit against his soul.

A temptation he could no longer resist.

Drawing himself upon the pallet and stretching out along Sera's body, he slipped one arm around her back and fit his length against hers.

He nuzzled his cheek aside her head, the tufts of her hair tickling his nose with the mingled scents of leather, winter, and woman. Slipping lower, he pressed his lips to her neck where just last night he'd fervently fed upon the poison. She initially cringed at the touch—perhaps his lips were cold—then let out a purr that told him she favored the contact.

"Angel," he whispered, without even questioning the label.

"Just Sera." She rolled to her back, her eyes opening to his wondering gaze. "Kiss me, Dominique. Make this day begin in a way I shall never forget, for I fear the night shall end in a way neither wishes to imagine."

He moved to lay on top of her, one knee pressed between her legs, their mail *scriffing* adjacent each other. "Don't think beyond the moment," he offered, knowing *he* should listen to such advice. He didn't want the night to come, for with it would bring the final de Morte. And Sera's departure.

But the dawn…it pressed his common sense. Made him imagine he deserved things he could not have. If the two of them could just remain in the moment…

Brushing his lips over hers, Dominique closed his eyes to the insistent flutter of want that tickled inside his brain, shuddered down his neck and shoulders, set his heart to a pleading tattoo, and wakened his loins to the passion contained in but a single kiss from an angel.

You must not.

But he did not listen to his conscience.

Sera's body stirred beneath his, answering the age-old way of nature. Her hips pressed against his, rubbing his leather braies and the hem of his mail tunic across his hardening cock. Squeezing his eyes shut, Dominique surrendered to the rush of desire and need that fired throughout his body.

Sera deepened their kiss, pressing her tongue over his lower lip and drawing it along the inside of his mouth. Hot and teasing, she slipped from his lower lip to his upper, then drew the tip across his tongue. An invitation to dance, to match the pulse of her heartbeat with his own, and to bring the solo rhythm pumping subtly in her hips to a duo.

He answered, gripping her tunic and easing it up over her hips. His fingers were rewarded with the hot, smooth texture of flesh. Blasphemy, he knew. But Sera's gasp erased further reluctance. Her primal gasp sucked a moan from deep within Dominique. Hardening the kiss, he drew up on his knees and pulled the mail tunic and, tugging the points free, yanked the wool undershirt over Sera's head.

She lay there in the pale light of the new day, her breasts exposed, the nipples rigid as ice pebbles, her smile taunting, yet promising. "Are you prepared to finish this quest, mercenary?"

Wicked woman.

"I am."

"Very well." She snuggled her hips up close to his. With an arc of her shoulders, which lifted her breasts into high mounds she silently pleaded his fealty.

Drawing his tongue over his lip, Dominique measured the teasing glint in her eye, then lowered his head to linger close to her breasts, yet not touching. His cock pounded for release, for satisfaction, for plunder.

Was he prepared for this quest into passion?

It had been a long time since he'd lain with a woman. Always, glamour had been used. He would not create a false impression with this woman. He must remain truthful. Though, he was still leery of revealing himself complete.

She did know he was Faery.

He touched his cloak, contemplated removing it, but did not. *Damn the truth. For now.* It *was* cold in the room. Instead he bowed to his mistress of temptation to serve her desires, hoping what little he could offer now would suffice.

Her nipple was a treat of utter indulgence as he slipped it back and forth between his lips and limned it with his tongue. Each stroke drew a gasp, a whimper, a satisfied groan from her mouth. Spurred by her vocal pleasure Dominique moved to the opposite nipple, and nipped and laved greedily. He spread a hand through her hair, relishing the spikes of darkness that teased at the sensitive spaces between his fingers. Drawing his hand over her face, he touched lightly upon her eyelids, skimmed the hard clean line of her nose, and traced the hot wetness of her mouth.

A nip to his finger startled. Dominique looked up from her breast. Sera had captured his hand with her fingers and sucked his thumb into her mouth. Oh…she was so wicked.

Sera flinched as a steel ring from Dominique's mail tunic grazed her moist nipple. So much to admire, to devour in this lovely man. She pressed a kiss to the meat of his palm and gasped, "I must feel you inside me. If you love me as you say, make the ultimate claim to my heart."

Dominique worked quickly, ripping the points from his shirt and codpiece, though he did not take the time to remove his cloak. Sera did not protest. There was a chill in the air. She just wanted him now. There would be time later to linger, to explore naked flesh—now was for bonding. He struggled to pull her chausses down her legs.

Sera reached down and found the exquisite hard shaft that jut from between his legs. A sword to slay her passions. Thrust mightily—

The vision of flames and shadowed horns playing across her chamber wall flashed in her head.

"No," she suddenly gasped. "Not this way." She shuffled out from under Dominique's body, at once fearful, and at the same time, so, so wanting. She wanted him, she did. But something wasn't right.

He damaged me, the damsel cried.

No, not Dominique, but Lucifer.

"Seraphim?" Obsidian strands of hair hung over his face, his violet eyes peering expectantly. He panted, as did she. Passion demanded its price.

She shook her head, chasing away the images, the damsel's trepidation. "It must be...different."

"Different from—ah. Indeed." He pulled himself alongside her and kissed her thigh. "I understand."

"You do?" She wasn't sure what to do. The room was cold, the lack of close contact had already brought a chill to her bones. "Because I'm not sure even I do. I want you, Dominique. I do—"

"But it must be different." He clasped his hands through hers and tugged so that she moved down on the pallet. As she moved, he shrugged up his shoulders so his head leaned against the wall. "You must be granted the control you did not have before. You cannot lie beneath me, you must...mount me."

"Oh, yes," she whispered, a smile curling her lips as the notion filled her head and chased away her fears. She would have the control this time. And what a man to offer such to her!

She swung a leg over Dominique's leg, straddling him. He did not move to touch her, so she reassured by taking his hand and placing it upon her breast. "I will have you now, Dominique San Juste. We will become one."

She moved her loins over his and guided his rigid member deep inside her heated folds. 'Twas no pain this time. Only pleasure. As their rhythm grew frenzied Sera closed her eyes and surrendered.

The damsel emerged, and released her voice in a splendid cry of triumph.

TWENTY-TWO

Baldwin did not return to the room until Dominique and Sera—lingering in each others arms after making love—had finally risen and dressed. Between kisses and caresses they pulled on the last piece of mail and accepted the loaf of rye bread Baldwin offered. Dominique excused himself to tend personal business. He led Sera to believe it was just a quick trip outside to relieve himself and pay the innkeeper, but after checking that Tor had been fed, he stepped around back of the stable. An alley no wider than the length of his arm sliced between two-story limestone buildings.

Closing his eyes and pressing the back of his head to the cold wall, Dominique had only to wait a few minutes before he sensed the otherworldly presence of the Oracle. The sweet fragrance followed, surrounding as a mist of fog enshrouds the newly risen ghosts of one's past.

"I have succumbed to my own base desires," Dominique said, his eyes closed.

Sera's scent lingered in his nose, the taste of her, on the tip of his tongue. The curves of her body remained imprinted in the whorls of his fingertips. Perfection. Too, too perfect.

"Damn the dawn and it's inexplicable hold it has on me! I've tainted her. I should have never continued this quest after seeing that symbol on her wrist."

"So you now know."

"You know that, too?" He searched the Oracle's eyes for surprise, some hint of unknowing, but found only subtle apprehension. "So much you have kept from me. And to know what I have done! I've taken a pure, heavenly form and tainted her with my lust."

"Can it not be love?"

"Love, lust, does it matter? She was not put on this earth to be treated in such a manner. Seraphim d'Ange lives only to bring Lucifer de Morte down. And when she has done so, she will then return whence she has come."

"Why say you that?" The Oracle shimmered closer, his constant gaze more discerning with a tilt of his head. "You cannot know her Fate."

"But I saw the mark on her wrist. She is an—"

"On this earth she is mortal. Those who have Fallen are then born anew. Remember only that, Dominique San Juste."

He had assumed as much. "Yes, but does she remember where she came from? Will she *ever* remember?"

"There will come a moment of Remembrance—brief, but telling—when she will recall her former life, her choice to Fall and fight Lucifer and his evil minions. It will come when she most needs it, but it will not last."

"How do you mean?"

"She will have the Remembrance, and then the knowledge will leave, as quickly as it arrived, never again to be excavated. Seraphim will always be but the mortal she was reborn to be."

"But that makes no sense at all!" Dominique fought the need to punch a fist into the stone wall of the tavern by clenching his fingers tight to his chest. "Why send a mortal to fight immortal demons?"

"The de Mortes do not become immortal until the fire demon is released. They are as Seraphim, Fallen to be born anew. Mere mortals, you see."

A frightening thought occurred to Dominique. "Does Lucifer know? Has he had the Remembrance?"

"I cannot say... Only that Seraphim needs you to complete her quest."

"And when she has succeeded?"

"You will know then what will be. You must now concentrate on the present. Delight in what you have, before it is too late."

"Delight? Ha! You speak of silly romantic pursuits when I am embroiled in a vicious holy war!" Dominique kicked the stone wall with a boot toe. "I've been seduced by that which I cannot have. Damn all the hells!" He swung on the Oracle. "And heaven, too!"

"You may not be of this mortal realm, but you guard your tongue, changeling."

Dominique drew in a breath. The Oracle had never addressed him so.

Wide brown eyes landed a fierce gaze upon him. "Do you really wish damnation to the heavens?"

Dominique tilted his head back and studied the cloud-littered sky. He could not see a mighty palace of gold and ivory floating in the gray velvet stratosphere. Could not even imagine a beautiful realm peopled with heavenly beings, harboring wings of white and haloes of gold.

But he need look no farther than the determined, hard blue gaze of Seraphim d'Ange to know that heaven did exist.

"Forgive me," he offered softly. "You are right, as usual. I will trust your wisdom, as I've no other source in which to place my faith."

"What of Seraphim?"

Dominique studied the Oracle with new wonder. He'd never thought of their situation that way before. Indeed, he could find a sort of faith in the presence of Seraphim d'Ange, a more personal, visceral faith. "She does give a man reason to trust in the power of faith. Faith in one's own strength. And I do choose faith over fear."

"It is always the wisest choice."

That Seraphim's blind faith had permeated his own confused beliefs was indeed a marvel. She had touched him in a special way. He lived only for her happiness now.

Damn his foolish need to learn of his Faery parents. Damn it all—no.

No. He *did* want that information. He must still cling to some part of himself. To lose himself completely to Sera would be dangerous. For if he lived only for her, how then would he know to give her happiness when he did not know it himself?

Yes, he would not surrender his soul completely in the pursuit of romance. Love was a partnership of two complete, yet distinctly separate souls. This he knew without question.

"Where will I find Lucifer's lair?"

"In the belly of Paris, the Marais. The entrance to his lair is but a small doorway painted in indigo and overlaid with gilded arabesques of a horrid nature. You cannot pass by without marking its presence."

"The final demon will die this night, I swear to it." Dominique smacked a fist into his palm, determination tightening his jaw. "But then, they are not demons, are they?"

"You suspect the de Mortes are—"

"Angels?"

The Oracle inclined his head. "Fallen from His grace. Deliberately."

"So this whole quest, this coming together of good and evil has been orchestrated for years? Even...decades?"

"When Lucifer and his brothers chose to Fall in pursuit of mortal pleasures, He recruited a Power to see they were punished."

"Seraphim is this Power," Dominique said, working through all this information as it ricocheted inside his brain. "I knew as much from the symbol on her wrist."

"Yes, a Power. One of the nine echelons of angels. The only angels He will allow to consort with mortals."

"But why so long? Why allow the de Mortes their decades long reign of terror? Could He not have sent her in adult form to battle them? And why without knowledge? Why only this Remembrance when it is most needed? Seraphim is tracking blindly through this quest with but the compulsion to avenge, yet she knows not the true reason."

"Without evil there cannot be good."

"Yes, yes, idiotic sayings which mean little. And are you of the same ilk? You know everything that happens between Sera and the de Mortes. Are you a Power as well?"

The Oracle closed his lips together softly and glanced up beyond the rooftops to the black veil of sky that bore no stars this eve. Enough to tell Dominique all he needed to know.

And how had *he* gotten involved in this almighty battle? He was a faery, a creature of the earth, and a changeling at that. What part in this holy war did he play? Was it what he had thought? That he was Sera's guide, the faery liaison leading the angel?

"You shall learn soon enough."

Dominique regarded the boy's knowing smirk. "I hate it when you do that."

"When you need to know, I will let you know. If you knew the things you knew now—then—the Fates would not have played your journey properly. Trust me, San Juste, all will come together. Much sooner than you can ever imagine."

An ominous foretelling. Dominique laid wager he would learn quickly, as the Oracle implied. But it could not be good, whatever should occur this dark eve. He felt the imminent evil touch his very bones with an icy shiver.

Drawing a deep breath through his nostrils, Dominique worked his sword inside its scabbard. He reached for his dagger; Baldwin still carried it. He must see to getting that back, for he would need all the weapons he could carry. He was ready to do battle. To end Lucifer de Morte's life, his bloody reign. And with that triumph he would then know where Sera really belonged. Whether on earth, or in the heavens, he would finally have that answer.

That Sera had been born to mortal parents—she *had* been born mortal. So what then was she?

"Mortal," the Oracle offered. "By God's grace."

"And what of the child she carries in her belly? Will that grow to be mortal or some demonic angel? That is it, isn't it? The connection!" Dominique stamped a boot against the crumbled stone at the bottom of the wall, and punched the air with his fist. "The blood connection between the One that would fell the demon de Mortes."

The Oracle glimmered, his image wavering and fading, before showing strongly. He nodded.

"So she really is?" Dominique asked, knowing the answer, but needing to be proven right. Or maybe, just maybe, wrong.

"There is *that* connection."

Damn. "She cannot face the demon alone."

"You were not hired to do any more than protect. Although——"

"And what is protection if I allow her to face Lucifer on her own?"

"You have…a point. That connection…" The Oracle's voice faded, as did his image. Just when Dominique thought the boy was leaving, he brightened and thrust a finger at Dominique's face. "I release you from your duty as protector. You've seen the black knight to Lucifer's playground. It is now your choice to either remain by her side and fight, or take the answers you wish and run."

He knew the exact words the messenger would speak before the lank, shivering soldier could crack open his dented helmet visor.

"Sammael is dead." Lucifer rolled a flawless ruby ball over the white damask cloth stretched on the table before him. Side to side the orb rolled, soundlessly ironing out a seam that had been missed by an inept servant. "Speak with my steward on the way out regarding payment for your services."

"Th-thank you, my lord." The man, somewhat taken aback that his message hadn't needed voice, backed from the room and pulled the door shut with his retreat.

Ruby beams sliced the air as the ball hit the door in the messenger's wake. The sound of glass hitting stone played a sweet melody in Lucifer's ears. He grinned, chuckled, then could no longer hold back the all-out laughter that bubbled up from his throat, deep and voluminous, and tinged with the wicked delight of success.

"I am next!" he declared to the raging fire that painted the room with an amber sheen. A wicked shadow of a horned creature danced across the fire-lit wall as Lucifer rose. Crossing his arms carefully over his broad chest, he approached the fire. The flames hypnotized his mortal eyes into a stare. Inside this shell of mortality the immortal demon rejoiced. Soon, it would be released. And his mortal servitude—punishment for his deliberate Fall—would finally be put to an end.

"Baldwin!"

Dominique rushed after the nimble-footed knight who strolled down the alleyway, whistling and jingling the bag of bones at his hip. A flock of scavenging ravens scattered as their path took them by the tavern's dump of rotting onions and a foul meat carcass. Just as Baldwin opened the door to enter the inn where they'd spent the night, the man turned and waved to Dominique.

"Wait!" Dominique yelled. "There is something I must tell you." He hooked an arm through his, and pulled Baldwin forcefully away from the doorway, into the shadows beneath the two-story building. A rat skittered along the high stone wall that separated the stable from the foul-smelling compost heap on the other side. "I must confide in you."

"Spit it out, man, Sera's waiting for me." He rubbed his hands together in surprisingly sanguine glee. "We strike tonight." The man had developed a bit of an immortality complex since passing through Sammael's lair.

"I know. Tonight."

Tonight. And then what? Forever? Or nothing ever again?

Dominique had refused the Oracle's offer of ending it all and walking away with the answers he so desired. He would see Sera to the bitter end. He wanted to be there when Fate played her hand. And his.

"It is about the connection." He glanced to both sides, assuring no one was within hearing range, and lowered his head, prompting Baldwin to do the same. "Do you remember I told you there was but one who could kill the de Morte demons, and that One had to have a blood connection to them?"

"Aye, but I still don't understand. How is Sera related to the de Mortes?"

"She's not related. Yet."

"Huh?"

"Remember yesterday morning beneath the plane tree? She was sick, but not from the poison."

"Sure she was. What else could it possibly have been?"

"There was not a drop of poison left in her body, squire, trust me."

"That's *Sir* Ortolano, if you please."

"Sir Ortolano, Sera was clean of Sammael's taint last night before we fled Meaux. I could sense she was well when I touched her body this morning. But I suspected something far more evil. I felt the light in her stomach."

"The light?" Baldwin scratched his jaw with dirty fingernails. "You confuse me atimes, San Juste."

"The beam of new life."

"Beam of—" His jaw dropped. He snapped it shut. "She's—"

"Yes."

"But—but you two haven't—I didn't think there was a chance—well, maybe this morning—I did linger in the tavern, thinking I shouldn't interrupt. How can this be?"

"It's de Morte's child, Baldwin. He propagated the blood connection the night he raped Seraphim. She carries de Morte blood in her belly."

The announcement swept over Baldwin's face in a fast play of horror, then nausea, then utter dread. "Hell."

"So there is bad news—" Dominique turned and pressed his back and head to the wall, paralleling his shoulders to Baldwin's "—and then—"

"Give me the bad news first," Baldwin said. "Not that anything could be much worse than giving birth to a demon baby. Ah, hell, will it be normal? I mean, will it look like a human?"

"I don't know."

Dominique didn't want to think that far into the future. Sera giving birth to Lucifer de Morte's child? The thought was too horrifying. On the other hand it would be a child born of two angels. Was that even possible?

"The de Mortes are angels, too. Fallen by choice, of course. Which I understand is an evil punishable by banishment from Heaven. But apparently there is release from that punishment, a release only granted by the One."

"You are speaking in strange tongues, San Juste."

"I know you don't believe that Sera is an angel—"

"I saw the mark when I gave her St. Benedict's bone. That proves nothing."

"To a mortal perhaps. But the de Mortes fell to earth, as well. Sera was sent to stop them—"

"Your eyes are bugging too far out of your skull, man." Baldwin assumed a presumptuous stance and spread his hand out between the two of them, all seriousness now. "Truth be told. What reason do you have to tell me such stories? If Sera was an angel sent to avenge these damned fallen angels, why the hell did she have to live two decades before doing so? You know the destruction the de Mortes have wrought upon France. No god I believe in would allow such."

"I don't understand that either, but it *is* true. Sera was reborn, as I understand it, into a mortal babe. Just as the de Mortes were, or so I assume. Anyway, the bad news is, that if Lucifer de Morte is unaware that Sera carries his child, he will have no reason to keep her alive. As soon as he sets eyes upon her, he will do everything in his power to slay the black knight, before she can slay him."

"Aye. So what is the good news?"

"I didn't say there was good news."

"But you just said—"

"You interrupted before I could finish. The even worse news is that if Lucifer is indeed aware of the child Sera carries, then he will very likely wish to keep her alive so she can give birth to his spawn."

"What are we going to do?" Baldwin whispered through sniffs. "We can't let her near that demon. Angel—demon—whatever the hell it is, it reeks of evil. So I'm calling it evil."

"A fair enough call. But we cannot run. Not forever. Lucifer will track Sera to all corners of the earth. She has to face him."

"Not alone?"

"I would never allow such. But she, and only she, must be the one that delivers the killing blow. I cannot do it. I've no blood tie to the man."

"Damn."

Indeed. It was then that the force of his emotion pushed beyond the mask of bravery and exploded out of Dominique's heart. He gripped Baldwin by the shoulders of his tattered tunic and pressed him against the wall. "I love her," Dominique gasped. "I would do anything to see she lives. I cannot imagine a life without her. Much as I know that cannot be so even if she does survive. *Mon Dieu,* but I love her."

"Baldwin?"

Both men stiffened at Sera's voice.

"Dominique?"

Dominique released Baldwin and the twosome turned to find Sera standing in the doorway to the inn. The firelight from across the room embraced her figure in a vibrant glow, gifting her with a surreal aura. That of an angel. He could not see her expression, for the back-light shadowed her face. Could not determine if she had heard his confession, or had only just come upon them.

"Evening draws upon us," she called. "It'll take time to track Lucifer. We must be going. I want to strike while it is dark."

"She didn't hear," Baldwin whispered imperceptibly. But loud enough to stab Dominique's heart.

"Yes, we should be off."

The squeeze upon Dominique's wrist was not seen by Sera as she turned and disappeared inside the inn. Dominique shrugged off Baldwin's fingers. But the man was insistent as he came around and stood before him.

"She *should* have heard." He squared his shoulders as Dominique made to push past him. "She needs to know exactly how you feel about her, before you advance to Lucifer's lair."

"I *have* told her I love her."

"Aye, but she took it as an easy answer to what you think she wants to hear. You must convince her of your love. It is the coward who will not bare his heart."

"And risk weakening Sera's resolve? She needs to be strong for this mission. I will not go spouting flowery proclamations, wilting her bravado for the sake of my own satisfaction."

"Baring your heart to Sera is what she needs right now. She loves you, too, Dominique, you know that."

Yes, she had said as much to him last night. Even knowing that he was of a race she had always despised. It could have been the passion speaking. Surely it was. "Mayhaps."

Baldwin released Dominique with a brisk shove. "You are both fools. What could be more powerful than the strength of two combined?"

"You speak of things that cannot be, Sir Ortolano." Marching past him, Dominique did hear the man's last words.

"And you are a coward."

·⚜ TWENTY-THREE ⚜·

The great rose window set into the south facade of Nôtre Dame filtered pale winter light in muted rays of indigo, carmine and viridian across the stone floor.

Sera marveled as she pulled off her gauntlets and splayed her fingers through a haze of red suspended in the air before her.

"Saint Chappelle drew our family on occasion," she whispered, as a twist of her hand painted her flesh in a rainbow. "But I've never been inside this great cathedral."

Dominique's spurs clicked on the floor, the *scriff* of metal across stone so loud as to seem sacrilege. "Neither have I." He walked down the central gangway toward the chancel.

Sera slid onto a bench and seated herself beside him with a *chink* of chain mail and a scrape of her sword across the floor. "This is not your faith?"

"Yes and no. My mortal parents were God-fearing, and as a child I followed their faith. But as I grew to my teen years my religious pursuits were drawn to nature, the death and rebirth of the seasons, the ebb and flow of the tides."

"The moon," she said, her bright gaze connecting with his and holding, caressing. "The time of the faeries?"

"Indeed. Though I had never the chance to learn the Faery rites. And I would not have dishonored my parents by pursuing such before them. But I cannot forgo the power of simple prayer instilled in me by my parents. Shall we?"

Together they knelt and pressed their clasped hands to fore-heads. Sera said a prayer to the blessed mother and beseeched the saints to lend an ear. She then asked for strength and per-severance. "And a bit of faery glamour," she added, with a grin at Dominique.

"I'll do what I can," he offered, and kissed the tip of her nose.

Then he remembered Baldwin's warning. *You are a coward.*

No, he was not. He was merely being cautious. He'd made the decision to be truthful with Sera; he would continue that. As best he could. He had not been completely truthful with her this morning as they had made love. There was still the one thing he was leery to reveal.

"You know that I do love you, Seraphim?"

She kissed him on the mouth, a full, gorgeous gift of passion. "I love you, too."

"You can love such a creature as myself?"

"Creature?" She quirked a brow, then rolled her eyes. "Enough of feeling sorry for yourself, changeling. To be truthful, I believe I've loved you from the moment I saw you romancing the moon outside Pontoise. If you can love a woman such as me, I can cer-tainly love a man such as you."

"I am honored to have your heart."

"Just don't drop it," she said, in a light tone. "It is a bit frag-ile right now."

"I'll use utmost care." He pressed a hand to her breast, his fingers conforming to fit the softness that he knew lived beneath the hard circles of linked mail. "I just wish I had not offended you earlier, in regards to your designs on marriage."

She nodded, gave a resigning shrug. "I've decided I should not require you to follow my own designs on the perfect proposal. That would make me like so many other desperate maidens. And I am not like other women, nor am I desperate."

"This I know. But there is your father's land."

"Yes, I should not wish to relinquish it to the English. So I just need to know…do you still agree to marry me when de Morte has fallen?"

Dominique's sigh bulleted through Sera's mail and tunic and punched a perfect hole through her heart. Right there, beneath his deceptively tender touch.

"Dominique? Tell me you have not changed your mind?"

He lifted her hand to his lips and pressed a seal there, then turned her fingers about to study her wrist. The blue marking bothered him, she knew. How could he possibly fear a devil's mark when he had so bravely chosen to stand at her side?

"I am not of the devil, Dominique."

"Of course you're not. But I have come to terms with the fact that we may not be together for much longer," he said, "so I shall enjoy this time we do have. Much as it requires defeating one particularly nasty demon."

"You don't believe we will be together after this. That's why you cannot accept my proposal."

"With all my heart, I wish to walk away from Lucifer's ashes with you by my side."

Dominique's face screwed into curious marvel as he looked her over. But it settled to dead serious too quickly as he turned toward the chancel and pressed his hands together in prayer.

"But no one can know their fate." With that, he bowed his head, and as he pressed his clasped fingers to his forehead, closed his eyes.

Conversation ended, by means of prayer.

Sera wondered what the moonlit knight prayed for. Perhaps gaining the knowledge regarding his faery parents burned so brightly he could not concern himself with petty measures such as marriage. Truly, that knowledge had been the paramount element in his taking on this quest. She should not burden him with even more to think on.

But as Sera settled to a pose of clasped hands and bowed head, she could not concentrate on prayer. Why had Dominique's parents abandoned him? *Had* he been hideous as the changeling that had been placed in her sister's cradle? And then grown to a fine and handsome man? It didn't seem feasible. She might like an answer to the question of his abandonment as well.

On the other hand, what good could it possibly serve to ask now of his past?

She moved a little closer, until their elbows and shoulders touched. Even through armor she could divine the tremor of his heart—quick and sure. It set her own heart to a desirous pulse. "Dominique," she whispered.

"Yes, love?"

He loved her, and yet…he made her feel as if he would not, could not, be there for her.

"There is something I must ask…but I don't wish to offend." She looked into his eyes. They were strangely dark now, not a glint of the royal violet she so often saw. It could be the shadows they knelt in, for the colors from the windows beamed high over their heads.

The warmth of his hand pressing over hers prompted her to speak.

"I was just wondering…regarding your own quest for answers. Why is it so important to know *why?* Now? After all this time?"

He tilted his head back, closed his eyes, and squeezed her hand gently. So difficult to face her, she sensed.

"If 'tis too personal…"

"It will just give me closure. Perhaps. Some sense of…belonging, when all my life I have always felt I stood just at the edge 'atween two worlds. Can you understand that?"

She nodded. "I know the feeling of not truly belonging, of being set apart from everyone else. But I've always been blessed to know I have a home and loving parents."

"I, too, had as much. But they were never able to teach me the ways of my kind. And even my mother, bless her soul, would often give me that downcast look, a little shake of her head, which meant, 'So sorry, I just don't know.'"

Dominique lifted Sera's hand to his face. Holding her palm cupped open, he smoothed it across his cheek and pressed it to the warmth that flowed within him. "We would sit for long minutes atimes, just like this. I'd hold her hand, trace the purple lines that had forged deeply into her palm by hard labor. She hadn't the soft whorls anymore, for years of work and toil had chiseled them away. Didn't matter, I loved my mother's hands."

Sera closed her eyes and laid her head against Dominique's shoulder. So right, this moment. Quiet, yet telling, beneath the rainbow haze of holy shadows.

"I'd press her palm to my cheek, like this, and just sit there, drawing in her essence." He closed his eyes and slipped into memory. "I could feel her difference, as I can feel yours—it's a definite speed the mortal heartbeat, much slower than my own.

"And then she would always say, 'So sorry, Dominique, if I

knew what you needed, I should move heaven and earth to grant it.' My heart would always clench at that moment. I so hated that my mother had to feel insufficient. She was so wise. I did need something."

He pulled Sera's hand to his mouth and pressed a hot, breathy kiss there. "I think I still do need something."

"The Oracle holds the names of your faery parents?" Sera whispered.

"He will grant me the answer when your quest is complete."

"Then you shall have that which you need, Dominique. I will do everything in my power to make it so."

She stood up, slowly pulled her hand from his cheek, then leaned in to press a kiss just below his eye. Long lashes fluttered across her nose. A faery kiss.

Without a word, Sera turned to exit the cathedral.

Indeed, the world was not right.

But it would be, soon enough.

The day was oddly warm, the sun bright as a copper shield as it settled closer to the horizon. "It'll be dark soon," Dominique commented, as they strode out from Nôtre Dame's west portal. "We should find Lucifer's lair before then. The horses—" He turned around on the slush-littered cobbles, spying the horses where they'd left them. "Where is our newly dubbed knight?"

With a sense of dread riding her spine, Sera rushed to Gryphon and Baldwin's mount, and found they had been secured to a ring with Baldwin's usual hitch knot. Tor stood close by, never needing restraint, for he was not Dominique's possession as the mercenary had explained.

Baldwin was nowhere to be seen. There were no taverns on this street, though she could hear the bawdy male calls from some establishment not far away. If that man had even thought to seek out a wench— "Baldwin!"

The press of Dominique's hand over her mouth confused Sera, until he pointed to the ground. Many sets of footprints in the fresh-fallen snow. And not just those of three people dismounting and two going on into the cathedral. A deep trench dredged through mud and snow-slush—like a man's feet, as he'd been dragged away.

"There was a struggle," she surmised. "Someone has taken Baldwin? I don't understand."

"I'll give you one guess as to who that was. Come!" Dominique quickly mounted Tor. "To the Marais. No doubt Lucifer has taken Baldwin as a means of bait."

"Bait?" Sera mounted Gryphon with absent regard, and secured her gauntlets. "That makes no sense. The man must know Sammael is dead. He is next. There's no need to lure the black knight."

"Perhaps he wishes to stack the odds in his favor in order to win the game between good and evil."

Much as he would have preferred to meet the black knight in battle this morn, with the dawn fresh and his strength at its peak, Lucifer did not mind so much now that he had a bargaining chip. Rather, a sacrificial lamb.

Sammael's henchmen had also reported the trio that rode for Paris. One of the three, the self-confessed black knight.

He paced before the bound captive. One eye was closed and swollen to a purple bloom, his lower lip was cracked. Lucifer hadn't been particular about the means of capture; 'twas a good thing his minions had not killed the boy. Though he was close to death, wasn't he?

A drop of blood trickled from the boy's nose and barely

missed splattering Lucifer's leather boot. He was surprisingly brave, considering the red hot tongs that Lucifer dangled cloyingly from the tip of his fingers.

"I shall repeat myself but once," Lucifer said. The upswing of the tongs almost touched the boy's chest—almost. "Who is the black knight? It is that man you travel with, am I correct?"

He did not even cringe to avoid the penduluming tongs. He could not, for the tightness of his bonds and the stone wall directly behind him. "You'll have to eviscerate me, and even then I won't talk."

"Evisceration," Lucifer drew out in slow syllables. He tilted his head, considering. "Tempting. Perhaps I'll save that for later."

This time he allowed the tongs to touch the boy's wool tunic, and in the instant of contact, the red metal singed through fabric and produced the most delicious aroma of burned flesh. The boy let out a yelp that caused the bats overhead to shiver in a mass of skittering black leather wings.

"The next swing will land just under your chin, boy, are you ready?"

"No!"

"You are ready to talk?"

"Damn! Mother of Mercy!"

"Come, child, there's no one to hear your blasphemous prayers down here."

"You'll meet the black knight soon enough, for the mercenary is determined to see him here."

"Ah yes, the mercenary. Fine man, he. He's one of my own, you know?"

"No, that's not—" The shock on the boy's face was a remarkable thing. His eyes bugged—rather, the one that was not swollen shut. "Dominique San Juste works for you?"

"I know not his name, only that he will do my bidding, and

deliver my release right to my hands. But which of the two is it? The man you started your quest with, or the man who joined it later?"

"Go to hell!"

"Indeed? I cannot wait!"

With that, Lucifer thrust the tong into the boy's gut, drilling it in until it stayed there, sizzling away at flesh and entrails.

"We've no time now," Dominique said to the vision of the Oracle that hovered before he and Sera. "Lucifer's lair." He pointed to the door ahead of them that sat like the door to the end of the world. Bright indigo lacquer coated it in oddly liquid design. Raised carvings of demons and angels were gilded—

Dominique stepped up to the door, placed a hand carefully upon one of the carved angels. "Angels?" he wondered aloud, as the other two silently observed. "Of course." He smoothed his palm over the horned head of a particularly nasty demon possessed of a grin that distorted its face. "They are Fallen, too."

Sera looked from the Oracle to Dominique. "What is all this talk of falling?"

"He casts out misfits and naysayers from his minions," the Oracle said on a shimmer. "As Satan Fell to the earth, so have millions of others. Though…the rebellious de Mortes purposely chose to Fall."

Sera approached Dominique and peered at the carvings. "You try to convince me that Lucifer and his brothers are angels fallen from heaven? That is idiotic!"

"As are faeries?" Dominique crossed his arms over his chest and met Sera's gaze. She must not go into Lucifer's lair with one shred of naiveté clinging to her soul. All fear must be banished before it was too late.

"But to fall," she said slowly. "Why stop here? Would they not fall to the bowels of hell to serve Satan?"

"I don't understand, but I can believe," Dominique stated.

Now would be a good time to tell Sera of her own falling—but no. Would that knowledge heed her in her final match against Lucifer, or prove a boon? He had yet to decide. Besides, she would never believe him. Never.

The Oracle had said there would be a time of Remembrance. He prayed with all his being that remembrance would come soon. Damn soon.

"It is time," the Oracle said. He floated above the slick cobbles, his indigo robes not even lighting on the glistening wet ground. "I promised Dominique an answer to his decades-old question in return for his accepting this mission. Now I shall give it."

"You've come to tell Dominique who his parents are?" Sera gave Dominique a bright smile.

The Oracle nodded.

"It can wait until Lucifer is dead, as we initially agreed." Dominique made to push by the boy, but he was stopped by a force that did not touch any part of his body so much as coax his brain to cooperate.

It didn't matter anymore who his parents were, or why they had given him up. It really didn't. Sera made him believe in himself. She infused in him a unique brand of faith that was all her own. If only for the length of time it would take to defeat Lucifer. After that, he would learn to cope without her by his side.

Maybe.

The Oracle stood between the indigo door and Dominique. He gave no intention of shimmering away. Try and step through me, he challenged with a bow of his head.

"You choose to tell me now because you foresee this quest bringing my death?"

"Nothing in this mortal realm can ever be known for certain."

So indeed, the Oracle did suspect Dominique would die inside Lucifer's lair.

Dominique exhaled heavily. If his life would be taken so that Sera might live...then so be it. "Very well, then. Who are they? Who are the parents who hated their son so much they would give him up for a mere mortal?"

"Your mother is known as Syr."

Syr? A name. Dominique swallowed, felt his mouth grow dry. Finally a name. All these years...and to now know her name.

He nodded that the Oracle continue.

"She is a beautiful faery who lives in the Valois Wood."

"That's where I—"

"Yes. She keeps watch over you."

"But—"Too incredible to process. "All these years?"

The Oracle nodded. "Syr is kind, yet ailing. She is not long for this mortal earth. She was cast out of Faery when she made you a changeling without permission from the elders."

"Faery?"

"It is the realm of your kind. Another dimension upon this very earth that cannot be seen with mortal eyes."

"I have felt it—it shimmers all about. But I have also felt entrance an impossibility. I suppose I will never see it?"

"Most likely not."

"Will I have a chance to see her—Syr—before..." He clenched his fingers into his palm. Of course not. His death would come at the hands of Lucifer de Morte.

Dominique felt his heart ricochet up to his throat. Syr. His mother. Alive, and had always been close. So close. He wasn't certain whether anger or joy stormed for release. But some emotion pried for freedom in the nervous jitter of his limbs. "Is there time yet to see her?"

"Perhaps. But you wish to know of your father as well."

So much information. So quickly. He needed to think it through, to comprehend his mother's presence. *Syr.* Such a beautiful name…

But he wanted to hear it all. "My father does not live with my mother?"

"He never has. Theirs was a brief affair. I dare say, it was Syr's choice to leave your father, and…to ensure that he never saw you by exchanging you with a mortal infant. You know…the mortal child perished before his first year."

"I care not for the child that replaced me—"

Dominique felt Sera's body stiffen beside his. Her sister— She had suffered much the same fate. How cruel that he did not now care.

"It died but months after Syr had claimed it as her own. She knew the boy infant hadn't more than a few months' breath in its sickly body. That is why she chose to take him from the San Juste couple."

Dominique stiffened. Sera slipped a hand through his loose fingers. Her presence calmed the darkness that usually raged at dawn. "She purposely selected a child that was to soon die?"

The Oracle inclined his head.

"That doesn't make sense. Why exchange her own son for a fragile mortal infant? Did she despise me so much? It must be more than just my appearance. Seraphim has said she sees the violet in my eyes."

"Oftentimes when a changeling has been found in an infant's cradle, it is because that mortal infant would not have survived beyond its first birthday. It is the way of nature."

Dominique could feel the perceptible change in Sera's body, her shoulders straightened, her fingers squeezed gently around his. To know such a thing was surely the Oracle's gift to her.

"Your mother had only your best interest in mind when she left you in the San Justes' home. She knew the couple would accept you as their own. She also knew that your identity would then be safe from your father."

"Why was it so important to conceal me from the man who fathered me? I don't understand?"

The Oracle hovered forward. He lifted Sera's hand and placed it upon Dominique's shoulder. The boy's warm smile of the ages enticed her to lay her head upon Dominique's shoulder as well. A comforting gesture. Preparation.

"Dominique," the Oracle said. "Your father is Lucifer de Morte."

TWENTY-FOUR

"Does that mean I have a fire demon raging within me?"

Sera tried to embrace Dominique, but he pushed out of her arms, stumbled backward across the cobbles, and pressed his fists against his forehead. "What will happen if *I* am not beheaded?"

"Dominique, don't say that."

"But I am half dem—no..." He lowered his voice and murmured to himself as he thought this all through.

But Sera heard it all.

"Lucifer Fell. It is not demon blood that courses through my veins, but...*mon Dieu.*" His eyes blazed in the darkness, the moon catching like diamonds in the blackness of those orbs. Black. Not at all violet right now. "This knowledge explains so much. All these years, the darkness within me—it is because my father is this murderous beast!"

"Your father's actions have not a thing to do with your nature. Damn you, San Juste, can't you see?" Sera stepped around in front of him, trying to catch his gaze. "You are only what you wish to be. You cannot be evil because you just now discovered your father is such. You were raised by kind mortals who loved and cherished you. It is their legacy that breeds within your heart, you know that. Do not allow this anger, this evil, to bore into your body and toy with your soul. Fight it!"

As she pressed her body the length of his, Dominique allowed his body to go limp beside hers. She snuggled her cheek aside his and joined her fingers within his at his sides.

"You would not allow vengeance to blacken my soul," she whispered. "Lucifer is only as strong as I will allow him to be. As well for you, you must not succumb."

Her tears dripped onto his cheek, but she did not sniff them away. A very long time passed as she gauged his breaths, listening as they calmed, and his muscles relaxed, releasing his strife. Hopefully.

"Sera, my angel." He closed his eyes as he whispered the prayerlike words over and over. They entered her thoughts as dreams on the wind. "You are my angel, you are my angel, always ever."

Yes, he must believe. He must pound that truth into his brain. His father had had no control over Dominique's life thus far; he would not allow Lucifer de Morte to latch onto his soul now. *Do not succumb.*

Could Seraphim have been sent for him, just as he had been hired to protect her? It was a ridiculous notion. To put himself on such an important pedestal. It was not for him she walked this earth.

But it was for her he walked the earth. *You are the liaison...*

Forcing aside his own troubles, Dominique resumed the courage he must have in Sera's presence. "I have sworn to protect you. I will not allow anyone to cause you further harm. That is a pledge that I will not—I *cannot*—break."

The trace of her fingers across his lips, over his jaw, worked like unseasonable winter flakes dusting the surface of a frozen pond. But a promise of beauty to an icy surface. She asked, "What will you do when you come face to face with him?"

"I don't know."

Could he look into the eyes that had been born to his own face? Was Lucifer even aware he had a son? Surely, he must not know. The Oracle said his mother had switched him at birth to keep Lucifer from knowing. But then, the demon lord must be aware his lover had had a child.

A child that had died. That is all the de Morte must know. And that may serve to Dominique's advantage.

"I cannot know what my reaction to Lucifer de Morte will be until I have looked upon his face and judged him myself. Will you allow me one moment to do so when finally we come upon him?"

"I will."

A hefty sigh released the remnants of his shock to the frigid air. It would not do to dwell on that which he could not change. "Then we should continue."

"Aye."

"But first." Dominique tugged on Sera's hand, bringing her to stand close. Her bright blue eyes glistened with the love and respect he craved. She was so strong. *So innocent of the truth.* If that he could be so uncorrupted, if his question might never have been answered…

But he had gotten the truth he'd pined for over the decades. And now he must accept and move on.

He pressed his hand to Sera's heart. "I beseech you to grant me some of this."

"What?"

"Your fire." He slipped his hand up under the armor and

spread his fingers to gauge her powerful heartbeats against his palm. Angel fire, born of this woman's determination to not become the usual, but simply, the remarkable. "I'm going to need it."

The heavy indigo paint and gilded arabesques beckoned as if a jewel-enrobed casket of treasures hidden deep within a nesting of plain, undecorated boxes. The entry was as the Oracle had said, no more than a door surrounded by four walls. Which only indicated that their journey would be down, into the earth.

Dominique clutched Sera's hand and squeezed. "Are you ready?"

"Are you?"

"The season is tumescent with snow that should not be. Angels have Fallen, and demons birth from their mouths. And a Changeling born of Faery and Heaven walks this earth. I know nothing anymore, Seraphim. Only that we must follow our hearts."

She searched his gaze, finding there a quiet confidence which seeped into her own heart. "It is a good path to take."

"Let us be to it then."

As if expecting visitors, an iron torchère flickered against the wall inside the entrance. No guards, not a single indication that someone wished them away.

Not a good portent.

But there seeped no poison from the walls, and she'd yet to sniff out brimstone—so she would take those as favorable signs.

Sera shook off the shiver that traced her body from neck to tailbone. She wished she had not abandoned the majority of her armor outside Creil. The steel shell would provide the protection she desperately craved. Though she wore the shoulder pauldrons, and gauntlets, the mail tunic did little more than warn of her approach with its minute chinks.

With a resolute sigh and a telling incline of his head toward the darkness, Dominique manned the torch, and Sera followed him down what might be hundreds of twisting short stone steps into the bowels of Paris.

The tunnel was literally carved out of the ground. The sweet smell of dirt and dry shale mixed with the torch's sulfurous perfume. To look over the curves and gouges of the floor and ceiling it appeared as if slaves might have dug out this passage with shovels. Sera pressed her hand against some particularly narrow gouges, curled her fingers, and found they slid perfectly into the four grooves. Perhaps the slaves had not even been allowed tools.

"We've come quite far," Sera said later, as the floor leveled out. Dominique paused to decide on one of two paths laid before them. She shrugged a hand over her arm, brisking some warmth into her chilled flesh. "Are you sure this is the place?"

"Positive." The stones on Dominique's cape *clicked* as he moved his torch from one opening to the other. "Now which would you choose? The path to the left, which appears to angle down, even deeper into the earth, or this one——" he flashed the torch before the opening "——that seems to be level, but it turns so quickly one can't be sure."

In the shadows of the flame, his eyes appeared black as hell. "Come, we'll go to the left, it feels just sinister enough to be the correct way."

He had taken on a hard edge since descending into the cold depths of Lucifer's lair. *His father's lair.* She must afford him his anger. Much as she felt it would not serve her vengeance, she knew it was what Dominique needed to face his rival. An enemy; his father.

How she wished things could have gone differently. But she would not renege Dominique's request to have but a moment to judge the man.

With only a few steps down, the twosome came upon a cavernous chamber hollowed out in the belly of the earth. Stalactites hung from the ceiling, seeping cloudy water, which eventually purled to drops that fell down a yawning crevice.

"Careful." Dominique caught Sera round the waist, halting her steps. "It's a long fall."

Immediately before her cut a crevice, dividing the room from end to end. Sera kicked a stone off the cliff. It disappeared into deafening blackness. The twosome waited for the sound of landing, but it never came.

"I guess we go back to the other path," Sera said. As she turned, the opening from which they had come sealed up with a thundering crash of stone against stone. "Dominique!"

"Don't panic." He rushed to the wall and pressed his hands over the surface, searching for evidence of the previous opening, perhaps a release mechanism.

"We're trapped!"

"Settle, Sera, I'll find a way out."

"You'd better hurry." The floor shook beneath her. She stumbled to Dominique's side and clutched him. "The cliff is moving!"

Dominique pulled Sera tight to his body and pressed himself against the wall behind them. Upon all wonders she had never seen anything like it. They both watched the edge of the cliff rattle and lumber backward, closing the distance between their feet and the growing crevice to but a few yards. And it gave no sign of ceasing.

"I love you," Sera gasped, as she studied his face. "We've come so far, and now it's to end." She didn't want to think in such a way, but——they now had but a stride of floor to go before free falling—— "If I must die without accomplishing my goal," she said, the tears already streaming from her cheeks. "I am honored to know it will be in your arms."

"Don't say that," he hugged her close. "There must be a way."

"Not unless you can fly——"

The earth gave way beneath their feet. Dominique's weight plunged into the darkness. Sera did not scream, only clenched tight to her lover's body and answered the call of gravity. Her sight was blackened by the flow of Dominique's black cloak as it slipped over her face and was ripped from his shoulders.

TWENTY-FIVE

One moment she was plunging into the mouth of hell, the next, Sera felt giddy and light. A warm glow coruscated all about her. The walls of the cavern were moving down before her eyes instead of up. She no longer clung to Dominique's body. Her fingers groped rushing air. Dominique was nowhere—

—and everywhere.

Aware that a force of bright light propelled her up toward the opposite side of the cave and a gaping opening in the wall, Sera clamped her hands over her shoulders and let out a shout of joy. 'Twas as if she had taken wing. Air rushed over her face and body in a thrilling shiver. This was freedom. This—felt very familiar.

In the next moment, her feet touched the ground on the opposite side of the crevice. Sera groped for purchase against the ebullience that made her tipsy.

With a glimmer of faery dust Dominique stood before her, tall and proud, his violet eyes bright with exhilaration.

"You never told me you could do that," she exclaimed, the thrill of her rescue making her words breathless gasps.

He shrugged; a sheepish grin made his expression so delectable. "I suppose a man must retain a bit of mystery about him."

Then she really looked at him. No longer did he wear the elegant black cape. Magnificent violet wings of a gossamer substance fluttered behind his shoulders. Sheer and voluminous, the wings, in four sections like that of a dragonfly, spread proudly out behind him. They were stunning. Beautiful. Beyond belief.

Sera reached to touch, but he flinched, setting the glitter-coated wings to a quiver.

"Please," she coaxed. "They are...incredible."

She reached over his shoulder. This time he did not move as she touched the tip of her forefinger to a diaphanous wing. It felt warm and soft, pliant. It vibrated with a pinging energy that tickled her finger, as if it possessed a life of its own and transferred that life-energy to her.

Stepping closer, Sera spread her hand wide and placed her palm to the thin violet fabric of Dominique's wing. It shuddered and swept a rush of sweet, meadow-scented wind over her face. Sera couldn't help but smile.

"You've kept them hidden...b-because of me?"

"I feared your dislike for my kind."

"No more," she hastened. "I love you whatever you are, Dominique. But...they are too beautiful to keep hidden."

"I have disguised my faery nature all my life. When I knew I would encounter others. It is not so easy to stride into a tavern with these things to draw attention. My cloak——" he glanced down the bottomless crevice where his cape had fallen "——was designed with a special pocket to gently tuck them out of sight."

"Your mother?"

"I've told you, she was so thoughtful."

Sera traced a finger along the delicately laced fringes that decorated the outer edges of the left wing. Her finger glimmered with faery sparkle. "I should wish to look upon them always."

When she pulled back, the ruby shard he'd once displayed to her from about his neck caught in one of her mail rings. "This was from your mother, as well?" she wondered, as she carefully untangled the leather tie from her tunic.

"My faery mother," he whispered. He reached for the ruby and clasped it between his fingers, rubbing it worshipfully. "Or so I've always assumed. My mortal mother found it tucked in the cradle beneath me. She kept it, believing it was from my mother."

"That your mortal mother was so accepting…"

"Indeed. But let us be on to the Dragon of the Dawn. I'm sure he lies in wait of our arrival."

"Your wings will not be damaged?"

He smiled, and as he did, Sera watched the elegant appendages fold down. With a peek around his shoulder she saw they had folded as a cricket's wings, tight to his back. His leather jerkin had been specially cut down from his neck to allow ease of movement. Impressive.

"I love you," she said, and sealed a jubilant kiss to his lips. "Will our children have such wings?"

"Children? Sera, you rush to the end of the story."

"Not the end," she said, "but a new beginning."

"I would like that. And, I am not sure if they will have wings or not. Only Fate knows for certain. Now come," he clasped her hand in his. "We've our darkest hour yet."

They stepped from the crevice ledge into another small, ovular room that featured five separate tunnel openings.

"I do believe we'll not even consider the left one," Sera said. "I have had enough of the sinister." She stepped before Dominique in perusal of the remaining four tunnels. "My turn to choose this time."

He bowed grandly, and with that movement, his wings shivered minutely against his back. "By my leave, my lady."

Their mood had become so mirthful, Sera now wondered should they be more serious. But as quickly as she could start to ruminate on that idea, a wall of stone slashed swiftly before her, bruising her extended palm with its rapid motion. "Dominique!"

Utter darkness surrounded in tendrils of icy unknowing. The wall had closed her off from her lover and three of the tunnels. Sera pounded the ungiving stone with both fists. When she paused to press an ear to the wall she could not hear an echo, nor a clatter from the opposite side.

Lucifer had to be controlling this trek, forcing her and Dominique apart to serve his own needs.

"I'll be damned if you think fantastical tricks will force me back. Prepare, Dragon of the Dawn, I will find you! It is not Dominique who can sever your crusty head, but me, the one d'Ange you were fool enough to allow life."

Sera paused, pressed her hands to the wall, then felt carefully to the side where she had last studied the tunnel openings. The thought occurred that should Dominique stumble onto Lucifer first the plan would not then go as perceived. He could not end the demon's life. Only she had the connection, that blood tie. Much as she was still uncertain that mere bloodspill counted...

What would Dominique do upon meeting his real father for the first time? And Lucifer not even aware of such a relationship?

Wait— Dominique *did* have a tie to Lucifer. He was the villain's very flesh and blood!

Her hand flaying out into the dark open tunnel, Sera stumbled forward and caught herself against the curved wall.

"Is it he that has the blood connection?" she spoke her thoughts as she sorted through them. "But then, what of me? How was I able to kill the first four brothers? Might there be two of us with the blood connection?"

She wondered now if Dominique had figured out the same.

He pressed his forehead to the cold stone wall that had emerged from out of nowhere to sever him from his lover's side.

The torch, forgotten in the calamity, flickered and sizzled on the ground at Dominique's feet. He pressed his palm flat to the wall, trying to divine the slow heartbeats of his lover on the other side. Nothing.

Would Sera fare on her own? Perhaps far better without him at her side, holding her back, wishing upon wishes that he could just steal her away to a distant island on this world. All for himself. No evil, fallen angels to battle. No quest to complete, and then answer to Fate. Life would be simple and sweet wrapped in the arms of his angel.

Blasphemous.

Indeed. Dominique clamped his arms across his chest. He coveted a heavenly being. He should press his own sword into his gut for such thoughts. He tilted his head, sensing the opening into the cave from which they'd come. He'd served the Oracle by bringing Sera to the end of her quest. He was no longer needed.

I love you, Dominique.

For that reason, he would not turn back. Sera needed him by her side. He would find her. Or die trying.

* * *

The air grew noticeably warmer with each careful stride down the dark tunnel. Sera pushed down her hood and scruffed her gloved fingers through her hair. Sweat drizzled down her back, but she would not give up her last shred of protection by removing the mail tunic.

Ahead, the path glowed with torch light. Most likely an opening into another chamber. As she descended two wide steps, she came upon another immense room, split down the middle by yet another crevice.

Sera swallowed, pressed a hand to the wall behind her, and did a scan at the base where it connected to the floor. It didn't appear as though the floor was disconnected from the wall, thus allowing for another plunge.

As the chill of déjà vu rippled through her system, she carefully took in the expanse of the room. On the opposite side of the crevice a round platform, set upon a shaved-off stalagmite, jut out from the cliff edge. A podium that could hold but one man—Baldwin—carefully balanced, for to sway one way or the other would plunge him to the dark depths below.

Her heart dropped to her gut at sight of the man. He was bound at the ankles, around the waist and wrists, and another rope cut into his neck and held his head to an awkward tilt. Blood stained his tunic, spittles of crimson flowed down his hose and puddled around his boots. He'd been tortured. Mercilessly.

An ache of betrayal cleaved into Sera's heart. She had not been there to protect this innocent young man from evils he should have never encountered.

Along the edge of the cliff paced a tall, thin man. Streams of liquid black hair flowed from crown to shoulder. Black tooled leather encased his legs and the diamond-studded doublet. Mail sleeves and a cowl *chinked* with his long, confident strides. A jagged-edge sword was clutched between the man's hands. The weapon glinted with every insectile step its master took. The Dragon of the Dawn.

At sight of Sera, Lucifer lifted the sword behind Baldwin's unwary figure.

"No!" She raced to the edge of the cliff, set a wary eye to the fall below, then shuffled back a few paces. She could hear the entrance of others from behind, and with a glance spied two henchmen in black leather.

The quivering knight inclined his head as Sera looked over the scene. *Don't spare me,* he said with the nod.

Foolish that he would believe Sera could be so coldhearted.

Lucifer was as she remembered. Even more imposing without the shadows and fire playing havoc on his demonic aura. A narrow face and jaw, and black, black eyes—but beguiling in his dark beauty.

Also immortal. Or rather, soon to be immortal, should she place her blade anywhere but his neck.

She must not forget. This creature who stood across from her, and wore the guise of a mere man was nothing like she had ever before encountered. Or wished to encounter again. A fallen angel? Could such wickedness possibly come from the heavens? Surely the Oracle was mistaken.

She had gone to hell with Lucifer once before. And had shivered and passively allowed him to violate her, for she had thought her death a surety. And now she must take that trip again, to save a man who had come to mean so much to her.

"He is innocent!" Sera yelled. Her rasping words echoed above and about her head for three or four repeats.

Strong hands gripped her upper arms from behind. She did not struggle against her captors. The wisest route would be to remain calm and not rile Lucifer. At least not until she was on the same side as he, and could meet him sword to sword.

"He did not have a hand in the murder of your brothers. Release him, and you may have me."

"But I already have you." Lucifer's eyes flashed red. So it hadn't been a trick of the flames in her room that night of the New Year. They really were demonic in color.

No, not an angel. Not in any way, shape, or form.

"I could slay both these men," she said of the guards gripping her arms, "before you might have a chance to order them to rip my arms from my body."

"Yes." Lucifer pressed his cheek against the side of Baldwin's head, and pouted a mocking lip. "But I, too, am swift with the blade."

"Obviously not so accurate," she commented, lifting her chin to completely expose the scar.

"Ah, I remember you now. I do have to wonder about that," Lucifer said, thoughtful now. Though his blade remained firm against Baldwin's throat. "I never fail. It is simply unthinkable. Perhaps it was meant to be, that I did not bring you to death."

She should have died. The cut would have severed any mortal man's head.

So why had it not hers?

Dominique's talk of fate and fallen angels and demons swirled her concentration into a stir.

"As I've brought your brothers to their deaths?"

"That may be the way of things. I never did care for Sammael's whining. You did me a great service by severing his head. How did you get through that blasted jungle of noxious plants?"

"Sammael may be an expert in poison but he is no match for a swift blade."

"Pity. Though...Mastema was always a dear. Ah! What is

done is done. All that matters now is that I have something that means the world to you, and you have nothing. You've no family, no home, no life. No voice either."

"What do you ask to spare Baldwin's life?"

Lucifer shrugged. Such a hideously mocking gesture from one so evil. "You. On your knees. Before me. Your life as well. But later, after we've both *spent* ourselves."

"No, Sera!" Baldwin managed. A narrow drool of blood trailed down his neck. He balanced precariously on the platform, his hands tied behind his back. "Leave while you can. I am nothing! You must complete the quest."

"The quest?" Lucifer snapped his sword to the base of Baldwin's neck as he backed away from the platform to firmer ground. "Ah, yes, the extermination of the de Morte clan. A most noble effort, I must give you that, black knight. Ha, ha! The black knight, a woman? Who could have ever imagined?"

"You made me what I have become."

"Did I?" A positive nod set his coal hair across his shoulder. "Perhaps so. Sometimes I do not recognize my own skill. Indeed a product of vengeance, you are. As dark and vile as the men you hunt. But if you think I will shiver and fall at the hands of a mere mortal—"

"No!" Dominique's words struck her frenzied thoughts. *Lucifer can be no stronger than you will allow him to be.*

He had not the skill to alter her destiny, to change her heart! If Lucifer had made anything of Seraphim d'Ange it was strength and determination. "Very well!" Sera quickly unsheathed the dagger at her ankle and laid it on the floor before her; she retained her sword, but held it blade down between her fingers in sign of surrender. "Release Baldwin and allow him safe passage from your lair. Only then shall I kneel before you."

"Surrender *all* your weapons."

"When I have your word that Baldwin will go free."

"You have it!"

"The devil speaks only in lies!"

Lucifer's droll chuckle echoed off the cavern walls and pounded like sharp-horned imps beating upside Sera's head. "I do appreciate the compliment, but I am not Satan. His second-in-command-above-ground, surely. But I've never quite been able to convince Him that I would do a much tidier job down here on earth."

"You take the Lord's name in vain!"

"Foolishly pious mortal. Using religion to justify your quest. I—" Lucifer pressed a hand to his chest—and then in a strange move, he thrust his wrist in display "—am an angel."

"Blasphemy!"

"Albeit, a Fallen One. You know, that Fall was something fierce. It took me decades to build up strength and to finally Remember."

"Baldwin!" Sera's shout startled the boy upright. He had been leaning to the left—so close to a death plunge. The boy's life must be spared; she owed him for the compassion he'd shown when he'd found her near-death after the raid.

"Very well," she complied, and tossed her sword. It clattered in echo to Baldwin's moans as it slipped out of sight and into the crevice.

"Done!" With a spin on his heels, the demon lord commanded his guards to bring Sera below. "And keep her alive. Circumstances have changed. I need to think."

The hands around her arms clenched like steel manacles. But Sera felt confident her sacrifice would not be in vain. Baldwin needed only walk out of here to safety. Dominique would find him and escort him through the labyrinth.

It was when Lucifer swung back around, his long hair swirling in a glittering swash of darkness, that she knew she had made the wrong choice.

·❧ TWENTY-SIX ❧·

Sera's scream clawed from her throat as the glint of Lucifer's *espadon* connected with Baldwin's neck. Blood sprayed the demon lord's grimacing lips. Crimson spattered the stone floor and rained down the dark crevice. Sera tasted Baldwin's life on her tongue. The newly dubbed knight's head toppled from his neck—his body followed in a soundless plunge into hell.

Lucifer wiped his fingers over the steel blade, pushing a stream of crimson from the blood groove out over the crevice. With a tilt of his chin, he granted Sera a satisfied smirk and a wink.

Then one of the guards blackened her vision with a well-placed fist.

The chamber was empty. But the overwhelming sense that he had just missed something rippled through Dominique's very soul. That horrid smell...

He rushed to the edge of the crevice that split a narrow jag through the cavern. Blood spattered the opposite face of the cliff-wall and the circular platform that jutted out from the stony ledge.

Plunging to his knees Dominique surveyed the hell-dark abyss. He did not have to look far to see Sera's sword caught up on a jag of stone.

"No!" He pressed his jaw tight and clung to the edge. Heartbeats galloped up to his throat. Everywhere the blood taunted in vicious streaks. She was dead? It could not be. Not so easily as that? And he nowhere near to offer protection?

Then he sighted a wilted leather bone bag clinging to a minute ledge below. "It is merely the squire." Then he corrected himself, "No, not *merely*."

At sound of the Oracle's voice, Dominique rolled to his back, then swiftly lunged forward to avoid a fatal fall. He sprang to his feet, tried to grip the boy at his shoulders, but his hands slipped through the vision.

Dominique's wings fluttered in rage. "Damn you! Tell me what has gone on here. Where is Sera?"

"She offered her life in trade for the boy's. Lucifer takes what he will and damn those who will challenge his authority."

"Why? Why did you allow me to lead her here when you obviously knew the outcome? She will die, but another soul ransomed to the devil's greed, insignificant and lost."

"Not insignificant," the Oracle said with disquiet ease. "You, Dominique San Juste—" he regarded the wings that shivered angrily between Dominique's shoulder blades "—need to start thinking with your heart, and not that thick skull of yours."

The words reverberated inside Dominique's head. He squeezed his eyelids shut, fighting the dull pound of pain. Had the Oracle betrayed him? No. He'd known from the start what had been required of him.

It is the Faery that serves as an angel liaison…

Yes. Perhaps the myth he had not given credence to really was truth. He would continue to guide. He would see Sera safely through this damned quest.

But there were important details he now needed to know.

"Yes, an angel," he cited the little knowledge he had to the Oracle. "But one with no memory, perhaps a memory that could provide her the skill to survive, when it seems Lucifer retains some power, some trace of his past. When will this Remembrance come?"

"She is the chosen One—"

"The chosen one? Bah!" His scaled gauntlet beat his chest; an angry action that he could not control. "Even I have more of a blood tie to Lucifer than Seraphim d'Ange. He is *my* father."

The Oracle raised a forefinger to his bottom lip as he perused Dominique's statement. "I know that. Though, I did not foresee—" The boy glimmered, his image, the colors of his flesh, his indigo robes, the gloss on his fingernails, fading to a chimerical wisp, then with a flicker, brightening to vivid flesh and blood. "Perhaps there can be *two* chosen."

Dominique felt a sickening quell roil his gut into a tight knot as he recalled pressing his palm to Sera's stomach beneath the snow-sheltered plane tree. "*Mon Dieu,* we both..."

"It appears that way."

The Oracle did not know this?

"And what if the demon should be released? Is Lucifer de Morte truly a demon, or some kind of angelic being? I cannot slay an angel. 'Twould be blasphemous."

"Have no doubt," the Oracle said, as he hovered before Dominique, "the only remnants of heaven clinging to Lucifer de Morte are but the remembrance of what was. If, or when, the Dragon of the Dawn's demon is released, it will be truly demonic. Forged from the sins of its keeper committed over the decades."

"Did Seraphim choose to Fall, or did He command she do so?"

"She fell of her own will."

"I thought angels had not their own free will?"

"It is not so much will, as the urge to protect. An urge planted by Him. Lucifer and his brothers had lived but a decade on this earth, when it was determined they would prove great devastation—beyond the usual—to the mortal citizens of France. It was decided that a Power would Fall to end what could only become a vicious reign of terror. Heaven works in mysterious ways. Sera chose this mission, Dominique, knowing that the Fall would erase all memory of her angelic life."

"But why is she refused knowledge of such? Has she no strengths, no supernatural powers that can bring the demon down, quickly and easily? Why wait this long? As Sera has said, so many have suffered under the cruel hand of the de Mortes. Why only now?"

"It is not in my knowledge. The Remembrance chooses the moment. And of course, Sera had to grow to maturity, gain the necessary strength of mind and body. That is all I can offer."

Hell of a paltry offer. Dominique clamped his hands over his opposite arms. From the corner of his eye he observed the Oracle's curiosity over his wings. Never had he been so unaware of his differences, so unafraid to just…be.

In a shiver of indigo and starlight the Oracle stood no more before him. Dominique stood alone in the vast chamber. Overhead, a bat squealed and swooped into the depths of the cavern.

He would not rest until Sera was back in his arms. Dead or alive.

"I will find and rescue her before de Morte has a chance to kill her. If he knows of the child she carries in her belly that may grant me some time."

Dominique turned to the crevice and looked down upon the glinting sword, barely dangling from a jut of stone. She had wielded it with such finesse and skill, such bravery.

She does not have her sword!

He stretched a hand over the yawning gap in the earth, and with a gesture of his fingers, raised Sera's sword up into his clutches. He shook off the faery dust from the blade, turned with purposeful strides, and marched out of the chamber.

Lucifer pushed aside the feeble wench who waited with wine and cheese at the side of his chair, toppling her against the wall in a clatter of silver and crystal. His boots strode the narrow tunnels of his lair with sure strides. *Crack* upon the cold, hard limestone. *Crack* upon the ancient debris. *Crack* upon the brittle spines of the mortals.

Up he climbed the stairs that twisted to the right to heed his enemies' swords from being drawn with ease. Around and around, until he was just below ground level.

'Twas but two hours from midnight. He could sense it. Though he was at his weakest, and would only become weaker before the surge of light that graced this earthly hell renewed his inner demon with the food it desired. Dawn promised full strength.

He'd had the black knight chained in the observatory, a round galley set three stories down into the earth. Windows set into the ceiling looked up to the sky. His shrine to the sun.

Lucifer strode through the darkness, the shiver of the open night barely registering on his flesh. Chains clinked against the stone wall as he entered the room. Strain as she might, there was no escape from the thrice-forged steel that bound her wrists and ankles.

* * *

Sera felt the icy touch of the Dragon of the Dawn before he even stepped into view. He entered with the quiet, eerie grace of a creeping insect, one that plants itself atop a person's head, then skitters down their neck, sending shivers like a jolt to the heart and causing one to claw maniacally at the unseen intruder.

She stiffened against the shudder that ran down her neck. The dull crack of Lucifer's boot heels across the stone floor of the chamber matched her heartbeats. Loud, deafening.

Memory rushed to the fore, much faster than reality would allow her to fight it back…

"This night you go to hell, pretty one." A wraith drawn up from a sealed tomb, the voice sounded, hollow and deep. So unwelcome.

The torch set into an iron bracket by her chamber door illuminated the growing shadow on the wall behind the intruder. Woken from a dead sleep, Sera grasped her senses quickly. It was a man, wearing armor. Great horns grew to the ceiling in the black shadows. Red flames danced in his devil-dark eyes. Long strands of sweat-soaked black hair snarled upon his forehead and chin.

The demon lord laid a palm against Sera's cheek. Her skin was cold as death. Winter had permeated her flesh. A growl, mixed with the rumble of laughter, curdled in his throat. He was going to violate her. *Again.*

"No!" Sera jerked her chin away from Lucifer's hideous touch. But he gripped her by the hair and held firm. She seethed as she fought against the visions of that New Year's night and tried to keep in mind the present. *That was then. This is now.* "Unhand me, beast!"

He drew a probing finger along the scar dashed from under her ear and down across her neck. "Pretty."

She tried to wrench from his grip but he would not relent. Her hands, tethered to the wall by chains, were useless. "It is your handiwork."

"Yes, but I've not the opportunity to admire such before. Most of my artistic endeavors are usually buried six feet under." A tilt of his head created a shadow of the left side of his face. Sinister in his quiet beauty. "I wager you can no longer scream. And if you cannot scream, then no one shall hear your cries for rescue. Pity. I do favor a woman who is vocal in her passions."

She jerked her chin up, defiantly fixing a smile on her lips. The man would not win this time. The black knight would not allow it. Lock the damsel behind bolted dungeon doors. Seraphim d'Ange would have her justice. Somehow.

Caught in the challenge of her enemy's stare, Sera summed up her opponent. He matched her in height, did not appear to possess the brawn that she had originally placed to such a blood-thirsty creature. In fact, he was thin, his face gaunt and his fingers long and bony. Skeletal, almost.

This was the man that had destroyed her entire family? This pitiful excuse for a man?

Sera wrestled within the manacles that held her to the wall. Thin, rusted chains garbled dull protest. If she had but an ax the aged chains would give way...

Lucifer paced before her. "You have hounded me for weeks and reduced my family by four-fifths, black knight, and yet I do not even have the pleasure of your name."

She straightened proudly, much as the chains fought to bear her down. Pride would serve no more than her downfall. "You forget your evil deeds as a snake disregards its shed skin. It is Seraphim d'Ange."

"Seraphim, eh? How ironic." He tilted his head. Torchlight danced up and down the length of his obsidian hair in streaks of blue fire. And in his eyes danced mystery.

Sera looked away.

"Indeed, I remember an altercation with the d'Ange family but a few weeks back."

"Altercation?" Her throat ached with every forceful utterance. But she did not allow regard for her pain. "You do not recall doing to my family as I have done to yours?"

"Indeed, indeed." Lucifer stroked the skin beneath her chin; much as she tried to wrest away from him, she could not. "It is very soft," he commented on the scar. "Like the smooth underbelly of a corpse slug. Ah, and 'twas you—" he inclined his head forward and tilted it—another insectile move—and pierced her gaze with the darkness of centuries "—the wench I had beneath my rutting cock. You bled so deliciously that day. From all orifices." Pressing the back of his hand to her chin, he lifted to study more closely his handiwork. "And such stamina to have survived the slash of my sword."

"'Tis the thirst for vengeance that kept me alive."

"Yes, yes, avenge your family. How noble. Seraphim, the Avenging Angel." Lucifer could not stop the chuckle that exploded over his perfectly straight, white teeth. "Doesn't that just figure? They have sent one from my very rank to stand against me on this mortal realm. Did Jehoel send you? But of course you don't know a thing about that, do you? Have you yet had the Remembrance? No…I don't think you have."

"You speak in riddle, and I've no desire to play your games."

"Seraphim of the Angels!" Lucifer declared grandly. The walls about him echoed the title. He whipped about and gripped her hand, turning it so she could see her own wrist. "Ah, you are but a Power."

"Release me," Sera croaked hoarsely.

Lucifer ignored her pleas. "A Power, chosen to Fall, but your memory erased, so you should not suffer desire for the heavens you once tread." He released her wrist with a twist of the bones. A thrust of his arm displayed his own wrist to her. Sera eyed the blue symbol, very similar to hers, but different. A true devil's mark?

"You still do not understand, eh?" he said. With a dismissive shrug, he strode away and began to pace before her. "That goes little distance in explaining your quest. I had thought you were the One. The one with the blood bond, chosen to either extinguish or release me from this mortal coil. But what bond do we share save the gift of wings and halo?"

"Blasphemy!" she raged. This man was toying with her mind. She must remain aware.

A new voice stirred the air; Sera lifted her head in surprise. "What of the child she carries in her belly?"

"Dominique?" she gasped. She wrenched around in her chains.

As Dominique entered the weak glow of the rush lamps, Sera saw the elegant wings that spread out behind the man. The violet appendages glittered in the soft light. A Faery king moving cautiously toward Fate.

Lucifer released her and stepped back a few paces. Overhead a bat shrieked out a warning as it skimmed the chill darkness.

"You say there is a babe, winged man? This wench is with child? Ah!" Lucifer delighted in the joy that giggled out his mouth in harsh bubbles. When his mirth calmed, he leveled a gleeful eye on Sera. "What a lovely scar upon His name. Sent to avenge the Fallen Ones, and fallen into the very sin He most prohibits. Oh, such joy!"

"Dominique, what are you saying?"

One broad step brought the mercenary into the moonlight that filtered through the windows overhead. He looked only at Lucifer, but placed a reassuring hand to Sera's shoulder. "You are with child, Sera. I have known since our escape to the plane tree."

She shook her head madly. "No."

"You claimed you were ill from Sammael's poison. But I took all the taint from your body, Sera. I was sure of that. I touched your stomach and felt the life. Forgive me for not saying something sooner. It is...Lucifer's child."

The demon lord stamped a foot on the floor and flung up his arms. Glee cracked deep radiating lines from the corners of his black eyes. "Of course it is mine, because you've not yet had her, have you, winged man?"

"This cannot be!" Sera shook and tore at the chains. "I shall hew the beast from my stomach with my own hands before I will give birth to such evil. Let me free of these manacles!"

Lucifer ignored her struggles, as did Dominique. Here he stood. Before his father. The Dragon of the Dawn. A tall, elegant figure he cut, dark brows overshadowing black as midnight eyes.

They are black as hell; not violet as they should be. But where I got them I do not know.

And now he did know. To look into the eyes of his creator and know whence he had come. The answers he had so desired all his life now stalked before him, despiteous, malicious, glowing in the red centers of Lucifer's eyes, menace slicing through the cut of his jaw.

"Now, tell me what you are," Lucifer coolly demanded. "I cannot determine if you are faery, or of the elf-kind for your dark coloring."

Dominique smoothed a hand over his sword hilt. His heartbeats had gone beyond speed, and had now merely become one big pulse. "What if it is none of the choices?"

"Get this babe from my stomach now!" Sera groaned.

"Will you silence, wench? I need to concentrate." A film of lid slipped over Lucifer's eyes as he stretched the tips of his fingers out toward Sera. Dominique observed as the man seemed to be divining the truth. A lugubrious smile pushed its way onto the dark lord's face. "Indeed…my child. Ah! A half-breed is better than none."

He turned and strolled into the darkness, exact center beneath the sky windows and pressed his chin into his palm for thought. A mortal gesture, yes. "And this man is half-breed as well. Perhaps faery *and* elf?"

"It matters not!" Sera rasped. "Release me, de Morte, and fight a fair battle to your death. Dominique will not interfere— he will give you his word."

"Will you now, Dominique?" Lucifer recited the name with perfectly mocking tone. "She speaks your mind for you? Quite the obnoxious ball of fire for a mere woman."

"It is not that I am merely a woman, but simply…a woman."

"A simple woman, yes, yes." Lucifer dismissed her declaration with a flick of his fingers. "Simple indeed, to trek to the bowels of the earth and present your demon lover with his half-breed child."

"You speak madness. More lies from the devil's mouth!"

"It's true, Sera," Dominique said. "I am so sorry."

"So you have purchased nine months of life," Lucifer offered with a tilt of his head. "I suppose I must see to your comfort. Cannot leave my child to freeze up inside your feeble corpse. And must keep you secure, for there is the trouble of your sneaking up from behind to behead me."

"Every chance I get."

"You would murder the father of your child?" Lucifer spouted mockingly.

"Don't speak that to me!"

"Why? You are not thrilled to hear of the upcoming joy? I thought all women rejoiced the process of bringing new life into the world."

"It will be as you are, a hideous demon disguised in mortal form."

"This mortal guise——" Lucifer drew splayed fingers up the length of his body "——is truly hideous, as you say. But I am not come from demon stock. If I must continue to remind, I am a Fallen One."

"That is enough!" Dominique announced. In a sing of challenge, he drew his sword from the scabbard and stepped before Sera, concealing all but her head from Lucifer's view with his widespread wings. "I'll not allow this beast to keep you any longer than the time it takes me to slay him and free you."

"Ah, so the hero reveals himself. Well, half-breed faery—whatever it is you are—I'll match your challenge." In a swift movement, Lucifer produced a crossbow from his back, set and ready to spring. With his free hand, he glanced the fingers across the hilt at his hip. "As well, my sword is in need of honing."

"You do not fear your death?" Dominique countered, his sword at the ready.

"How can I? *You* are not the one with the blood bond. Right here——" the demon lord drew a line across his neck with his forefinger "——aim carefully."

Lucifer raised the crossbow, prepared to blast an arrow at Dominique, but held back at the glint of violet in the man's dark eyes. "Ah, a faery. I should have suspected as much. So *you* are my mercenary."

"*He* is your mercenary?" Sera wondered.

"He lies," Dominique hissed.

"Quite the revelation, isn't it? The very man you trusted to protect you is the one who had been chosen to deliver you to my hands. Oh, the joy of it all!"

"You twist your cruel tricks back upon yourself, Lucifer,"

Dominique said. "The Oracle has released me from my mission. From the start, he did not once request I harm Sera. So you see it is you who has been tricked."

"Doesn't matter, I have the wench. So I have won. Come now, let us be done with the preliminary battle, so I may then prepare a nest for my future child."

With careful forethought, Dominique swung his blade. The damascened steel *chinged* against iron and released Sera from her restraints. She wrestled with the chains, but could not release the manacles. "Your sword is here," he called.

Sera lunged for his scabbard, short lengths of chain beating the air beneath her wrists. She then declared to Lucifer, "You would not harm your own son!"

The villain halted at the echo of Sera's gravel-laced plea. Lucifer's thumb lifted from the crossbow trigger.

Dominique cringed. His wings shivered violently, then settled to calm. To hear the truth so blatantly declared, and before the man in question, tore at his soul, put a terrible ache in his gut.

"My...son?" Lucifer growled out in a tone so sepulchral it chilled Dominique to the bone. The demon lord inclined his head, a night beast listening with acute hearing and sharpened eyesight. "How can this be?"

"Much as I'd rather not lay claim to such parentage—" Dominique displayed his sword at the ready "—the Oracle has told me as much."

"The Oracle. Hmm..." Lucifer rubbed his jaw, the crossbow now relaxed in his hand, though certainly he could bring it to the ready with a jerk of his wrist. "You mean that child of a wraith that comes at the snap of a finger?"

A crisp snap found the Oracle shimmering before the threesome.

Maliciously pleased that his command had brought forth the figment, Lucifer crossed his arms over his chest, the glistening arrow aimed haphazardly at Sera.

"You told me you serve neither good nor evil," Dominique blasted at the floating child. "What is this now that you come at the devil's beckoning?"

"I'm flattered that you all think me The Old Lad Himself," Lucifer said, with a glance to Sera. "You tell him."

"Supposedly," Sera gasped, "he is not."

"A moot point." Dominique, sword at the ready and one eye on Lucifer, approached the Oracle. "Have you deceived me all these years, only to lead me in the fore to evil's reign?"

"I have not," the Oracle answered.

"He insists I am the mercenary he hired."

"Yes, and no," was the Oracle's reply.

"You always were so frustratingly noncommittal, Leviticus. It matters not whether he is my mercenary. The final result is as I have desired." Lucifer sneered. "But is this…faery…really my son?"

"Syr gave birth to him six and twenty years ago," the Oracle stated.

"Syr," Lucifer whispered, "she never said a thing."

"She exchanged me with a mortal babe to keep me from your hands," Dominique raged. "Because of you I never had a mother's love—"

Dominique paused, clamped his jaw tight, suddenly wished he could take back his words. He *had* had a mother's love. A father's love as well. His mortal parents had loved him as their own. Even though he was not of their kind, something so strangely different from them. Yet they had loved him without question.

"Dominique?"

Sera's voice wavered in the back of his thoughts. Dominique turned, his sword tip dragging across the stone at his feet.

"I am not needed anymore," the Oracle proclaimed. "What shall be, will." He vanished with a dulcet chime.

"I remember Syr well," Lucifer cooed. "Slender and lithe. Wings of finest gossamer. A delicious feast for many a man's pleasures. But that babe died three months after she gave birth. I know, boy, I kept close watch."

"Obviously not close enough, for you did not see my mother make the switch. The babe you saw die was a mortal infant."

Lucifer held curious hold on Dominique and Sera's fighting positions. Both held arms at the ready, feet planted in preparation to lunge. "So you are a changeling, then? Discarded from the Faery kingdom?"

"Only because my mother wished to protect me from you."

"I would not have harmed my own son." Lucifer bristled, bringing his shoulders square and the crossbow in line with Dominique's heart. "I would have taken you underwing—so to speak—and made you a fierce warrior at my side. Not this miserable excuse for a mercenary who must keep a woman at his side to fight his battles. Aye, I am ashamed to look upon you as my own."

"I will not feel an ounce of shame in severing your head from your body!"

"Dominique, no!" Sera lunged to stop the arrow that clicked from the demon's crossbow. Her sword glanced off the leather gauntlet wrapped round Lucifer's wrist and dove deep into Lucifer's heart. At the same time, the arrow pierced Dominique's shoulder and felled him to his knees.

"Blessed mother, forgive me," Sera gasped.

"What is it?" Dominique managed to ask. He fingered the arrow. It had pierced flesh and bone and had torn through his left wing. When he looked up, he could not keep his jaw from dropping.

Lucifer de Morte's body hung suspended before them, motionless, blood streaming from the heart where Sera's blade had entered. With a bone-shattering sound that would forever live in Dominique's memory, the head snapped back to release a torrent of fire.

❧ TWENTY-SEVEN ❧

The twosome could but stand, utterly transfixed, as they witnessed the fire beast undulate and wend before them. Dominique held his sword—but he was not aware, could not think beyond the moment. Too late for regret. The match he had feared now hovered before him.

Flame crackled and hissed as the liquid fire began to form and take on the shape of a man's body, complete with flowing hair and Lucifer's face. The limbs started to lengthen, the fingers grasping and clutching at the air, as if drawing in oxygen to fuel its formation. A horrible roar bellowed out from the beast's mouth. 'Twas hell declaring its release from the earthly cage of flesh and bone.

Here be no angels. Save the frightened woman that stood but two paces from Dominique's side, completely unaware of her origin.

He stepped quickly, touching Sera's elbow with his own, but remaining aware of every twitch, every motion from the writhing, changing fire beast.

"Forgive me," she whispered. "We are doomed."

"Never." Even as he spoke Dominique felt bold fortitude blaze through his veins. He was ready for this battle. This day he had discovered the answer to a decade's old question. And this day he would cut through that long-spent longing with his sword.

Flames began to zing around the surface of the formed beast, sizzling out in snaps of red light, until there were but a few sparks flickering on the ground before the unnaturally long talons curled before them.

Tall, black, and elegant, the creature stood before them. Tattered wings stretched from hell to the glass ceiling, and the narrow limbs appeared flesh burnt to the bone. Eyes of red looked down upon Dominique and Sera with a glimmer of malice blinking the crisp black lids.

Still the beast changed, and moved, and grew.

"It appears to grow in size with every breath," Dominique managed.

One winged appendage stretched forth and clasped before Sera's face. "Become my wife, fellow angel," the beast growled in a simmering song of flame and icy sharpness, "and we shall rule the dawn with our babe at our side."

"I am no angel," Sera pressed through a tight jaw.

"Please *remember,*" Dominique whispered, more to himself, than Sera. When would it come? Surely she was not expected to fulfill her mission as a mortal being?

"But I will be," Sera continued, unaware of Dominique's prayerful hopes, "your worst enemy!"

The laughter that rumbled from the beast's jaws beat against the cavern walls with hideous disregard. "And I yours."

Lucifer bent before the two, his body folding neatly, supple like a willow branch, and pressed his sulfurous visage in the air before Sera and Dominique. Indeed it had swollen to twice its original size in but a few breaths. "If I cannot seduce my child's mother into servitude, perhaps this half-breed faery will serve his father?"

"I will see you dead and in hell where you belong," Dominique declared.

"Ah!" The beast straightened, drawing up to its full height, until its tattered wing-tips clicked against the windows overhead. "Is not the midnight your time, faery child?"

"Enough!" Sera raised her sword before her. "Time to die, Lucifer."

She swung, slicing a clean line across the foot of the beast, which released a thick ooze of black. In the next instant, the wound sealed up and formed a molten scar.

The mercenary stepped forward and swung, only to have his sword tapped away by the beast's agile wing.

"What do we do now?" Sera called to Dominique.

He knew the safest route—and was not averse to taking it. "Retreat!"

Sera looked to the narrow tunnel they had come through. Back to the monstrous beast, who had again doubled in size. In minutes the creature would be that of a dragon in size, and after that—she swung her gaze back to the tunnel opening. If Lucifer were to get stuck… "Let's do it!"

A ruffle of amber flame licked at Sera's heels as she dashed to the tunnel. Dominique's footsteps followed close behind. She sensed he ran backward, still battling the beast with the feeble sword he held. They were no match to this fire demon, unless they could trick it.

"Don't stop!" she called back as they entered the tunnel.

The ground shook beneath her feet. Lucifer's massive bulk rushed after them, his expanding body bruising the limestone walls and shaving away the tunnel in half the time it would have taken myriad slaves to do the same.

"Wait!" Dominique caught Sera in a run and slammed her against the wall. "We must kill him, Sera. I still believe he can be defeated by taking his head."

"Indeed," she gasped. "We just need to keep him on our heels. If he does get stuck, that will provide chance to sever his head."

She felt him slip his fingers through hers and squeeze, hard. Sera returned the squeeze, wishing she could just close her eyes and wish herself back to Dominique's enchanted cottage in the forest. Away from the horror that currently crammed its head inside the tunnel.

The walls vibrated. Stone shards broke away from the ceiling, and the floor cracked beneath them. Another impact shook the entire cave as Lucifer tried his entrance over and over.

The furious beating of demon wings against the cavern wall stirred up debris in the tunnel. Sera choked and clung to Dominique. If they had gauged incorrectly, and Lucifer were able to navigate the tunnel—

"He is wedged firmly," Dominique whispered. "I'll do it."

He released Sera and approached the struggling demon. Sera bit hard on her lip, not caring that blood ran down her chin. Nor caring who would wield the killing blow. They were both possessed of the blood connection. One perfectly placed stroke is all it would take. Unless—

"Run!"

She gripped Dominique's hand as he lunged toward her, and stumbled behind him, sword in hand. "What is it? Did you place the stroke?"

"It is changing. Liquefying. Listen!"

"I'll take your word for it!"

Sensing the temperature rise in the tunnel, Sera could only

guess that the dragon had transformed into its fiery state. If they didn't run, they would be burned to char.

With Dominique's hand pressed to her shoulder, Sera ran toward the minute glow that shimmered at the end of the tunnel. Another chamber. They were far below the surface of the earth; escape was many passages and chambers away.

The crackle of Lucifer's fiery roar singed Dominique's heels. The beast was so close. Yet, it seemed more that it merely followed, instead of trying to attack. Pressing them into the chamber that lay ahead. The chamber in which he and Sera had plunged into the crevice.

Knowing the jump would be long, Dominique skrit ahead. The tunnel opened into the chamber. Indeed the crevice was wide. But Sera hadn't time to stop. Catching her under her arms, Dominique took the jump—flapped his wings—and they landed solid ground.

"This is the chamber—" she said, shaking off the landing and looking about "—with the moving floor!"

"Stand back," he said, and drew his sword from its sheath in preparation. The motion of drawing blade against his own flesh and blood slowed in his mind. But now was no time to think, only react.

Lucifer's roars rumbled out from the tunnel. Lightning crackles and spatters of fire preceded his entrance into the cavern. Fire had become black flesh and tattered wings. The fallen angel spread out his wings until the spiny tips scraped the walls of the cavern, but his torso and legs were still encased in the tunnel. Trapped, for the moment. The head was now monstrous, its jaws capable of scooping up a small cottage. A great roar shook the cavern walls. The sound sent a razor-sharp ripple down Dominique's spine.

"Surrender," bellowed out from the beast's skeletal jaw. Great spumes of fire glittered out from its nostrils. 'Twas dragon-form now. Every breath spewed fire. Every inhale shook the walls and loosened stone from the ceiling.

Dominique reached back for Sera. He did not touch her, but felt her near, for he glanced his fingers across the severed chain that still clung to her wrist. The glimmer of her sword flashed in his peripheral vision. But it was the sound of steel drawing over stone that startled him around. "Seraphim?"

Her back pressed to the wall, she held her fingers to her forehead. Chains dangled before her. Eyes shut tight, she strained then stretched her mouth wide to shout, "Dom-Dominique…the pain. Oh!"

He scrambled to her side, gripped her fingers. She was hot. Feverous. Sweat dripped from her scalp. Her jaw was so tense. "Sera? Please…we must flee."

"No," she said. "The light…it is…so bright."

Flames licked at Dominique's heels. Dragon's breath. "Sera, will you let me fly us out of here?"

"No!" She pushed out of his grasp and stood. For a moment she just stared at her wrist. The symbol— "I remember!"

Blue-ice eyes flashed open upon Dominique's gaze. He heaved in exhaustion. The heat of the fire beast's flames singed his wingtips. "You…" he gasped, "remember?"

"Everything," she stated in the coolest, most confident tone he had ever heard. No rasp to this feminine voice, only the determined hardness of an avenging angel.

"You—you know?" he managed. "That you were—are—"

"Indeed."

Sera looked beyond him to the demon. Dominique could visibly gauge the change in her features. Courage washed away the fear that had spurred her retreat. Integrity honed by torment and compassion rose to the surface. And for a moment—so brief, but that which burned itself to his memory—he saw the valiant glory surround her spiked black hair in a radiant arc.

"You will not see another dawn, Lucifer!" she announced grandly. "I have come to see your end. Prepare to fall to the depths you should have reached decades ago."

Sera rushed past Dominique. He hadn't time to stretch out a hand and touch her. Fiery rage spurred her forth, her path set for the dragon's gaping jaws.

"No," Dominique hissed. He gripped his sword, but he was suddenly so tired. The heat drew the sweat from his body and made it impossible to hold the steel. His wings felt heavy, cumbersome. "Do not sacrifice yourself," he whispered. "Please."

But as he spoke the words, he knew it must be so. This was not his war; he had merely been the guide.

The icy clack of demon teeth, set in a crocodile jaw, snapped a chill shudder down Dominique's spine. Sera had run inside the demon's mouth.

As Lucifer twisted and writhed against the inner intruder, Dominique could but stagger to his feet and sway at the cliff's edge.

She was gone. His Sera. Brave, honorable, passionate. Sacrificed for the good of mortal-kind.

You have served your purpose. You, faery, have led the angel to Destiny.

Yet still the demon lived. Was there no killing this beast?

The ground rumbled beneath Dominique's feet. Fiery death cries, tipped with flame, filled the air. Suddenly, the glint of steel burst out from the neck of the beast. Sera's sword.

Dominique stumbled backward, pressing his fingers to the stone wall for purchase against the moving floor. He tried to cry out, but the sweltering heat wilted his voice. Morgana's blood, did she yet live?

Lucifer snarled and snapped his head down, landing it across the crevice, smoking nostrils to one side and neck to the other.

The horrid sound of steel rending through dragon flesh and scale filled the cavern. The hideous stench of evil blossomed and consumed the air with fetid darkness. Sera's sword worked its way from the original protrusion, down, sawing its way through and across the neck. Dragon-scale was hewn open in serrated cuts. Thick black blood oozed out in viscous drops.

A blood-slimed head emerged from the slice in the beast's neck, coughed, then a hand groped up out of the throat. Hope blossomed in Dominique's heart.

The dragon's eyes rolled to the back of their sockets. The heavy emerald-scaled lids closed. A quiet death, this.

"Sera, be wary!" Dominique yelled. But it was too late.

Sera's hand slipped over blood-slimed scale, and the rest of her body was purged from the beast like an infant born to the world. Yet she was not grasped by loving hands and a cooing kiss. Instead, she fell into the mouth of the crevice.

The vibrations of the moving cliff shook the demon's body over the edge, where it tumbled down the black mouth of hell. Right behind Sera.

Transforming to light, Dominique flew down, squeezing his way past the massive bulk of the beast and past Sera to catch her mid-fall. He strained against gravity, pumping his wing muscles. Faery dust enveloped them in a sparkling mist. The light from above was snuffed out by Lucifer's body.

Surging upward, Dominique deftly avoided the beast with an agile dodge. Surfacing, he hovered with Sera in the safety of his glow until he spied an escape tunnel. He moved briskly through the tunnels, Sera clinging to his shoulders, her legs wrapped around his hips, retracing the steps they'd taken, until the doors of the entrance flung wide before them and he landed Paris, topside.

Setting her down inside the small room through which they had first entered, Dominique then carefully cleared away dragon's blood and slime from his angel's face.

A little tipsy, she staggered, but clamped a firm hand upon his shoulder. "That," she gasped—and smiled, "was most hideous."

Dominique could not help but smile himself. Relief welled in his heart. He pressed a kiss to her bloodied forehead and squeezed her tight. "That…was most brave."

"Are you hurt?" she wondered, pressing a hand to his shoulder. The arrow had pierced flesh, but he did not bleed. "Your wing, it's been damaged."

"Worry not, it will heal. But, I must go back."

"What—" she heaved, spat out a glob of dragon slime "—for?"

"I want to ensure the beast is dead. I also want to see if there's a way of closing up these underground chambers forever. Will you be aright until I return?"

"If you are not long."

"I will not be." But before he left, he must hold her. To know, to feel, to possess. For one last moment. *Don't take her from me now,* he thought. But he knew that was not in his command.

"Sera?" He smoothed his lips over her dragon-slimed mouth. "You remembered."

"Remembered what, San Juste?"

He pulled away and looked into her blue eyes. Innocence had returned to the clear sparkling orbs. So she had forgotten again. The way it must be, he supposed. For now.

"It's nothing. Stay here, I won't be overlong."

* * *

When he emerged from the lair of Lucifer de Morte, Dominique felt confident that no more would the man—demon—Fallen One—torment the country of France.

He'd flown down to the bottom of the crevice and had looked over the remains of the fire beast. Singed to char, and still smoking. The skull had shattered upon landing the sharp stones of the abyss floor.

His father. But only through the action of copulation. Yes, a simple clinical action that could not have involved love. Had Lucifer loved Syr? There was no way to know. But Dominique must not even wonder.

Only one man had been his true father, Phillipe San Juste.

As he'd flown up out of the crevice the walls had rumbled and the floor had once again moved. This time to seal up the opening in the earth that had become Lucifer's grave.

The demon angel would meet his just end in Hell, Dominique felt sure of that.

When he topped the stairs he saw that Sera did not wait in the small entrance. She must have gone outside, perhaps for a breath of cleansing air. The stench from below coated Dominique with foul reminder of how close he and Sera had been to their own deaths. The Remembrance had come just when she had needed it.

That had really been cutting things closely.

Dominique stepped outside to the cool, fresh air. Midnight was illuminated with the sprinkling of goosedown snowflakes. So glamorous and pure. 'Twas the time of the faeries. His time.

Heavy snowflakes fell upon his face and melted into tears of newness and good. And for the second time in his life Dominique allowed the hot tears to flow from his eyes and mix with the cold snow. And if felt so, so right.

'Twas a sign, Dominique knew it in his heart. Evil was to be covered over, and beneath, new life would spring forth. Nature had taken back her throne.

Ah, but to think of new life... There was a new life yet to be born that would not be so welcome.

Swiping away the tears, Dominique strode around the side of the indigo door and spied Sera crouched against a wall. Moonlight caressed her silhouette in worshipful reverence. Her hair and shoulders and legs were covered with snow. Chains hung from her wrists and traced the snow. Her face was lifted to accept the kiss of nature's triumph.

He approached her slowly, taking measured carefulness in observing this quiet moment. This angel had triumphed against all odds. And he felt sure, had the Remembrance never come, she would still have been the successor, so determined and brave she was.

"All will be right now?" she wondered, without opening her eyes or looking up to him.

"It feels that way." Dominique crouched beside her and traced his forefinger through the melting flakes on her cheek. "You are so beautiful, Seraphim."

She tilted her head to the side and opened her eyes to beam a mysterious gaze up at him. Without a word, she then lifted her hands to show Dominique the blood she held.

He rushed to check for wounds, on her stomach, her arms, her thighs, but stopped as she retracted her hands. "Sera, you are...injured?"

She gently tilted her cupped hands before him. The pool glistened with a coating of fresh snowflakes. "'Tis the babe," she said. "It has been purged from my body."

He swallowed, noticed the blood that stained her chausses was bright crimson, not dark as the dragon's had been. "I—I'm sorry."

"It is what must be."

She leaned forward and placed the mass on the ground before her feet, then carefully swept a pile of snow over it. Making the sign of the cross, she then blessed the babe with a promise that the snow would melt and baptize it even in death.

"This child shall not be judged by the sins of its father," she whispered. "Nor shall you." She looked up to Dominique. "Are you aright?"

"I will be," he reassured. He touched a strand of dark hair that spiked straight up from her head and had amazingly avoided the bloodbath. "I only wish we could have saved Baldwin."

Sera sniffed—Dominique witnessed the struggle on her face as she fought against her pain—then she surrendered and out flooded tears from the soft depths of her eyes. "He did not deserve to die that way. He was a brave man."

"Somehow," Dominique smoothed his hand across Sera's shoulder, "I believe he would have been proud to know he died to save you."

She smirked, swiped the back of her hand under her eyes. A slash of blood blazoned across her cheek. "We must go to Nôtre Dame," she said, "and say a prayer for Baldwin Ortolano, knight of honor and valor."

"We shall."

Feeling the tears flow anew, Dominique bowed his head to Sera's forehead. The two remained, silent, shedding their pain in clean hot tears for long minutes.

With a whistle, Tor and Gryphon appeared to retrieve their masters. Much as Dominique simply wanted to hold Sera close and wish them both back to his cottage with the blink of an eye, he wanted to honor Baldwin as much as she.

A candle was lit on the nave in the cathedral, and silent prayers were whispered. They followed their trail of bloody boot prints out into the chill darkness of Paris, and with a touch of her hand to his, Sera said, "Take me home, Dominique. I want to go home."

Water shushed across the hot pool in minute waves, lapping against Dominique's chin. Seraphim sat across from him, her eyes closed, her arms floating upon the surface. A blacksmith had been roused from sleep at the edge of the Marais, and a few coins had enticed him to free Sera of her last bond to Lucifer. Eight hours had passed since they'd emerged from the bowels of hell, triumphant.

In that time no words had been exchanged, only silent consolation. Blood had flowed, and an innocent life had been sacrificed. Now all would be right.

Yes, all.

Sera had not been taken from this earth. The Oracle had been right. She knew nothing of her previous life, would never know. The symbol on her wrist remained but a curious marking to her. She would remain on this earth until mortal death returned her soul to heaven.

Not a single trace of the de Mortes remained on this earth.

Save himself.

"You are thinking about what your future holds?"

Dominique tilted his head, amazed at Sera's perception. Though he should not be so surprised, they had become close in so little time. "I am."

"I wager you could sleep through the dawn for all you've been through."

"You think so?"

"We shall soon enough see."

Yes. For if he could sleep through the dawn that would mean the darkness planted by his father's seed would be lifted. Just as the child in Sera's belly had been purged upon the demon's death, so then might he be released from the Dragon of the Dawn's evil legacy.

"You will never be like him. You mustn't even worry of it."

She glided through the water and pressed her knees to either side of his hips. The hardness of his body joined easily with her softness. Sera's whimper released the tension that had been riding Dominique's scalp.

"We have triumphed. Nothing can ever again do us harm. And if we should be faced with such a challenge, we will face it together."

"The black knight and the half-breed faery?"

"You are whole in my eyes, Dominique. Look at me," she said with sudden urgency.

Dominique allowed her to tilt his chin up so the rush light flashed in his eyes. Sera's cry of surprise startled him. "What is it?"

"Your eyes. I did not notice in Paris because I was too exhausted. The darkness is lost, Dominique. They are now brilliant violet."

He pressed her hand to his cheek. "You tell me true?"

"He is gone from you," she whispered, and pressed a kiss to each of his eyelids.

With that knowledge, Dominique pulled Sera close to his body and nuzzled his face into her neck. Her hips began to work a desirous rhythm against his loins. "Thank you," he murmured into the soft curve of her ear. "For sharing your fire."

EPILOGUE

Dominique woke in Sera's arms. She purred softly beside him, her legs twined within his. A pansy petal had snapped off and lay upon her hair. He plucked it up and trailed the violet petal across her lashes. She did not stir, and so he carefully slipped his legs from hers.

Nearby, the fire crackled to a glowing simmer. Raspberry wine, opened and half-emptied in their bellies, carried a heady scent from the table to the bed. Pushing aside the wolves' fur counterpane, he sat up and reached for his discarded braies.

The chirp of a bird outside the cottage sounded the first call of spring. Surprising to hear after the relentless weather that had been attacking France the past few weeks. He'd known that nature was out of balance.

And this morning he did not sense that misbalance. Everything felt…right.

Padding barefoot to his door, Dominique opened it carefully to avoid the creak that would wake Sera. He bent low to pass under the short threshold. His toes sunk into melting snow and water-logged green grass. The sun blasted him with a hot kiss—it hung high in the sky. He'd missed the dawn!

Rushing forward through slush and grass, Dominique looked about. A conglomeration of robins chirped in the elm tree overhead. The snow, thick and frothy days ago, had been reduced by half. 'Twas springlike. A sweet gift from nature.

Pushing his hands up through his hair, Dominique then stretched his arms out wide and embraced the clean beauty of the day. His wings expanded and breathed in the heady, pure forest air. The darkness had been lifted from his soul. The woman he loved slept like a contented kitten in his bed. And—

A luminescent violet glow shimmered before him. It undulated and took shape, releasing a pungent floral scent, like that of a rose bursting open beneath the sun. Not the Oracle.

Curious, Dominique stepped forward, wanting to touch this unfamiliar apparition. But it solidified so quickly, he was soon aware a living being stood before him on the snow.

She was beautiful. Tall and slender, with long gray hair that coiled at her hips. A diaphanous blue tunic clung to narrow shoulders and flowed to the ground in a delicious stream of color. Her eyes glowed violet.

"M-mother?"

"Yes."

Words would not form on Dominique's tongue. Nor did this lovely woman appear compelled to speak. But he could not resist the compulsion to touch, and so he plunged forward to hug her. Their bodies melded, and heartbeats matched. Yes, mother. His kind. The soft breeze of wings briefly folded about his shoulders before stretching proudly behind her back.

Now, all was right.

"Dominique?"

Behind him, he sensed Sera. With a glance he saw she stood in but his shirt, her toes wiggling in the depths of slush outside his door. Innocence had not been lost after all, for it glowed upon Seraphim's face.

"I want you to meet my fiancée," he whispered in his mother's ear, and proudly stepped aside.

"She is very pretty." Syr's voice was liquid, pearled with breaths of love.

A weary smile tickled his lover's face. She bowed her head in shy acceptance of Syr's statement.

"She is Seraphim," he said, guiding his mother forward. "Seraphim d'Ange. She has consented to become my wife for every day to come. And we will make many grandchildren for you, and sleep through every dawn."

"Your children will be blessed," Syr said in soft whispery tones. "With the goodness of Heaven and Faery."

A gown of red damask—formerly Rosemary San Juste's—swished between Seraphim's legs as she strode across the ice-crusted meadow to the berm of snow that surrounded the Valois Wood like a castle's curtain wall. Cold and bright this day; but for the sun Seraphim did not shiver.

Birdsong fluttered through the skeletal canopy of the nearby forest. Branches creaked as the melting snow, heavy and wet, strained the dry winter wood. The expanse of snow that coated the lands glittered like a dragon's hoard.

Stretching her arms wide and lifting her face to the sky, Seraphim closed her eyes and breathed out an exhale of iced air. A smile, unbidden but so welcome, curved her mouth.

Free, she felt. Released from the powerful vengeance that had carried her from one de Morte to the next in a rain of blood and fire.

Now, her family avenged, a bright future awaited. Mayhap, a new family would grow from the love she had won from a faery. With Syr as witness, she and Dominique had handfasted themselves at daybreak. And in her husband's brilliant violet eyes Seraphim had found her home.

Unlike her former home. That very distant, untouchable place. Parasongs away...

Opening her eyes, she searched the crystal white sky. Not a single cloud marred the perfect stretch of air. Reaching up, she grasped, curling her fingers gently and brought her coiled fist to her chest.

"No one need know," she whispered. "Heaven. Still in my heart."

* * * * *

*Return to the world of Changelings next year
when the sister who was lost is found!*

An interview with Michele Hauf

What does fantasy mean to you?

Fantasy is any world not my own. It can be simple or spectacular, daring and dangerous, but it's always got to be a step out of the ordinary. And it must make me believe.

Why do you write fantasy?

It's that whole dream-fulfillment thing. I was born into the wrong century. (Or rather, this time around isn't quite as exciting as my previous lives.) So I create the worlds that fascinate me, and people them with characters that walk and talk for me. And those characters always get to swing a big sword. :-)

Who are your favorite authors?

I think the first time I read Anne Rice's *The Vampire Lestat* I walked around in a daze for about a week. It was like discovering a new drug. A really good drug. Recently my fantasy fetish is being fed by Terry Pratchett and Neil Gaiman. I must have that first-day-in-the-store copy of Gaiman. I must!

As well, anything Brian Froud produces is a must-have. This man talks to faeries. He creates the most delicious images of faeries. I want to live in his fantastical world!

Through the shadowlands and beyond...

Three women stand united against an encroaching evil. Each is driven by a personal destiny, yet they share a fierce sense of love, justice and determination to protect what is theirs. Will the spirit and strength of these women be enough to turn back the tide of evil?

On sale May 25.
Visit your local bookseller.

LUNA

**Bestselling Harlequin Historical™ author
Deborah Hale has created a beautiful world
filled with magic and adventure
in her first fantasy novel.**

**"An emotional richness and depth
readers will savor."
—*Booklist* on *Carpetbagger's Wife***

Visit your local bookseller.